TETHERED

SPIRITS

AHARI

OSELIEN

LIBERA

ATREA

MALFRAM

DEVEAURAL

N

ERYTHYR

ALSO BY T. A. HERNANDEZ

THE SECRETS OF PEACE TRILOGY
Secrets of PEACE
Renegades of PEACE
Survivors of PEACE

OTHER WORKS
Calico Thunder Rides Again
Whispers of Shadow and Starlight

TETHERED SPIRITS

SPIRITS

T. A. HERNANDEZ

This book contains varying degrees of the following:
Mild language, violence, depictions of death, references to self-harm and
suicidal ideation, exploration of trauma and mental illness, discrimination,
torture, imprisonment, terminal illness. Please read safely and responsibly.

TETHERED SPIRITS

Copyright © 2021 by T. A. Hernandez

The Sanita Street Publishing name, imprint, and logo are trademarks of
Sanita Street Publishing

This is a work of fiction. Names, characters, places, and incidents are a
product of the author's imagination or are used fictitiously. Any resemblance
to actual people, living or dead, or to businesses, companies, events,
institutions, or locales is completely coincidental.

Cover art and design by T. A. Hernandez

ISBN: 978-1734033014

Sanita Street
Publishing

For my Grammie, who was a
shining flame in my darkest days.
Thank you for helping me find
hope and healing.

Part I

The man who could not die

AMAR

WHAT DID SHE WANT WITH US?

Amar dipped his quill into the small pot of ink at his side and let his gaze drift across the pages of the journal in his lap. The pale light of dawn and the dying embers of a campfire illuminated his hastily scrawled words, and he read them over again. Even after pouring all his thoughts onto paper, and even though he'd pondered the question ceaselessly in the four days since the altercation, he was no closer to finding answers.

He scowled and swept his shaggy black hair away from his eyes. What *had* the Visan girl wanted with them? She'd attacked out of nowhere, without provocation, and all he had for clues were the memories of her face and the fight that had followed.

And, of course, the fact that she was a Tarja, which was especially unusual considering there were no natural born Tarja among the Visan people—at least, not as far as Amar knew. She must have formed a Bond then, sharing her life with the spirit of a dead Tarja in order to gain magical power. It wasn't a common practice, but seemed the only explanation for her magic, given her heritage.

But then, that detail was also an assumption. She looked Visan and wore Visan clothing, but she might have had some Kavoran or Atrean blood as well.

None of that provided any clear motive for her assault, though. She hadn't even seemed angry that night, just single-minded in her focus. Amar had no idea who she was, and Mitul and Saya hadn't recognized her, either. But if she didn't have some kind of personal vendetta against any of them, why had she attacked?

He glanced across the remains of the campfire. Mitul and Saya lay on the ground a few paces apart from each other, their breaths slow and even in sleep. He should probably wake them. The dull light of morning was already seeping into the sky behind the greenery of the forest, and Saya would be impatient to get moving.

A fond warmth spread through Amar's chest as he watched the young warrior sleep. If not for her, he might have been taken captive that night. Their assailant had cornered him in a cave where they'd taken shelter from the rain, trapping him inside some sort of magical barrier. Mitul had never been much of a fighter, and it was only because of Saya's quick reaction to the attack that Amar had been able to break free. Together, they'd driven away the Visan girl, but it had been a hard fight. They were lucky no one had been hurt—or killed.

The thought sent a shiver down his spine. He picked up his quill again and set it to the page.

I have to protect them.

After all, neither of them would even be here if not for him.

Maybe that was it. He frowned at the line above the words he'd just written.

What did she want with us?

Us. What if it wasn't about *all* of them, though? What if it was only about *him*? What if the Visan girl, like Saya, had only tracked them down because of what Amar was?

It sounded a little egotistical…but maybe not. Saya had tracked him down after hearing about his unusual condition—something she thought might be useful, once they learned more about it. What if the Visan girl had the same idea? She *had* gone after Amar first that night, trapping him in that barrier like she was trying to take him prisoner.

What did she want with us? Amar jotted down two more words. *With me?*

Across the campfire, there was a shuffling in the grass as Saya stirred and sat up. Amar corked his bottle of ink and stored it, the quill, and the journal back inside his pack.

Saya looked up at the rosy dawn sky, then turned her golden-eyed gaze on him. "You didn't wake me to take my watch."

He shrugged. "I wasn't tired."

"I don't believe you."

Amar put some more kindling on the glowing embers. He coaxed the fire back to a low blaze while Saya shook Mitul awake.

"Morning already?" Mitul said, sitting up. He yawned and twisted his neck until it cracked, then combed his fingers through his long graying hair and beard. The creases at the corners of his eyes deepened as he smiled at Amar. "Sleep well?"

"Not with you snoring all night," Amar replied with mock gruffness.

"Ha! You're one to talk," Mitul shot back. "Your snores were as loud as a roaring tiger during my watch. I was relieved to wake you so I didn't have to listen to it anymore."

Amar flicked a chunk of bark from the forest floor at him, but it hit Saya instead. She sighed and muttered something under her breath in her native tongue, then stood and began packing up her belongings. Mitul followed suit. Amar, already packed, started to reheat last night's rice and lentils over the coals for their breakfast.

"Your haseph markings are looking pretty faded," Mitul said to Saya. "Thought you might want to know before we reach Tarsi."

"Thanks." She took a small bone container from her satchel, sat cross-legged in front of the fire, and opened it. Inside was a layer of an earthy red paint roughly the same consistency as clay. Saya wet her fingers with some water from her canteen and dipped them into the pigment, mixing it until she was satisfied. Then she swept her long brown hair behind her shoulders and raised a single index finger to her face. With practiced precision, she traced over the blotchy remnants of the lines already there.

"Better?" she asked, turning her face toward Mitul and Amar. The familiar, deep red markings were stark against her bronze skin—two lines below her right eye, a half-circle curving around her left, and another straight line down the center of her chin.

"Better," Mitul said. Amar nodded his agreement.

"How much farther is Tarsi, anyway?" Saya asked.

"Not far." Mitul picked up his saraj and cradled it lovingly in his arms. He began to softly pluck at the seven strings over its rounded body. Rich, fluid notes filled the air as he slid his fingers down the neck of the instrument. "We should be there this afternoon."

"And how confident are we that this Tamaya will have the information we need?"

"Very," Mitul said with a grin. "This is the most promising lead we've had in a long time. Don't you think, Amar?"

"I guess."

"Oh, come on. You have to be more excited about it than that. Good fortune won't find you on its own unless you send that hope out into the world. Believe in the possibilities!"

Amar only grunted in response. Mitul was always spouting off poetic nonsense like that. It would have been unbearably obnoxious, except that he genuinely meant it. His optimism was usually enough to pull Amar out of his more cynical thoughts, but not today. Today, his stomach was a mess of knotted coils, the same way it always was whenever they met a Tarja from the ever-growing list of names in his journal. Even if he'd shared Mitul's beliefs about sending hope and positivity into the world, it wouldn't have made a difference. He didn't have much hope left to give.

But he couldn't tell either of his friends that. Not when they both still depended so much on the promises of that hope.

He took the food off the fire and divided it onto three copper plates Saya held out. She took one for herself and carried a second to Mitul. He set down his saraj to eat, and in the silence left without his music, the knots in Amar's stomach only tightened further. He tried to distract himself with his own breakfast, but his appetite was already gone. After all the dead-end leads they'd already chased down, he wasn't sure he could take another disappointment.

Still, it wasn't like he had any better options. He could keep up the chase and hold onto the belief that Tamaya or some other Tarja could tell him what he needed to know, or he could resign himself to an eternity of confusion and struggle and loss.

Faced with such a bleak alternative, he had to keep going, even if he no longer held anything more than the faintest flicker of hope.

They arrived in Tarsi that afternoon, a small but busy city carved out of the forest, where commerce thrived and traders often stopped to barter with local merchants. They immediately went in search of Tamaya, but hours later, they were still no closer to their goal. No one seemed to know where she lived, or if they did, they wouldn't say. Most people refused to even talk to them, not if they weren't buying something. As far as Amar was concerned, the answer to such a simple question should have been free.

A headache pulsed between his temples as he led the others to the end of the crowded market street. The shouts of merchants hawking their wares and buyers negotiating for better prices still echoed in his ears, but at least here, the noise was subdued enough that he could hear himself think. It was a sweltering hot day typical of Kavoran summers, and his arms felt heavy as he lifted them to wipe sweat from his brow. The shade of a nearby building offered little respite from the heat, but at least it was something.

"Where to next?" Mitul asked, his voice as chipper as ever.

Amar sighed. They were getting nowhere like this, and as annoyed as he was by the idea of paying for information, maybe that was what was required to get this over with. The trick would be to pay as little as possible.

A trio of laughing boys darted past, and Amar's hand shot out to grab the last one by the shoulder. Ignoring the uneasy look Mitul gave him, he spun the boy around and fished a single brass jitaara out of his pocket. He held the coin up so it gleamed in the sun. "Want it?"

The boy's eyes went as round as the coin. He glanced over at his friends, who were watching from a safe distance.

Amar loosened his grip on the boy's shoulder and rotated the coin in his fingers. "Well?"

After another moment's hesitation, the boy nodded.

"Good. I'm looking for a Tarja woman. Tamaya Takhar. Can you tell me where she lives?"

Round eyes widened even further, and the boy shook his head.

"Why not?" Amar's voice came out in a deeper growl than he'd intended, and the boy took half a step back, as if he were afraid.

"I'm so sorry." Mitul said. He put a hand on Amar's wrist and shot him a pointed look. Amar shrugged and backed away. If Mitul really thought he could do a better job of getting the information they needed, let him try.

Mitul crouched down so he was eye level with the boy. He held his hand over his shoulder until Amar dropped the coin into it. And then, without even making the boy answer the question, Mitul pressed the money into his tiny palm. Amar swallowed the protests beginning to form in his mouth. Now the kid was going to run off, and they'd have nothing to show for the coin they'd given him.

But the boy only stared at the coin, his mouth hanging open. In a city like Tarsi, it was probably the first time anyone besides his parents had ever done him a kindness without expecting anything in return. His little brows furrowed as he shifted his gaze back to Mitul.

Mitul smiled at him with the same genuine warmth that seemed to charm everyone he'd ever met. "It's very important that we speak to Tamaya," he said. "No one else here has been able to assist us, but you look like a responsible, helpful child. Would you please be so kind as to tell us where we can find her?"

Again, the boy glanced at his friends, but they stayed where they were, cautious and silent. At last, he said, "She doesn't like us talking to outsiders about her."

"Ah, I see," Mitul said. "Well, we wouldn't want to upset her, but it really is very important that we find her. We wouldn't even have to say it was you who told us. You wouldn't be in any trouble."

"I can't," said the boy, then sheepishly added, "I don't even really know where she lives."

"You don't know which house is hers?"

He shook his head. "It's not here. It's far, I think. In the woods somewhere."

"That's very helpful, thank you. Do you know anyone else who could tell us where to find her?"

The boy cocked his head to one side, thinking.

Amar crossed his arms. This was a waste of time. The child clearly didn't know anything useful. Most likely, he was just trying to come up with a way to get another coin from them. From all Amar had seen, everyone in Tarsi was more concerned with their own prosperity than they were with basic courtesy.

"I know someone!" the boy said, a gap-toothed grin splitting across his face. "Come on, I'll take you to her."

He darted away, into the crowded market street. His friends bolted after him, and with a sigh, Amar followed. He kept a close eye on the boy's yellow cap as he wove between the people crowding around stalls and carrying baskets full of newly purchased goods.

Amar nearly lost him around a corner, but he caught a glimpse of one of the boy's friends squeezing through a narrow side street and chased after them. He wasn't sure if Mitul and Saya were even still behind him, but if they couldn't keep up, he'd find them later.

After a few more quick turns around wood and thatched-roof houses crammed together, the boy and his friends abruptly halted in front of a two-story structure with a sign over the door that marked it as an inn. A small pen and shelter for animals were attached to the side of the building, and a few goats and several chickens wandered the area. A bent figure crouched underneath the low shelter, gathering eggs from a small coop into the basket at her feet.

"What are we doing here?" Saya asked as she and Mitul came to rest beside Amar.

He shrugged. The boys approached the fence and called to the person inside the pen. "Kesari!"

"Is that you, Pujit?" She twisted around to smile at the children, hazel eyes gleaming in the sun. Black hair hung around her face in thick waves that landed in jagged edges against her shoulders. She couldn't have been older than fifteen or sixteen, and her voice carried a faint accent. Atrean, maybe, though she looked as Kavoran as Amar with her inky hair and brown skin a few shades lighter than his own. The heavy frock coat she wore certainly seemed to be of Atrean make, though it was absurd for anyone to be wearing such a garment in this heat.

"I hope you're not here to distract me again," the girl went on. "Your mother still hasn't forgiven me for—" Her gaze shifted to Amar and the others, and she stood up quickly. "Oh, you brought company. I'm so sorry. If you'll follow me inside, I can fetch the hostess for you."

Pujit laughed. "They're not here for a room, Kesari."

The girl raised an eyebrow and bent to brush the dirt off her knees. A lantern hanging from her coat swung forward as she did so, causing the flames inside to ripple and flutter.

Amar scowled. What kind of person carried a lit lantern in broad daylight?

"They're looking for Tamaya," one of the other boys said.

Pujit nodded and flashed the coin Mitul had given him. "And they gave us money. Maybe they'll give you money, if you help them."

Amar let out a huff. It always came down to money, and they were running short on it as it was.

"Well in that case, I thank you for bringing them to me," Kesari said. She reached deep into her pocket and pulled out a small pouch that jangled when she shook it. She plucked out a single brass coin for each boy and handed them over one by one. She ruffled Pujit's hair as his fingers closed around the money. "Run along, then. Go buy yourselves something yummy."

Chattering delightedly amongst themselves, the three boys headed back to the market street with their prizes clutched in tight fists.

"So," Kesari said, returning her attention to Amar and the others. "You're looking for Tamaya?"

"We've been looking for her all day," Amar grumbled. "No one here will tell us anything."

She stooped to pick up her basket of eggs. "She doesn't like to be disturbed, and the locals don't like to get on her bad side."

"Why?" Mitul asked. "Are they afraid of her or something?"

"Sort of. She's easily the most powerful Tarja in this province, and one of the most powerful healers in Kavora, maybe in all of Erythyr. Someone whose good graces you want to remain in, especially if you might need a favor from her someday."

"But you can help us find her?" Saya said.

"For a price."

Saya's lips pressed together in a thin smile. "Of course."

Kesari shrugged. "A girl has to put a roof over her head and food in her belly somehow."

"And you're not worried about getting on Tamaya's bad side?" Amar asked. "If everyone else is, why not you?"

"Oh, I'm not from here," Kesari said. "Just a traveler passing through, like you."

"Then how do you know where she lives?"

Kesari shrugged. "I'm persistent. It took some time, but I found her home. I've made the trip there several times now."

Amar reached for his coin pouch. "How much do you want? Tell us where she lives, and we'll be on our way."

"It's better if I take you. Make sure you find it all right."

"Fine," he replied shortly. Maybe he shouldn't be so quick to trust a stranger—especially one as odd as this girl—but they'd wasted enough time already. "How much?"

"Twenty jitaara."

Amar bit back a retort about extortion and counted out the coins. It was nearly everything he had left, and Mitul and Saya didn't have much more. With a grudging twist in his stomach, he dropped them into Kesari's waiting palm. "Lead the way."

ALEIDA

IT WAS NEARLY SUNSET BY THE TIME ALEIDA AND VALKYRA RODE into Tarsi. Despite this, the market street was still noisy and crowded as vendors called out reduced prices and promises of quality in an attempt to make a little more coin before nightfall. Aleida slowed her horse from a gallop to a walk and patted his sweat-dampened neck. "Good boy. We made it."

The horse only let out a soft snort in response, probably too tired to do much else. Aleida slid off his back and wrapped the reins around her hands. She'd pushed him hard this afternoon, hoping to reach Tarsi before nightfall. Her quarry couldn't be too far.

All they had to do now was find him in the teeming mass of people that packed the street ahead.

"Where should we look?" she asked Valkyra.

The small, furry dragon pulled her tiny claws free from the shoulder of Aleida's tunic, where they'd dug in to allow her to maintain her perch even with the horse's jostling strides. She unwrapped her tail from around the base of Aleida's neck and stretched her white, silky body before responding. "Start asking around. Maybe one of the vendors saw them earlier."

Aleida squeezed her way into the crowd with the horse following along behind her. He was easily the largest animal in the market, and their passing disrupted the natural flow of foot traffic. More than a few people cast irritated glances in their direction. Several times, their expressions only darkened further when they saw who was leading the horse.

"No shame, dear," Valkyra whispered in her ear. "Not for them."

"Not for anyone," Aleida finished.

She held her head higher and set her mouth in a firm line. Let them stare. Let them take in the sight of her ash brown hair and pale blue eyes shining against even paler skin—features that immediately marked her as Visan. Features that so often drew confusion and even hatred into the gazes of the Kavorans around her. But she could handle their stares along with their judgments, so let them judge.

No shame.

Besides, the fact that foreigners were a rarity here could work to her advantage. The things that made Aleida stand out in Tarsi were the very same things that would make her quarry stand out, too. The man who couldn't die had the same black hair and deep brown skin as these people, as did the musician. But their other companion, a Sularan warrior, was as much an outsider here as Aleida and would have drawn just as much attention.

A stern-faced old woman met Aleida's gaze for a moment before shifting her attention back to her work. Chickens squawked in cages lining the wall behind the woman. Others hung by their necks from the top of the stall, already plucked and ready for cooking. The smell of blood pressed against Aleida's nostrils as she approached the stall.

"Excuse me," she said. "I'm looking for some people who may have passed through here. There's a young man and a Sularan woman, both about my age. The Sularan wears red paint on her face. They would have been with an older man, perhaps forty. He carries a saraj."

"I haven't seen anyone like that," the woman replied. She turned around and grabbed a struggling chicken from one of the cages. "Good fortune to you, though, and goodbye."

Her response was so quick and rushed Aleida doubted whether she'd really paid attention. "Please, if you could think about it for a moment. The older man may have played some music in the street, or—"

"Are you going to buy a chicken?" The woman turned the point of her knife toward Aleida, her other hand still clutching the flapping bird by its legs.

"I—well, no, I only—"

"If you're not going to buy anything, you should leave. Your horse is blocking my stall."

Aleida opened her mouth, but Valkyra's feathery wing brushed against her cheek before she could speak. "Come," the dragon said. "Let's ask elsewhere. There's no sense wasting any more time here."

Aleida shot the woman a parting glare before tugging on the reins and trudging forward.

The other vendors were no more helpful, and some even less so. One man spotted Valkyra and, presumably thinking she was an ordinary pet dragon, grabbed Aleida by the wrist and led her to the back of his stall where several of the creatures sat in cages. Like Valkyra, they were furred and feathered, with long necks and horns curving gracefully behind their heads, but they were brown and gray and black instead of white. Aleida told the man she didn't have the money to buy one and wasn't interested in breeding hers, but he wouldn't take no for an answer. At least, not until Valkyra bit his finger. Aleida ran from the stall so quickly she almost left her horse behind.

Irritated by this encounter, she continued down the street, repeating her questions with even less patience than before. Everyone she talked to quickly dismissed her. All they seemed to care about was money. Unless her quarry had handed some over to one of them, they'd probably stared right past him and his friends.

The sun sank lower, and Artex painted a sunset of peachy oranges and rosy pinks in the sky. It was gorgeous, the kind of sunset that deserved to be watched and admired until it faded into night, but Aleida didn't have time. So much time had already slipped away from her, and she was still no closer to finding the man who couldn't die. She had to keep going.

Still, she spared a moment to offer a silent prayer to her god. *Please, Artex, help me find them.* As an afterthought, she added, *And thank you for the beauty you're sharing with us this evening.*

"Are you sure you don't want to rest?" Valkyra asked.

"Not yet," Aleida replied.

"You've been pushing yourself so hard these last few days. You must be exhausted."

"I'm fine." She would have to be. And besides, whatever fatigue she felt now was nothing compared to what Tyrus was going through.

"We can always start fresh in the morning. If it turns into another fight, you'll need your strength. We're outnumbered."

"I said I'm *fine*." This was her chance, so close she could almost feel it in her fingertips. She wouldn't let her own weakness be the thing that held her back. For Tyrus' sake, she couldn't afford that.

The merchants were starting to pack up their wares now. If there were any answers to be found here, she was running out of time to find them. She approached the closest man, who was packing fresh vegetables into a handcart. "Can you spare a moment to talk? I'm looking for some people. Maybe you've seen them. There were two men, one about my age and one older. And a Sularan woman with red markings painted on her face."

The man continued his work, not even so much as acknowledging Aleida's presence. This was a waste of time. He wasn't going to tell her anything. She pulled on the horse's reins, ready to walk away.

"Wait," the man said. He met her gaze for the first time, a greedy glint in his dark eyes. "Nothing in the markets of Tarsi is free, you know. Not even information."

"Are you saying you've seen them?"

The man clicked his tongue and rubbed his thumb and forefinger together like he was holding a coin. Aleida sighed and reached for the small bag under the hem of her tunic. She counted out five jitaara— more than a quarter of the money she had left—and passed the coins over to the man. He counted them quickly and raised an eyebrow as if asking for more, but Aleida stared back at him coldly.

"They were here earlier this afternoon," he said. "Three of them, just as you described—a Sularan woman, a young man of about the same age, and an older man carrying a saraj. They were asking about Tamaya Takhar."

"Who is that?"

"She's the best Tarja in this region. People say she drew all the waters out of the Mayuka River to flood the enemy's camp during the siege of Jakhat."

What could the man she hunted possibly want with such a powerful Tarja? Aleida pushed the question to the back of her mind and voiced a far more important one. "Where can I find Tamaya?"

The man flicked one of the coins Aleida had given him into the air and caught it again. "Seems you're trying to get more information than you paid for now."

Something cold and desperate uncoiled inside Aleida's gut and slithered into her heart. She dropped the horse's reins and took two steps closer to the man. Annoyance flickered in his eyes as she invaded his personal space. He opened his mouth, but her hand shot out and closed around his throat before he could speak.

A frosty chill rose within her like a tidal wave, and she took a deep breath to quell her anger before channeling altma. The magical energy flowed through her Bond with Valkyra and into her limbs, lending her extra strength, which she used to shove the man against his cart. She brought her face to within mere centimeters of his. His eyes were wide, his lip quivered, and his pulse raced beneath her fingertips like a frightened rabbit.

Valkyra's tail lashed back and forth against Aleida's shoulder, and she leaned in to whisper in her ear. "That's it, dear, stay in control."

The man's eyes darted to Valkyra and back to Aleida in sudden understanding. "Your dragon—it's not just...you're Bonded. You're a Tarja."

"Let's try this again," Aleida said evenly. "I asked you a question, and you're going to answer me. Where can I find Tamaya?"

The man sputtered and continued to squirm beneath her grasp. "I can't. She doesn't like outsiders. If I make her angry, she—"

Aleida drew on more altma, this time channeling it into an electric jolt that tingled in her fingertips. It shot out in tiny, blue sparks to shock the merchant. He whimpered in pain, and Aleida's conscience winced, but she didn't heed it. She couldn't afford to, not when she was closing in on her quarry. No shame. No guilt. Not for anyone.

"Right now," she said, "you're making *me* angry. And you don't want that, do you? Tell me where she is."

"East," the man rasped. "Outside the city."

Aleida let go of his throat so he could speak more easily. "Go on."

He coughed a few times. "Follow the road until you cross over the creek. There's a narrow trail that leads up into the hills. When you reach the falls at the top, go east again, through the trees. Her house is in a clearing not too far in. It's a long trek on foot. If you hurry, you might catch up to the people you're looking for before they get there." He looked up at her with pleading eyes. "Tamaya never has to know I sent you."

"If you're lying to me," Aleida hissed, "you'll have bigger problems to worry about than Tamaya." She took hold of the horse's reins, mounted, and wheeled him around to head east. Everyone they passed stared, but now their expressions were full of fear rather than disdain. They backed away and pressed themselves against each other as she rode by.

A gentle whisper brushed against Aleida's conscience. She shouldn't have used her magic to intimidate the man like that. He was only trying to make a living, like anyone else. And for that, she'd hurt him. She'd damaged another one of Artex's most precious creations simply because she'd been too impatient to come to an understanding with him.

We are all children of the Artist, beautiful works created by His hand. It's our duty to treat each other accordingly. Mama's voice, a memory as clear as still water in Aleida's mind.

Guilt floundered inside her like a fish dragged out of the sea. Torturing a man for any reason wasn't something the girl she used to be would have done. It wasn't something that girl would have even considered. But between the invasion of her homeland, her parents' deaths, Tyrus' illness, this pursuit—somewhere along the way, she'd let it all turn her into a person she barely recognized.

But that was who she'd had to become to survive. The girl she'd been before never would have been able to claw and fight and scrap for not only her own life, but her brother's as well. The girl she'd been before would have given up on saving Tyrus long ago, as soon as the hunt became too difficult. The girl she'd been before would have put all her trust in ideals that offered nothing but vain hope and quickly shattered comfort to those foolish enough to cling to them. The girl she'd been before was weak, and Aleida hated her.

A small part of her also mourned that girl's passing.

Valkyra shifted on her shoulder, settling back down into a relaxed, sprawling position. Her claws hooked into the fabric of Aleida's shirt. "You handled that situation well. I sensed your anger, but your power was perfectly controlled."

"I scared him."

"Was that not the objective?"

"It was. But I shouldn't have hurt him."

"Oh, my darling, you only did what you had to do." Her voice was as soft and soothing as the fur that brushed against Aleida's cheek. "There's too much at stake to waste time on other people's comfort. You saw the way they looked at you. Do you think he would have hesitated to force answers from you if your roles had been reversed?"

"No."

"Then don't let it trouble you. Focus on what lies ahead. What will you do when you catch up to the man you seek?"

Aleida set her jaw, recalling the disastrous outcome of their fight four nights before. The musician had never been a threat, but she hadn't bargained on going up against a Sularan warrior, and the man who couldn't die was a better fighter than either she or Valkyra had anticipated.

This time would be different, though. This time, she wouldn't give any of them a chance to fight back. "I'll take them by surprise," she said to Valkyra. "And then I'll kill them all."

She urged the horse into a gallop. A short stretch of road and some hills were all that now stood between her and the man who couldn't die. Only once she had used his power to save Tyrus' life would she finally allow herself to rest.

KESARI

THE JOURNEY TO TAMAYA'S HOUSE WASN'T A PARTICULARLY DIFFICULT one, and the three strangers Kesari had picked up in Tarsi could have found it well enough on their own if she'd given them directions. But this would work out better for everyone. Sure, she was selfishly using them for her own gain, but escorting the trio to Tamaya herself meant they'd be spared some time and guesswork along the way. As an added bonus, they could potentially provide her with a chance to earn Tamaya's favor, and Kesari *needed* Tamaya's favor. A rewarding arrangement for all involved, and one she'd played out with other travelers on at least half a dozen prior occasions.

Of course, none of those occasions had panned out the way she'd hoped, but Kesari had a good feeling about these three. She glanced back at them, trailing behind her on the narrow path through the forest, and smiled to herself. Yes, there was something very unique about these three. Something special. The kind of special that might finally capture Tamaya's interest.

"How much farther?" Amar asked gruffly as he reached Kesari's side. Of her three new companions, he was the one she kept the closest eye on. He didn't seem to like her very much; his dark eyes had watched her with suspicion from the moment they met. His face was fixed in a stern frown that made him look much older than he really was—only a couple years older than her, if she had to guess. An ancient-looking sword with a basket hilt hung at his waist next to a modern flintlock pistol, and he carried himself with the quick, strong grace of a fighter. Not someone she wanted to cross.

"We'll get there a little after nightfall," she told him.

On that note, Tamaya probably wouldn't be pleased about receiving visitors so late, especially if they turned out to be unremarkable. Kesari needed to find out more about them before they arrived. She didn't want to irritate the old woman any more than necessary, and she could always slip away if need be, once she brought the three travelers safely to their destination.

The older man, Mitul, would be the easiest to talk to. Amar clearly wasn't the friendly type, and the Sularan woman, Saya, was even more intimidating with her tall frame and muscular physique. But Mitul had a kind, honest face and smiled easily. It wasn't much to base her judgment on, but she had to start somewhere. She slowed her pace until she fell back beside him, allowing Amar and Saya to take the lead.

She opened with a polite, easy question. "How long have you been playing…" She nodded to the instrument slung across his back. "I'm sorry, I forget what it's called."

"The saraj," Mitul replied. "I've played it since I was a boy. Almost as long as I can remember."

"That's a long time. You must be good."

"Good enough to earn an honest living, which is all I really need."

Kesari eyed the instrument curiously. It looked complicated with all its strings and frets. "I always thought it would be fun to play music, but I never learned."

"What kind of instruments are most popular in Atrea?" Mitul asked. "That's where you're from, isn't it?"

Her smile began to slip a little, but she recovered, adopting her most cheerful, friendly voice. "That's right. How could you tell?"

"Your accent," Mitul said. "You speak Kavoran well for a foreigner, though."

"My mother's Kavoran. I learned some from her before I came here."

"I see. Did she come with you?"

A chill bloomed inside Kesari's chest. What was she supposed to say to that?

"I'm sorry," Mitul said at the lull in the conversation. "I don't mean to pry. You just seem young to be out on your own, so far from home."

"I'm sixteen," she said, as though that were a perfectly normal explanation. Her high, nervous voice sounded pitifully childish. This wasn't how the conversation was supposed to go. *She* was supposed to be the one asking questions, not the other way around. She needed to get things back on track.

"Why do you need Tamaya's help?" she asked. If she had to guess, it was something to do with the haseph markings painted on Saya's face, but the woman hadn't spoken a word since they'd left Tarsi.

Mitul began to stammer a response, but Amar cut him off. "Who says we need her help?"

Kesari shrugged. "Why else would you be going to see her?"

"That's our business." Amar's voice was low and harsh. "We paid you to show us the way, not to ask questions."

"There's no need to be rude," Mitul said, casting an apologetic look at Kesari. "I'm sorry. His manners could use some work, but he's right. It's probably best if we keep that to ourselves. You're a nice girl, and I'm sure you're perfectly trustworthy, but..."

"But we don't owe you an explanation," Amar finished sharply.

Well, *that* was an interesting response. What was making him so guarded? She glanced down at the lantern hanging from her coat. Two dark voids in the center of the flame stared back at her. No doubt Lucian had several thoughts about their new companions, but for now, it was best he stayed in the lantern, away from gawking stares and the questions and judgments that always followed.

Kesari raised her hands in a placating gesture. "I only asked because Tamaya tends to be picky about the work she'll take on from outsiders. She turns most people away at the door. If you're looking for help with some common problem that could be solved by any ordinary Tarja, you're wasting your time."

"So we've heard," Mitul said, adjusting the strap of his saraj over one shoulder. "But our problem is a very unique one. We've talked to other Tarja—a lot of them—and no one has been able to figure it out yet."

A smile pulled at Kesari's lips, but she did her best to conceal it. "Good. That's good. A magical mystery—she'll like that." And if she was the one to bring this magical mystery right to Tamaya's doorstep, the old Tarja would surely owe her a favor.

They crossed a narrow bridge at a spring that met with the road, Kesari taking the lead once more to guide the others onto a rocky trail along a jagged hillside. They walked single file, Amar following directly behind Kesari, then Mitul and Saya bringing up the rear. The colorful sunset had faded to a dusky gray, and Kesari unhooked the lantern from her coat to light the path ahead.

"How is it that the fire in your lantern is so bright and yet never seems to burn out?" Amar asked, his voice laced with the same mistrust he'd regarded her with all afternoon.

"Magic." It wasn't a lie, though it wasn't exactly the truth, either.

"Magic," Amar repeated. "I've never seen magic that could be sustained for so long without a Tarja to maintain it. Unless *you're* the one keeping the flame alive."

The two black eyes inside the lantern stared back at Kesari, unblinking. She let out a short, forced laugh. "I'm no Tarja. I don't even know enough about magic to explain how it works." Another lie—she knew plenty about magic—but lies were so much simpler than the truth.

They walked in silence for a while, conserving their breath for the laborious hike up the hillside. When they reached a small waterfall at the crest, Kesari paused to catch her breath. The others did the same without protest.

"How much farther?" Mitul asked.

Kesari pointed across a swath of tall grass into the forest beyond. "Not far. It's a little way into these trees."

Amar nodded. "Let's go, then."

She'd barely taken three strides when the flame inside her lantern surged bright and hot—a warning from Lucian. Kesari didn't have time to react. He burst into the night in a flurry of curling flames and crackling sparks.

A chill settled over her. Lucian had revealed himself, and now there would be questions—the ones she always tried to avoid. She whipped around, taking in the others' shocked expressions, and opened her mouth to explain.

What she saw behind them made her stop. A young woman charged up the hill, the rush of the waterfall drowning out the sound of her footsteps. Blue lightning sparked between her palms, and every inch of her was tensed like a predator on the attack.

She was nearly upon them. Kesari barely had time to shout a warning to the others. "Behind you!"

AMAR

THE FLAMES HAD A FACE.

For a few frozen seconds, that was the only thought in Amar's head as he stared at the fiery thing that had burst from Kesari's lantern. It hovered in the empty air a second longer, then rushed between Amar and Mitul, past Saya still behind them.

It had a *face*.

Kesari shouted something, but before Amar could ask what was going on, Saya called his name. "Amar!"

He whirled around. The fiery being spread out like a wall behind Saya. On the other side, a thin figure skidded to a stop.

It was *her*. In the light of the orange flames, stark shadows played across the sharp planes of the Visan girl's face. On her shoulder, the white dragon Amar assumed to be her Spirit Tarja bared its tiny fangs.

He gritted his teeth as the same question screamed in his mind. What did she want with them? Why was she so determined for a fight, especially when the odds were stacked against her?

It didn't matter. He couldn't have her endangering him and his friends anymore. He drew his pistol, took aim through the fire, and squeezed off the single shot he always kept loaded in the weapon.

The white dragon moved in a blur. Rather than hitting the girl, Amar's shot struck the creature square in the chest, and it jerked back with its wings unfurled. But there was no blood, and it quickly righted itself in the air. He hadn't hurt it at all.

It was impossible to hurt something already dead.

Beside him, Saya nocked an arrow to her bowstring. The Visan girl didn't give her a chance to shoot. She raised a hand. A stream of water flew from the nearby falls and plunged through the wall of fire. The burst struck Saya, knocking her off balance, and scattered droplets soaked into Amar's clothes. Steam billowed around the Visan girl as she dashed through the remaining flames.

Amar holstered his gun and drew his sword, calling over his shoulder. "Get out of here, Mitul!" Whether Kesari took cover as well was her choice.

Their opponent was forming a barrier between her palms—the same kind she'd trapped him with four nights ago. Saya loosed an arrow at the iridescent energy taking shape in hands, but the other girl dodged with unnatural speed. Amar closed the distance between them. His sword flew in a series of practiced thrusts and slashes, but she evaded each blow with ease. The barrier in her hands continued to grow.

The fiery thing from Kesari's lantern danced around them. What *was* it, anyway? Some kind of magic, but it seemed alive, its movements following the fight to illuminate the darkness around Amar as though it were helping him of its own free will. But that was impossible, unless...

She *was* a Tarja, and not an ordinary one. Like the Visan girl, she was Bonded to a Spirit Tarja, but hers took the form of a flame.

Why had she lied?

A question for another time. He couldn't let himself be distracted now.

Too late. His blade slid through empty air, and the Visan girl seized his wrist. His skin burned on contact with hers, and a shock travelled through his entire being. Every muscle tightened in searing pain, limbs so rigid he felt he would shatter.

As suddenly as the sensation had begun, it was over. His body was like ice, frozen midair in the swirling mist of the Visan girl's barrier. He couldn't move, couldn't speak. Was he really such a fool that he'd let himself be trapped again?

The fiery Spirit Tarja shot past Amar and straight into the girl's face. She flinched, giving Saya an opening. An arrow cut across her outer thigh. The girl cried out, and the barrier rippled, weakening. She propelled herself backward with magic before Saya could fire another shot. The maneuver was clumsy compared to the effortless grace she'd shown before.

This was his chance. Amar strained against the weakened barrier and managed to take a swing at it with his sword. A much slower, weaker swing than he was normally capable of, but it was enough. The barrier dissipated, and he fell. He landed on his feet and launched himself at the retreating girl.

He was closing in fast. A few more steps, and he could end this.

Lightning crackled in the girl's hands as she extended a glowing palm. Amar skidded to a stop and dove to the side. A sparking bolt struck the ground where he'd just been, scorching the grass.

Recovering his stance, he faced his opponent again. Her breath remained calm and even, but her expression was visibly strained. Blood soaked through her torn pants where Saya's arrow had grazed flesh.

"Who are you?" Amar called out between labored breaths. He didn't expect an answer, but he was tired of playing this game without knowing its purpose. "What do you want with us?"

"Why don't you surrender and find out?" she called back in heavily accented Kavoran.

"Why would we surrender when we have you outnumbered?" Saya challenged. She let another arrow fly.

Amar darted in for an attack while the girl was distracted. The fire Spirit Tarja hovered overhead, but the white dragon launched itself straight into the flames. Neither one could harm the other, but that didn't stop them from trying. They flew high into the air, darting around each other in a frantic sort of dance, and the world around Amar went dark except for the glint of his blade and the flickering glow of lightning from the Visan girl's hands.

No more games. He'd given her every chance to retreat. If she was going to keep coming after them and putting his friends' lives in danger, he couldn't hold back. He had to put a stop to this. Now.

He quickened the pace of his attacks to an almost reckless fury, but his opponent still matched each movement. Was she even feeling any of this? Judging by the speed and grace of her movements, he doubted it. She was using her magic to strengthen her own body—something that was just as dangerous for her as it was for him. Magic could numb pain, but she wouldn't be able to heal her wounds until the fight was over, and she couldn't maintain this pace forever.

Saya closed in to join the fight, now wielding a set of matching dual daggers. The reach of Amar's sword gave him an advantage, but with the Visan girl's concentration now split between two foes, they were wearing her down at last. She switched tactics, using her magic to defend rather than attack.

Saya and Amar drove their opponent back to the river. Her foot faltered on the rocky bank. Saya seized the opening, slicing at her throat with a dagger. The Visan girl spun away at the last second, colliding with Amar. She grabbed his sword arm, and jagged lines of blue lightning curled around his wrist. As pain shot up his arm, she wrenched his sword from his weakened grasp with magically amplified force.

She was going to kill him. It was too late to change that. She was too close—too fast and strong—and he was unarmed. Saya wasn't going to be able to stop her in time.

The blade slashed across his stomach, tearing through flesh and the organs underneath in a savage sweep.

Warm, wet blood seeped into his clothes and spread across his skin. Someone screamed his name—Saya, maybe, or Mitul. Pain followed, hot and agonizing in its sharpness. The world swayed and lurched. His body collapsed in what felt like a delayed, lazy motion. He landed on his knees before toppling onto his side. His sword rested in the grass before his eyes, glistening with his own blood.

Footsteps thundered past him, and he caught a glimpse of a retreating figure skidding down the hillside. His vision swam as something wet slipped down his cheek. More blood? He tasted salt. Tears.

Why was he crying? He wasn't going to die—not really. He *couldn't* die. This probably wasn't even his worst death. He couldn't remember, but he was almost certain he'd experienced greater pain than this before, more gruesome deaths, more painful violence.

A figure knelt on the ground beside him, and Mitul's face came into focus. His deep brown eyes were brimming with anguish. A new ache filled Amar's chest as Mitul placed his hands over the wound, trying in vain to stop the bleeding.

"Can't you do something?" Mitul pleaded. His voice was muffled, far away.

Another set of legs came into view. Amar tried to force his gaze upward, but his strength was ebbing, and even that simple movement was exhausting. He only managed to get his eyes high enough to glimpse the bottom of a blue frock coat.

Kesari. She'd stayed. A fight that wasn't hers, and she'd stayed anyway. Brave kid, that one.

Amar closed his eyes. Mitul's voice spoke again. "You're a Tarja! You can save him. Please, I can't lose him."

You won't lose me, Amar wanted to say. *I'll always be here.* But he was tired, and the ground, which had been so cold just moments ago, was now warm and soft and welcoming.

It would be easier if he didn't fight it.

He wasn't sure where that thought had come from, but instinctively, it felt right. This was familiar. He had been here before, done this before, and the outcome was always the same. Why fight it?

He forced his eyes open one last time and summoned every last shred of energy he had to smile at Mitul. He wasn't sure whether it worked, or if Mitul even saw it, but that was all he had left to give.

He closed his eyes again, let the soft warmth of the ground envelop him, and slipped into oblivion.

KESARI

"YOU'RE A TARJA! YOU CAN SAVE HIM. PLEASE, I CAN'T LOSE HIM."

Mitul's hands were wet and red. He stared up at Kesari with wide, frantic eyes, but she couldn't move. She couldn't speak. All she could do was stare at the young man sprawled out on the grass at her feet, watching his blood pool beneath his body and the uneven rise and fall of his chest as he sucked in his last breaths.

A memory began to flicker at the edges of her consciousness. Kesari squeezed her hands into fists. Not now. Please, not now. But the more she tried to push it away, the stronger it became, until it was all she could see.

Like she was right back *there*.

A man carries a young woman onto the street. Her eyes are wide, her face streaked with ash, her dress torn and bloody. He lays her on the ground and pleads through sobs. "Stay with me. Please, Susanna, stay." His hands, clutching hers, are covered in blood.

The woman sucks in a shuddering gasp, then goes still.

"How is he?" Saya's voice broke through the memory. "Is he—"

"Not yet. But if we don't get him some help soon..." Mitul looked around. "The Visan woman?"

Saya knelt next to Amar and placed her hands over Mitul's, applying pressure to the gaping wound. "Rode off on a horse. I put an arrow in her back, but it didn't stop her. What do you need? How can I help?"

An orange glow fell over them as Lucian drew near. He hovered beside Kesari and spoke into her ear, but she couldn't make out the words, only the fiery crackle beneath his voice. It rose to a roar, and suddenly, everything was on fire.

People pour from the burning building, coughing, screaming, and clinging to one another. Bodies shove and press against her in their frenzied efforts to escape the flames. The smell of smoke fills her nostrils, suffocating her.

"Kes?"

Death. Horrible, painful death, everywhere she looks. And no sign of Rajiv anywhere.

Her fault. All of it is her fault.

"Kesari!"

She blinked until the fire disappeared, and it was only the dying man and his friends in front of her.

"Don't just stand there!" Saya yelled. "You're a Tarja. Do something!"

Something strong and sharp clamped down on her lungs like the jaws of a wild creature, refusing to let her go. "I can't." Her voice was barely a whisper.

"Try," Mitul said. "Please."

"I can't."

"Kes." Lucian's voice.

She shut her eyes. If she looked at him right now, if she saw the fire, she wouldn't be able to block out the memories. They would consume her. Still, his voice was a comfort, something familiar to keep her grounded where she was. Not back *there*, on that day. But here, now, on a wooded hill in Kavora, not far from Tamaya Takhar's house. A man was dying, and his friends wanted her to save him.

"Kes," Lucian whispered. "It's all right. You're safe. Amar is dying, but we might be able to help him. I can walk you through it. You can give him a chance."

"What if I make things worse?"

"They can't get any worse," Lucian said.

"Please try," Mitul urged.

She wanted to. A small, frail part of her, locked away deep down in the dark, wanted nothing more than to help him, to use her magic and save his life. The stronger part of her was sick at the idea.

"I can't."

Saya glared up at her, the muscles in her neck and shoulders taut as she shouted. "What's wrong with you? He's going to die, and you're going to stand there and—"

"Enough!" Lucian roared back, growing as big as a wolf and swooping down in front of Saya. She jerked back, eyes wide. Lucian shrunk back down to his usual apple-sized ball of flame and spoke more gently. "If she says she can't do it, she can't do it. I'm sorry."

"It doesn't matter anymore," Mitul said quietly. He pulled his hands away from Amar's wound. "He's gone."

The night pressed in on Kesari, threatening to strangle her. Amar was dead, and she had done nothing to stop it. She pulled down the sleeves of her coat—Rajiv's coat—and wrapped it a little tighter around herself. "I'm sorry."

"It's done now." Mitul wiped his bloody hands on the grass and stood up. His eyes were wet, but no tears fell. "How much farther did you say it was to Tamaya's house?"

Kesari exchanged a glance with Lucian. Mitul's voice was weary, his expression tense, but aside from that, he was almost calm. Saya didn't seem particularly distressed, either. She looked at Kesari as if waiting expectantly for her answer. They'd just lost a friend, but already they seemed eager to move on.

Kesari hesitated. "Shouldn't we…take a moment, or something?"

Mitul looked at Saya. "If we can get him to Tamaya's house before he revives, she can see for herself. That might be helpful."

"It would," the warrior agreed.

"I'm sorry," Lucian interjected. "What do you mean, *before he revives?*"

Mitul took a deep breath and looked at Saya again, but she only shrugged. "That's what we wanted to see Tamaya about," he said. "Amar can't die. Not permanently, at least. He always comes back."

"Back to *life?*" Lucian exclaimed.

Mitul nodded. "I know it sounds absurd, but I've seen it twice before this. He's dead now, but he won't be for long."

"He might as well be," Saya said bitterly. "If everything else you've told me is true, he won't be the same when he comes back. He won't remember anything."

Mitul winced at this, casting a forlorn look at Amar's body for the briefest moment before composing his features once more. "We've been through that before," he said softly. "We'll get through it again."

"So you've never seen this phenomenon yourself, then?" Lucian asked Saya. "Yet you believe it?"

"I do. A man I know saw it once, years ago. A man I trust."

Lucian drew closer to Kesari's ear. His glowing heat warmed her cheek as he whispered. "They're out of their minds. They have to be. We should leave before they turn their madness on us."

"What if they're telling the truth?" Kesari hissed back.

"It's not possible. Even the most powerful magic has limits, and death is one of them."

"It's ludicrous," Mitul said, attempting to wipe the blood off his hands in the grass. "Trust me, I know. You're giving us the same looks I've seen on the faces of every Tarja we've told about this. But I don't need you to believe me. I only need you to take us to Tamaya. That was our bargain, wasn't it?"

He made a fair point. Kesari looked at Lucian.

"I don't like this," he murmured.

She turned back to Mitul. "I'll take you. What are we going to do about him?"

"I'll carry him." He nodded to Saya. They both knelt back down, and Saya helped Mitul hoist Amar's body over his shoulders. His thin legs shook as he rose, but then he stood tall and strong. A dark stain was already spreading over his shoulders as Amar's blood seeped into his clothes. "Lead the way."

They set off through the forest. The undergrowth was thin and the trees were spread out in this part of the woods, so it wasn't a difficult trek. Mitul walked next to Kesari much of the way with Saya taking the rear again, watching their backs for any sign of their attacker's return.

Amar's dangling arms flopped haphazardly against Mitul's body. Kesari shook her head and whispered to Lucian in Atrean, not wanting to offend her companions in case they could still hear her. "This is all a little morbid, isn't it? It seems disrespectful."

"Maybe, but we're too far into this madness to turn back now." Below the two empty black spaces that formed his eyes, a wide, jagged shape split open like a fanged mouth—his version of a smile. "Think of it this way. Whether they're telling the truth or their minds are completely addled, Tamaya won't be able to deny that this is all very interesting." The smile faded, and in a softer voice, he said, "You'll finally get your answers."

Answers he didn't necessarily want her to have, despite spending the last two years seeking them with her. "Lucian…"

"It's all right, Kes. I lived my life. I won't take away your freedom to live yours however you see fit."

Mitul hurried a few paces to catch up with them, breathing heavily and struggling under the weight of Amar's corpse. It was amazing he'd managed to carry him so far already without complaint. They were roughly the same height, but Mitul was thin and lanky while Amar had a more muscular physique. He had to be heavy.

"Are we close?" he huffed.

Kesari pointed to a bulky shadow through the trees ahead. "That's her house."

Tamaya's home was a squat, mud brick structure with a thatched roof. A few chickens stirred and clucked at their approach, and Kesari motioned for the others to tread carefully past the garden. At the door, she rang the heavy iron bell hanging from an exterior wall.

They waited, but there was no answer. Kesari rang the bell again.

"Are you sure she's even home?" Mitul asked, shifting Amar's weight. A few drops of blood hit the dirt at his feet.

"She's home," Kesari said, ringing the bell more forcefully now. "She's always home."

And there it was. A faint light seeped through the underside of the door, which was flung open to crash against the wall a moment later. Behind it stood Tamaya Takhar. She stared up at them all with small dark eyes and a drooping frown. Her gray hair was piled on top of her head in a big, round bun, the top of which barely reached Kesari's nose. Her skin was as dark and as creviced as the bark of a teak tree, and in one withered hand, she balanced a magical orb of pale, yellow light.

She raised the light higher to examine her visitors' faces. Her eyes immediately found Kesari's, and she made a guttural sound like she was trying to dislodge something unpleasant. "You again! Won't you let an old woman have some peace and quiet?"

"I'm sorry to disturb you." Kesari touched her palms together in front of her and made a slight bow. "I wouldn't have come if it wasn't important."

"That's what you say every time," the Tarja grumbled. "Well, out with it then. What kind of trouble have you brought me now?"

"Something interesting," Lucian said. He floated over to illuminate Mitul, Amar, and Saya.

Tamaya's lips turned down lower as she peered between their faces. Her gaze lingered on Amar's body for a moment before darting back to Kesari. "I've seen plenty of corpses, girl, and I don't much like the idea of one bleeding all over my doorstep. You have tested my patience for weeks now. I'm finished! If I ever see you here again—"

Kesari thrust out her hand to stop the door from closing. "Wait! Please, hear me out. None of the people I brought here before were half as interesting as this group is. You said you wanted something that wouldn't be a waste of your skills. If what they're saying is true, then this is something worthy of your time."

Tamaya crossed her arms, her toe tapping impatiently, but she said nothing.

"Just listen to what they have to say," Kesari pleaded. "If I'm wrong, I swear you'll never hear from me again."

Tamaya's eyes narrowed, and for a few moments, her jaw moved back and forth like she was chewing on something. She pointed a gnarled finger at Kesari's face. "I will hold you to your word, girl. You understand?"

"Of course."

"Bring them inside, then."

She held the door open, and Kesari stepped through, followed closely by the others. Tamaya jerked a nod to a room on the left, and inside, they found an empty bedroll spread out on the floor. "You can lay him there," she said.

Saya helped Mitul maneuver Amar's body onto the bedroll. Kesari's stomach churned at the sight of his wound and the exposed parts beneath it. She took deep breaths through her mouth to avoid the iron scent of blood.

Tamaya approached the bed with grim curiosity, shaking her head. Her thin fingers searched for a pulse at Amar's neck, then again at his wrist. She muttered something to herself before turning to face Kesari and the others. "Now that I've invited a corpse into my house in the middle of the night, would someone care to explain what all this is about?"

Tamaya fixed her gaze on Kesari, and Mitul looked at Saya, who stared back at him with a shrug. Kesari shifted her eyes to the floor before anyone could start demanding answers from her.

Mitul cleared his throat. "Well, to start with, he's not exactly a corpse."

Tamaya raised an eyebrow. "I've seen a lot of dead bodies in my time. Seen a lot of *nearly* dead bodies, too. There's a difference. Your friend here is most certainly dead."

Mitul nodded. "For now. But I've seen him die three times now. He always comes back to life the next morning, but when he does, he can't remember anything from before he died. That's why we came to see you. We want to know what's happening to him."

"And you thought I'd find *this* more convincing, is that it?" She gestured to Amar's body.

"It wasn't supposed to happen like this," Mitul said. "I'm truly sorry for the inconvenience, and the mess. We were attacked on the way here. But if you can wait until morning, you'll see for yourself."

Tamaya looked at Saya. "And you—you've seen this as well?"

"No," she said. "But I know Mitul to be an honest man. I believe him."

The old Tarja grunted and began to mutter under her breath, casting dubious looks at all of them. After a short pause, she sighed. "I'm going to bed. Wake me up when he's alive again." She shuffled past Kesari and Lucian on her way to the door.

"You believe them?" Lucian asked with a hint of amusement in his voice.

Tamaya's hunched shoulders shifted forward in a shrug. "No magic I know of can bring back the dead, but I learned long ago not to assume anything's impossible. Besides, what's the harm in waiting to see how this plays out?" She shot a glance back at Mitul. "True or not, I can see *he* believes what he's saying. Which means either he's right, or he's gone mad. Either way, this is the most intriguing riddle I've been faced with in a long while."

Kesari's heart leaped. "Does that mean you'll answer my questions?"

"I suppose it does," Tamaya muttered. "But not now. Even an old woman needs her beauty sleep." She swept aside the colorful woven cloth hanging in the doorway and left the room.

"What now?" Lucian asked, floating down a little lower to hover at Kesari's shoulder.

She leaned against the wall with her hands behind her back. "Now, I suppose we wait."

ALEIDA

WITH EACH OF THE HORSE'S FOOTFALLS, THE SHARP POINT OF THE arrow embedded in Aleida's lower back seemed to be digging itself deeper, one hair's breadth at a time. Her fingers itched to pull it out, but that would only worsen the bleeding, and she couldn't stop to deal with her injuries yet—not until she was far away from that Sularan warrior and any chance of being pursued.

What she really needed was more strength and less pain. Magic could help with that. She drew in altma from her surroundings—the trees, the grass, any living energy source she could sense—and channeled it through her entire body. The effect was minuscule. Maybe she'd finally reached her limits. Maybe her emotions were in too much turmoil to command her magic after coming so close to death. Breathing techniques and calming meditations could sometimes be useful in reestablishing control, but not so much with an arrow in her back and a wide, raw gash across her thigh. Or maybe she was simply too feeble-minded to focus, in this condition.

She tried again, but the altma she did manage to channel was weak and quickly slipped from her grasp. She tilted her head back and roared into the starry sky above.

"Stop here," Valkyra said.

They were only halfway back down the trail they'd followed into the hills. "We should keep going."

"You *can't* keep going like this. I doubt they'll pursue us this far on foot. We should be safe enough."

She was probably right, and stopping to rest and heal would be a welcome respite. Aleida pulled back on the reins. A new wave of pain shot up into her shoulder blades as the arrow in her back shifted. Skies be damned, she just wanted to get the thing *out*.

With a cry, she forced her leg over the saddle and slid clumsily from her horse's back. Despite her best efforts not to lean on her injured leg, it still burned and oozed fresh blood when she put the slightest pressure on it. She stumbled forward and barely managed to catch herself on her hands when she hit the ground.

"We need to get that arrow out before we can heal your injuries," Valkyra said, hopping off her shoulder. "You won't be able to get a good angle to pull it straight out. It might be better if I do it."

Aleida grit her teeth and dug her fingers deep into the grass and the cool dirt beneath. "Do it."

Valkyra went around to Aleida's back, then stretched up and placed her tiny, clawed forelegs on either side of the shaft. There was a tight pressure around the wound as she pushed against Aleida's body to give herself more leverage, then an intense pain and a slow squelching noise as the arrowhead came free. Aleida sucked in and bit down on the insides of her cheeks to stifle a scream.

Valkyra fluttered to rest in front of her with the arrow in her jaws. Red blood smeared across the pristine white fur at her muzzle and feet. She dropped the projectile onto the ground. "We need to start by mending the tissue underneath. Do you think you can do that?"

Aleida started to nod, but stopped herself and shrugged instead. Healing oneself was said to be twice as difficult as healing someone else, and healing magic had never been one of her strengths. She could channel altma with a force that rivaled some of the best Tarja soldiers in the Kavoran army, but healing required a different kind of precision. Valkyra had once said it hadn't been a great skill for her, either, when she was alive. That partially explained why it was difficult for Aleida, even under the best of circumstances. Those Bonded to the spirit of a dead Tarja were often limited by the same skills—or lack thereof—that person had once possessed in life.

Could she heal herself now, in this condition? She had no choice but to try.

She reached around and gingerly touched the wound in her back. It didn't feel so bad on the surface, but there was deeper damage underneath. She closed her eyes and tried to seek out the underlying injury with her magic, but there was nothing, no sensation at all. It was as if all her power had abandoned her, leaving her empty. She focused on her connection with Valkyra, who served as a bridge between her abilities and the energy she channeled. Even that didn't seem to help.

"I can't do it."

"You need to calm your mind," Valkyra instructed.

"I am calm!" She tried again, but still felt nothing.

"If that were true, my dear, you wouldn't be struggling to channel your altma now. Take a breath. The danger is past. There's nothing left to fear."

"I'm not afraid," Aleida growled.

"What, then? Something is distracting you."

"Of course something's distracting me. This *hurts!*" Her eyes burned, but she blinked away the tears before they could fall.

Valkyra dipped her head in a nod. "That's good. Acknowledge it. We don't fight our pain. We don't ignore our emotions. But we don't let them overpower us, either. We acknowledge them, accept them, and stay in control."

Aleida fought the urge to strangle the dragon. How easy it must be for her to spout off lessons about control when she wasn't the one suffering. She'd been dead long enough that she probably couldn't even remember what physical pain felt like anymore.

"You're angry," Valkyra observed, meeting Aleida's glare with her usual serene repose. "You're angry at me, and you're angry because we didn't succeed tonight."

"We almost had him," Aleida hissed. "Damn it all, I even managed to kill him. If I'd killed the Sularan, too, we could have taken him, and this would all be over. We could have been on our way back to Tyrus right now. But I failed. *Again.*"

"They were more prepared for us after our last fight, and we never accounted for the Tarja who was with them today."

"I know, but Tyrus is…" An image of her brother's too-thin legs and twisted posture flashed through her mind. She swallowed the lump that rose in her throat. Tyrus was dying. She couldn't bring herself to say it out loud.

"That's it," Valkyra said soothingly. "Acknowledge your feelings and accept them. You can't change what was, only what's to come."

Aleida didn't want to acknowledge her feelings. It would be far less painful to shove them down and pretend they'd never existed. But as she'd learned time and again in the two years she'd been Bonded to Valkyra, burying her emotions would only interfere with her ability to use her magic.

She took a deep breath, closed her eyes, and opened herself to the full force of her inner turmoil. Her physical wounds hurt less than the guilt, disappointment, and fear warring inside her heart. Memories of the fight and everything she could have done differently replayed in her mind. She couldn't afford to make those kinds of mistakes. Tyrus was counting on her, and she'd let him down, wasted time he didn't have.

What if she couldn't succeed before his time ran out? What if he died, leaving her all alone in the world, the sole survivor of her family?

She let it all crash over her in waves until tears began to roll down her cheeks.

For a few minutes, she allowed herself to cry, giving her pain the time it needed to be recognized. Then she raised her chin and wiped away her tears with the back of her hand. She was doing the best she could, and Tyrus was still alive, still counting on her. She couldn't change what was already done. All that was left was to keep going. She'd do better next time.

Valkyra nodded. "Try again."

Aleida reached around to touch the wound at her back, channeled her altma, and sought out the underlying layers of damaged tissue. The magic flowed freely this time. A soothing coolness bloomed inside the wound and spread. The bleeding stopped as muscle and skin knit themselves back together, forming a raw, raised scar on the surface. She pulled her hand away. She could still sense injured muscle and flesh beneath the surface, but the pain was much more bearable now.

She mended her leg next, following a similar process. An angry red line remained across her thigh when she was done. It would split open and bleed again if she wasn't careful, but at least for now, the worst of the damage had been repaired and some of the pain had subsided.

"You did well," Valkyra said. "Now sleep. Magic did most of the work, but your body needs rest to fully heal."

Aleida shook her head and stood up stiffly. She tested her weight on her injured leg. Not as strong as it should have been, but it would have to do for now. "How can I sleep when we're so close? If we go back now—"

Valkyra spread her wings and glided over the grass to the horse. She nipped him in the ankle with her tiny fangs. His ears flicked back, and he let out a panicked whinny as he shot off down the trail.

"Why did you do that?" Aleida cried. "That horse was our best chance of catching up to them!"

"I'll track him down later. Right now, you need to rest, and since you're too stubborn to listen, I decided to take matters into my own hands."

"I'll walk, then."

"And how far do you think you'll get on that leg?"

"Farther than I'll get sitting here."

Valkyra sighed. "Aleida, please. Listen to reason. Even if you could reach them, you're in no condition to fight, and they'll be on their guard now more than ever. We need to reevaluate our plan, and you need to rest."

She was right. Aleida hated every word of her little speech, but she was right. She lowered herself back onto the grass and stretched her injured leg out in front of her.

Valkyra meandered over and sat down, feathery wings folded demurely behind her back. Her silky tail wrapped around her legs. "I know how much you want to save Tyrus," she said gently, "but that man and his friends have outmaneuvered us twice now. We need to be smarter."

"Amar," Aleida said. "His name is Amar."

For so long, the man who couldn't die had been only a story to her, and then only a face. Now he had a name, too—the one the Sularan woman had called out to him during their battle. Somehow, knowing that simple fact about him made him seem more real, more human.

More like her.

But she couldn't let herself think like that. In the end, if it came down to Tyrus' life or Amar's, she would do whatever it took to save her brother.

"Are you certain he's the key to helping Tyrus?" she asked Valkyra. They'd had this discussion many times before, but sometimes it was comforting to hear it all again. Valkyra was always so sure and steadfast, and that confidence was a rock on which Aleida could stand when her own doubts rolled in like storm clouds.

"I'm sure," Valkyra said. "Once we learn the secret to his immortality, we should be able to replicate whatever magic is causing it."

"And Tyrus will live," Aleida said. "But will he be healed?"

"I have every reason to believe so. The information I've gathered indicates that any injuries or illnesses Amar suffers are healed quickly, even when the injury is fatal. That must be part of what prevents him from ever truly dying."

She still didn't understand how it was possible. Before the Kavoran Empire had invaded and conquered Vis, she'd never ventured outside her home city of Libera. There were no natural born Tarja among the Visans, and while Tarja from other nations sometimes passed through the coastal city, magic had been largely a mystery to her. It still was, in many ways. She knew enough of how it worked to call on it herself, but even now, many of the feats accomplished through magic looked like miracles to her.

Sometimes, it was easier for her to think of magic as a kind of faith. She didn't always understand it, just as she didn't always understand Artex's workings, but she believed in the possibilities both offered. She believed Artex would watch over Tyrus and keep him safe while she was away. She believed that Valkyra knew what she was doing, and that once they captured Amar, they could use his unique ability to save Tyrus' life. And if, in the end, that meant using Amar or trading his life for her brother's, then so be it. The fact that she now knew his name changed nothing.

"You really should rest," Valkyra said. "Lie down, sleep. Give the altma in your body a chance to do the rest of its healing work."

"I don't think I'd be able to sleep now even if I wanted to," Aleida muttered, but she lay down anyway, wincing as the muscles in her back stretched around the arrow wound.

"Try." Valkyra took a few steps closer to her, curled up on the ground, and began to sing softly. It was an old Visan lullaby, something her mother used to sing to her and Tyrus. It didn't sound quite the same in Valkyra's Kavoran accent and low voice, but when Aleida closed her eyes, she could almost see Mama sitting beside the bed she and Tyrus had shared as children, stroking their hair while Papa looked on from the doorway.

It was only a memory, and those days were long gone, never to return. But for a moment, Aleida allowed herself to sink further into the comforting illusion it provided. If the only place she and her family could be together was in her dreams, then, for a little while at least, that was where she wanted to be.

AMAR

HE WOKE WITH A GASP, AS THOUGH STARTLED FROM SLEEP. WAS IT A bad dream? What had he been dreaming? Or perhaps it was a noise, though everything was quiet now.

Pale sunlight filtered through a window overhead. It must be dawn, or early evening. But when had he gone to sleep?

No answers came to mind. Not a good sign. He let his gaze drift around the room, searching for something familiar. The doorway was covered by a colorful woven cloth, and a man he didn't recognize dozed against one wall. The bed beneath him was little more than a roll of heavy blankets spread on the floor, and nothing covered him except…

He pressed a hand to his abdomen. There was something thick and dry caked into the fabric of his clothes and flaking from his skin. He raised his fingers to his face. A dark red substance coated them.

Blood.

His? He didn't think so, but where else could it have come from? He sat up carefully just in case. Nothing hurt, but the front of his shirt had a long, ragged tear. He raised the bottom hem to his shoulders to examine the flesh underneath. No wounds, not even so much as a scar.

Someone else's blood, then. Why couldn't he remember?

His gaze darted back to the man sleeping against the wall. A neat, graying beard covered his chin and jawline. Half of his dark hair was pulled back in a knot behind his head while the rest hung loose around his shoulders. His clothes were simple, made of homespun cloth that hung in loose folds over his thin frame. One hand rested on the saraj laid out beside him.

Who was this man? He still had no idea, but he got out of bed and approached him anyway, bending to get a better look at his face.

The stranger stirred, blinked, and looked up. "Amar," he said in a voice still groggy with sleep. "You're awake."

Amar. A name that didn't belong to him. His name was—

His *name* was—

Why couldn't he remember? His heart pounded, and he backed away as fast as his feet would take him.

"It's all right," the man said, pushing himself up off the floor. He held his hands up and slightly outstretched, like he was approaching a wild animal. "You're safe. I know this is all very strange, but I can explain everything. Would you like to sit down?"

Whatever was wrong with his mind, this stranger could have had something to do with it. He wasn't going to stick around for him to continue whatever unpleasantness he was plotting. His eyes found the door, and he ran to it. The man made no move to stop him as he flung aside the colorful fabric.

Another figure stepped in front of him, blocking his path. Red lines crossed her face, not quite dark enough to be blood, but they gave her a fierce appearance nonetheless. He threw a punch at her.

She dodged the blow as if she'd been expecting it. His fist only grazed a few strands of her long brown hair. "Amar, stop!"

He lashed out again, but she caught his arm and attempted to twist it behind his back. Skies above, she was strong. He wrenched free and aimed a kick at her torso. At the same time, she dropped into a crouch and made a sweeping motion with one of her legs. Her stiff foot hooked around his ankles. His legs flew up, and he landed on his back. All the air in his lungs whooshed out in a ragged grunt.

"We just want to talk," said the man from the room, coming to stand over him. "No one is going to hurt you."

Still gasping for air, he grabbed the stranger by the ankle and yanked him down. Then he made a break for the nearest door.

The woman was faster and blocked his path again. "You need to listen, Amar."

"That's not my name!"

"Can't an old woman get any peace and quiet in her own home?" a new voice shouted from another room. The tapestry over the doorway shifted, and a short old woman emerged, hair disheveled and mouth twisted in a disgruntled frown. Her eyes met his. "The dead man rises. It seems your friends were telling the truth."

"He's alive?" said another voice, and a girl with black hair poked her head out of the same doorway. How many people were in this house?

They were all talking to him like they knew him—or knew about him, at least. But he didn't recognize any of them. Who were they? Who was *he*? What did the old woman mean by *the dead man rises*? What dead man?

His eyes shifted between them all. Aside from the taller woman who'd knocked him down, none of them looked particularly dangerous. Maybe his situation wasn't as dire as he'd thought at first. Now he only had questions, too many to count. It might not be such a bad idea to at least hear what they had to say.

"Who are you people?" he asked. "What's happening to me? Where are we?"

The bearded man laid a gentle hand on his shoulder. "Come sit down, and I'll explain everything."

He gestured to the room they'd both awakened in, and they all filed inside. The shorter girl with the dark hair had a magical hovering fire that provided a little more light to see by. A Tarja, then. He'd have to keep a close eye on her. She could be even more dangerous than the taller one.

The man sucked in a breath and held it, as though he couldn't quite figure out where to begin. "I think some introductions would be appropriate," he said after a few moments. "I'm Mitul. Our gracious host is Tamaya Takhar, an esteemed Tarja in this province." He gestured to the older woman beside him.

"My name is Saya," said the tall young woman. "I'm sorry for knocking you down earlier." Her amber-colored irises gleamed in the firelight, and the red markings painted across her face looked suddenly familiar, though she herself didn't. Those were Sularan haseph markings.

How was it that he could recall information like that but couldn't remember anything about himself?

"I'm Kesari," said the other girl. She stuck her hands into the pockets of her long blue coat and nodded to the fire hovering beside her. "And this is Lucian."

"A pleasure to formally meet you," the fire said, and there seemed to be the hint of a face within its flames. Not an ordinary magical fire, then. He had to be a Spirit Tarja, though it was taboo for a Spirit Tarja to Bond with a person as young as Kesari looked. But that was a question for another time.

He felt like he should say something, perhaps give his own name, but he still didn't know it. Amar was as good a name as any for now, but he wasn't about to start introducing himself that way. Instead, he said, "It's nice to meet you all," even though that couldn't have been further from the truth.

"Your name is Amar," Mitul said. "Or at least, it has been for as long as I've known you. Twenty-eight years now. This is the third time I've seen you die, and the third time I've seen you come back to life."

Come back to life…was that what Tamaya had meant? *The dead man rises.* But that was impossible. He shook his head. "I don't understand."

"Let me start at the beginning," Mitul said. "You and I met in Jakhat when I was fifteen. You were a couple years older, or you appeared to be. When we met, you couldn't remember who you were or where you'd come from."

"Sounds familiar," Amar muttered.

Mitul nodded. "Neither of us had anyone else, so we looked out for each other and did what we could to make a living for ourselves. I taught you to play music. You kept us safe and out of trouble. I always thought of you as an older brother."

Brother. He said the word fondly, like it meant something important to him. The way he was looking at Amar, it clearly should have meant something to him, too. But it didn't. He broke their gaze and stared down at the floor.

"We grew up," Mitul went on, "but as the years passed, you never seemed to change the way I did. After a while, people assumed *I* was the older one. We used to laugh about it, like it was a trick we were playing on everyone else. But it bothered you, after so many years."

"What do you mean by that? I didn't change like you did."

"You didn't age," Mitul said. "You never have. Even now, you look exactly as you did when we first met."

Amar frowned. Mitul claimed they'd met nearly three decades ago. The lines in his face and the gray strands in his dark hair reflected that. But according to him, Amar himself still looked like a teenager. "That's not possible."

In the corner of the room, Tamaya let out a snort.

"It gets even more impossible," Mitul said with a hesitant smile. "You and I made a pretty decent living for ourselves playing music in Jakhat. We mostly performed on the streets, but we were often hired to play for wealthy families and even some of the nobility. We were starting to do well enough for ourselves to attract unwanted attention. A gang of thieves broke into our house one night, and things got out of hand. You tried to fight them off—all six of them. I did the best I could to help, but…they killed you."

His eyes drifted to the floor. "I sat with your body for hours. In my shock, I didn't know what else to do. You had no heartbeat. You went cold. You were *dead*. And then suddenly, you weren't. Come morning, you were alive again, and your wounds had vanished." He shook his head. "It was the most incredible thing I'd ever seen, and it was terrifying."

Amar narrowed his eyes. The sincerity in Mitul's voice was almost convincing enough to make him believe this outlandish tale. Almost. Mitul himself certainly seemed to believe it, which could only mean he'd lost his mind. But the others were listening with rapt attention, giving no indication that they found his words false or humorous or otherwise unbelievable.

Maybe they'd all lost their minds.

As unbelievable as the tale was, there didn't seem to be any harm in entertaining it a little longer. He still wanted to learn what had happened to make him end up in this strange house without his memories. "So, then what?" he asked.

"You didn't remember me," Mitul said. "After you came back, you didn't remember anything. When I told you what had happened, you didn't believe me."

A scoff escaped Amar's lips, and he barely managed to stop himself from rolling his eyes.

"That's it—that's the very same look you had on your face back then. But when we went out, everyone greeted you like they knew you. We came across one of the men who had killed you, and he ran away as if he'd seen a ghost."

A faint shiver fluttered across the back of Amar's neck. This entire story was based on the word of a madman, but there was something uncannily familiar about one part of Mitul's statement. Amar looked around the room at Kesari and Lucian, at Saya, at Tamaya, and then back at Mitul.

Everyone greeted you like they knew you.

"After that," Mitul went on, "our lives continued mostly the same as before. We moved to Valmandi for a time. I'm not sure you ever completely believed me about what happened to you—not at first. We never talked about it. But after a while, you noticed the same signs. My body continued to age while you stayed young. You decided you wanted answers, so we set out to find them. Together."

Amar scoffed again. "How noble of you to leave everything behind to help a poor soul like me."

Mitul winced and twisted the metal cuff around his wrist. "You're my brother, Amar. And you needed help. Whatever sacrifices were made, I made them out of concern for you."

"No one does anything out of pure selflessness," Amar retorted.

Mitul simply shrugged. "You can believe what you choose. I'm only telling you my version of what happened."

"Fine. What next, then?"

"We started our search in Valmandi. This is obviously some type of magic, so we sought out any Tarja who might know what was happening to you or how to get your memories back. We found a few good leads, but in the end, no one there could help us." He sighed and ran a hand across the back of his neck. "After another year, we left Valmandi and started travelling all over Kavora. We've been doing so ever since, though when you died the second time, we had to be more careful."

"And how did I die the second time?" Amar asked.

"I'm not entirely sure," Mitul said. "I wasn't there, or I probably would have been killed, too."

"You had a run-in with a mercenary," Saya chimed in, crossing her muscled arms. "One of my people, an outcast. He told me stories of a man he once killed in Kavora who rose from death completely unharmed, like some kind of demon. As soon as I began my haseph, I went searching for you."

"Haseph." Amar turned the Sularan word over in his mind for a few seconds. A ritual of some kind, if he was remembering correctly. A rite of passage all Sularan youth were required to complete. "You're supposed to bring something back to your people—something of value. What does that have to do with me?"

"Whatever magic is affecting you could help save my people. I want answers as much as you do."

"She's been very helpful," Mitul said. "I'm not sure we would have survived these last two attacks without her."

Amar frowned. "What attacks?"

"Well, that's how you died yesterday. There's a young woman, about the same age as Saya. Visan, we think. She attacked us five nights ago, then again last night. She's Bonded to a Spirit Tarja—a white dragon."

Lucian floated a little closer, and a dark, jagged mouth in the center of the flames opened when he spoke. "They're powerful," he said, his voice crackling like sparks. "Most Spirit Tarja aren't capable of taking the form of a living creature. Even my own form is fairly complex. Whoever those two are, they make for dangerous enemies."

Amar jerked a nod at Kesari. "And how exactly did you two come into this story, anyway?"

"We were your guides," Kesari said. "We were bringing you here to see Tamaya when we were attacked."

"Tamaya's one of the best Tarja in this province," Mitul said. "We were hoping she could explain what's happening to you."

Amar looked to the old woman. "Is anything he said even possible?"

Tamaya lifted one bony shoulder. "I don't believe in impossible. As soon as you start saying something's impossible, the world finds a way to prove you wrong."

"So you believe them?"

"I believe what I saw with my own two eyes. You were dead last night, split open like a slaughtered goat. And now you live, completely healthy aside from the memory loss."

Amar pressed his palms against his eye sockets. This was all so much to take in. How was he supposed to sort out what was true and what wasn't if he couldn't even remember anything? The story Mitul had told was so unbelievable, and yet, the others all seemed to accept it—even Kesari, Lucian, and Tamaya, who claimed to have just met him.

There had to be a more logical explanation, but he couldn't figure out what it was yet, or alternatively, why these people might be lying to him. What did they have to gain by it?

"You still don't believe it," Mitul said.

"How am I supposed to believe something so ridiculous?"

Mitul said nothing, but he walked over to the wall where he'd been sleeping earlier and bent over two bags on the ground. From inside one of them, he pulled out a leatherbound book and a slender wooden box. He tore a page from inside the book and handed it to Amar with the box. "I want you to write something for me."

Amar sat down on the bed, opened the box, and took out the feather quill and bottled ink inside. "Why?"

Mitul folded his arms, the book clasped against his torso. "Please, humor me."

Amar shrugged. He uncorked the bottle of ink and dipped the quill inside.

"Write these words exactly," Mitul said. "*My name is Amar. Or at least, that is what I've been called these last eighteen years.*"

A strange thing to write, but it would be interesting to see what Mitul thought the point of this little exercise was. He scrawled the words across the page.

Mitul went on. "*I'm writing this to myself so I can remember. If I die again and forget who I was, I want to have some kind of proof, even if I'm too stubborn to believe it.*"

Amar finished writing the words and stared down at the page. "This proves nothing."

Mitul opened the book and laid it out on the bed next to Amar.

"What's this?"

"Read."

Amar picked it up. The words inside were exactly the same as those he'd just written. Not only the words themselves, but the lettering, too. The slope of the lines, the thickness in the curves—they were nearly identical, written by the very same hand. *His* hand. His stomach dropped.

"You wrote that," Mitul said. "Right after we decided to leave Valmandi. You made me memorize the words. You said if you ever lost your memories again, I should have you write those words and show you the journal."

Amar shook his head. "It's not possible." But his voice sounded far less convincing now, even to himself. "It's a trick."

Mitul knelt down in front of him. "You can deny what's happening and make excuses for the things you don't understand. But this is real. I've always been completely honest with you."

"And I'm supposed to just believe that?"

"Not yet, but in time, I think you will."

Unlikely, but Amar kept that to himself. He looked back down at the book and continued to compare the words there to the ones he'd written. They really did look uncannily similar.

Mitul tapped a finger against the journal. "There's more in there—things that may help you understand. You should read it." He motioned for the others to follow and made his way to the door. "We'll give you some space. Come find me when you're done if you want to talk."

They left the room one by one, leaving Amar alone with the book and dozens of unanswered questions.

KESARI

KESARI TRAILED TAMAYA DOWN THE HALL, LEAVING SAYA AND MITUL outside Amar's door to converse quietly with each other. The old woman didn't stop until she exited the house. Kesari squinted against the morning sun's brightness and cleared her throat. "Excuse me, Tamaya. I was wondering if we could talk."

Tamaya's mouth puckered. "Oh, what is it now, girl? Be quick. I've got a magical riddle to puzzle over."

"Yes, about that. You remember our deal, don't you? I brought you something interesting, like you wanted. You have to hear me out now."

"Yes, yes. I suppose you've made up for all the annoyances you brought me before." She placed her hands on her hips. "Let's hear it, then."

Kesari glanced at Lucian hovering silently over her shoulder. His expression was unreadable, which was nothing new, but she'd heard enough about his opinion on the matter to sense his disapproval. Still, he made a little dip, like an encouraging nod. "Go on."

She swallowed and clasped her hands together to stop their trembling. "We want to break our Bond. Or, I guess, *I* want to. I don't know if it's even possible, but if it is, I was hoping you'd help us."

Tamaya's jaw hung open for a moment, and then she began to laugh. The sharp, cackling sound seemed to echo in the silence of the surrounding forest. "You want to break your Bond? I know you were raised in Atrea, girl, but surely you're aware that forming a Bond is a permanent decision. There is no going back. This is exactly why the practice is forbidden until the living partner has reached adulthood."

Kesari raised her chin. "As you said, I'm not from Kavora. I don't see why I'd be expected to follow your customs."

"Fine, but *he* should have known better." She jabbed a thin, gnarled finger at Lucian. "What kind of self-respecting Tarja forms a Bond with a *child?* I hope your shame haunts you until the day your spirit leaves this world."

"I'm sure it will," Lucian replied evenly.

Kesari winced. No doubt that decision was already haunting him. He deserved better than to be Bonded to someone like her.

The old woman clicked her tongue. "Do you have any idea what you're asking? To undo magic as powerful as that—the results could be disastrous." She shook her head, frowning in disapproval. "You share a life. Tampering with the Bond could hurt you. It might even kill you. Not to mention the fact that you traded half your life for the gift of magic, and there's no guarantee of getting that back now that the deal is done. To throw away what you got out of the bargain would be foolish."

These were the same arguments Kesari had heard from Lucian a hundred times before. His eyes flickered with a knowing look that screamed *I told you so.* But those answers weren't good enough—not when she'd come all this way. "You're saying it's possible, though."

"Why not? Magic makes many things possible that wouldn't be otherwise. But just because a thing is possible doesn't mean it should be done. Why would you even want to?"

Kesari ignored the question. "If it's possible, that means you can help me. You're a powerful Tarja. Surely you—"

"No!" Tamaya snapped, drawing herself up a little taller.

"You *can't* do it, can you?" Lucian asked, staring at the old Tarja woman intently. "Even if you wanted to, you wouldn't be capable of it."

She didn't answer, but her lips pressed together in a thin line.

"Your magic is fading," Lucian went on, and there was a hint of satisfaction in his voice at having realized this new piece of information. "You can't channel altma the way you used to."

"I'm just getting old," Tamaya grumbled. "It happens to all Tarja. At least, to those of us who didn't trade half our lives to gain our power." A hint of jealousy flashed in her eyes.

"That's why you don't help outsiders anymore," Kesari said. "Your reputation—you can't risk it. You're not as—" She clamped her mouth shut. Better not to finish that sentence. Tamaya might not be as strong as she once was, but she still wasn't someone to cross.

Something squeezed at her chest as she looked at the old woman anew. Should she say something else? Apologize maybe? But it wasn't *her* fault Tamaya's magic was fading. At her age, that was perfectly normal. It happened to all natural born Tarja near the end of their life, a transition that allowed the soul to leave the physical realm upon death, rather than being tethered by the altma still connecting the body and spirit. If that connection to their magical energy didn't fade, and a Tarja died prematurely, their spirit would linger. That was what had happened to Lucian.

If Tamaya's connection to her altma was already fading, she couldn't have much time left. A few years, maybe, but to have death looming so inevitably, like a pistol aimed and waiting to be fired...

"Don't look at me like that," Tamaya snapped. "I don't want your pity."

Kesari averted her eyes. "Sorry."

"You're right. I can't help you. But even if I could, I wouldn't."

"Then at least tell me where to go. Surely you must know someone who can help."

"No. It's blasphemy, and I want no part of it. You'd likely kill yourself in the process and gain nothing from it."

"Peace," Kesari said.

"What?"

She forced her gaze to meet Tamaya's but took care not to look at Lucian. How could she, when she was talking about *this*? "That's what I'd gain from breaking my Bond. Peace."

The old Tarja was silent for a few seconds. Then she reached up and took Kesari's jaw in her hand, pulling her closer to peer into her eyes. Tamaya's were shrewd and prodding, like she could see straight into

Kesari's soul and was trying to make sense of what she found there.

"What happened to you, girl? What are you so afraid of?"

The echoes of distant wails filled Kesari's head. She clenched her fists, dug her nails into her palms, and turned her focus to the sounds around her—the faint rustle of wind in the trees, the whistles of birdsong, the gentle babble of a nearby stream winding its way over stone.

"Will you help me, or not?" she asked in a shaky voice.

Tamaya pulled her hand away and sighed. "I won't. I'm sorry."

Kesari gritted her teeth. "We had a bargain! I did my part. You can't go back on your word now."

"Do not accuse me of breaking a deal, girl. You never said you wanted to do anything so reckless."

"You never gave me the chance!"

It wasn't fair. She'd been searching for a way to break her Bond for so long and had been sure this was the end of her journey. Now, the one person who could help her was refusing to do so, after everything she had been through to get here. Her throat tightened, and her eyes burned as tears welled up inside them. She blinked them away furiously, but one managed to escape, streaking down her cheek until she caught it on the sleeve of her coat.

"You can't do this." Her voice came out hoarse and desperate.

Tamaya crossed her arms. "I won't say any more about it." The look on her face was clearer than her words. No amount of pleading, raging, or crying was going to change her mind.

Kesari glared at the woman and swallowed the knot in her throat. "Enjoy your magical riddle, then. I hope you have more help to offer them than you gave me." She turned on her heel and walked away.

Lucian hovered along beside her. "Kes—"

"Go away. I want to be alone."

"I'm not sure that's a good idea right now," he said gently.

"Why not?" she spat back, but she knew. It had been almost a year since she'd talked about or even thought of taking her own life, but he still feared for her.

"I just want to make sure you're safe."

Kesari marched on, burrowing her fists deeper into the pockets of her coat. "Right. Because if I die, your spirit fades away, and you'll finally have to face whatever comes after. You're an even bigger coward than I am."

"That may be true, but that's not why I'm worried."

"Why, then?"

"Because I care about you. Surely you know that by now."

Kesari clenched her jaw and tried to hold back the new tears forming in her eyes. She did know that, and his concern was more than she deserved. How much time had he spent, letting her drag him across half the empire so she could find a way to get rid of him? And all because she was too weak to face what she was, what she'd done.

She was a burden, broken beyond repair. Lucian deserved better, but it was too late to make different choices. Too late for either of them.

Tamaya's house was barely visible through the trees behind them now. Kesari walked a few more paces until she reached the edge of the stream. She sat on a slab of rock with her boots squelching in the mud. Lucian still hovered beside her. "Leave me alone," she muttered, instantly regretting it. She didn't actually want him to leave.

"I'm not going anywhere," he said. "But we don't have to talk about it. We don't have to talk about anything."

She wrapped her arms around her stomach with her hands slipped inside the opposite sleeves of the old coat. Her fingers brushed over the raised scar lines on her forearms, permanent reminders of all the times she'd tried to escape the pain and intrusive memories with the blade of a knife. Sometimes, she still longed for that escape. Skies above, she longed for it *now*. But dealing with the shame and guilt that always came afterward would have been unbearable.

Having Lucian nearby made it easier to resist some of her more destructive impulses, though she'd never found the words to admit that to him. She liked to think he already knew, which was why he stayed in spite of the rage she threw at him in her worst moments. And he'd taught her other ways to manage those feelings. Ironically, they were the same techniques that would have helped her channel altma, if she were still using her magic.

She let out a long sigh, releasing some of her anger along with her exhaled breath. She inhaled again, slowly, and focused on the sound of the stream in an attempt to clear her mind. Her thoughts kept drifting to her argument with Tamaya, the sight of Amar's lifeless body, and the chaos of the night she'd left home. Again and again, she brought her focus back to the stream, and after a few minutes, everything else faded away.

There was only the water, and she was only a girl in a forest, and whatever came before or after ceased to matter.

AMAR

My name is Amar. Or at least, that is what I've been called these last eighteen years. I'm writing this to myself so I can remember. If I die again and forget who I was, I want to have some kind of proof, even if I'm too stubborn to believe it.

I asked Mitul to read and memorize these words, though he may not even be around should I need them someday. If my guesses about my own immortality are correct, I'll outlive him. I also can't ask him to continue this search with me if he decides to leave. He's already sacrificed too much—more than I should have allowed him to. He's a loyal friend. I've come to trust him even more than I trust myself. If I forget everything else, I hope some part of me will at least remember that much.

More than anything, I hope we find answers before I forget again. Some men might relish the idea of immortality, but I don't. There's something terrifying about the prospect of watching everyone around me age and die while I remain frozen in time for eternity. I can't let that be my fate.

Amar ran his finger over the journal's page as he read the entry again, trying to dredge up some memory of the man who had written it. Himself, or whoever he'd been in a former life. But the words were as unfamiliar as the name the others had given him.

Except for that last line. *I can't let that be my fate.*

Some deep-seated fear squirmed through every fiber of his being. The sensation was almost familiar, and he sat with it for a moment.

Where had that fear come from? It wasn't tied to anything specific—at least, not as far as he could tell. All he knew was that he didn't want anything to do with immortality, no matter how invincible it made him. Right now, it was the *only* thing he knew about himself.

He flipped through the rest of the journal's pages. A few were written as neatly as that first entry, but most of the book contained haphazardly scribbled notes. There were lists of names, some of which had already been scratched off and some that directed him to different pages in the journal. Tamaya was on one of these lists. The names must have belonged to Tarja he and Mitul thought could be helpful, with those they'd already visited crossed out in dark, angry slashes.

He skimmed through the rest of the notes, but none of them meant much to him. There seemed to be more detailed entries recounting his travels over the last ten years, but he'd read those later. Right now, it was all a little overwhelming.

He flipped back to the first page. The handwriting there matched the copy he'd made so well. Not perfectly enough to be some magical duplicate, though he still hadn't ruled out magic as a possible means of deception. The only other possibilities were that Mitul knew a very good forger, or that Amar had indeed written those words himself in another life.

He was more inclined to believe the latter, despite the unlikeliness of Mitul's story. A few doubts still lingered, but it wasn't like he'd managed to come up with a better explanation. And he couldn't see any good reason why the man might be lying to him. At least, not yet. He'd have to be cautious, stay on his guard, but for now, it seemed his best option was to go along with Mitul and the others.

He sighed, then stood and crossed the room to the pack Mitul had pulled the journal from. He needed some clean clothes. Rummaging around, his fingers brushed against fabric. He pulled out the bundle and unrolled it to find a single shirt, a pair of loose pants, and a set of undergarments. He held them to his nose. Clean enough, and anything would be better than the blood-stained tatters he currently wore.

Amar peeled away the layers of ruined clothing and used a basin of cold water in the corner to wash himself. When he was finished, he donned his new attire, smoothing the soft, well-worn fabric of the shirt over his chest.

Like the one that had been destroyed, it was a plain wheat color and hung just below his hips. He tucked it into his pants, made of a darker and sturdier material, and strapped on the same belt he'd been wearing before. There was a holster for a pistol and a small pouch filled with spare cartridges, but the weapon itself wasn't among any of his belongings.

He combed through his thick hair with wet fingers. It needed a good wash, but for now, at least he was a little more presentable. He walked to the doorway, pausing to listen to the whispers in the hall. They were too quiet for him to understand.

He stepped out of the room, and Mitul and Saya immediately ceased their conversation. They both stared at him, then Saya gave Mitul a nod. "I'll give you two some time." When she headed outside, sunlight streamed through the open door to illuminate Mitul's face. There were shadows under his eyes, and the smile he gave Amar seemed strained.

"I imagine you still have some questions," he said, leaning back against the wall with his hands behind him.

Amar nodded. Where to begin? There were so many questions swirling around in his head, but most were related to what had caused his condition and why it had happened. Mitul didn't seem to know any more than he did regarding that, so instead, he chose a question the man could answer. "Why are you still here, after all this time? Why would you help me?"

Mitul shrugged. "Why does anybody help someone they care about?"

I've come to trust him even more than I trust myself. The words from his journal flashed through his mind, but standing here beside Mitul, Amar felt none of that trust. "You're telling me you gave up years of your life to follow me on a personal quest that's led nowhere?"

Mitul gave a small shrug. "Yes."

"That seems like a dreadful waste of time. Why stick around?"

"Because, Amar, your problems are mine, too. You're my brother."

There was that word again. *Brother.* A word loaded with some sentimental history Amar had no ties to. It grated on his nerves. "No," he said flatly. "I'm not."

"Maybe not by blood, but we're family all the same. I couldn't send you off alone knowing you could die and forget who you are all over again." His brows knit together, and something fearful came into his eyes. "How long would it take you to discover the truth on your own? How long have you wandered already, not knowing who you really are or where you came from?"

"It isn't your problem."

"But it is. The memories you lost were ones we shared, and without them, I'm just another stranger to you." Before Amar could respond, Mitul pushed himself away from the wall and motioned for him to follow. "Come. Let's see if Tamaya's managed to think of any solutions to your predicament."

They found the Tarja outside in her garden. She crouched on her hands and knees between the neatly cultivated rows, plucking out weeds with dirt-coated fingers and tossing them behind her in a pile. Saya stood at the other end of the house, scratching the ears of a striped cat that sat on a fence post. In her other hand, she clutched a sword by its scabbard, and there was a flintlock pistol tucked into the sash at her waist. Probably the same pistol that belonged in Amar's holster, but he couldn't blame her for taking it as a precaution.

"Excuse me, Tamaya," Mitul said. "We wondered if you'd given any more thought to Amar's situation."

She continued her gardening without so much as a glance in their direction. "What do you think I've been doing out here?"

"My apologies. We didn't mean to interrupt, but the woman who attacked us last night could still be on our trail."

"Hm. You're saying you brought trouble straight to my doorstep, is that it?"

Mitul rubbed at the back of his neck and gave Amar an uncomfortable look. "I suppose we did. I'm sorry. We didn't mean to, but the sooner we leave, the better. Or we can make preparations to defend ourselves here, if you'd rather."

Tamaya grunted and continued to tug at a particularly stubborn weed. "Don't trouble yourself. Whatever fight that girl brings, I can handle myself. As to your question, I do have a few ideas." She finally yanked the weed free and brushed off her hands, then held one out to Amar. When he didn't move right away, she frowned and said, "Come on, boy. Help an old woman up."

Boy. He was at least as old as Mitul, and for all they knew, he could be older than her. He offered his hand and pulled her up. She was even lighter than she appeared.

She gave him a reproachful look as she set about brushing the dirt off her clothes. "What I would give to be as old as you must be and have a body that wasn't falling apart."

How old was that, exactly? Fifty? Sixty? A hundred maybe, or even a thousand?

So many years lost from memory. The idea of it was dizzying, like staring down into the sheer drop of a bottomless abyss. He shook his head and pushed the thought from his mind. Best not to dwell on it too much.

"I'm afraid I don't have all the answers you're looking for," Tamaya said. "But I do have a few theories, and better yet, I know exactly where you need to go to find out more."

Mitul's entire face lit up in a smile. "That's wonderful. Saya, come listen to this."

She walked over to stand beside Amar, then passed him the sword and pistol with a pointed look, a clear warning of what might happen if he tried anything. He nodded to her in understanding, but she kept her eyes glued to his hands as he slipped the gun into its holster.

He was still buckling on the sword when Kesari came stomping around the opposite corner of the house with Lucian hovering faithfully beside her. The girl's hands were clenched around the cuffs of her too-long coat sleeves, and her entire body was rigid. Her narrowed eyes focused their gaze on Tamaya.

"I'm not leaving," she said, her voice tense. "Not until you give me what I came for—what I *earned*. We had a deal. You can't expect—"

"Silence, girl!" Tamaya's arm shot forward, and a gust of air tore across the grass to slam Kesari in the ribs.

She stumbled back a few steps, and Lucian's flames rippled frantically as he grew to twice his usual size, then shrunk back down just as quickly. They exchanged a glance with each other before approaching more slowly.

"Now then," Tamaya said primly, "if you can remain civilized and silent, you can stay and listen to what I have to tell the others. Maybe you'll hear something useful."

Kesari scowled and opened her mouth like she was about to protest further. Lucian whispered something in her ear, and she stayed silent, placing herself beside Saya with her arms folded.

"Now where was I?" Tamaya muttered.

"You know where we need to go next?" Mitul offered.

"Right. But first, I have a theory I think you might be interested in. Last night, I told you that no magic I know of can bring back the dead, and that's true. But magic is an ancient art, and there are practices that have long since been lost through time. There's one type of magic in particular that might explain what's happening to you, Amar."

"What's that?" he asked.

"I'm not an expert on the subject, but if I had to guess, I'd say it's a curse."

Mitul frowned. "Like the ones in stories? Sleeping princesses and cursed objects and true love's kiss? I thought curses were a myth."

"And where do you think myths come from? There are hints of truth in all stories if you look closely enough."

"Do you have anything more to go on than that?" Saya asked.

Tamaya nodded. "There was a historian at the academy where I studied who believed curses may have been fairly common at one point. His research suggested they may have been outlawed during the reign of Emperor Harish."

"But that would have been at least five centuries ago," Mitul said.

"Yes, but as we all saw for ourselves this morning, Amar is immortal. Which means he could very well be centuries old."

"Old enough to have lived in a time when curses were prevalent," Lucian said.

"That's what I suspect."

The world seemed to freeze around Amar. Five hundred years old. Maybe more. *Probably* more. He'd known this was a possibility, but hearing it spoken aloud somehow made it heavier.

"And how does one remove a curse?" he asked Tamaya.

"That, I can't answer. But I do know someone who might be able to help. Years ago, when I was still part of the academy's training program, I had an apprentice, Jameson Weatherford."

"That's an Atrean name, isn't it?" Mitul asked.

Tamaya nodded. "He lived in Kavora for a few years to study magic.

I've had many students over the years, but Jameson was unique. He was capable of channeling more altma than even I could after decades of practice, and his skill with healing magic was beyond anything I've seen before or since. He was a prodigy, not that it mattered much."

"What do you mean?" Lucian asked.

Tamaya shook her head and let out a short laugh. "He was always far more interested in magical theory than he was in its practical application. He spent all his time in books studying how magic worked, why it worked, what differences existed between certain branches of magic, and so on." She clicked her tongue. "It used to infuriate me. All that raw power and talent, but the only thing he ever put any real effort into was reading those books and scribbling his notes. He could have taken a prestigious position at the academy if he'd wanted, but he refused."

She was rambling now, and none of it was helpful. Amar cleared his throat. "But you think he'll be able to figure out this curse?"

"I'm not sure, but he's the best chance you have. Maybe he even knows some way to break Spirit Tarja Bonds safely." She cast a sidelong glance at Kesari and Lucian, who exchanged a look of their own. Kesari bit her bottom lip like she was holding back a smile.

"Where do we find him?" Saya asked.

"He moved home to Atrea, last I heard. Some lakeside town. Malfern or Melfarm or something like that."

"Malfram?" Kesari asked.

"Could be. Of course, he'll want nothing to do with anything that takes him away from his studies, but if you say I sent you, he should at least hear you out."

With that, she promptly knelt back down and returned to her gardening. Apparently, the conversation was over as far as she was concerned.

Mitul and Saya looked at each other, then at Amar. "Well," said Mitul, "what do you think?"

He frowned. "Atrea's a long way to go looking for answers this Jameson might not even have."

"He's right," Saya said. "Besides, we haven't exhausted our search here in Kavora."

"No, but it's not like that's been going so well," Mitul replied. "This is the first solid lead we've had in years—certainly the best we've had since you found us."

"Maybe so, but a curse?" Saya shook her head. "It sounds a bit unbelievable."

"It does, but it makes more sense than anything else we've heard." Mitul turned to Amar. "I think we should go."

An image of the pages from his journal flashed across his mind. All those lists of names, dozens upon dozens that had already been scratched out. Their search in Kavora had clearly been unsuccessful. Would it be such a bad idea to follow a lead elsewhere?

On the other hand, was it wise to give up the search here? "Atrea is so far," he said. "And it's summer. We'd have to cross the desert during the hottest part of the year. Or go around, which would take even longer."

"That won't be a problem with Saya's help," Mitul said.

"That's true," Saya agreed. "The desert is my home. I can get you through quickly and safely."

That took care of one problem, but there were others. "We don't speak Atrean. At least I don't." Amar could identify other languages floating around in his head—a few snippets of Sularan and various Kavoran dialects, along with some other language he couldn't name. But there was nothing that matched the blended, lilting sounds that belonged to the Atrean tongue.

"I don't either," Mitul admitted. He looked at Saya expectantly.

She shook her head. "Just a few words—not enough to help us get around."

Kesari took a timid step toward them. "I might be able to help with that."

"What are you doing?" Lucian hissed.

She ignored him. "I know the language and the customs. I'm from Atrea—from Deveaural, specifically, but I know Malfram. I could get you there. And it sounds like Jameson could help me, too, so why not travel together?"

Mitul turned back to Amar and shrugged. "Whatever you decide, I'm with you."

"As am I," Saya agreed.

Amar clenched his jaw. His gut instinct was to ditch the whole lot of them and set out alone. He didn't want the company of these strangers who claimed to be his friends. But Mitul seemed harmless enough, and Saya and Kesari could be useful.

"We'll go to Atrea," he said. "I'd like to meet this Jameson and find out if he's really as smart as Tamaya says he is."

"Oh, he is," the old woman muttered from the ground. "Too smart for his own good, if you ask me."

Mitul turned to her with his palms pressed together and made a low bow, even though she couldn't see him with her back turned. "Thank you for your hospitality," he said. "We owe you more than we could ever repay, but I left a few jitaara on your table."

"Unnecessary, but thank you."

"I guess we'll be on our way now."

"Good," she replied. "Things were a lot more peaceful around here before you all showed up. I wish you safe travels. And if you do see Jameson, please remind him it wouldn't hurt to write an old woman a letter every now and again."

Mitul smiled. "Of course."

They went inside to collect their things while Tamaya continued her gardening. She didn't even look up when they trailed past a few minutes later, leaving her and her humble home behind.

ALEIDA

THE HOUSE IN THE FOREST STOOD ALONE BETWEEN TALL, THIN TREES that made it look smaller than it actually was. As far as Aleida could tell, the old Tarja who lived there was alone, too. It seemed Amar and his friends had already moved on.

She swung her leg over the horse's saddle. It was still sore, but between her healing magic and the full day of rest she'd had, her injuries were much improved. She clenched her jaw. She'd needed the rest, but maybe if she'd woken up earlier, she and Valkyra could have arrived here in time to catch Amar.

Aleida glanced at the Spirit Tarja perched on her shoulder. "You shouldn't have let me sleep all day."

"I should have let you sleep longer. You still don't look entirely well."

"I'm fine." A lingering tiredness seemed to have seeped into her very bones, but she wasn't about to admit that.

All lights in the house were out. Hopefully that meant the old woman was sleeping. Aleida looped the horse's reins around a tree branch and crept forward through the darkness. A rustling wind muffled the sound of her steps through the forest undergrowth, and she soon reached the low fence surrounding the house.

"Be careful," Valkyra warned. "She may be alone, but that doesn't mean she'll be unprotected. She's bound to have a few defenses set up to ward off intruders."

"I know." She reached over the fence and unhooked the latch holding the gate. It swung open with a low creak. Taking a breath, she sharpened her focus on the altma within and all around her, ready to channel it should the need arise. Then she stepped through the gate and headed for the house.

All was silent. She tried the door, but it wouldn't budge. Probably bolted shut from the inside. Valkyra would want her to use magic to unlock it, but that would take more time and finesse than Aleida had the patience for. Not when she could simply break it down.

She pressed her hands against the door and sent a burst of altma through her palms. The blast of energy shattered the wood into dozens of splintered pieces, leaving the entrance clear.

A horrible shrieking noise filled the air. She clamped her hands over her ears. Where was it coming from?

A diminutive old woman appeared in front of her. Aleida readied an attack, but the distraction of the high-pitched noise had disrupted her connection to her altma. The old woman's onslaught came faster. Shards of splintered wood rose from the ground and shot toward Aleida. She barely managed to block them with a barrier. Several fragments flew past her and through the open doorway.

Before she could react, Tamaya threw out a hand, and a gust of air slammed into Aleida's barrier with such force that she stumbled back. Another blast came a split second later. Aleida pushed against it. Time to go on the offensive.

She lowered the barrier and channeled altma into her fingertips. Tamaya thrust her hand out again, but this time, there was barely enough air to ruffle Aleida's hair. She was losing steam already.

Aleida extended her own hands and released her magic. A blue glow filled the house as jagged tendrils of lightning passed through Tamaya's semi-translucent form and struck the wall behind her.

Not the *real* Tamaya. An illusion.

Aleida whirled around. A dark, round shape flew at her. She managed to throw up another barrier, and the heavy kettle bounced off it to clang against the floor.

Where had that come from?

A pan came flying from around the corner. Aleida blocked that, too, then ran to the corner and darted into the adjacent hall.

It was difficult to see anything in the dark. Too difficult to be natural. She sent a flash of lightning to illuminate the hall, but even that couldn't permeate the shadows. Another illusion, maybe. Tamaya could be anywhere.

"There," Valkyra whispered against Aleida's ear. "In the room to your right, where the shadows are blackest."

Aleida gave a slight nod but didn't look. Not yet. Instead, she continued to glance around the hall, shooting off flashes of lightning in every direction. When she did let her gaze drift to the room, it was only briefly, but there in the far corner stood the faintest outline of a person. Tamaya. The illusory shadows were bent so expertly around her that she was all but invisible.

Aleida looked away and continued her inspection of the hall, pretending she hadn't seen the other Tarja. She channeled altma into her legs until her muscles tingled with power.

Valkyra's claws tightened around the fabric of her shirt. Aleida released the magic in a single surge and dashed into the room. She stopped just short of colliding with Tamaya and pinned the old woman's neck against the wall with violent force. The shrieking noise immediately ceased.

Before she could recover, Aleida threw up another barrier. This one went around Tamaya—a temporary shield of magical energy that would prevent her from using her powers, at least for as long as Aleida could maintain it. No trouble at all if she stayed focused and kept her emotions under control.

Fear flickered in Tamaya's dark eyes, but only for a moment. Her brow furrowed, and wrinkled skin tightened over a clenched jaw as she glowered at her captor. Her pulse pounded beneath the pressure of Aleida's forearm, strong and steady.

Despite all that, she still looked old and frail. Older and weaker even than the sickly neighbor woman Mama had cared for when Aleida was very young.

We are all children of the Artist, her mother had often reminded her, *and it's our duty to look after each other.*

Her cheeks burned. Artex would not want her doing this.

But surely Artex also wouldn't want Tyrus to die. Besides, Tamaya wasn't as frail and helpless as she appeared.

Aleida brought her face closer to the old woman's. "Where are the people who were here before?"

Tamaya's lips curled in a sneer. "Lots of people have been here before. You'll have to be more specific."

No time for riddles. Aleida gripped the woman's wrist with her free hand and shot thin tendrils of lightning up her arm. She groaned in pain. A familiar guilt started to rise up inside Aleida, but she shoved it back down. Doing so was unnervingly easy. She was becoming too used this.

"You know exactly who I'm talking about," she growled. "Where did they go?"

A slimy glob of spit landed on her cheek. Tamaya smirked with all the smug satisfaction of a cat who'd just caught a mouse.

Aleida's face grew warm, and her grip around Tamaya's arm tightened. Foolish old woman. She channeled her altma into another shock. Tamaya's entire body stiffened, and when it was over, she slumped against the wall, sinking to the floor with a faint whimper. Aleida went down with her.

What was she doing, torturing an old woman like this? What kind of monster had she become?

"The barrier," Valkyra said into her ear.

It was starting to weaken and had slipped away entirely in some places. Aleida took a breath. She could dwell on her moral quandries later. For now, she stowed away those feelings in a dark corner within herself and quickly reformed the barrier, but it wasn't as strong as before. The sooner she could wrap this up, the better.

Tamaya remained motionless against the wall, but her chest rose and fell in steady breaths. At last, she coughed and raised her head, her gaze defiant. "Bloodthirsty heathen."

Some of Aleida's guilt died away. "Don't talk to *me* about heathens," she hissed. "It was Kavoran Tarja like you who destroyed my home and slaughtered my family. Do you think I'll hesitate to kill you if you don't give me the answers I need?"

"Is that supposed to scare me?" Tamaya spat. "I've stood against entire armies of Tarja more powerful than you. I trained some of the best of them. It was I who taught Nandini Kumar, and I know *that* name means something to you."

On her shoulder, Valkyra's body tensed. A chill ran through Aleida's blood, and in that brief moment of broken concentration, her barrier fell. Tamaya seized the opportunity to make an escape. She wrenched free of Aleida's grasp, and a metal washbasin came flying from the other side of the room. Valkyra knocked it aside before it could make contact.

Aleida lunged at Tamaya and reformed her barrier, then sent a powerful shock through the old woman's body. She writhed and screamed, and even as Aleida let the lightning die, she was torn between wishing she hadn't done it and wanting to hurt Tamaya even more. This woman had mentored Nandini Kumar, a former imperial advisor said to be responsible for the invasion of Vis.

The same invasion that had resulted in the deaths of thousands of Visans, including Aleida's parents.

"I ought to kill you," she said through gritted teeth.

"So do it. I'm not far from death anyway."

The stubborn defiance in her eyes was too genuine to be a bluff. Aleida took a breath to keep her frustration in check, then leaned in closer. "I can make it the slowest, most painful agony you've ever experienced." She tightened her grip around the old woman's wrist, letting the faintest shock jump between their skin.

Tamaya flinched. "There's no need for cruelty," she muttered.

"Then tell me what I want to know. The visitors you had earlier—what were they doing here?"

Tamaya gnawed on her bottom lip for a few seconds, as if mulling over her options, then answered the question. "They were seeking respite after their fight with you, as I understand it. One of them was dead when they arrived on my doorstep, and alive again when they left. I expect you know that already, though, or you wouldn't be hunting him."

"They were headed here before we fought. Why?"

"They had questions." Tamaya pursed her lips and didn't elaborate.

"What questions?" Aleida prodded.

"The girl wanted to know how to break her Bond with her Spirit Tarja."

"I don't care about the girl. What about the man? Amar. What did he want?"

"His memories back, I expect. He was very confused when he returned to life this morning. I'm not sure he even really knew what he wanted."

Aleida frowned. "What do you mean?"

"When he rose this morning, his physical wounds were gone, but he couldn't remember anything. Not his name, or where he was, how he'd gotten here, or even who his friends were. They were like strangers to him. They said it happens every time he dies."

Another oddity about Amar's immortality. How would that affect Tyrus once they found a way to give that same immortality to him? Perhaps Valkyra would know, but that could wait until she was finished here. "What answers did you give them?" she asked Tamaya.

"Not many. I suspect the man's under some kind of curse, and I don't know anyone in Kavora who could handle a problem like that. I told them they'd be best off going to Atrea to speak to an old student of mine—Jameson Weatherford. That's where they were headed when they left here."

"Where does he live exactly?"

"Some lakeside town. The Atrean girl called it Malfram. I'd draw you a map if it would get you out of here quicker, but I expect you can find it well enough on your own."

Aleida's eyes narrowed. Atrea was a big country, and a long way off. Hopefully she'd catch up to Amar and the others before then, but if not, she needed to be sure she was headed the right way. "How do I know you're telling the truth?"

The muscles in Tamaya's neck tightened. "You've already tortured it out of me, so I'm not sure what other proof I can give you. I have no reason to protect them. Believe me or don't, it's your choice."

"You put up quite a fight for someone who has no one to protect."

"I can't defend myself and my home?" A fierce anger returned to her eyes. "You're the one who broke in and attacked me. You'll forgive me if I didn't feel too cooperative after that."

Aleida released the old woman's wrist but continued to channel altma into the magical barrier as she stood and backed away. Tamaya braced one hand against the wall and the other on her thigh, then slowly pushed herself up. Aleida started to reach out a helping hand—an instinct the gentle girl she used to be still remembered—but caught herself and hastily drew back. Tamaya probably wouldn't welcome her help, anyway. Easier for both of them if she kept up her role as the violent intruder.

"If I find out you're lying—"

"Oh, enough already," Tamaya muttered. "Go on, leave an old woman in peace. You've done enough damage and I don't have anything else for you."

Aleida exchanged a quick glance with Valkyra and strode to the open doorway. Behind her, Tamaya muttered under her breath—something about repairs and setting up better defenses. Aleida paused in the threshold and turned around. Her eyes met Tamaya's for just a moment. The hatred there was all too familiar.

Bloodthirsty heathen.

She opened her mouth to apologize, then recalled what Tamaya had said about teaching Nandini Kumar and stopped herself. It was hard to feel true sympathy for anyone so directly connected to person who'd destroyed her homeland.

She turned on her heel and walked outside, taking no care to avoid the neat little garden between the house and the gate.

"You could have killed her," Valkyra said as they headed back to where they'd left the horse. "It would have been understandable."

Aleida swallowed hard, but the tightness in her throat remained. "It wouldn't have done any good." She wondered, though, whether there would have been some satisfaction in it, a sense of justice being served. "Do you think she was telling the truth?"

"I do. I've heard of Jameson Weatherford. He's young, said to be a prodigy, and possibly the best Tarja Atrea has ever known."

Aleida nodded. "And if Amar's immortality is a curse, can we still use it to save Tyrus?"

"I think so. We wouldn't be able to recreate it, but there are certain methods of transferring magic from one person or object to another. In theory, we could do the same thing with a curse."

In theory. Not quite the guarantee Aleida wanted, but probably the best she could hope for, given the circumstances. She channeled her altma into an orb of light around her hand to help her navigate through the trees. "What do you think it means that he can't remember anything after he comes back to life?"

"I'm not sure. It could be part of the curse, or maybe some unintended consequence of tampering with magic so powerful."

"Will that happen to Tyrus if we transfer the curse? Will he forget?"

Valkyra brushed a soft wing against Aleida's cheek. "I'm sorry, my dear, but I honestly don't know. Would that stop you from saving him? If he has to forget you to keep his life, is that a price you're willing to pay?"

"Of course," she replied without hesitation, but her heart squeezed painfully. Tyrus was all she had. They'd been through so much together, just the two of them against the world. If he forgot all of that—forgot *her*—would any of this be worth it?

She hated herself for even thinking such a selfish thing. What did it matter if he forgot her? He would be *alive*, and he might return to how he'd been before his illness. He could live a long, happy life without having to worry about sickness or crippling pain ever again.

They had been through so much together—so many horrible, painful things. Perhaps it would be better if he forgot.

"Look," Valkyra said, a hint of alarm in her voice. "The horse."

Aleida brightened her orb of light and directed it ahead. The horse lay on the ground, head drooping from the reins still tied around a tree branch. Its neck glistened with dark, wet blood. More blood ran in thin streams from wounds along its back and sides—wounds created by jagged shards of wood that had once been a door.

Tamaya's attack. Aleida had managed to block some of the projectiles with her barrier, but the rest had shot straight out the open doorway she'd been standing in.

She tightened her jaw as she set about gathering her belongings from the horse's saddlebags. Better the animal be the victim of Tamaya's attack than her, but that didn't make the new setback any more bearable. With the horse, she'd had a good chance of catching up to Amar and his companions quickly. Now, that was going to be much more difficult.

She sent out a silent plea to Artex. *I could really use some help, if it's not too much to ask.*

But of course, it *was* too much to ask. How many times now had she gone directly against Artex's desire for peace and goodwill by inflicting harm on others? She quickly amended her prayer. *If you won't help for my sake, then at least do it for Tyrus. He's good and kind and still has so much to offer this world—you know that. Whatever happens to me doesn't matter, but at least let me help him.*

She used her magic to push out some of the dirt from beneath the horse's other side so she could reach under for her pack. It was stuck. She yanked the straps harder and fell back with a grunt when it came free.

"Are you going to bury it?" Valkyra asked.

Aleida stood and stared down at the dead animal. Poor thing. He'd served her so well over these last few weeks. Maybe she should bury him, but she'd wasted enough time here already. "Tamaya killed him. She can bury him herself." She steeled her heart and turned away from the carcass. "Where to? I assume Amar and his friends will need supplies if they're travelling all the way to Atrea."

"Yes. They'll likely head for Valmandi first. Perhaps Sharmok after that."

"We'll have to catch them before they reach the desert." With the Sularan woman in their company, they'd have a trusted guide to take them across the inhospitable terrain rather than being forced to go around the long way. Aleida and Valkyra were not so fortunate.

But it didn't matter. She *would* catch up to them before they reached the desert. She had to. And the next time she faced them, there would be no mistakes.

AMAR

AMAR WOKE AT DAWN THE MORNING AFTER THEY'D LEFT TAMAYA'S, startled out of sleep by a dream he could only recall the end of. He'd been running from something, or maybe *toward* something. Something he couldn't see. He hadn't made it far, almost as if he'd been held back by invisible chains. The feeling still lingered, accompanied by a sense of dread and powerlessness.

He pushed himself up and rubbed at his eyes. Saya sat on a nearby rock with her back to him. The forest wasn't quite as dense on this stretch of road, and her long hair shone in the peachy glow of sunrise. "You're awake," she said without turning around.

"I can go back to sleep if you'd like," he replied.

She stood and stretched her arms. "No. We should wake the others and get going. I still worry about that Visan woman being so close on our trail."

She went to shake Mitul, leaving Amar to wake Kesari. The girl had pulled one arm free of her coat to drape it over her body like a blanket. Her brows were creased, and her jaw was tight. Maybe her dreams were troubled, too.

"Kesari," he said, touching her shoulder. "Kesari, wake up."

Her eyes opened and darted across their surroundings. "What's going on? Where's Lucian?"

Amar looked around. Where *was* the fiery Spirit Tarja? He'd spent much of the previous day in Kesari's lantern, but that was empty now.

"He doubled back to make sure we're not being followed too closely," Saya answered. "He should be back soon. We may have to leave without him, but I'm sure he'll catch up."

Kesari sat up with a frown and adjusted the lapels of her coat. "You shouldn't have sent him off alone."

Saya shrugged. "It was his idea. And it was a good one. I would have told you, but he didn't want to wake you."

Mitul dug around in his satchel and began to pass out dried mango slices and hunks of bread for their breakfast. Amar took the food and nodded his thanks without meeting the other man's eyes.

"We can eat as we walk," Saya said, hoisting her satchel over one shoulder. "Let's go."

"You're in a hurry this morning," Amar said, his tone intentionally prickly. He was famished, and now that he'd had some time to recover from his nightmare, he was starting to feel drowsy again. They'd walked late into the night, and he couldn't have had more than a few hours of decent sleep. Was the danger really so great that they couldn't rest a while longer?

Beside him, Kesari yawned and gave a slight nod of agreement. "It's barely morning."

Saya jabbed a finger down the path in the direction from which they'd come. "There's a dangerous, violent Tarja after us. We may have thrown her off for now, but I'd prefer she didn't catch up with us again. Or have you all forgotten what happened the last time our paths crossed?"

Amar looked up at her, fighting to keep his expression neutral. "Actually, I *did* forget."

Saya's eyes widened like she'd been slapped across the face. "Amar, I'm sorry. You know I didn't mean it like that."

"I don't *know* anything," he shot back. "I don't remember. I don't know who you people are, or who I am, and I don't know who this Visan woman is, either. I don't see why we have to go rushing off so soon. Who put you in charge, anyway? Isn't the whole point of this journey to find out what's happening to *me*? Shouldn't I have some say in where we go and when?"

His petty arguments made him sound like a child, but he couldn't stop himself. There was a caged wolf inside him, and now that its door was open, it burst out, ready to tear apart everyone in its path.

Mitul's hand fell on his shoulder. "Amar, please. We're only trying to help."

"I don't need your help," he snarled, pulling away.

The man held up his hands in resignation. "Look, none of this is fair, and I'm sure it's all very confusing and overwhelming. But I'm asking you to trust us. Saya's right. We should go."

A simmering heat continued to roil inside Amar, but he held it back. This wasn't worth fighting over. He even agreed with Saya and Mitul. He didn't remember the enemy they spoke of, but he'd seen the blood on his clothes in the aftermath of their last fight. She wasn't someone he wanted to run into again.

But that didn't mean he was willing to admit he was wrong. And he didn't appreciate Saya's comment about his forgetfulness, intentional or not. It wasn't *his* fault he couldn't remember anything.

"Fine. Let's go." He stuffed his food in the pocket of his tunic and went to get his pack. His sword and pistol sat atop it, and he belted both around his waist. The weapons felt familiar there, comfortable in a way that helped to quiet the growls of that wolf inside him.

For now.

They walked in silence, lingering tensions stifling all conversation. Saya and Mitul took the lead with Kesari right behind them. Amar brought up the rear, hanging back to avoid interaction with the others.

Kesari kept glancing back over her shoulder, her brows knit together with worry. He was about to ask if she had a problem with him and why she couldn't just mind her own business, but then she put a hand to the lantern hanging from her coat. Of course it wasn't him she was worried about. She was waiting for Lucian.

The Spirit Tarja finally made an appearance around mid-morning. He floated past Amar without a word, coasting to a slower pace when he reached Kesari's side. Her entire face brightened when she saw him. "You're back!"

"Did you see anything?" Saya asked.

"I saw many things," he replied with a sly cheekiness that brought a smirk to Amar's lips. Saya muttered something under her breath, and Lucian quickly added, "No sign of our friend, though. If she's still following us, she's farther behind."

"Oh, I'm sure she's following us," Saya said. "But I'm glad she's not close. Thank you for looking."

They walked on into the afternoon, stopping to rest only when the sun was high overhead and sweat began to bead on their skin. They gathered under the shade of a cluster of trees near the road's edge, and Mitul once again passed out food to the others. Saya and Kesari thanked him graciously, but Amar said nothing and found a place away from the others to eat.

After they were finished, they set off again. Amar tried to hang back alone like before, but Mitul lingered until he'd caught up. "How are you doing, my friend?"

Amar's teeth ground together at the man's choice of words—*my friend*. "I'm fine."

"Are you sure? You seem a little on edge."

"I said I'm fine."

"All right," Mitul said brightly, seemingly unfazed by the harshness in his tone. "I just wanted you to know that I'm happy to answer any questions you have or talk about whatever you'd like. Maybe share some memories, when you're ready."

"And what's that supposed to do? You'll tell me a few stories about the man I supposedly used to be, and we'll go back to being friends again?"

Mitul shrugged. "I thought it might help you feel more like yourself."

"More like the person you think I am, you mean." Amar cast him a sidelong glance. "You must not like this new version of me very much."

Mitul's amiable smile fell, and he turned his eyes to the road ahead. "I'll always like any version of you, Amar. Even the one that hates me."

Before he could respond, Mitul quickened his pace and fell into stride with Saya again. She cast a glance back at Amar, an angry frown pulling at her lips, but her eyes were sad. He looked away and pretended to be fascinated by the trees and the birds.

It wasn't that he *hated* Mitul—or Saya, for that matter. But the way they watched and hovered over him was enough to aggravate anyone. They spoke to him like they knew him, but that familiarity only went one way. He hated feeling so off-balance. He didn't need any more reminders of how very incomplete he was without his memories.

He wasn't the old friend they wanted him to be. Not anymore. And what was the point of forging friendships if he could die at any point and forget them all over again? Or worse, if he *didn't* die—if they grew old and he didn't, until he outlived them and was left all alone with only bittersweet memories to cling to.

Something inside him constricted in a way that brought on a wave of nausea. He couldn't recall a specific time he'd lost someone close to him, but it must have happened at some point if he was as old as Tamaya thought he was. He wouldn't set himself up for that kind of heartache again. Mitul would just have to get used to the distance between them.

Voices drifted from the road ahead, and Lucian retreated into the lantern hanging from Kesari's waist. He'd done that a few times already, always when they came upon someone else on the road. Like he was ashamed, their Bond a secret they both needed to hide. Odd behavior, but considering how young Kesari was, maybe there *was* some element of shame.

The strangers they passed turned out to be a pair of merchants. They barely acknowledged Amar and the others from the seat of their wagon, and as soon as they'd disappeared from view, Lucian reemerged from his lantern to hover at Kesari's shoulder.

What was their story, anyway? What strange circumstances had led to them forming a Bond, and why were they so secretive about it now? Tamaya had suggested that Jameson might be able to break Spirit Tarja Bonds, and that seemed to be what Kesari and Lucian were after. But why, when forming a Bond with a Spirit Tarja came at such a high cost to the living partner?

Amar continued to mull over these questions as they continued on their journey. They didn't stop again until well past sunset. Mitul and Saya split the night's watches between them, declining Kesari's offer to help with an exchanged glance of uncertainty. Amar had offered to take a turn the previous night, but Saya had made an excuse about his needing to rest, and Mitul had backed her up. The more likely reason was that they didn't trust him not to run off and abandon them in their sleep.

To be fair, he had considered doing exactly that, particularly as Mitul's pitying looks became more frequent and insufferable.

If they didn't want his help, so be it. Let them wear themselves out on half a night's sleep if they were too worried to trust anyone else. When he'd finished his meal of salted pork and dried berries, Amar found a relatively comfortable spot in the grass to sleep and turned his back to them all without a word.

The next day progressed much like the one before, and again, they walked late into the night. Mitul was stumbling over his own feet by the time they stopped. Kesari was yawning every few minutes, and even Saya's squared shoulders had begun to droop with exhaustion.

"Do you want to take the first watch again, or should I?" Saya asked Mitul as they laid out their blankets.

"I will," he replied, but he didn't sound happy about it.

Lucian hovered between them. "It's foolish for you both to waste your energy walking this far on so little sleep," he said in his low, crackling voice. "I don't need sleep. I can keep watch all night."

"He's right," Kesari agreed. "You don't need to tire yourselves out like this."

Saya frowned and said nothing. Mitul kept his eyes on his blanket, smoothing out the same wrinkles over and over again.

"They don't trust us," Amar said. He stared directly at Mitul, waiting until the man's gaze rose to meet his before continuing. "You claim we were friends and ask me to trust you, but you can't do the same for me?"

"It's not like that," Mitul replied.

"Isn't it? What are you so afraid of? That we'll murder you in your sleep? Or that we'll steal everything you own and disappear without a trace?"

"Amar, please…" Mitul didn't finish the sentence, just shook his head and let out a longsuffering sigh.

"We don't trust you because you're not yourself," Saya said. "And I don't care if that upsets you—it's true." She turned to Kesari and Lucian. "I don't mean any offense to either of you, but we barely know each other."

"What does it matter if I leave?" Amar spat back. "You and Mitul spend so much time whispering about me and trying to tiptoe around my feelings. I'm sure you'd both be happier on your own."

Saya leaned forward, her eyes cold and hard. "Oh, I'm sure we would be, if you're going to keep acting like some ignorant, self-centered *pashlik*."

Amar didn't know exactly what the word meant, but it was obviously an insult. Before he could respond in kind, Mitul stepped between them, his hands raised. "Stop this, both of you. We all want the same thing. There's no reason to fight." He turned to Saya. "Lucian's right, and so is Amar. We're going to have to start trusting each other a little more if we want this journey to go smoothly."

Saya hissed a rapid string of Sularan words under her breath, then looked at Lucian. "Fine, then. Take the watch. But you'd better wake us the moment something happens."

"Of course," Lucian replied with a wicked grin. "There's nothing like a few singed eyebrows to get people up and out of bed in a hurry."

"Oh, stop it," Kesari said, but her mouth turned up at the corners. Saya glowered at them both, and she quickly added, "He'll do no such thing, I swear."

Saya shook her head, lay down on top of her blanket, and closed her eyes. Mitul looked at Amar before resting his head on his pack. "Goodnight," he said with a conciliatory smile.

Amar merely grunted in response and lay back with his hands behind his head. Within minutes, his companions were fast asleep, their deep breaths breaking up the night's silence. Amar, however, lay awake. After trying everything he could think of to quiet his mind and drift into sleep, he finally gave up and rose from the ground.

Lucian hovered several paces away, and he turned to face Amar at the sound of his stirring. The Spirit Tarja's fiery body stood out in stark, jagged orange against the night, but his eyes and mouth were as black as the sky. "All that fuss about making sure you don't wear yourselves out, and now you're not going to sleep?"

"I *can't* sleep," Amar replied. He went to stand beside Lucian and followed his gaze out into the dark beyond the trees. "You do this every night? Just wait here alone for hours while she sleeps?" He nodded to Kesari, who dozed peacefully nearby.

"Usually," Lucian said. "It's been more interesting these last few nights, having Saya or Mitul to keep me company. And tonight, I find myself with the most interesting company of all." His dark eyes seemed to narrow. "A man out of time, cursed with immortality. I've never met someone quite so…unique."

There was a question there—one Amar didn't want to answer or even contemplate. Time to change the subject. "You're pretty unique yourself, aren't you?"

Lucian's eyes seemed to widen, but it was hard to read his expressions in the flickering flames. "What do you mean?"

"Well, you speak Kavoran as well as any native. But Lucian is a Visan name, isn't it?"

"It is."

"I didn't think there were any natural born Visan Tarja." There was the woman who was hunting them, but she seemed to have gained her abilities from a Bond. Only natural born Tarja could become Spirit Tarja, and only if they died prematurely.

"How can you remember something like that and yet remember nothing about your own life?"

Amar gave him a wry look. "That's what I've been trying to understand myself."

Lucian's chuckle was dry and brittle. "Well, you're right. No Visan I've ever heard of was born a Tarja. But I'm not Visan—not really. I'm not sure where I came from. A Visan woman found me shipwrecked near her village when I was a boy, too young and scared to tell her my name. She and her wife raised me as their own."

"Generous of them," Amar said.

"Well, what else were they going to do? Throw me back to the sea?"

"Some people would have."

Lucian grinned. "You're very pessimistic, aren't you?"

He shrugged. "What happened when they found out about your magic?"

"They did their best to understand, but I don't think they ever really did. And of course, in Vis, magic made me more of an outcast than I already was. I tested for placement in a Kavoran Tarja academy as soon as I was old enough and never looked back."

"Not even to visit your parents?"

"They weren't exactly supportive of my decision. Can't blame them, given how Kavorans see Visans as heathens just because they aren't *blessed* with the ability to channel altma." He said this with derision, like the idea was absolutely ludicrous. But there were plenty of people in Kavora who believed it.

"People fear what they don't understand," Amar said.

Lucian gave him another amused smile. "You sound very sure about that."

"It's true enough, isn't it? Why else would you hide in a lantern every time we see strangers on the road?" He glanced over his shoulder at Kesari. "If they saw you Bonded to someone so young, they wouldn't understand, would they? They might be fearful, or even angry."

"They might." Lucian's smile disappeared, and his dark eyes simply stared out at the road.

Amar waited a few seconds before prying further. "Why *did* you two decide to form a Bond? And why are you looking for a way to break that Bond now?"

"Ah, you picked up on that, did you? It must seem a strange thing to seek after."

"Well?" he prodded when Lucian offered nothing further.

The Spirit Tarja turned his gaze to Kesari, her limbs curled beneath her coat. "I was only thirty when I died," he said. "It happened while I was in Atrea, where natural born Tarja are far less common than they are in Kavora. Most people there have little understanding of magic, and few would choose to give up half their life for that power. If a Spirit Tarja doesn't form a Bond with a living person within a few days of their death, they fade away, and I didn't have time to search for the perfect partner. I wanted to live, and Kesari wanted magic more than anything. We thought ourselves lucky to have found each other."

"But that changed," Amar said. "You're trying to break your Bond, and I haven't seen her use her magic at all since I met you both."

"She never does," Lucian said quietly. "She hasn't for a long time now."

"So what happened?"

"It's not my place to say."

"I guess I'll have to ask her then."

"I doubt she'd tell you, and I strongly suggest you don't ask at all." The implied threat in his voice was as sharp as a knife's edge. "It's none of your business, and I'd hate to make an enemy of you when I was just starting to like you."

Amar's fingers curled into a fist. "She let me die," he said, a new heat flaring up inside him. "She could have used her magic to save me, but she didn't. And now, because of that, I can't remember who I am."

Lucian stared at him with a frown that looked even more menacing than his usual demonic grin. "Because of your *curse*, you can't remember who you are. Kesari had nothing to do with it. And just because she didn't try to save you doesn't mean she would have succeeded if she had."

"She still should have tried."

"I think a part of her wanted to."

"Then why didn't—"

"Because she *can't*. That's all I'll say about it."

Amar sighed and ran a hand through his hair, exasperated. "I'm only trying to understand."

Lucian grew larger and pushed himself closer to Amar's face. His flames curled and fluttered like a gust of wind had torn through them. "You're trying to find someone to blame. I can understand the impulse, but I won't allow you to put that blame on Kes. She doesn't deserve it, especially when she's done nothing but help you."

Amar had no response for that. He was still bitter that Kesari had made no attempt to save his life, but Lucian was right. It may not have made a difference at all, and blaming her for it now wouldn't change anything.

With nothing left to say, he turned on his heel and headed back to his bed.

"For what it's worth," Lucian said, "I think you might be saving *her*, even though she couldn't do the same for you. Going to see Jameson, returning to Atrea—it's something she needs to do, and she wouldn't be doing it if not for you."

Somehow, his words only made Amar feel worse.

KESARI

THEY WALKED AT THE SAME UNYIELDING PACE FOR ANOTHER FIVE days, by which point Kesari's feet were covered in blisters and her legs ached unceasingly from the moment she woke up until after she fell asleep. Whenever she or one of the others complained, Saya would remind them of the need to put as much distance between themselves and their pursuer as possible. An understandable precaution, especially considering she'd killed one of them the last time they met.

The road began to wind its way back to civilization, and they crossed paths with other travelers more and more frequently. Lucian was confined to his lantern more often than not. He claimed it didn't bother him, but Kesari winced a little every time he retreated inside. If he'd Bonded to someone else—someone more confident and less broken— there would be no need for hiding. Underage Bonds were frowned upon, but it wasn't like they never happened. She was the one who couldn't bear the stares and whispers they attracted.

He was still in his lantern when they finally reached Valmandi. A cluster of ramshackle huts and tents were the first structures to come into view at the northernmost edge of the city. These made up a Visan refugee camp, which seemed to have expanded since the last time Kesari had travelled this way. A wooden fence had been haphazardly erected around the encampment, its edges pushing right up against the road. Several Visans stood along the path, attempting to sell various commodities to passing travelers. Many wore brightly colored Kavoran clothes rather than their more subdued traditional attire, but their pale skin, eyes, and hair made them easily distinguishable from the Kavoran travelers with darker complexions.

Saya stopped in front of a pair of boys who couldn't have been older than ten. Dirt smeared their faces, and their worn clothes hung loose on too-thin bodies. They offered her a misshapen clay pot decorated with tiny shells. A useless trinket, but she smiled at them and traded some of the food in her satchel for it. Kesari waited for her to finish up the transaction, but Amar walked on, Mitul trailing on his heels.

Kesari and Saya had to scramble to catch up with them and avoid getting lost in the thickening foot traffic. As bodies crowded around her, Kesari glanced over her shoulder at the two boys. They had split the food between them and were devouring it like they hadn't had a decent meal in weeks.

Her chest tightened. There must be dozens of children here like them, displaced and possibly orphaned by the invasion of their homeland. She hadn't seen her own home in years, but at least she had a home to go back to. At least her parents were still alive.

The road had widened now that they were near the city walls. Two steady streams of traffic flowed into and out of the open gates as merchants, carts, horses, riders, patrolling soldiers, and more went about their business. When Kesari and the others reached the gates, the guards standing to either side looked them up and down with stony expressions but let them through without a word.

Kesari took in a deep, contented breath as Valmandi's lively streets opened up in front of them. Multi-story buildings rose up in every direction, their walls decorated with vibrant tapestries and painted murals. The rich hues seemed to glow in the sunset's intense orange light. The sound of thousands of voices filled the air, punctuated by laughter and music and animal noise. Children ran through the streets chasing after a leather skin ball while their parents and grandparents watched.

A handful of Tarja fit in among the people here as naturally as anyone else, but Kesari's eyes were drawn to them as she scanned her surroundings. Two Tarja children made a game of seeing how high they could jump by channeling extra strength into their legs. A Tarja man lit a blazing cookfire with a simple touch of his hand against the wood. A Tarja grandmother wove magical illusions into her story while a captive audience of children and adults alike watched and listened at her feet.

Kesari's smile fell. Not so long ago, she would have given anything to do magic like that. Now she had the ability but couldn't bring herself to use it.

She followed the others though streets that wound their way farther into the city. They passed by the larger homes of wealthier families and into the military district, where barracks housed and trained the soldiers who patrolled Valmandi in pairs and small groups. Beyond these were more houses, a bustling market, and temples and shrines where people gathered to meditate and reconnect with altma. Although Tarja were the only ones who could channel altma to perform magical feats, the energy could be found in all living things and was viewed as sacred in mainstream Kavoran culture.

The largest of these temples stood near the center of the city, a stone's throw away from the gates to the palace. When they reached it, Mitul stopped so abruptly that Amar nearly crashed into him.

"Watch where you're going," he grumbled.

Mitul didn't answer. Kesari followed his gaze to a large, colorful mural painted on the tallest side of the temple, which faced the palace. Her breath caught as she admired the artwork, a portrait of a beautiful young woman with thick brows, full lips, and long lashes. Her eyes were closed as if she were sleeping, and her hands were clasped together loosely over her chest. A beaded veil draped over her raven curls and fell loose behind her shoulders, disappearing beneath the colorful, delicate flowers surrounding her.

It was the most stunning painting Kesari had ever seen, but her heart sank a bit as she studied it more closely. There was something mournful in the slight downturn of the woman's mouth, and her brows pinched together a little, as though she were troubled.

"She looks sad," Saya said, tilting her head to one side.

Kesari and Amar both nodded in agreement, but Mitul gave no response, his gaze lingering on the painting.

Amar nudged him in the shoulder. "Do you know her or something?"

Mitul blinked quickly, like he'd been pulled from a trance. "Princess Priyani?" He gave a slight chuckle. "No, of course not."

So *that* was who the woman was. Kesari had heard the story many times throughout her travels, though the details varied depending on where she was. Princess Priyani was the late daughter of Bhajan and Indira Sharma, the king and queen of Valmandi and rulers of Kavora's second-largest province. She'd been well loved and was said to have been gracious and benevolent, taking time out of each day to personally address the concerns of the common people.

Her marriage to Emperor Akraja some twenty years prior had been widely regarded as a good match, despite their vast age difference. The union had solidified the ties between Valmandi and the empire's central power in Jakhat, and those ties only grew stronger with the birth of Akraja and Priyani's son, Savir.

From there, the story became murky. The emperor's sister, Dashiva, would have been his successor, but that changed with Savir's birth. A few months later, Akraja fell sick and died, leaving Dashiva to rule as regent until the young heir came of age. But after two years, Priyani and the boy were murdered by enemies of the empire in a bloody assassination. Dashiva was crowned empress and had ruled ever since, though there were still occasional rumors that the young Prince Savir had somehow survived the attack and would one day return to claim his throne.

It was almost certainly nonsense, but looking up at Priyani's portrait, Kesari could see why some might cling to those rumors. The princess' death had been an unthinkable tragedy. If she'd been half as kind and beloved as the stories said, of course people would want to believe some piece of her was still alive out there.

"Ready to go?" Saya asked Mitul.

"A moment longer, if you don't mind." His voice was sad, and his eyes had taken on that vacant, trance-like look again.

Amar gave an exasperated sigh. "It's just a stupid painting. If you didn't know her, why do you care so much?"

"I know the man who painted her," Mitul replied. "Or at least, I used to."

Amar looked sullen, but he didn't say anything else. His hand went to rest on the hilt of his sword, fingers tapping the pommel irritably.

"Who was he?" Kesari asked Mitul.

"Kamaal Ruman. His work has become quite famous. You may have heard of him before."

She hadn't, but she didn't keep up with that sort of thing. Besides, that wasn't what she'd been asking. "I mean, how did you know him?"

Mitul blinked in that strange, waking-up sort of way again, then turned to her. "He was my partner, for a time. We might have been together for the rest of our lives, if…." He trailed off, fingers brushing over the turquoise cuff on his wrist, then let out a sigh. "If things had been different. But I loved him, very much."

There was a pained note in his voice, and for a second, Kesari had the urge to put an arm around his shoulder and tell him it would be all right. Instead, she asked, "Where is he now?"

"I don't know, but I hope he's happy." He shifted the weight of his satchel and turned to Saya and Amar. "We should find somewhere to stay before nightfall."

They kept walking, skirting around the walled grounds of the palace to find quieter, emptier streets. The sky had darkened and lights were beginning to appear in the building's windows as people retreated indoors for the night. Mitul was now rambling on about an inn he knew somewhere nearby, which allowed guests to play music, dance, and share other talents for the entertainment of their fellow patrons. It was customary for spectators to tip the performers, and Mitul claimed to have once made enough money there in a single night to live on for a week.

"Besides," he said, "I haven't been able to play in weeks. I wouldn't want to forget how." He laid a gentle hand on the instrument hanging at his side.

Saya shook her head. "You know perfectly well it wouldn't have been safe to play out there these last few nights. You might as well have shouted to tell our pursuer where we were."

She was right, but Kesari had been hoping to hear Mitul play every day since meeting him. Perhaps tonight she'd finally get the chance.

"How much farther is this inn of yours?" Amar asked. "Are you sure we're going the right way?"

"Of course," Mitul replied. "You don't remember, but we lived here for years. I know this city well."

"This looks exactly like the last ten roads we've been down."

Kesari had to agree; she'd long since lost track of where they were in the maze of Valmandi's streets. The area they currently occupied was empty except for a few closed shops, and there didn't seem to be anyone else around.

Saya broke away from the others and slowed. Mitul stopped when he realized she was no longer following him, as did Amar and Kesari. Amar let out an exasperated sigh and muttered under his breath. "Oh, skies above, what now?"

Kesari followed Saya's gaze down a narrow side street, where a pair of uniformed city guards loomed over a Visan woman and her child. They stood too close, invading her space with brazen authority. Her posture was stiff as she shrunk away from them, and her son clutched at the fabric of her shirt with tiny, balled fists.

"If you don't have a permit," one of the guards was saying, "we'll have to take you into custody."

"Please," the woman said, "I was on my way home. I can be out of the city in five minutes if you'll let me—"

"Do you know what would happen if we made exceptions for every Visan heathen we caught inside our walls after sunset?" The contempt in his voice churned Kesari's stomach. No one deserved to be spoken to like that, and the woman was clearly terrified. If only there was something she could do to help.

But she was just a girl. A small, powerless, coward of a girl.

When the woman didn't respond, the second guard answered his companion's question. "It would be absolute chaos." He took a step closer to the woman, reaching a hand toward her face. She flinched, but he grabbed her jaw and forced her to look up at him. "We're only trying to keep everyone safe, you know."

By the time he finished his sentence, Saya had closed half the distance between herself and the guards. Her muscles were as taut and wiry as a stalking panther's as she nocked an arrow to her bowstring. Mitul hissed her name and took a few steps after her, but she continued without hesitation, calling to the guards. "Is there some kind of trouble over here?"

Neither of them so much as looked at her. "It's nothing you need concern yourself with," the first one said.

"You're harassing this woman. That's enough to make it my concern."

Kesari's jaw dropped. These guards were practically giants with their burly physiques and bayoneted rifles. Was Saya seriously going to start a fight with them? She may have been a Sularan warrior, but she was much smaller than either of these men, and what was her bow supposed to do against their guns? And yet she stood, tall and proud, undeterred by their icy glares or the authority of their uniforms. Did she have a death wish?

Kesari glanced at Amar to see whether he was as shocked as she was, but he was busy picking the dirt out of his nails, his expression flat and bored.

The first guard turned to face Saya with slow, deliberate movements. He unslung the rifle from his shoulder and made a show of examining the sharp point of the bayonet. "You'll leave us to our business, girl, or you'll find a blade stuck through your guts while you wriggle like a worm."

"And detaining innocent people is your business now, is it? I'm so glad you're out here protecting us from terrifying criminals like those two." She nodded to the woman and child. "What did they do? Who did they hurt?"

"There's a curfew. All Visan refugees are to be out of the city by sunset unless they have a permit."

"If it were up to me," said the second guard, "there ought to be a curfew for you wretched Sularans, too."

"Fortunately, it's *not* up to you, is it?"

Both men bored into Saya with glares as sharp as their bayonets. Kesari's insides wilted. She didn't want to be here anymore. Her legs urged her to run, get as far away as she could before the fight broke out. But she couldn't abandon the others to face down two armed guards on their own.

Except of course she could, because what good was she doing here anyway? She wasn't standing bravely by Saya's side or using her magic to persuade the guards this wasn't a fight they wanted. She was hanging back, cowering like a scared little mouse. Even the rapid pitter-patter of her heart felt like tiny mouse feet scurrying away.

Amar sighed and cracked his neck a few times. Then he unholstered the pistol at his hip with one hand, unsheathed his sword with the other, and strode forward until he was standing right next to Saya. He kept both weapons pointed at the ground, but his hands were firm and sure around their grips. Mitul took up a position on Saya's other side, unarmed but still bold enough to stand by his friends.

Kesari's heart continued to race. Why couldn't she be that brave?

"You heard her," Amar called out to the guards, extending his blade to point at the nearest. "Clear off."

One of them pressed the stock of his rifle against his shoulder. "Make us."

Something warmed against Kesari's leg through the heavy fabric of her coat—Lucian's lantern. Before she could open the door for him, he sprung from the small gap in the top and rushed in front of Amar, Mitul, and Saya, expanding until he was as tall as a person and three times as broad. Shock widened the guards' eyes as they stared at the demonic face within his flames.

There was no hanging back now. Legs shaking, Kesari forced herself to move until she stood beside Mitul. There was a bit of exhilaration mixed in with the fear now. She wasn't nearly as brave as her companions, but she could pretend to be, and even in pretending, she felt a little bolder.

Behind the guards, the Visan boy whimpered. His mother clutched him closer to her, but there was a look of triumph on her face as she watched the guards' reactions.

Their steady hold on their rifles had faltered, the weapons now aimed at the ground. Clearly, they hadn't anticipated this much resistance. They might have been willing to put up a fight against a middle-aged man and two armed teenagers, but a Tarja, too—no, they hadn't counted on that at all.

Never mind that Kesari hadn't actually used her magic in two years. *They* didn't know that, and sometimes the mere threat of what she *might* do was enough to scare people off.

The nearest guard turned to his companion with a thinly veiled mask of fortitude. "Come on, our shift's almost over. It's not worth the trouble."

The second man looked disappointed, maybe even a little angry, and he jabbed a stiff finger at the Visan woman's face. "Don't ever let me catch you in this city past curfew again. You won't get off so easy next time."

With that, they stalked off. Lucian gave Kesari a wink as he shrunk down to a smattering of sparks, then retreated into his lantern without a word. The Visan woman thanked them all in a quick, clipped accent. Amar asked her for directions, which she delivered before taking her boy's hand and hurrying off. She gave Kesari a wide berth and an almost fearful look as she passed.

When they'd gone, Saya turned to Amar with a curious tilt of her head. "You backed me up."

He shoved his pistol into its holster with a noncommittal grunt, avoiding her gaze.

"Why?" Saya pressed.

"To get it over with," he muttered. "Come on. Let's keep moving, or we're never going to reach this inn."

He and Mitul led the way in the direction the woman had directed them, and Kesari fell into stride beside Saya. "That was really brave, what you did back there."

Saya shook her head. "It was stupid. I could have gotten us all into serious trouble. If you and Lucian hadn't stepped in at the end, I'm not sure what would have happened."

"Why did you do it, then?"

"Because it infuriates me, the way they treat them."

"Who? The Visans?"

She nodded. "It's not right. And it's like that guard said—if they had their way, those same restrictions would be imposed on my people. Sometimes it seems like it's only a matter of time before that happens."

"What do you mean?"

Saya frowned. "Kavorans put themselves above everyone else. They think everything in Erythyr is theirs for the taking, and they don't care what they destroy or whose lives they ruin in the process."

Kesari's eyes swept over the red marks painted on Saya's tawny skin, the determined set of her jaw, and the fierceness in her amber eyes.

Whatever magic is affecting you could help save my people.

The words she'd spoken to Amar at Tamaya's house echoed through Kesari's mind, and the pieces began to fall into place.

"Your haseph—you want your people to become immortal?"

Saya shrugged. "Maybe. Some of them."

"Why?"

"The Kavorans outnumber us. Their armies are bigger and stronger. They think they can take whatever they want because no one has been strong enough to stop them. It's what they did to the Visans, and it's what they'll do to us when they tire of the current arrangement." The planes of her face were sharp in the stark light from a nearby window. "But if our warriors were immortal, if we could rise from death to fight in battle again, the Kavorans' advantage in power and numbers wouldn't matter."

Kesari nodded but said nothing. It wasn't an unreasonable plan, and had she been in Saya's position, she might have come to the same conclusions. But when she looked ahead at Amar, an immortal man trying to rid himself of that curse, she couldn't stop the shiver that rippled across her skin.

AMAR

MITUL EVENTUALLY LED THEM ALL TO AN INN CALLED THE SAFFRON Fox. As promised, it was the kind of establishment which catered to those who wanted good food and entertainment in addition to a place to lay their heads. Low tables and cushions for sitting filled the building's ground floor, with a space set up along one wall for performers. A woman and her trained dragon were performing when they arrived, and the audience's applause followed them up the stairs to the two rooms they'd rented for the night.

The rooms themselves were small but comfortable. Mitul and Amar took one while Saya, Kesari, and Lucian took the other. No sooner had they set their belongings inside than Mitul pulled his saraj from its case. He softly plucked at the strings, occasionally turning the knobs at the end of the instrument's neck to adjust its tune. "I'm going to go down and see if I can earn us a bit of money for the rest of our journey. You're welcome to join me, if you'd like. Your kanjira should still be in your pack."

Amar had seen the small handheld drum among his other belongings, but he'd barely touched it, let alone attempted to play it. He wasn't about to start now. "No thanks."

"Oh, come on, it might be fun."

There was that same warm familiarity again. Like they were friends.

Like they were family. Amar crossed his arms. "You're the musician, not me. Go on and play, since that's all you've been able to talk about today. Just leave me alone."

Some of the warmth left Mitul's eyes. "All right then," he said, turning to the door. "I will."

He walked out, and Amar pushed down the nagging feeling that started to rise from the pit of his stomach. He had nothing to feel guilty for. Mitul meant well, but he was trying too hard to force whatever connection they'd supposedly once had. They didn't need to go everywhere and do everything together. In fact, some time apart might do them good.

Amar turned to his pack and opened the clasp at the top. He dug through its contents until he found his coin pouch. He needed a new tunic to replace the one that had been ruined in his fight with the Visan girl. More importantly, he needed a stiff drink.

His fingers brushed against the cloth-wrapped bundle at the bottom of the pack. His kanjira, the one Mitul had wanted him to play. He pulled it out but didn't unwrap it, instead setting it on the bed. He placed his journal alongside it, then unsheathed his sword and laid it out across the thin mattress.

A frown pulled at his lips. He'd read his journal from cover to cover and had been through his belongings dozens of times over the last week, hoping something might help him remember the man he used to be. But of course, nothing came. Nothing certain, anyway. But with these three items, there was always a vague sense that were important somehow. Like he'd be sad to lose them.

With the journal and the kanjira, that feeling made sense. The journal connected him to who he was and what he wanted. It was proof that he hadn't simply lost his mind and that there was some truth to what the others had told him of his past. And in that past, he had once made a living playing music on the streets with Mitul. The drum would have been a significant part of his life at one point, and even if he couldn't remember the details, there seemed to be a lingering attachment to the instrument.

The sword, however, was a mystery. Until today, he couldn't remember ever having cause to wield it. He'd worn it at his side as a precaution more than anything, and because it brought him some peace of mind, but he hadn't felt like a swordsman until this evening when he'd stood next to Saya, weapons drawn and ready for battle. He'd been inexplicably calm despite the threat, confident that if a fight came, he would walk away victorious.

He wrapped his fingers around the hilt. Even now, it felt comfortable in his hand, like it had always belonged there. He didn't get that same feeling from the pistol, despite it being an arguably superior weapon.

He held the sword up and examined its design more closely. A lotus flower surrounded by delicate bronze leaves adorned the basket hilt, which showed no signs of age or tarnish. The slightly curved blade was perfectly balanced and honed to razor sharpness at the edge. He stood and tested the feel of it with a few practice swings. It cut through the air with a gentle *whoosh*, and he grinned. It felt good, familiar, like an extension of his very being.

Amar cleared his mind and allowed his body to guide him through a series of practiced movements. His muscles remembered the motions even though he couldn't bring up the memory of learning them. For the first time since he'd awakened in Tamaya's house, he knew who he was. Not entirely, not in all the important details, but with his sword in his hand, he could sense some of the broader strokes. It was the closest he'd come to feeling like himself.

He slashed the blade in a wide arc, turning enough to see the doorway. Saya stood there watching him, Kesari right behind her.

Amar froze with the blade still in the air, heat burning across his face. Then he turned away, shoved the sword back into its sheath, and tossed it onto the bed.

"I've always admired your skill with a blade," Saya said softly. "You must have had a lot of practice to learn to wield it like that."

The compliment stung. He should have remembered that practice, those years of training, but he didn't. And he didn't know what to say in response that wasn't bitter and mean, so instead, he stayed silent.

"Do you want to come downstairs with us?" Saya asked. "We were going to get a hot meal and listen to Mitul play. You know how excited he's been. I'm sure it would mean a lot to him if you were there."

Amar's jaw clenched, and he had a sudden urge to be anywhere else but here. He snatched up his coin pouch and shoved past Saya on his way out the door. Kesari scurried to get out of his way.

"Where are you going?" Saya called after him.

"I'll get my own food," he replied, and he hurried down the stairs and out the door before she could say anything else.

"More sohra," Amar called to the barman from his chair in the corner. He downed his last swallow of the alcoholic beverage and slammed the copper mug onto the table. His head was already buzzing, and his voice had an unnatural thickness to match the clumsiness of his tongue. He'd had more than his fill already, and a wiser man would have stopped a long time ago. But he had absolutely zero interest in being wise and every interest in becoming as blissfully drunk as possible.

That should be an easy enough feat in an establishment such as this, which wasn't nearly as clean or as cozy as the Saffron Fox where'd he left his companions. Several of the other patrons exchanged raucous stories while the rest were already passed out on various tables, cushions, and benches around the room. Amar expected to be among the latter before too long. The sooner the better.

A long belch escaped his throat, and he called out again. "I said, bring me more sohra."

The barman wiped his fingers on his tunic and approached the table, emptyhanded. He bent over Amar. "I think you've have enough, boy."

"*Boy?*" Amar let out a chuckle. Compared to how old he must be, this man was barely more than a child. "I'm not a boy, I'm an old man. Can't you see?" He grinned, amused by his own joke. Of course the barman couldn't see. No one could.

"Come on, time to go home. You're much too young to be throwing your life away in a place like this. I'm sure your parents don't want you out this late. They must be getting worried."

At this, Amar broke into boisterous laughter. It came out in loud, guffawing bursts that drew stares from the other customers. Amar howled at the uncomfortable looks on their faces. The whole situation was absurd. He was older than anyone in this room—probably older than anyone in the entire world, for that matter—and here was some stupid barman trying to curtail what he thought was a boy's reckless drinking and send him home to mommy and daddy.

He was still laughing as he stood up. The room spun all around him, and he gripped the back of the chair to steady himself. Once his surroundings had stabilized a little, he grabbed his empty mug and began making his way to the kegs lined up against the far wall. "It's all right," he said. "I'll get it myself."

The barman grabbed his arm. "I can't let you do that."

Amar tried to wrench free, but the room lurched with his sudden movement, making his stomach churn. "Let go of me," he snarled, but the barman's grip remained firm. Amar raised the mug in his other hand and attempted to hit him over the head with it.

"Oh, no you don't!" The barman blocked the slow, off-balance attack easily and grabbed Amar's wrist with his free hand. There was a brief scuffle in which Amar was too dizzy to really know what was happening, and then he suddenly found himself being thrown out into the street. He had barely enough time to throw his hands out in front of himself to cushion his fall. His palms scraped against the dirt, and his teeth cut through his bottom lip as his chin struck the road. The metallic taste of blood seeped into his mouth.

Behind him, a door slammed shut. He'd have to find somewhere else to drink now, but he'd seen a couple of other pubs on his way here. It shouldn't be too hard to find them again.

With a groan, he pushed himself off the ground. The road seemed to lurch beneath him like a ship in a storm, making his insides roil. Or maybe that was the sohra.

Someone grabbed him by the arm and tried to help him stand. Amar started to look up to see who it was, but nausea chose that very moment to overcome him. He doubled over, spewing all the contents of his stomach onto the person's sandal-clad feet.

An exasperated sigh preceded a familiar voice. "And I *just* took a bath."

Amar glowered up at Mitul. "If you didn't want to get dirty, you should have stayed—" He wretched again, barely managing to direct his expulsions onto a bare patch of ground. He didn't know whether to be appalled or impressed that his stomach could hold so much.

"There," Mitul said soothingly. "Get it all out."

Couldn't the man leave him alone? Amar wanted to shout at him but couldn't manage more than a croak in his current state. He put his hands on his knees for support as his body shuddered. Finally, he gave one last dry heave, spit the sour taste of sick and alcohol onto the ground, and straightened.

"We should get you to bed." Mitul put a gentle hand on his shoulder. "Come on."

Amar pulled away. "I don't want to go to bed." He hated the way his own voice sounded, like a child whining about his parent's perfectly reasonable request.

"Enough of this, Amar." Mitul's voice was firmer now. "You've clearly had enough to drink already. Sleep it off. You'll feel better in the morning."

"No I won't!" He took another step back and let all the resentment and anger that had sent him out drinking in the first place come spilling out. "I'll *never* feel better—not while you're around. You act like you're my older brother or something, but I don't know you. I don't know any of you. Whatever responsibility you think you think you owe me, you don't. And I don't owe you anything, either."

"Amar, you know that's not true. I *do* know you. Right now, I know you better than you know yourself, and I—"

"Stop!" Why wouldn't he just *stop*? Why did he have to keep reminding Amar of everything he was missing, of how damaged he was? "I don't have to listen to you. You're nobody. You're a sad, lonely man desperate for a friend who doesn't even want you. Do you understand me? I don't want you."

Mitul opened his mouth, took half a step toward Amar, and then stopped. He said nothing, only gave him a woeful look like an old dog that had been kicked. Fiery hatred blazed inside Amar. He ought to knock that pitiful look right off the man's face.

He clenched his fist and threw a punch. Mitul ducked aside with surprising speed, or maybe *that* was the sohra, too. The blow missed, and Amar stumbled. He barely managed to right himself, his insides burning even hotter than before, eager for a fight. But he wasn't going

⌘ 100 ⌘

to get it. Not when he was so drunk and sick he could barely stand. This could wait until tomorrow.

Or not. He didn't want to ever see Mitul again.

"Don't follow me," he growled, shoving his shoulder into the other man's as he passed.

To his great surprise and bitter relief, Mitul didn't.

ALEIDA

FOR DAYS, ALEIDA HAD KEPT A DOGGED PACE, RISING EARLY TO start her travels each morning and only stopping at night when her feet refused to carry her another step. Amar and his friends must have been doing the same, because she hadn't caught up to them. Or, more worrisome, perhaps they'd managed to acquire mounts.

The idea consumed her with every step she took, as did her frustration with losing her own horse. Twice, she had come infuriatingly close to catching her quarry and failed. If he got too far ahead now, would she ever find him again, and would it be in time to save Tyrus?

Time. It slipped through her fingers like dry beach sand, escaping her grasp no matter what she did. The ever-present weight of losing precious hours and days seemed to crush her from the inside out, but there was nothing she could do. Nothing except press forward, ignoring her body's tired protests.

They were only a day's travel from Valmandi now, and shortly after dark, Valkyra began her usual arguments for Aleida to rest. "You've barely had the energy to eat these last few nights," she said. "Let's get a nice hot meal in you, something fresh to help you recover your strength. You can stay here and make the fire while I hunt."

A hot meal *did* sound wonderful, and it wasn't like she could go much farther anyway. So she simply nodded and found a decent spot off the road to make camp. Valkyra flew away into the trees, and Aleida set about making a fire. With the help of her magic, it didn't take long. She found a comfortable place to sit, kicked off her boots, and dug into her pack until her fingers found the flat leather case tucked under her spare clothes.

She pulled it out and untied the cord that held it shut. Inside lay a stack of loose papers bound between more leather, a tiny bottle of dark ink, a few quill pens, and several sticks of charcoal wrapped in cloth. She inched a little closer to the fire, took out a stick of charcoal and a sketch she'd started weeks ago, and examined her prior work.

The lines of the sketch were so light she could barely make them out, but that had been the entire point. Until two weeks ago, she'd never laid eyes on the man who couldn't die and had only had Valkyra's descriptions of him to go on. Those descriptions had been vague at best, and the features she'd sketched were equally indistinct. But now, a detailed image of Amar was seared into her memory.

She closed her eyes and conjured up the way he'd looked at her the night they fought beside the waterfall. There had been such a burning intensity in his eyes, enhanced by the fiery glow of the Spirit Tarja who accompanied him. She could still see the tension in his knit brows when he'd yelled at her. *What do you want with us?*

Did he really not know? Did he really not understand the gift he had, and how fiercely she and others might be willing to fight to gain even a lesser version of that gift?

She set the charcoal to paper and sketched out the lines of his face in more confident strokes. She could still hear the crackling fire and see its light dancing across her paper, but everything else seemed to disappear as she drew. Even the scattered, anxious thoughts that had previously consumed her fell silent. There was only her and the paper and the charcoal in her fingers, and for a few precious minutes, she found some semblance of peace.

Valkyra returned before she had finished her drawing. She swooped in with a dead rabbit in her clawed forelegs and laid it on the grass next to Aleida. "Here's your supper, dear."

Somewhat reluctantly, Aleida set her drawing aside and knelt in front of the fire. "Thanks," she said, picking up the rabbit. She made quick work of skinning and dressing it, then stuck it over the fire to roast. She washed her hands with some of the water still in her pack and returned to her drawing. Valkyra settled on her shoulder to watch her work.

"That's very good," she said, brushing the back of Aleida's neck with her tail. "It looks exactly like him."

"Almost." There was something in the shape of his nose and the curve of his mouth that didn't look quite right yet. She sketched a few new lines over the ones she'd previously made, and, once satisfied, laid them down with a little more pressure. After that, she started shading, emphasizing the planes and subtle curves of Amar's face until she had a portrait that was, if not an exact likeness, at least close enough to be recognizable.

By the time she was done, the rabbit had finished cooking. She touched her fingers to the paper and channeled a bit of altma to help preserve the drawing. It wouldn't last forever, but it would at least prevent some smearing.

She set her drawing supplies on top of her pack and took the rabbit off the fire. It was still too hot to eat, and she was about to use magic to draw out some of the warmth when a faint rustle in the trees overhead caught her attention.

"Ah," said Valkyra. "It's Feros."

Perched on a low-hanging branch above them, an owl-like creature blinked his large, pitch-black eyes twice as he stared down at Aleida. She held out an arm for him to come to, but he stayed where he was and extended a wing, preening at his feathers as if he had all the time in the world.

"Get down here, you stupid bird," Aleida said.

Feros let out an irritated screech and fluttered down to rest on her arm. He dug his claws in a little harder than necessary, but it was impossible to tell whether the act had been intentional. Aleida glared at him and opened the small tube strapped to his back. She pulled out the rolled paper inside and barely managed to get the tube shut again before Feros turned a greedy eye to the heap of discarded rabbit entrails next to the fire. He hopped down and began picking at them.

Aleida wrinkled her nose. Strixes were faithful creatures, and highly useful with their unique intelligence and ability to channel limited amounts of altma for tracking. But there was something unnerving about their taste for blood and their proclivity for ripping the innards out of their prey. The legends didn't help. In Libera, older children had told her stories about the wild strixes of old who loved nothing more than to tear human infants apart from the navel and gobble up their insides.

She shuddered. Tyrus would have said she was being ridiculous, and he would have been right, but he'd always been more attached to Feros than she was. It probably had to do with the fact that she hadn't been very kind to the strix when she was a child. She was constantly trying to shut him out of the house, and on more than one occasion, she'd accidentally shut the door on a leg or a wing or his face. She'd always been terrified of him, sure she'd wake one night to find him ripping into her own stomach. She couldn't count the number of nightmares she'd had about it, and to this day, she was still half-convinced that Feros hated her.

But he was useful—incredibly useful—and so she put up with his more unpleasant qualities. For Tyrus' sake.

Trying to ignore the moist, squelching noises a few paces away, Aleida unrolled the message Feros had delivered. There were two sheets of paper. The first was a letter, written in Hasan's hand and completely unintelligible to Aleida, who had never learned to read. The second contained a few of Tyrus' ink drawings.

She held the letter up for Valkyra. The Spirit Tarja shifted her weight forward and began to read it aloud. "Dear Aleida, how are you? I'm sorry I haven't written in so long. Hasan's been busy and couldn't help me until today. He kept saying I should write it myself because it would be good practice, but it's hard to think of what I want to say when I'm trying to concentrate so much on the letters. Or maybe I'm just being lazy. Anyway, I hope you're doing well, and I hope I didn't worry you by taking so long to write."

Aleida frowned. How long *had* it been since she'd sent her last message to Tyrus? Five weeks, maybe six. Normally he was quick to send back a response, and the delay might have worried her if she hadn't been so preoccupied with everything else going on lately. Worrying about it would have done her no good, of course, but still, she should have noticed.

Valkyra kept reading. "Things have been quiet here. Hasan keeps teaching me to read and write and do numbers, and I keep ducking out of lessons every chance I get. Of course, that's a lot harder to do with wobbly legs and feet that won't cooperate. I can't get far when I try to run away these days."

Aleida's frown deepened. The last time she'd seen her brother, he'd barely been able to walk, let alone run.

"That was a joke, by the way," Valkyra read. "It's all right if you laugh."

Aleida rolled her eyes, but the corners of her lips quirked up a little despite herself. He knew her too well.

"In all seriousness, I'm doing fine, all things considered. Hasan has been trying some new treatments, and the pain hasn't been as bad the last few days. I even did some drawings for you. They're not as good as yours, obviously, but here's a little glimpse at what life is like here in Chatanda in the summer. I hope you get a chance to come and see it for yourself. I miss you, but if you can't come home yet, I understand. I know you'd be with me if you could. Please be safe out there. I love you. Tyrus."

Aleida tucked the letter behind the second sheet of paper and studied Tyrus' drawings with a concentrated scowl. There was one of Feros, ruffle-feathered and slit-eyed as he dozed on a branch. A second drawing showed a trio of young children running while a pair of dogs cavorted about in the third. The fourth drawing was an exaggerated caricature of Hasan, his heavy brows drawn together in a stern expression. Words were scrawled beside his open mouth in Tyrus' own unpracticed letters.

Before Aleida could ask what the words read, Valkyra spoke. "That one says, 'You really need to practice your writing, Tyrus.'" She did a fair impression of Hasan's low voice, then gave a musical little laugh. "I doubt this is what he meant when he said that."

Aleida forced herself to smile. Once, the drawings might have made her laugh, too. Looking at them now only tied knots in her stomach. Like her, Tyrus was a decent artist, and the physical deterioration caused by his illness was plain in the state of his work. What once might have been captured with strong, broad strokes had now been rendered in shaky lines and minimal detail. Inky smudges and haphazard streaks were scattered at random across the page, left there by accident when he'd struggled to maintain control of his quill. Something that would only happen more often as his illness progressed.

But he wouldn't want her dwelling on that. He'd want her to recognize the joy and humor in his pictures. She studied them again and allowed a more genuine smile to spread across her face. He was showing her pieces of his life, opening a window for her to see into his world even though she couldn't be physically present in it. This was their own unique way of communicating, and she was grateful to still have that binding them together even when they were so far apart.

They hadn't ever had the chance to learn to read or write—not until Hasan began teaching Tyrus. Aleida had never bothered to learn and still had no interest in doing so. She didn't have the time, and she preferred the drawings to the letters, anyway. Words were clearer and more specific, but the drawings were more personal.

She carefully folded up the pages and set them aside. The rabbit had cooled enough to eat now, and she closed her eyes to offer a quick prayer to Artex.

Thank you for the food, and thank you for allowing Tyrus' letter to reach me safely. Please watch over him while I cannot.

She cut off a piece of the meat and took a bite, chewing slowly. The fresh, warm meal was a welcome improvement over the stale biscuits and dried berries she'd been subsisting on for the last several days. The fire burned low as she ate, and her thoughts drifted to Libera and Tyrus and the parents they'd both lost in the invasion.

Valkyra hopped down from her shoulder like a cat and stretched her legs and wings in front of the fire. "You're quiet," she said. "Usually you're happy to get a letter from your brother. What's wrong?"

"What if he's not doing as well as he says he is?"

Valkyra tilted her head to the side. "If something were wrong, I'm sure Hasan would have written about it."

"It's the drawings," Aleida said. "I think his hands must be hurting him, or he's losing more control of his muscles."

"That's to be expected, knowing the progression of Storm Withering Syndrome."

"That doesn't make it any easier to accept," Aleida muttered.

"I'm sorry, dear. That's not how I meant it. But this isn't anything out of the ordinary, you know that. He still has time, but there are going to be some bad days along the way. Perhaps he drew those pictures on a bad day."

Aleida took another bite and chewed slowly, trying to concentrate on the flavor of the meat and the smoky smell of the fire to hold back the tears pricking at her eyes. "I wish there was more I could do."

Valkyra stretched up to rest her forelegs on Aleida's knee and looked her in the eye. "Oh, sweet child, you're much too hard on yourself. You're doing everything you can to help your brother. I can only imagine how terrifying this must be after everything you've both gone through, but what you're doing now will save his life. Think of how happy you'll both be when you make him immortal and take away all the fear and uncertainty this illness has brought on both of you."

Aleida nodded and wiped at her wet lashes with a finger. She went back to her food, not speaking the question that still loomed in her mind. She didn't dare give voice to such an awful idea, but it haunted her long into the night, even after she closed her eyes to sleep.

She was racing against a merciless disease that was slowly ravaging her brother's body and would eventually claim his life if she didn't stop it. She was doing everything she could, pushing herself to the very brink of her limits, but that same question kept dragging her down as if she were a stone cast into the sea.

What if it wasn't enough?

AMAR

THE TOUCH OF SOMETHING WET WOKE AMAR. HE TURNED HIS HEAD and inhaled the hot, rancid breath of whatever had woken him. A dog, he saw as he cracked one eye open. The beast was muddy and matted, skin sucked tight against a bony frame. He'd probably already picked up a few fleas just from being so close to it.

It went in for another lick at his face. Amar pulled back. "Stop that."

The dog barked, and the noise reverberated painfully in his ears. He pushed himself up and put his hands to his head, which seemed to pound with increasing strength the longer he was awake. Had anyone in the entire history of humanity ever been *this* hungover before?

He forced his eyes open a little farther to examine his surroundings. The dog sat panting a few paces off. They appeared to be in an alley. The shadows cast by the tall buildings on either side shielded Amar's sensitive eyes from the full strength of daylight, but he could see a bright blue sky and sunlit streets ahead. The conversations of the people who walked past filled the air with grating noise that made him long for silence.

He was still in Valmandi, at least as far as he could tell, but he knew no more than that. The previous night was a blur. He'd gone to a tavern to drink, and then he'd gotten into a fight with the barman, who threw him out. There had been some vomiting and some yelling, and he'd wandered off in search of more drink, but even those parts were fuzzy. Anything that might have happened afterward was a blank space in his memory, but he had plenty of those already. What was one more?

The part about the vomiting and the yelling seemed important though. What was it he'd been yelling about?

The crestfallen look on Mitul's face floated into his mind. *You're a sad, lonely man desperate for a friend who doesn't even want you.*

Ah, that was it. A wave of guilt started to rise with the memory of those harsh words, but he quickly shoved it down. All he'd wanted last night was to be left alone. Mitul should have known that. If he didn't like the response he got when he came looking for Amar, that was his own fault.

More details were coming back to him now. After his conversation with Mitul, he'd gone in search of not only more drink, but supplies for a journey to Atrea—a journey he had intended to make all on his own. A colossally stupid idea, he realized with the effects of the sohra wearing off. Atrea was still so far away, and getting there would mean going all the way around the Sular Desert, or crossing right through it in the height of summer.

Going through was the faster option, and a far more appealing one given his growing impatience for answers. But he couldn't do that on his own, and hiring a guide meant entrusting his safety to a complete stranger. There were about a hundred different ways that could go wrong. Saya was obnoxious at times, but at least they had a history. He couldn't remember it, but it was a starting point, and she'd proven trustworthy enough. Better to cross the desert under her guidance as they'd already planned than to put his life in the hands of anyone else.

Unfortunately, that meant he'd have to go crawling back to others in this sorry state. Whatever scraps of dignity he had left fell away in apprehension of their disapproval.

But why should he care what they thought? He *didn't*. Did he?

Amar sighed. The sooner he got it over with, the better. He pushed himself up, trying to ignore the throbbing pain in his skull. He patted the dog's head on his way past, then braced one hand against a wall for support as he made his way to the adjoining street. With his other hand, he shielded his eyes against the bright, mid-morning light.

It took him a few minutes of wandering to figure out where he was. He made his way to the palace grounds and then to the temple with the mural of Princess Priyani. From there, he was able to find his way back to the Saffron Fox.

The others were waiting outside the inn when he arrived. Mitul had his saraj out and sat near the step playing the instrument. His fingers seemed to dance across the strings as he sang in a gentle, melodic voice. It stirred something in Amar that almost made him wish he'd stuck around at the inn last night, if not to play with Mitul, then at least to listen.

Saya was the first to spot him as he approached. She said something to the others, and they followed her gaze to him. Kesari stuck her hands in her pockets and gave him a nervous smile, but Saya's face was fixed in a scowl. Mitul ended his song, and a few nearby listeners tossed coins into the center of the olive-green sash at his feet. He thanked each of them, barely glancing at Amar.

"I was starting to wonder if you'd ever show up," Saya said when he reached them.

"What happened?" asked a low voice from the lantern clipped to Kesari's coat. "You look absolutely horrific."

"Shhh," Kesari hissed, looking mortified.

Saya glanced down at Lucian. "You should be glad you don't have a nose. He smells absolutely horrific, too."

"I'm back now," Amar said flatly. "Let's go."

"Oh, *let's go*, he says. As though it were that simple."

Mitul put a hand on her shoulder. "Just drop it."

She shrugged away from his touch. "No. He needs to understand. What about the supplies we needed? What about our plan to leave first thing in the morning so we could reduce the risk of running into that murderous Visan woman?" She put her hands on her hips and glowered at Amar. "You didn't think about any of that, did you? You think it's fine to go wandering off, doing whatever you want. But now—now that *you're* ready to go—*now* we can leave?"

Behind Saya, Kesari nervously shifted her feet, her hands still stiff in her coat pockets. Amar dug his nails into his palms to stop himself from unleashing the anger that seemed to have become his default response to almost everything. That anger would get him nowhere. Nothing Saya had said was false, and her frustration with him was perfectly justifiable. He'd been stupid and selfish and far more immature than a man his age should be.

"I'm sorry," he said.

The animosity in Saya's eyes melted away, but it was quickly replaced by suspicion. She let out a long sigh. "You know we're only trying to help you, right? That's all any of us have been trying to do this entire time. Especially him." She pointed to Mitul. "And you've treated him the worst. He puts up with it because he cares about you, but I can't stand it anymore. You can't keep behaving this way."

Amar nodded solemnly. She was right. He'd been prickly and standoffish at best ever since they'd left Tamaya's house. Beyond that, he'd been downright hostile at times. His anger about his situation had made him mean, and he'd taken that anger out on them, hating them for knowing more than he did about himself. Skies above, a part of him he *still* hated them for it.

But that wasn't their fault. And despite everything he'd thrown at them, they stayed. They were still trying to help him, and they certainly didn't deserve the hostility he'd shown them.

"I'm sorry," he said again, looking at each of them in turn. "I've acted poorly, and none of you deserve that. I'll do better."

Saya nodded. "Thank you."

"Thanks," Kesari echoed, her eyes darting up from the ground to meet his.

Mitul started to reach forward like he was going to put a hand on Amar's shoulder, then seemed to think better of it and lowered his arm. "I appreciate the apology. If you ever want to talk, I hope you'll let me know."

Amar almost dismissed the idea out of hand but stopped himself from speaking. Instead, he nodded. Perhaps eventually, it would be nice to talk to Mitul about who he'd been before all this.

"We should get going," Saya said.

"What about the supplies we needed?" Amar asked

"Do you really think we wasted the entire morning sitting around here waiting for you?" she replied.

"We bought enough supplies to take us to Sharmok," Mitul explained. "That will be our last stop before the desert. We'll need to restock once we're there."

Saya gave Amar a penetrating look. "It would be nice if you could avoid throwing all your money away on drink next time."

A familiar surge of anger rose within him, but it ebbed away just as quickly. Between waking up in a dirty alley and the splitting headache still throbbing in his skull, he didn't want to touch another mug of sohra for a very long while.

ALEIDA

ALEIDA WALKED THE LAST STRETCH OF ROAD TO VALMANDI UNDER a brilliant sunset sky that quickly melted into gray twilight. By the time she reached the city gates, the torches had been lit, and the guards barred her entrance with unfriendly scowls.

"And where do you think you're going?" one asked, sidestepping to place herself in Aleida's path.

"I need to get into the city," she replied. "I'm looking for someone."

"Do you have your travel papers?"

"What?"

The guard gave a longsuffering sigh. "If you don't have travel papers, you don't have permission to enter the city."

Aleida frowned. The man who'd gone through the gates ahead of her hadn't had to present any travel papers. "I'm not sure I know what you mean."

"No refugees allowed in the city after sunset. Come back tomorrow."

Now she understood. A familiar heat burned through her. She wanted to scream at the injustice, but she fought the urge, not wanting to give the guards any more reason to dislike her or reinforce their preconceived notions about her.

No shame. Not for them, not for anyone.

She raised her chin and took a breath. "I'm a traveler, not a refugee. I promise I won't make any trouble, but it's really important—"

"Didn't you hear me?" The guard took another step into Aleida's personal space. She spoke slowly and deliberately, as if Aleida were too stupid to understand. "I said no Visans allowed in the city after sunset without travel papers. No exceptions."

That *wasn't* what she'd said, exactly, but to most Kavorans, being Visan was the same thing as being a refugee, and they didn't have much tolerance for either. Aleida clenched her jaw. There wouldn't even *be* any Visan refugees if the Kavoran empress hadn't decided to invade and claim their lands seven years ago. But pointing this out to the guard wasn't likely to make much difference.

"Please," she protested again. "If you'll just—"

The guard shoved her shoulders hard enough to make her stumble backwards. "I'm not going to explain myself again. Get out of here. Or perhaps you'd rather be arrested?"

Altma crackled in Aleida's fingertips, but the needle-point press of Valkyra's claws at her collarbone gave her pause. "It's not worth it," the Spirit Tarja hissed in her ear. "Let's go."

Aleida let her altma slide back into dormancy and forced herself to turn around. A few Kavoran travelers snickered and whispered amongst themselves as she walked back down the road the way she'd come. She pressed her lips into a thin line and did her best to ignore them.

The refugee camp she'd passed earlier was already in sight, and with no better ideas in mind, that was where she headed. "What a ridiculous rule," she muttered to Valkyra, still seething. "No other Kavoran cities have a curfew for Visans."

In fact, most refugee camps had dissolved entirely in the years since the invasion as more Visans migrated into the cities to find jobs and housing. Not so in Valmandi, where they were intentionally kept outside the walls and the refugee camp seemed full to bursting.

She cast a dark glance back at the gate and the guards. "What's the point of shutting us out when most of the people living in that camp work inside the city anyway?"

"The rulers of this province are stubborn," Valkyra replied, a hint of derision in her voice. "They always have been, constantly straining against the imperial court in an effort to maintain their own power. They didn't agree with the invasion of Vis and refused to contribute troops to that effort, so in their minds, the Visan refugees aren't their problem to deal with."

"Not their problem?" Aleida scoffed. "There's a huge camp right on their doorstep."

"And there it will remain, at least until the laws change and Visans are allowed to move inside or build permanent residences here on the outskirts. There are good jobs in the city, and plenty of merchants and nobles willing to hire Visan laborers. But I fear King Bhajan is too proud to ever admit his own foolishness."

Aleida rolled her eyes. This was just another setback she couldn't waste time on. She had to find a way into the city, and quickly.

She followed the crooked fence line around the border of the refugee camp until she found an entrance. The two men standing guard there let her pass with friendly nods. Their worn blades and ill-fitting attire seemed especially pitiful compared to the new guns and fresh uniforms of the Valmandi city guards. They might be able to protect the camp against an animal attack or a single, careless thief, but beyond that, their effectiveness was limited.

Cookfires were already blazing to life inside the camp, and Aleida stopped in the light of the nearest one to rummage through her pack. She pulled out her leather case and flipped through the pages inside until she found the drawings she was looking for. In addition to her portrait of Amar, she also had less detailed sketches of his companions, which emphasized their attire and most noticeable features. She put the rest of the pages back, slid the case inside her pack, and pressed on with the drawings clutched in one hand. "Let's see if anyone here has seen our friends."

"That's a good idea," Valkyra replied.

She started with the nearest tents, approaching anyone she saw and showing them the sketches with the same question on her lips. "Have you seen these people?" Some looked mildly annoyed at her interruption of their tasks, but they all took the time to study the drawings and consider her question. Most knew what it was like to search for someone who was lost, even if their motives differed from hers in this particular case. But one after another, they all denied having seen Amar or his companions.

She continued through the camp, weaving her way between tents and shacks as an odd mixture of emotions churned within her. It had been a long time since she'd been among so many of her own people, and having them all around her now was familiar and soothing. Snippets of conversation in her native language and the scent of foods she'd grown up eating put her at ease in a way she hadn't realized she'd longed for. But these were not the proud, stone structures of Libera, and the grief and adversity etched into the faces of the people who lived here served as a harsh reminder of all they'd lost. There would be no going back to the days of their former glory. Not anytime soon. Probably not ever.

Eventually, she found a woman who recognized the people in her drawings. She and her son had had an encounter with them the day before, and she was even able to tell Aleida where they'd been headed—to an inn called the Saffron Fox. A few more inquiries about travel papers and ways to get inside the city after dark earned her a crude diagram showing hidden entry points sometimes used by smugglers.

Aleida thanked the woman and wove her way back through tents and around campfires, reviewing what she'd learned with Valkyra along the way. "I think our best option will be the breach in the wall, assuming it's still there. It's closest to the Saffron Fox and it will be the easiest to get to."

"Sneaking into the city like that is going to be dangerous."

Aleida bristled at the warning in her voice. "You don't approve?"

"I'm not sure rushing into this is such a good idea."

They exited the camp the same way they had come in, and she shot the Spirit Tarja a sidelong glance. She didn't have a mother anymore, but sometimes Valkyra acted enough like one to infuriate her. "What else are we supposed to do?"

"We don't even know if they're still here. They were yesterday, but they could have left already. It might be better to keep moving."

"And what if they haven't left yet? This could be the perfect opportunity to capture Amar. We can't walk away from that—not without knowing for sure."

"If you get caught, it's going to set us back even further. Is that a risk you're willing to take?"

It was a fair point, and one worth considering carefully, especially since she didn't want to waste any more time. None of her options were ideal, but at least if she followed up on this lead as soon as possible, she'd have the facts she needed to make a more informed decision. Maybe, if luck was on her side, she'd even walk away with the prize she was after.

"No risk, no reward," she said. "I'm going."

Valkyra didn't respond right away, and in her peripherals, Aleida could see the tense frustration in her draconic eyes. When she did speak, it was in a low voice heavy with objection. "Then I suppose I have no choice but to follow and try to keep you out of trouble."

They couldn't find the breach in the wall marked on their diagram, not until Valkyra pointed out a patch of discolored stone that was less overgrown with moss and vines. The opening must have been patched up, but thankfully, the next location they tried was still an option. On the eastern side of the wall, a series of narrow climbing footholds had been carved into the rock. Aleida could barely make them out in the pale moonlight, faint shadows darkening the recessed hollows.

Valkyra flew down from the top of the wall to rest on Aleida's shoulder. "I still don't like this."

"Is there a path all the way to the top, or not?"

"There is, but it's not a very good one. You could fall to your death in about a dozen different places if you don't do this exactly right. I really think we should wait until morning."

Aleida ignored her and stepped up to the wall, placing her hand in the first hold. Her fingers curled around the narrow ledge, which barely reached her second knuckles. The toes of her opposite foot fit into a space about knee-high.

This wouldn't be so bad. It was almost like scaling the cliffs back home in Libera. She and Tyrus used to jump into the foaming ocean waves below, whooping from the thrill of it all the way down.

Except now, there was no water below to break her fall.

She channeled altma into her hands and feet to improve the strength of her grip. Then she began to ascend.

Even with the assistance of her magic, the climb was more difficult than she'd expected. These were not the rough, craggy walls of a seaside cliff. This stone was smooth and straight, and the handholds chipped into its surface became narrower and farther apart the higher she climbed. Soon, she could barely see them in the dark. Valkyra hovered around her, pointing out where the next ledge was and directing her on how to position her feet. Whatever misgivings the Spirit Tarja still had about this plan, she mercifully kept them to herself.

Sweat beaded on Aleida's forehead, and her hands began to feel clammy. She was about to risk wiping them on her shirt when the narrow ledge under her right foot gave way. She held back a cry as she shifted her weight and scrabbled for new purchase against the stone.

Valkyra put her own back underneath Aleida's dangling foot. Her wings beat in mighty gusts as she guided the foot to a new recess, this one much higher than the first. Aleida strained to reach it and at last managed to hoist herself up, gasping. Her muscles burned, but she tried to ignore the ache and kept climbing, focusing all her attention on the wall and on putting one limb in front of the other.

There was only her and the stone. Tyrus was depending on her. She could do this. For him, she could do anything.

After several more minutes, Aleida's fingers found a ledge that was wider than all the others. She looked up and saw only the night sky yawning wide and unobstructed above her. She'd reached the top of the wall at last. She pushed herself up the last stretch and hoisted her body over the parapet, then dropped down onto the wooden walkway below.

All she wanted was to lay here a moment and rest, but that wasn't an option. There was a fire a fair distance off, which highlighted the silhouette of a passing guard. She forced her shaking limbs to move and pressed her back against the parapet. Where to next? It didn't matter as long as she could get off the wall and away from here before a patrol spotted her.

"Over here," Valkyra whispered, and Aleida turned to find her standing at the edge of the walkway several paces behind her. "There's a building below. You should be able to drop to the roof."

Aleida darted to Valkyra's position and looked down. Most of the building was sheltered under the walkway, but there was a small wooden overhang she should be able to reach. Carefully, she dropped to her stomach and scooted feet first over the edge of the walkway. She lowered herself down until she was hanging by her fingers, which still ached from the climb.

"That's good, dear," Valkyra said. "Let go."

Aleida let her fingers slide off the walkway. The drop lasted a split second longer than she'd expected. She landed with an unceremonious grunt, then stumbled and rolled off the edge of the overhang to thud against the ground below. The air left her lungs in a sudden *whoosh*.

She lay there, gasping and dazed, until Valkyra landed on her chest and peered down into her eyes. "Are you hurt?"

Aleida wheezed out a breathless laugh and shook her head.

"Then let's go before someone comes to investigate all the noise you made."

She got up and raised the hood of her cloak to hide her fair skin and mousy hair. Above, the sounds of hurried footsteps were already drawing closer as guards approached. Valkyra nestled into the folds of Aleida's cloak at her shoulder, and together, they slipped into the shadows of the city, leaving the wall behind them.

It wasn't yet midnight, and there was still some activity in the streets. Aleida kept her head down and avoided looking anyone in the eye. A few of the buildings nearby still had lanterns lit outside their doors, and she stopped underneath one to examine her diagram.

The woman from the camp had marked where the Saffron Fox should be in reference to the palace grounds and Princess Priyani's temple. Aleida compared it to where she'd climbed over the wall and set off in what must be the right direction. When no one was around, she tore the paper to shreds and used sparks of altma to burn the pieces, letting the ashes drift behind her.

She walked for what felt like a long time, keeping a watchful eye out for patrolling city guards and avoiding their paths as much as possible. She was beginning to wonder if she was going the right way when she spotted a flash of color in the glow of three braziers that stood near a large Kavoran temple.

The fire illuminated a magnificent painting on one of the walls, and Aleida sucked in an awed gasp as she drew nearer. This was the work of Kamaal Ruman, one of the greatest artists in all of Erythyr. Once, when Aleida was very young, he'd traveled to Libera to do some studies of their architecture and the seaside cliffs that characterized that region. He had even gifted some of his work to the city in gratitude for their hospitality, and one painting had hung in the cathedral where Aleida and her family attended worship services.

She used to beg her parents to take her to see it. She would stare at it for as long as they would allow, studying every brushstroke and every pigment, wondering if her own skills would ever come close to matching his. She still wondered that sometimes, when she wasn't worrying about more important things—which was all the time, these days. Right now, she would have loved nothing more than to have the luxury of admiring the mural for hours, studying every subtle line and hue, learning as much as she could from the work of this master.

But those were the wishes of the carefree girl she'd been before. She had no time for such indulgences now.

She redirected her eyes to the streets ahead and continued on her way.

There were several larger buildings in this part of the city, and many had signs hanging over the doors or in the windows. Some had pictures to indicate what sort of establishment they might be, but Aleida couldn't read the others. "Do you see the place we're looking for?" she said to Valkyra.

"Not yet, but I think we must be in the right area. There are a lot of inns and taverns here."

They kept going, eventually coming to a wide street with several buildings still lit from the inside. The tallest had wooden sign over the door which depicted a fox, its tail carved in bold Kavoran lettering. The sounds of music and laughter drifted from the door, which was cracked open to let in the cool night air.

"This is it," Aleida said.

"What now?" Valkyra asked. "You won't be able to sneak in there without being seen."

She was right. There was far too much activity inside, and it didn't look like things were going to die down anytime soon. "You could fly in through one of the windows," she suggested. "Have a quick look around, see if they're still here."

"A dragon flying around loose in an inn? That's bound to draw unwanted attention."

"So don't let anyone see you."

"You make it sound so simple," Valkyra murmured, but she bounded into the air anyway and flew to an open window on the second floor. She perched on the sill for a moment, peering inside, then disappeared into the building.

Aleida waited. Inside the inn, a new song started up, and when that one ended, another. Valkyra did not return. Aleida nudged a rock back and forth between her shoes with mounting impatience. Judging by the size of the building there must have been dozens of rooms, and searching them all was going to take some time. Most likely, Valkyra wouldn't even be able to check all of them properly. Some would be closed off, and some areas would be too crowded for her to sneak past unseen.

This wait was unbearable. A more direct approach would speed things along. Aleida didn't have any travel papers, but no one else knew that. The fact that such a thing existed at all meant it wasn't completely out of the question for a Visan to be in the city at this hour. She might draw a little attention to herself, but what did that matter? She'd be gone soon enough, and she hadn't seen any guards around for a while.

She squared her shoulders and headed for the door. There was a lively crowd inside, but no one even so much as glanced in her direction when she entered. They were all too busy listening to the singer atop a low stage in the corner of the room, or calling for more food and drink as servers rushed by balancing wide platters over their heads.

"Can I help you?" said a voice to her right. A broad-shouldered man sat behind the counter, the quill in his hand poised over the slim book he'd been writing in. He peered at her from below a pair of thick eyebrows, and when she lowered the hood of her cloak, his eyes widened a little.

"I'm looking for someone. I was told he's staying here." She pulled out the sketches in her pocket. The pages were wrinkled and beginning to tear at the edges, but the drawings were clear. She held one out to show the man. "His name's Amar. He was here yesterday, and he might be still. Do you recognize him?"

"I don't make it a habit to say who my customers are," the innkeeper said, not looking at the drawing. "People like their privacy."

"Of course," Aleida replied. "But he's a friend of mine, and it's very important that I find him. I have some time-sensitive information he needs to hear."

The innkeeper narrowed his eyes. Aleida tried to maintain an expression of innocence. After a few seconds, he sighed, looked down at the drawing, and nodded. "I remember him. He was here with a few others the night before last, but they left this morning. A shame, too. The saraj player was quite talented. He drew in a lot of customers."

She was too late. Again. "Do you have any idea where they might have gone?"

"They were talking about getting supplies for a journey through the desert. Sounds like a bad idea this time of year, but one of them was a Sularan, so I suppose they'll manage."

Aleida returned the drawings to her pocket. "All right. Well, thank you. You've been very helpful."

She turned quickly, colliding with the solid, uniformed torso of a city guard. Throwing her hood up over her ears, she tried to slink past him with a mumbled apology, but he gripped her shoulder and barred her path to the door.

"Is this one giving you any trouble?" asked the guard.

"Not at all," the innkeeper replied. "Aren't you off-duty? Come sit down and have a drink."

Aleida cast a look of gratitude to the man over her shoulder, but the guard didn't release his grip. He pulled down the hood of her cloak and nodded. "Visan. I thought so. You're not where you're supposed to be, are you?"

Aleida's heart thundered inside her chest. "I—I was only—" Her mind stumbled over excuses, but she couldn't get anything coherent out.

"There's no need for all this," the innkeeper said. "She wasn't causing any trouble, really."

The guard ignored him. "Where are your travel papers? Or are you foolish enough to think you can walk around this city without them?"

Aleida's eyes darted around the room. There was no help to be found among the inn's patrons. They were still listening to the music, oblivious to what was going on behind them. But the door was *right there*. So close. If she could get through it, she was sure she could outrun the guard.

She channeled her altma at the same time she tried to duck out from beneath his grasp. When that didn't work, she put a hand around his wrist and sent heat and electricity into the exposed skin between his glove and his shirt sleeve. He let out a roar of pain and released his hold on her.

Aleida ran—or started to. She'd only taken a single step when she tripped over the guard's outstretched leg. She didn't have time to catch herself and landed hard, scraping her chin against the rough wood floor.

Before she could scramble to her feet, the bulky weight of the guard's body was pressed against her back. He pushed her head down with one hand and used his other to shove something soft and wet against her mouth and nostrils. Aleida could barely breathe through it, and she thrashed frantically in an effort to break free. She clawed at his arms, his legs—anything within reach. It was no use.

After a few seconds, he let go of her face. She sucked in a gasp and blew air out her nose, shooting chunks of something orange and slimy onto the floor. Then she reached for her altma again, ready to tear the entire building apart so she could escape.

But there was no altma to reach for. Or, if there was, she couldn't sense it. She tried again to no avail. It was as if all the altma had simply been ripped from her and the world around her.

The guard wrenched her arms behind her back and hauled her to her feet. "You're under arrest for trespassing and assaulting a city guard."

"What did you do to me?" she asked, trying over and over again to channel her altma. "Why can't I—what did you *do*?"

The guard chuckled. "Your first experience with daravak, I take it? Well, now you know how surprised I was when you tried to use your magic on me. I've never heard of one of you heathens being blessed by altma, but I suppose there's a first time for everything. Now move."

He shoved her forward, and without her magic, Aleida was powerless to do anything but go where he directed.

PART II

THE GIRL WHO FEARED THE FIRE

KESARI

AT MITUL'S SUGGESTION, KESARI AND THE OTHERS BOOKED PASSAGE on a merchant ferry that could carry them downriver most of the way to Sharmok. Mitul charmed the ferry master into letting them pay their way with their own labor, which allowed them to save the money they'd need to buy supplies later. Kesari and Amar spent their days on board cooking and cleaning for the crew while Saya and Mitul helped sort through inventory in the cargo hold.

True to his word, Amar seemed to be making more of an effort to treat them all with less hostility. Sometimes he was even kind. He and Lucian got along especially well, and when no one else was around to see or hear the Spirit Tarja, the ferry's galley filled with the sounds of their banter. Kesari kept out of these conversations, but her heart warmed at seeing Lucian make a connection with someone who wasn't her. The two of them had always gotten along well enough, but there was a certain burden of responsibility between them that Lucian didn't have to carry with Amar.

She was happy for him. He deserved to have those positive connections with others, and so much more. More than she could give him. She pondered that as she lay awake on their third night aboard the ferry. With every passing minute, they drifted closer and closer to Atrea, to home. They still had a long ways to travel, but the fact that she was going at all still filled her with a strange mixture of surprise and apprehension.

She rolled onto her side and shifted her arm beneath her head, staring at Lucian's flames as they flickered against the glass of his lantern. They might be headed to Atrea, but that didn't mean she had to go all the way home. Malfram was nowhere near Deveaural where she'd grown up. She didn't have to go back there and face what she'd left behind.

Memories flickered in the back of her mind like tiny sparks, and the silence was suddenly unbearable. "Lucian," she whispered.

"Yes?"

"Tell me a story."

"It's late, Kes. You should sleep."

"I can't."

"You're not even trying. And aren't you getting a little too old for bedtime stories?"

"Mum says you can never be too old for stories."

Lucian's mouth curled up in a smile. "A very wise woman, your mother."

Kesari tried to smile back but found she had to fight back tears instead. Most days, she could deal with the pain of missing her family. All she had to do was shut out the images of Mum and Dad, Navya and Rajiv, and remind herself that they were better off without her. But sometimes, missing them would hit her out of nowhere, a sudden yearning that pushed against her lungs until she could barely breathe.

She should be with them now. She should be asleep in her own bed, not here on a Kavoran ferry lying awake in the dark. If only she had made different choices. If only her childish heart hadn't longed for magic. Maybe then she wouldn't have Bonded with Lucian, and they both could have been spared their current burdens.

"Tell me what's really keeping you awake," the Spirit Tarja said gently.

Kesari swallowed the knot in her throat. "Do you ever wish you'd made a Bond with someone else?"

"Never," he replied without hesitation.

"I'm serious. Someone stronger, maybe. Or braver."

"Kes, you're one of the strongest, bravest people I know."

"I'm not." The certain truth of the words brought back the knot in her throat, and her voice became shaky. "I'm terrified, all the time. Amar, Saya, Mitul—they're all so brave. I have all this altma inside me waiting to be used, but I can't bring myself to use it. I'm not even brave enough to keep our Bond."

"There are other kinds of strength and courage."

She gripped the cuffs of Rajiv's coat a little tighter. "You don't have to say that to make me feel better. I know this isn't what you wanted when we made our Bond. Just tell me the truth."

His dark eyes locked with hers. "The truth about what?"

Kesari took a breath. She hadn't ever dared ask him this before. Already, she feared the answer, but if she didn't pose the question now, maybe she never would. "Do you resent me for rushing into making this Bond and then wanting to break it?"

He made himself a little bigger and pressed against the glass so she could see his face more clearly. "All I wanted was a chance to live a little longer," he said. "You gave me that. How could I resent you?"

"Because this isn't what we agreed to. A Bond is supposed to be permanent."

The dark voids of Lucian's eyes flickered a little. "It wasn't fair for me to ask you to form a Bond when you were so young. I never should have put you in that position."

Kesari frowned. "It was my choice."

"You were a child, and I knew better. Besides, if it was your choice then, it should still be your choice now. It's your life, after all."

"And yours."

"No. I'm only here because I'm leeching off the borrowed time you gave me." He shrunk a little, and his voice grew softer. "I still worry about what will happen to you if you go through with this, but if it's what you really want, then that's what we'll do."

Kesari nodded and dabbed at her eyes with her coat sleeve. "But what will happen to you?"

"I'm not sure. I suspect I'll fade away, like any other Spirit Tarja without a Bond."

"You mean you'll die."

He grinned, flames twisting into jagged teeth below his eyes. "I'm already dead, you know."

"Yes, but…you'll be gone." A hollowness opened up inside her chest. Until now, she hadn't given much thought to what breaking their Bond might mean for Lucian. There hadn't been any point in speculating on it until they knew it was possible. But if it was, and if she really went through with it, she might be killing Lucian in the process. His altma still tethered his soul to the physical world, but without a physical body to attach itself to—without that Bond to *Kesari's* body—he probably would fade away into a true and permanent death.

"Don't worry about what happens to me," Lucian said. "I had my shot at living, and I've cheated death long enough already. I'll be all right."

Kesari nodded and closed her eyes, but that hollow ache followed her into a restless sleep filled with nightmares of smoke and falling ash.

The ferry master dropped them off at a bend in the river not far from Sharmok. The fast-moving water had carried them far in three days' time, well outside the deciduous forests that characterized much of Kavora and into the flatter, drier terrain of the country's southern border.

The summer air was hot and dry, and as they walked, Kesari's skin grew damp with sweat. She kept her coat on anyway. She could handle a little warmth. Beneath the coat, her tunic sleeves barely reached her elbows, and she was less certain of her ability to handle the stares and questions her companions might have upon seeing the self-inflicted scars that covered her forearms. She could change into something more comfortable once they found lodgings in Sharmok.

The town itself was smaller than both Valmandi and Tarsi, but as the only major Kavoran settlement this close to the desert, it served as a hub of trade and travel. Several Sularans mingled with the Kavoran locals, and Saya held out her hand to them in silent greeting as they passed, palm low at her side and facing forward. The other Sularans returned the gesture, often with a brief nod. Like her, a few of the

younger ones bore the same painted haseph markings on their faces—
two lines under one eye, an unfinished circle around the other, and a
third line from the lower lip to the chin.

Kesari and the others followed Saya's lead toward the center of
town. A Sularan woman with thick, graying braids caught her gaze and
turned a palm out to her. Saya nodded but didn't mirror the hand
gesture this time, and Kesari did a double take as they passed. The
haseph lines on the older woman's face weren't painted on, but were
instead carved out in raised scars that glistened a shade lighter than the
rest of her skin. Reflexively, she touched her own cheek. That had to
have been painful.

She waited until they were out of earshot to ask Saya about it. "That
woman back there—who cut those markings on her face?"

"Probably someone from her tribe, unless she had the courage to
do it herself."

The hairs along Kesari's forearms prickled, and she resisted the urge
to run her fingers along her own scars. "Why?"

Saya gave her a sidelong glance. "We're required to complete haseph
before we can be fully accepted into our tribe. The markings we paint
on our faces show that we've started that pilgrimage. When we return
home and if our offering is accepted, we wash those markings away
forever. But some don't complete their haseph, or they bring back an
unsuitable offering. They wear the mark of their failure forever and can
never fully be one with us."

"That seems..." Kesari struggled to find the right word, not wanting
to offend Saya.

"Harsh?" the warrior offered.

She shrugged. "A little."

"We're given plenty of opportunities for success. If the first offering
is insufficient, we can seek out another, and there's no specific
timeframe for when the haseph must be completed."

"Then why would anyone let themselves be marked like that?"

Saya shrugged. "The reasons are different for everyone, I suppose.
It's not easy, leaving home and being separated from everyone you
know. We live among strangers who often have little respect for our
customs and beliefs. For some, it becomes too difficult."

"Isn't in just as hard to never be fully accepted in your own tribe."

Saya considered this for a few seconds. "Maybe. I know a man who has those same scars. He resented our leaders for not accepting his offering, and he didn't take the opportunity continue his haseph out of pride. For some, I think it's easier to be an outcast at home than to be an outcast among strangers."

"I'm not sure I understand."

"Neither do I. As much as I miss home, I don't think I could ever face my people if I knew they'd never fully accept me."

That was a sentiment Kesari could understand all too well.

A few minutes later, they came upon a public well near the center of town and stopped to rest a while. Each of them took turns drawing up cold, clear water from its depths to refill their canteens, and Kesari splashed some of it over her face and neck to cool her skin. When they were finished, they gathered in the shade of a nearby building to eat and discuss what supplies they needed.

"How much money do we have between us?" Saya asked, pulling out a pouch of coins from the red sash around her waist. Kesari dug around in her pack for her own stash. It was far lighter than she'd hoped, but it seemed the others didn't have much to offer, either. Amar held out only three jitaara on an open palm.

Saya frowned as her eyes darted to each person's hand. "We're going to need more than that. We can hunt some of our food in the desert and I can forage around the area here before we leave, though it will slow us down. And it won't sustain us for the entire journey. You'll all need different clothes to protect yourselves from the heat, and I was hoping to get a donkey to carry our water and other supplies."

"I'm sure we can earn a little money here," Mitul said brightly. "Everyone loves good entertainment. While you look for food, Amar and I can play some music and hope a few coins are tossed our way."

"I don't play music," Amar muttered.

"Oh, come on," Lucian said from the lantern at Kesari's side. "How hard can it be? All you have to do is bang your hands on some drums."

"You do it then." Amar's voice was harsh, but a teasing glint lit his eyes. "Oh, that's right. You can't because you don't have any hands."

Lucian chuckled. "That's all right. I don't miss my hands nearly as much as I miss my sense of taste."

"*That's* what you miss most?"

"Among other things. The world is a delicious place, Amar. Don't take it for granted."

Amar shook his head and turned back to Mitul. "All right. I'll play with you. But don't expect me to be any good."

Mitul's face split in a wide grin. "Oh, you'll do fine. As soon as we get that kanjira in your hands, it will all come back to you."

"What about me?" Kesari asked.

"Well, there's always work for a Tarja," Saya said with a tentative smile. "Repairing whatever's broken, healing a few scrapes or broken bones, lending your strength to make difficult tasks a little easier. You could do a lot of good with your skills, and people would be willing to pay for it."

A cold chill ran across Kesari's skin. Saya was right, but there was no way she was going to do any of that. She couldn't risk it. "I can't."

"Are you sure?" Saya asked, her voice gentle and encouraging. "You could start with something small, see how it goes."

Kesari shook her head. "No, I'm sorry."

"Why not?" Amar asked.

Kesari's stomach dropped as she searched for some excuse. Before she could say anything, a warning hiss came from Lucian's lantern. "Leave it alone, Amar."

He shrugged. "I think we deserve some answers. You keep refusing to use your magic when it could help us most. What if we need it when we're crossing the desert? What if one of us gets hurt out there? Are you going to help, or are you just going to sit there and watch that person suffer?" His voice took on a hard edge. "Maybe even watch them die?"

"That's enough!" Lucian shouted, his flames growing to fill the entire lantern.

Amar clamped his mouth shut, but every muscle in Kesari's body tensed. She wanted to run, to be anywhere else but here, but she couldn't move. Amar was right. She was useless, and she wished so badly she wasn't that her fingers started to itch with the desire to channel altma. She could feel her connection to it, right there, so close...

A wave of memories slammed into her, and she recoiled in disgust, pushing her altma back into the darkest corner of her being where it wouldn't be able to escape.

She *couldn't* use her magic. Not now. Not ever again.

Maybe the others *did* deserve to know why, but she couldn't bring herself to tell them. How could she possibly explain? They'd be horrified if they knew what she'd done. She put her hands in her pockets and stared down at her feet.

After a few seconds, Amar broke the silence. "I didn't mean to push, but I don't understand why you would—" His voice was still strained. "Never mind. It's none of my business."

Mitul put a hand on his shoulder. "We should find somewhere to play before the day gets away from us."

He nodded, and the two of them left, Mitul scrambling to keep up with Amar's brisk steps.

Saya turned to Kesari and Lucian once they were alone. "I'm sorry about that. If I'd known how much it would upset you, I wouldn't have brought it up."

"Don't worry about it," Kesari said quickly.

Saya shook her head as she watched Amar and Mitul's retreating figures. "I know he's angry and confused, but he shouldn't be taking that out on you. Are you all right?"

Kesari started to nod, but something about the genuine concern in Saya's eyes gave her pause. It was like the older girl could see straight through her, and that brought down a piece of the wall she'd built up. "He's right," she said softly. "I should have tried to save him before. Maybe then he wouldn't have died and lost all his memories."

"Or maybe things would have turned out exactly the same." Saya took a step closer and put a hand on Kesari's shoulder. "None of this is your fault. You know that, don't you?"

After a brief hesitation, Kesari nodded, because in that moment, with Saya's confident reassurance, she *did* know.

"I don't understand why you can't use your magic," Saya said, "and I won't ask you to tell me unless you want to. But I can see that it troubles you, so if you do ever want to talk about it, I'm here to listen. We all have burdens. None of us should have to carry them alone."

A gentle brightness warmed Kesari's heart, chasing off some of the shadows that lingered there. "Thank you."

Saya shielded her eyes with a hand and looked up at the sun. "The day's getting old. I'm going to see if I can find any game outside the village. Lucian, it would be helpful if you could scout from above and let me know what you see, take some of the guesswork out of the hunt."

"Do you mind, Kes?" Lucian asked.

"No, that's fine," she replied. "What should I do while you're gone?"

"You could look at prices for the supplies we'll need from some of the local vendors," Saya suggested. "I'm not sure how much money Mitul and Amar will manage to earn in a town this size, but I suspect we'll have to be careful about how we spend it."

"Sure," Kesari said, eager to help however she could. "What do we need?"

Saya ran through a list of various supplies, and Kesari repeated them back to her to make sure she wasn't forgetting anything. "I think that's everything," Saya said. "We can meet you back here later this evening."

"I'll see you then. Good luck with the hunting."

Lucian exited his lantern to fly alongside Saya, and the two of them headed off, leaving Kesari to her task. Her assignment wouldn't directly get them the money or the food they needed, but it was still important. She could still be useful to the others even without her magic, and knowing that, she walked down the street with her head a little higher and her spirit a little lighter.

AMAR

A<small>MAR'S FISTS WERE CLENCHED AS HE WALKED AWAY FROM HIS</small> companions. Perhaps he'd been too harsh with Kesari, but why was *he* expected to participate in some musical exercise just to earn a little money while those same expectations didn't apply to her and her magic? What secret was she hiding that was so terrible she couldn't talk about it?

He kicked a rock down the street and watched it bump along a few paces, then kicked it again when he caught up to it. What was the point of making a Bond with a Spirit Tarja if she wasn't going to use the power that came with it? Especially given that she would have cut her own life short in making that Bond. Magic was useful. It could help them—help *her*. And yet, even the briefest mention of her using her gift brought terror to her eyes.

Maybe it *wasn't* any of his business, but she hadn't used her magic to save him, and he'd died. Maybe her efforts wouldn't have made a difference, but she hadn't even tried. He only wanted to understand why.

"Wait," Mitul called from behind him, and Amar stopped to let the man catch up. "You're in a big hurry for someone who doesn't seem to know where he's going."

Amar shrugged. "Just trying to find a good place to play."

"Did you see somewhere?" Mitul asked. "I noticed a wide street on the way in. Plenty of people, good visibility for those who might want to stop and watch. But if you had something else in mind, that's fine."

"No," Amar said. "Your place sounds perfect."

"Wonderful. It's this way."

They found the street Mitul had suggested and set up at the corner of an intersection with a lot of foot traffic. Amar dug through his pack until he found the wrapped bundle containing his kanjira. While Mitul set about tuning his saraj, Amar studied the small drum.

It was no larger than the span of his hand from palm to fingertips. A circular wooden frame was left open at one end while a drumhead of taut, scaly lizard skin stretched across the other. Amar tapped the surface, then turned the kanjira over in his hands. His fingers curled around it, thumb reaching through the open back to clasp the frame tight in his left hand. It seemed to fit there, a sensation that reminded him of drawing his sword for the first time in Valmandi. Familiar, like it belonged there.

Mitul turned to look at him. "There you go. You're remembering already. Now hold your fingers apart, like this." He held his own hand up to show Amar. "That's right. When you hit it, your fingers should bounce right off the surface. Go on, try."

With a swift, almost instinctual motion, Amar struck the surface of the drum with his right index finger. A low note reverberated in the air for the space of half a breath. He struck the drum again, this time allowing his fingers to move in a series of practiced movements he hadn't even known he could do. A smile pulled at his mouth. It sounded...not perfect, but not half bad, either.

"Keep going," Mitul said, beaming at him. He began to strum a few notes on his saraj.

Amar tried to hammer out a steady rhythm to match the melody Mitul played. For a minute, it sounded like it was starting to come together, like they were actually making music. Amar stared at his hands. Where had he even learned this?

The moment he started searching for that memory, the music faltered. He stopped to listen to Mitul's jaunty tune and tried to come back in, but he couldn't seem to pick out the right rhythm. It was all a mess.

Mitul played a few more notes to bring the song to an end and turned to Amar. "That was great!"

"It was terrible." He was half tempted to throw the drum to the ground and give up. This had been a bad idea anyway. He was no musician.

Mitul shrugged. "It fell apart at the end, but for a little while, we had it. Didn't you feel it? It was almost like bef—" He cut himself off and gave Amar a sheepish look. "Sorry. Look, don't overthink it. Don't worry about the mistakes or whoever's watching. Just play."

Amar sighed and stared down at the kanjira. It seemed to thrum against his palm, as if begging to be played. And for a little while, they *had* pulled something decent together. "All right," he said. "Let's do it again."

"Try this one." Mitul plucked a few notes on the strings of his saraj. His long fingers danced deftly over the frets along the instrument's neck. "It was your favorite when we played in Jakhat. Maybe it will come back to you."

Amar let Mitul play alone for a few seconds before coming in. He tried not to think too much about what he was doing, and once he stopped trying to analyze every single beat, the rapid rhythm of his fingers against the drumhead swept away the doubts still lingering in his mind.

The song Mitul had chosen was a lively one, and before long, a few people had gathered around to listen. Mitul walked back and forth in front of them, stopping every now and then to nod or smile at one of the onlookers. They smiled back, listening even more keenly once he had moved on. One stern-faced old woman let out a coy, girlish laugh when he paused in the middle of his song to wink at her.

Amar snorted. He hadn't known Mitul for long, but he got the sense that the man could charm his way into the good graces of anyone he met. He was certainly more charismatic than Amar would ever be.

There, now he'd lost his rhythm again. His fingers faltered for a few seconds, and Mitul glanced over his shoulder at him but kept playing. Amar tapped his foot, found the beat, and resumed his drumming. If the audience noticed the slip, they didn't show it.

By the time the song ended, the crowd of onlookers had doubled in size. They clapped enthusiastically, and Mitul took a few humble bows. "Oh, thank you. You're too kind." He gestured to Amar. "Let's hear some appreciation for my friend here. This is his first time performing in front of anyone, and he gets a little nervous. I think he's doing a fantastic job, though. Wouldn't you agree?"

The spectators clapped and whistled. Amar's cheeks grew hot, but he raised a hand to wave at them and gave what he hoped was a gracious smile.

"Now then," Mitul said, raising his voice so the entire street could hear him. "What shall our next song be? Any requests?"

The onlookers turned to each other, some whispering amongst themselves, but none seemed to want to be the first to speak up.

"Come on, don't be shy," Mitul said. "Anything you like."

A young woman finally called out a request. "Do you know the one about the little lost prince?"

Mitul's face took on a somber expression. "Ah, the Lament of Prince Savir. Yes, I do know it. A beautiful tune, tragic as it is. But, if that's what you want, it would be my honor to play it for you." He turned to Amar. "I think I'll do this one alone, if you don't mind."

Amar nodded and laid the drum in his lap as Mitul began to play. The low, sad melody sent a hush over the onlookers, and a few more people from the street drew near to listen. Then, in a voice as soft and as soothing as a warm blanket on a cold day, Mitul began to sing.

Bright as dawn, new hope is born,
An heir destined to unify.
He will grow in strength and wisdom.
An alliance will be fortified.

Where he leads, our nation will follow.
When he calls, we will obey.
Sleep now little prince, no darkness to haunt you.
We await your noble rule one day.

In the night a shadow slinks,
Darker than the blackest sky.
In the night, a woman whispers,
Gives her babe a kiss goodbye.

Where he has gone, none may follow.
When he will come home, none can say.
Sleep now little prince, no darkness to haunt you.
We await your noble return one day.

In the woods or by the sea,
A babe grows safe and far from harm.
Far from home and those who love him,
He will grow in strength and charm.

Where he has gone, none may follow.
When he will come home, none can say.
Sleep now little prince, no darkness to haunt you.
We await your noble return one day.

In a time not far away,
He will come to claim his throne.
A prince once lost but never forgotten,
We will receive him as our own.

Sleep now little prince, no darkness to haunt you.
One day we'll receive you as our own.

By the time the last notes of the song had faded away, the crowd around them had grown to a respectable size. They clapped as Mitul took a bow, and several people tossed coins into the sash he'd coiled on the ground in front of them. Amar shook himself, trying to pull away from the spell Mitul's voice seemed to have put him under.

"What's next?" Mitul asked the crowd. "Maybe something a little more lively?"

A few people called out different songs now. Mitul grinned and turned to Amar. "Looks like we've got our work cut out for us. You think you can keep up?"

Amar couldn't help smiling back at him. "I'll try."

They played until sunset, the crowd of onlookers ebbing away and rising again throughout the afternoon. By the time Mitul suggested they wrap things up, Amar's hand was starting to cramp from holding the kanjira, but a part of him wanted to keep playing through the night. There was something freeing about the music. For the first time he could remember, he'd actually been having fun. Pure, carefree, undisrupted enjoyment. He didn't want to let that go.

"We did pretty well for ourselves," Mitul said, gathering up their coins and dropping them into his pouch. "You were excellent. I never draw as many people on my own as I do when I'm playing with someone else, and it's been a very long time since you and I played together."

"Didn't we play together before?"

Mitul shook his head. "Not since before I saw you die the second time, which was about five years ago. I couldn't ever talk you into it. I held onto your kanjira hoping you'd change your mind, and I may have sneaked it into your pack when you were lying dead at Tamaya's house."

"I'm sorry it took so long," Amar said, though it felt strange to apologize for some previous version of himself he'd never known.

"No, it's all right. I'm just happy we were able to play together today. I've missed it." A hint of sadness tinged his voice. "Music was how we met, you know. You stopped to listen to me one day, and you came back to listen every day until I finally asked if you wanted to play with me. I had to teach you the kanjira." He laughed. "You weren't very good at first, but you were stubborn enough to keep trying."

Amar put the drum back in his pack. What was he supposed to say to that? He couldn't remember any of it, nor the sentiment that went with Mitul's words. That same, familiar anger boiled up from his gut, he clenched his jaw to hold it in.

"Forgive me for being nostalgic," Mitul said. "I thought sharing those memories might bring you comfort, but it seems I've only upset you."

Amar relaxed his shoulders. It wasn't fair to be mad at Mitul. None of this was his fault. "You keep telling me about all these things I used to do, and I *should* remember, but I don't."

"I can only imagine how frustrating that must be." He sighed. "I know I expect too much from you sometimes, and I'm sorry. You lost all your memories, but I lost something, too, and I haven't been handling that loss very well. I've been impatient to get my old friend back, but I need to appreciate you for who you are now."

Amar scuffed the toe of his boot against the ground. "And what if I can't ever be that old friend you miss?"

Mitul clapped a hand over his shoulder. "We'll get there. We always do, but it takes time."

Amar forced himself to raise one corner of his mouth in a small half-smile. If only he had the same conviction Mitul did.

ALEIDA

ALEIDA PRESSED HER FACE AGAINST THE COOL METAL BARS OF HER cell, peering down the dark halls of the guardhouse as far as she could manage. With no one in sight—not even the hulking dog that sometimes patrolled the area—she wrapped her hands around the bars and attempted to channel altma.

For the briefest moment, there was a flicker of something in the center of her chest, a familiar stirring that might allow her to reconnect with her magic. She snatched at it desperately, but nothing happened. Nothing ever happened. Not since that infernal guard had arrested her at the Saffron Fox.

Maybe one of Valkyra's bridging exercises would do the trick. Aleida hadn't needed to do one of those in a long time as her magic came so naturally now. But perhaps whatever the guard had done to her had disrupted the pathways between her mind, body, and spirit. Those three elements of the self had to be in harmony for a Tarja to effectively channel altma. She didn't *feel* like any of them were misaligned, but it certainly couldn't hurt to attempt the exercise. It wasn't like she had anything better to do.

She inhaled a deep breath through her nose and exhaled slowly out of her mouth. Closing her eyes, she focused her other senses on her surroundings. Water dripped against stone somewhere outside the cell.

The smell of sweat and human refuse seemed to cling to the very walls, and the metal bars were smooth and cold against her palms. The occasional disruption slipped into her thoughts to interrupt her focus—worries about the three days she'd lost sitting in this cell, questions about where Valkyra was, the ever-present fears about Tyrus' health. Once, she might have attempted to push these thoughts out or beat them into submission. Now, she gave them only the barest acknowledgement and let them drift in and out of her mind like gentle waves breaking against the shore.

She stayed like this for a while, honing her focus until she could feel a noticeable change within herself, a calm stillness that was ideal for channeling altma. Again, she reached for her magic.

Nothing happened.

"Damn it!" Aleida slammed her palms against the bars of the cell and shook them. But of course, they didn't budge. She snarled in frustration, pressed her back against the metal, and slumped down onto the floor.

They'd taken away her magic. Somehow, the guards in this place had a method for stripping a Tarja of their powers. It made sense. There were enough Tarja in Kavora that those who enforced the law would need some trick to subdue them, but Aleida hadn't ever given the idea much thought before. What was it that guard had used, back at the Saffron Fox? Daravak, he'd called it, but shouldn't it have left her system by now? The guards stationed here hadn't repeated the procedure. They could have put something in her water, but that hadn't tasted any different than usual, and she'd refused to eat anything else they'd brought her.

Her empty stomach clenched painfully at the reminder.

She wrapped her arms around herself, wincing a little as her arms pressed against bruised ribs. The guards had questioned her twice in the past few days, wanting to know what she'd been doing in the city after dark and how a Visan girl had come to be a Tarja. One of the guards, who happened to be a Tarja himself, had tested some of her belongings to see if any one of them was actually a Spirit Tarja Bonded to Aleida. A reasonable assumption; it was common for Spirit Tarja to take the form of inanimate objects since anything more complex required a considerable amount of power and skill to achieve.

When that didn't turn up any answers, they'd called her a half-breed and demanded to know which of her parents had been Visan—or in their words, the *filthy heathen*. Then they took bets on what nationality her other parent might have been. When she had refused to give them any information, they'd spit in her face and tried to beat the answers out of her with their fists. The captain of the guardhouse had come in and put a stop to that the second time, but not before Aleida had a swollen eye and bruised ribs to match the scrape on her chin from her scuffle at the inn.

Aside from the daravak, nothing they'd done should have interfered with her ability to channel altma. So what was wrong with her?

A cold pit opened up inside her stomach as her mind conjured up a question she hadn't allowed herself to consider until now. What if they'd stripped her of her magic permanently?

Before she could sink into panic, a soft whisper drew her attention. "Aleida."

She shifted around. Valkyra sat on the stone floor outside her cell, white fur gleaming in the moonlight. Aleida let out a shaky breath. "You found me."

"No thanks to your poor decisions," Valkyra replied. There was only a slight hint of disapproval in her voice. "Come. It's time we leave this place."

"How? My magic is gone. I can't get out."

The Spirit Tarja unfolded her wings, bowed down, and shook herself. With a metallic jangle, a ring of keys slipped off her back and over her neck onto the floor. "I expect these will help."

Aleida's eyes widened. "How did you get those?"

Valkyra gave her a sly smile. "I have my ways. Now hurry. We only have a small window of opportunity to make our escape."

Alcida reached through the bars and picked up the keys. There were more than a dozen of them. She held her breath as she tested them in the lock one at a time, flinching whenever they clanked together. If anyone was around to hear, they didn't seem to find the noise suspicious. No one came running, not even the dog.

At last, she found the right key. It turned with a quiet *click*, and the lock pulled free.

She swung the door open, and Valkyra fluttered up to rest in her usual place on Aleida's left shoulder. "I've already secured your belongings. They're outside with the horse."

"You got us a *horse*, too? You've been busy."

"I have."

"How did you manage—"

"Shh. Later. Right now, we need to focus on getting out of here. Through the door up ahead, on your right."

Aleida pushed the door open a crack and listened, but there was no sound from the other side. She exited into the cool night air and found herself standing on a wooden balcony. A flight of stairs led to the ground. There was still no sign of anyone.

"Where are all the guards?" she asked as she took the stairs two at a time.

"Their attention has been diverted elsewhere."

"Your doing again, I suppose?"

Valkyra ignored the question. "Keep going, dear. That way, toward the river."

Aleida headed for the water. They were outside the city wall, near a wide pathway marked by wagon tracks and hoof prints. Not a main entrance into the city, but still a route that must have been busy during the day. The sound of voices drifted from around a bend in the road.

"Hurry," Valkyra hissed. "That might be the guards on their way back."

Aleida broke into a jog, trying to keep her footfalls as light as possible. The voices drew nearer, along with the sound of heavy boots crunching against gravel. She crossed to the other side of the road and slid down the grassy bank to the river below, then pressed herself flat against the ground. Hopefully, the shadows would be enough to conceal her.

For a few brief moments, she dared to peer up over the rise of the bank to watch the road. Five city guards approached, speaking to each other in disgruntled voices. Aleida put her head down and listened, her heart pounding against her sternum.

"What a complete waste of time that was. The man's grown cowardly in his old age."

"That, or foolish."

"Probably both. He's a loon."

"Silence, all of you! Magistrate Ashaya was chosen for the imperial council by Empress Dashiva herself, and the Empress tolerates neither fools nor cowards."

"He's not on the imperial council anymore though, is he?"

"Right. How did he end up here if he was on such good terms with the Empress?"

"Wasn't he friends with that other advisor? The Tarja woman, the one who was executed for treason after all that mess with Atrea."

"I thought that was because of what happened in Vis."

"Are you talking about Nandini Kumar?"

Aleida stiffened at the mention of that name, and a chill spread through her veins.

"Yes, that's the one."

"Maybe Ashaya fell out of the Empress' favor when Kumar did."

"Enough of this. You're all a bunch of fools, and you have no business speculating on the dealings and intentions of the Empress. The Magistrate is an honorable man, and however he came to be assigned here, we should be grateful for his work. He's certainly more competent than his predecessor."

One of them made a joke Aleida didn't fully catch, and the sound of their laughter faded away as they continued down the road. She waited a few more seconds before sitting up. "Where's this horse?" she asked Valkyra, more eager than ever now to leave Valmandi far behind them.

Valkyra extended a foreleg to the left. "That way, not too far. We should be able to avoid being seen if we stick to the edge of the river."

Aleida slid down the bank the last few paces to the water's edge. She stood, brushed herself off, and started walking at a brisk pace. "Now are you going to tell me how you managed to get me out of there? And what took you so long, anyway?"

"I would have come sooner if I could have," Valkyra said. "It took me a whole day to find out where you'd gone, and then two more to organize your escape."

"And how did you do that?"

"I had a little help from an old friend."

Aleida's heart sank. "The Magistrate, by chance?"

"Yes."

"I didn't realize you knew anyone here." She didn't quite manage to keep the annoyance out of her voice.

"I know many people in many different places, as do you. Does that bother you?"

"You should have mentioned it."

"Ah, I see," Valkyra said gently. "You're upset by what those guards said."

"Why would I be upset?"

"Well, if Magistrate Ashaya was a friend of Nandini Kumar, perhaps now you're wondering if I was a friend of hers, too."

"Were you?" Aleida growled. There was so little she knew about Valkyra's life before she had died. She must have been a great Tarja, and it seemed likely that she'd been friends with other great Tarja in high places. People like Nandini Kumar, who had used her high position to orchestrate an invasion that had ended thousands of Visan lives.

"I knew her," Valkyra admitted quietly. "But we weren't friends."

Aleida clenched her jaw, unable to stop the sudden surge of emotion that swirled inside her like a hurricane. "You never told me."

"I didn't think it was anything worth telling."

It wasn't. It was nothing Aleida had needed to know and nothing that had any real impact on her relationship with Valkyra. So why did it feel so much like a betrayal?

"I'm sorry, dear," the Spirit Tarja said. "I didn't realize it would upset you."

"It doesn't matter." She had more pressing concerns right now anyway. "I'm not sure what they did to me back there, but I haven't been able to use my magic since I was arrested."

"Daravak," Valkyra replied. "It should wear off in a day or so."

"What is it?"

"It's a type of fungus, mostly harmless, but it does inhibit a Tarja's ability to channel altma. It's a common means of subduing dangerous prisoners. When it's fresh, inhaling it is enough to suppress a Tarja's power for an entire day."

Aleida frowned. "It's been more than a day since they used it on me."

"You slept while they had you locked up, didn't you? All they would have had to do was put a little of the stuff in front of your nose while you were dreaming to renew the effects."

"Oh." A weight seemed to lift at the realization that her powers would return. She'd only had them for two years, but in that time, they'd become an integral part of who she was. She wouldn't have been able to bear it if her magic was truly gone forever.

"There's the horse," Valkyra said.

A handsome bay was tethered to the slender trunk of a young tree. Aleida clicked her tongue softly to the animal as they approached, and he nickered in return. She patted his neck as she stepped around to examine the saddle. Her own small pack hung over one of the saddlebags, and the other was filled with enough food to last several days.

She untied the horse's reins and swung up onto his back. He carried her up the gentle slope of the riverbank and back to the main road, which was empty now. It was only then that she realized she didn't quite know which way they should go. Amar and his friends had doubtless moved on from Valmandi. They could have reached Sharmok by now. Maybe they'd already started into the desert.

"Where are we going?" Valkyra asked.

"I'm not sure. We could try to follow them through the desert, but you seemed to think that was a bad idea."

"Without a guide we can trust? It's a terrible idea, especially in the middle of summer. Even under the best conditions, there are a thousand ways to die in that place if you don't know what you're doing or where you're going."

Aleida bit her lip. The alternative was to go around the desert, but that would only waste more time. "I don't want any more delays."

"Perhaps you should have considered that before you went charging into that inn without me."

Aleida suppressed the urge to roll her eyes. "We'll have to go around, I suppose."

"A wise decision. You won't be able to do anything for your brother if you're dead in the middle of the desert, after all." In a gentler voice, the dragon added, "Going around will take us near Chatanda. We could stop by and check in on Tyrus. I'm sure he'd appreciate the visit."

Aleida's mood brightened a little at the thought, and she nudged the horse forward with her heels. She hadn't seen Tyrus since last winter—far too long ago for both of them. As much as she hated the idea of more delays, it would be good to pay him a visit. He always claimed to be doing well enough in his letters, but this way, she could see for herself, and she wasn't opposed to that.

KESARI

AFTER A RESTFUL NIGHT AND A HOT BREAKFAST IN A LITTLE INN NEAR the outskirts of Sharmok, Kesari led the others to the various vendors she'd scouted out the day before to buy supplies. They spent all but a few coins acquiring everything they needed, including a stocky little donkey which Saya named Berna. Then they drew water from the well until they'd filled every single one of the extra canteens they'd purchased and loaded them onto Berna's back with their other supplies.

They left Sharmok and travelled for a few hours before stopping to eat and swap out their clothes. Kesari and Saya stood behind the donkey to change while the men watched the road for travelers. Their new attire was light and loose-fitting, meant to allow plenty of airflow while shielding as much skin as possible from the burning rays of the summer sun. Kesari shucked off her heavy coat and the close-fitting garments beneath it, then stuffed them all into her pack.

Saya held a new shirt and pants out to her. "These should fit you." Kesari took the clothes, and Saya's eyes drifted to the dozens of scar lines running up both her forearms.

Her cheeks grew hot, and she quickly averted her gaze to avoid meeting Saya's. What was she going to think of her now? How was she supposed to explain? *Should* she explain, or just leave Saya to her own speculations?

"It's not as bad as it looks," she blurted out, then quickly shoved her arms through her sleeves and tugged the ends down as low as she could. "I mean, I did it to myself, but…I don't do that anymore."

Her stomach twisted. She shouldn't have said anything. They were starting to become friends, and now she'd ruined it. Saya wouldn't understand this. How could she, when Kesari barely understood it herself?

She allowed her eyes to flit up from the ground to the older girl's face. Whatever she'd expected to find there—disgust, pity, judgment—Saya didn't show any of it. Instead, she gave Kesari a small, kind smile and said, "I'm glad."

Some of her body's restless tension melted away, and she stopped tugging at the cuffs of her sleeves. *I'm glad.* No blame, no revulsion, no lectures or demands for an explanation. Only acceptance. Was that even possible?

For some things, maybe. But there was still plenty Saya and the others didn't know about her—things that were best kept to herself.

After Amar and Mitul had changed, they continued down the road with Saya leading the way. The foliage grew thinner, and the road turned to little more than a trail as they started into the desert. Far ahead, rocky mesas rose up at sharp angles before ending in high, flat plateaus. As they drew closer, Kesari could make out the individual hues of the cliffs' many layers, from pale tan to warm orange to a deep rusty red.

They didn't see another living soul until late afternoon, when a few Sularan traders passed by, presumably on their way to Sharmok. They greeted Saya with the same open-palm hand gesture Kesari had seen in the village. After that, they were completely alone, and soon the trail they'd been following disappeared entirely. Saya led them on, confidently following a path only she could see. Kesari hooked her lantern to one of the packs Berna carried, and Lucian came out to hover beside her as they walked.

Kesari had always pictured the Sular Desert as being barren and empty, with nothing but sand and sun as far as the eye could see. Perhaps there were places where it was like that, but so far, there had been a lot more to look at than she'd anticipated. Short scrub bushes and prickling cacti stood out in vibrant greens and yellows against the reds and oranges of the sand and rocks. A few of them bloomed with brightly colored flowers, adding flecks of pink, blue, and purple to the warm earthy tones.

The landscape was undeniably beautiful, but the longer they walked under the merciless heat of the sun, the more Kesari started to hate the desert. Her face burned, and her dark hair was hot to the touch when she reached up to brush it out of her eyes. Saya stopped for a moment to wrap her head and face with the red sash she usually wore around her waist and shoulders. She helped Kesari, Mitul, and Amar do the same with similar garments they'd purchased, but it didn't seem to help much. When Kesari began to sweat, the fabric of her clothing clung to her body with an uncomfortable stickiness. She would have stripped down to her undergarments if she thought it would do any good, but Saya had warned them that exposing their skin to the sun would only make it burn.

The air finally started to cool late in the evening when the sun began to slip behind the cliffs to the west. They walked a little while longer in the gray dusk as stars flickered into view overhead. As the night grew deeper, little glowing lights sprang to life in the surrounding desert. They were coming from some of the plants, and Kesari bent to examine one closer as they passed.

The plant itself was some kind of bush, with long, blade-like leaves extending from a central mass. A spray of flowers rose up from the middle on a long stem, and it was from the center of these flowers that the plant gave off a soft, blue glow.

Kesari gently lifted one of the blooms. The altma within her swirled up like a sudden gust of wind. She dropped the flower and skittered away from the plant with a short yelp.

The others stopped and turned to look at her with concern. Lucian hovered in front of her. "What's the matter?" he asked.

She eyed the plant warily. "What *is* that thing?"

"Mesala," Saya replied. "It means torch."

"Sularan torches!" Kesari said. The sudden stirring she'd felt when she touched the plan made sense now. "I've heard of those. They're full of altma."

"Aren't all living things full of altma?" Mitul asked.

"Yes," Lucian replied. "Though usually only in small quantities. Tarja and some plant and animal species have unique adaptations that allow them to draw in additional altma and channel it for their own purposes. In the case of this plant, that means glowing flowers."

Saya nodded. "The glow attracts ghayat and other animals, which eat the flowers and spread their seeds."

"Ghayat?" Kesari asked.

"A type of antelope that lives here. Perhaps we'll see some during our travels." She looked up at the stars for a moment, then back at the surrounding landscape. "This is as good a spot as any to make camp for the night. We'll leave early, so get some rest."

They set out the next morning well before dawn. Kesari was still yawning and trying to wake herself up as she followed Saya through the brush and over rocky terrain. Lucian had enlarged himself and now hovered overhead to light their path, but Kesari's tired feet still stumbled a few times. The sun began its ascent over the horizon, and the chill that had set in during the night steadily began to dissipate, replaced by the same dry, oppressive heat as the day before. Saya encouraged them all to drink plenty of water, even the donkey, and Kesari purposely let some of it drip down her chin and neck.

They stopped before noon under the shade of some tall, jutting rocks. At Saya's suggestion to them all, Mitul scooped away the top layer of brush and sand, then flopped down on the cooler dirt beneath with a satisfied sigh. Kesari removed her boots and dumped what must have been entire handfuls of sand from them. Saya forced Amar to drink a little more water despite his protests that he wasn't thirsty. They ate a quick meal and lay down to sleep in the shade while Lucian watched over the donkey and their belongings. He woke them up before sunset to continue their journey, and they didn't stop again until well after dark.

The next day passed much the same as the day before, as did the following. They travelled during the cooler parts of the day and rested when the sun was hottest, but still, Kesari was certain she'd melt into a puddle before they reached Atrea. The vegetation grew sparser as they walked across cracked, hard-packed ground, and by the evening of the fourth day, they'd come upon an expanse of sandy dunes that slipped and shifted under their every step. They would slide down one only to have to trek all the way up another, and with every three steps Kesari took, she was certain she was slipping back two more.

"Are you sure this was the best way to come?" Amar grumbled as they labored up the rise of a particularly high dune. "Why didn't we head down that washed out riverbed we saw this morning?"

Kesari had been wondering the same thing. Instead, Saya had taken them on what seemed like a detour, heading farther west than a straight path to Atrea should have taken them.

"The storm," Saya replied, pointing to the overcast sky that now stretched behind them. The occasional burst of distant lightning flared against heavy clouds. "That wash goes into a canyon. There are flash floods when it rains."

"And you're sure that wouldn't have been easier than this?" Amar asked.

"I'm sure. That's exactly why I took charge of this little expedition. You'd have gotten yourself killed five times by now without me."

"Probably true," Mitul wheezed, trying to coax Berna a few more steps up the slope.

Kesari forced her legs to push her to the top of the dune. Upon reaching it, she gasped at the view on the other side. A few more small sand dunes rose from the expanse of open land in front of them, which was illuminated by the blue glow of mesala flowers. There were hundreds of them, far more than they'd seen anywhere else. It was as if the light of the stars above was being reflected off the sand below. Kesari's first instinct was to stand and admire the view for a few minutes, but something else drew her attention.

At the bottom of the slope, a group of shadowy figures bent over several of the mesala plants. Moonlight glinted off their blades as they cut the long, flowering stems and stuffed them into pouches at their sides. When one of the stems was cut, the flowers' glow faded away in seconds.

"What are they doing?" she asked Saya, pointing.

Saya's face twisted with rage, and she tore down the slope at a run, shouting as she went. "Hey! Stop that right now!"

Two of the figures ran, clutching their bags tight as their feet kicked up sand. The other three turned, brandishing knives and pistols.

On their way to Saya's aid, Lucian, Amar, and Mitul went rushing past Kesari and down the slope. She stood frozen, heart pounding, torn between following them and running away. She didn't *want* to run, but what else was she supposed to do? She had no weapon. She wasn't a fighter.

Neither was Mitul, but Saya was his friend, and she was Kesari's, too. Before she could talk herself out of it, she hurried after them.

A gunshot sounded. The sand near Amar's feet sprayed up from where the projectile had struck, but he didn't flinch. A warning shot, or an accidental miss? It was impossible to say, but Kesari's heartbeat raced even faster as she continued on.

Saya reached the man who'd taken the shot as he fumbled to reload. She had him on the ground with her knee against his chest and a knife at his throat before Kesari could so much as blink.

His companions lowered their weapons and began to plead with Saya, their voices mingling so that it was difficult to distinguish one from the other. She didn't make a move to hurt the man, but she didn't release him either.

Amar and Mitul skidded to a stop on either side of her, and Kesari stood behind with Lucian hovering overhead at an impressively intimidating size. His orange glow illuminated the terror in the strangers' faces as they glanced at each other and then back to their friend on the ground. All of them had the deep brown skin and black hair that was typical of Kavorans.

"What are you doing here?" Saya hissed, shifting her knife so the tip pressed against the soft skin under her captive's jaw.

"N-nothing," he stammered. "Only passing through. I swear."

"What are those, then?" She nodded to the dropped bag lying beside him.

"Please, we're simple traders. We didn't mean any harm."

"That's the same excuse you people always make." Saya's voice was a hiss, low and dangerous.

Maybe she was going to hurt him after all. Kesari's stomach

churned.

"We're only trying to make a living. We all have families to take care of. Surely you can understand that."

"At the expense of *my* family?" Saya shouted. "You have no right to be here taking what doesn't belong to you. Do you have any idea the damage you've done?"

"Let me go," the man said, his voice trembling. "I swear I'll never set foot here again."

"I've heard promises like that before."

"Saya," Mitul said quietly. "Please, you're better than this."

She stayed there a few seconds longer, her body as tense as a drawn bowstring. Then, almost as quickly as she'd pinned the man down, she pulled her knife back and stepped away from him. "Leave this place," she growled. "Now."

The man scrambled up. He left his bag lying in the sand and retreated to a safe distance with his friends. They backed away quickly, keeping wary eyes on Saya as they returned to their mounts and the two other men standing several paces off. Then they rode away into the night.

Saya muttered something under her breath as she watched them go. She hiked back up the dune to where Berna stood waiting. The donkey laid her ears back and brayed in protest, but Saya eventually coaxed her into coming down. She asked Lucian to follow the Kavoran traders to ensure they cleared off like they'd promised but said nothing more about the encounter.

A stifled silence settled over the group as they made camp and ate their supper. Amar, Mitul, and Kesari had all chosen spots next to each other on a slab of rock facing the fire. Saya sat cross-legged in the sand on the other side. The flickering light made her frown seem deeper and fiercer than it really was.

Amar was the first to break the silence. He gave Mitul and Kesari a sidelong glance, then fixed his gaze on Saya. "Do you want to explain what all that was about?"

"It doesn't matter," she replied flatly.

Amar raised an eyebrow. "You looked like you were ready to kill that man, so I'd say it *does* matter."

She sighed and kicked one leg out in front of her. "Turn around."

"What?"

"All three of you. Turn around." She nodded pointedly to something behind them.

Kesari turned to face the sea of glowing blue that stretched out behind them. She held in a gasp, not wanting to startle the trio of animals that stood a few dozen paces away. "Are those—?" she whispered to Saya, but her words faltered on the name she couldn't remember.

"Ghayat, yes."

Kesari craned her neck to get a better look at the creatures. One of them, the largest, stared at her with big, dark eyes. Two long, ridged horns rose over its head and curved around to its back, where they gleamed in the blue glow of the mesala flowers. In the night, it was hard to tell exactly what color it might have been, but most of its body was covered in sleek, dark fur. The underside of its belly and the inner parts of its legs were considerably lighter, and that same lighter color ran in four vertical stripes down its face. The chin and cheeks were also light, with a single dark line running from its lower lip to the bottom of its chin. In a way, the lines reminded Kesari of the haseph markings painted on Saya's face.

"They're pretty, I guess," Amar said hesitantly. "But you're not answering my question."

Saya was quiet for a few more seconds, watching the ghayat. "Every year," she said, "Kavoran traders come through here to harvest as much mesala as they can possibly carry. It's the ghayat's primary food source, and most of the mesala that grows here comes from seeds that have been digested by the ghayat. It's a cycle. They need each other to survive. Just as my people need the ghayat to survive."

"What do you mean?" Amar asked.

"They're an essential part of our lives. We eat their meat. We use their hides for tents, blankets, beds, shoes, and clothing. We make tools and weapons from their bones and antlers. But with so many Kavorans harvesting the mesala, there hasn't been enough regrowth for the ghayat to thrive. Herds are dwindling, and if nothing changes, it will be only a matter of time before my people begin to dwindle away with them."

"But what do the Kavorans want with so much mesala?" Kesari asked.

"You felt something when you touched one yesterday, right?" Saya asked. "The flowers can enhance a Tarja's magic. Our own healers have used them for centuries to strengthen their abilities and perform feats that would have otherwise been impossible. It's only natural that a nation with so many Tarja would want such a resource."

"Why now, though?" Amar asked. "Kavora has always been full of Tarja. Why are they suddenly so interested in the mesala?"

"For a long time, outsiders avoided the desert, and my people had very little interaction with other nations. We kept our way of life secret. When the Kavorans did learn of the mesala and its unique properties, our leaders were able to negotiate a suitable trade agreement." Saya took out one of her knives and began sharpening the blade against a rock. "For centuries, we've carefully cultivated the mesala and watched ghayat herds to ensure stability even as we traded with the Kavorans. And that arrangement worked well for a long time. But things have gotten worse since Empress Dashiva took the throne."

"How so?" Kesari asked.

"The military," Mitul said, and Saya nodded. He turned to Kesari to explain. "Empress Dashiva has been enlisting more and more Tarja in the imperial army. She's used that power to bring Kavora's provinces more securely under her control, as well as to absorb more territory. Like Vis, and the borders of the desert. Sharmok was an independent colony ten years ago. The military threatened to take it by force, but the people opted to surrender instead."

"They've been encroaching on the desert more and more," Saya said. "We've kept them at bay through careful negotiations, which often involve giving them more and more mesala for the promise that they won't invade our lands. But poachers come in to take more than they're allowed, and the Empress does nothing to stop them. With the ghayat herds dwindling, we can't afford to give them any more than we already are. Especially when it's only making their armies stronger." She stared darkly into the fire, her jaw tight. "My people are outnumbered and outmatched. If the Kavorans wanted to march in and take our lands away from us right now, they could. We'd fight back, but in the end, we would still be overrun."

Kesari recalled Saya's words to her in Valmandi. *If our warriors were immortal...*

"That's why we have to help Saya with her haseph," Mitul said, looking at Amar. "What our nation is doing to her people is wrong, and your immortality might be the key to stopping it."

"How?" Amar asked, frowning.

"Imagine an army of immortal warriors," Saya said in a low voice. "No one would dare take advantage of us then."

Beside Kesari, Amar tensed. He stared into the fire without speaking, but the muscles in his jaw worked like he was grinding his teeth.

"I know you don't understand," Saya said. "We argued about it a few times, before you died."

"You're right," he replied. "I don't understand. I'm doing everything I can to find out what happened to me so I can get rid of this curse, and you want to inflict it on your own people?"

"I don't *want* to. If there was a more effective option, of course I'd do that instead. But as far as I can tell, there isn't. And immortality is a far better alternative to annihilation."

"You have no idea what you're talking about," Amar growled, his fingers tightening around the edge of the rock he sat on.

"And you do?" The pitch of Saya's voice rose. "How can you say that living forever is really so terrible when you don't even remember most of your life?"

"Exactly. I don't remember. So how is it you think this is going to work out? What happens to your friends when they die in battle and come back with no memory of who they were before? Is that really the kind of fate you would condemn them to?"

"I'm not condemning anyone. I'm giving them a *choice*. A choice to fight for their families and their way of life instead of watching it all be stripped away from them one piece at a time. And you do *not* get to judge me for that, Kavoran."

Amar glared at her through the flickering firelight. He shook his head, stood up, and began to walk away.

Mitul rose and took a step to follow him. "Amar, where are you going?"

"I need to take a piss," he said flatly, "if that's all right with you."

Mitul sat back down without a word and shifted his gaze to the fire.

Saya poked at the coals with her knife, its sharpened edge reflecting the orange glow of the firelight. "He was almost starting to come around to the idea before," she muttered, glancing at Mitul. "I really wish that woman hadn't killed him."

"So do I," Mitul said, "but there's no changing it now." He lifted his saraj into his lap and began to play, and Kesari let the music lull her into a welcome sense of contentment as she watched the flames die down.

KESARI

Kesari's days ran together more and more the longer she and her companions travelled through the Sular Desert, until she was no longer certain how long ago they'd started this journey. Eight days, maybe, or nine. She'd stopped wondering whether they would ever make it out and had simply accepted the fact that this was now her life—sand and sun and walking until the sand filled her shoes and the sun rose to its highest point, when they would stop a few hours before walking some more. Only Saya, Lucian, and the donkey seemed unaffected by the stifling heat and the vast emptiness all around them.

One morning—ten days into their journey, or maybe eleven—Saya began to hum as she passed out their breakfast. A smile lingered in the corners of her mouth, even when Amar began to grumble again about the heat.

Lucian bobbed along beside her. "You're in a good mood today."

"We should all be in a good mood," she replied. "We're almost there."

Kesari sat up a little straighter. "We're almost to the other side?"

Saya laughed. "No, not quite."

Kesari immediately deflated.

"Why would you even say something like that?" Amar muttered

sullenly through a mouthful of bread. Lucian chuckled a little, and Amar shot him a glare.

"Sorry. I should have been more specific. We're almost to Hayathu, where my family lives. It's our biggest settlement. We'll be able to restock our supplies and rest in comfort before we continue our journey."

"Out of curiosity," Mitul said, "how much farther is it from there to Atrea?"

"At least another two weeks," Saya replied.

Kesari held back a groan. She'd been so hopeful that they were nearly done with this miserable place, but at least they'd get some reprieve before the long, final stretch.

They finished their food and started walking before the sun had fully risen. A few hours later, a cluster of jagged rocks came into view, protruding from the sand at sharp angles. "There it is," Saya said, a grin breaking across her face as she pointed to the rocks.

"I thought you said it was the biggest settlement," Amar said, shielding his eyes against the sun. "I don't see anything."

"You will."

Sure enough, as they drew closer, tents of all shapes and sizes came into view between and behind the rocks. Dozens of them clung to the shade cast by enormous slabs of stone, more than Kesari had imagined there could possibly be in this empty landscape. Goats, donkeys, and even a few ghayat wandered the area, munching on the mesala, cacti, and other plants that grew more abundantly here than anywhere else they'd seen in the desert.

A few Sularan men stood on the tallest rocks outside the settlement, armed with bows and muskets. Saya raised a hand as they approached and called up to them in Sularan. They shouted something back down to her, and she laughed.

She led them through the shade of the rocks and into the settlement of Hayathu. Sularan adults worked outside their homes, sewing ghayat hides, fletching arrows, and weaving fibrous plant material into baskets. Children chased each other through the sand, squealing with laughter and unrestrained joy. Most of the people had the same tawny skin and dusty brown hair as Saya, though there were several with darker complexions and hair as black as night.

Many of the tents had been pitched around a large pit that opened up in the center of the settlement, rimmed with jagged rock that protruded horizontally over the empty air. No, not a pit, exactly, Kesari realized as they got closer. One side wasn't enclosed, instead merging with the sheer drop of a large cliff. A rushing sound came from inside the chasm.

"Is that…water?" she asked.

Saya nodded and motioned them forward. They walked to the rim and looked down, where an underground river emerged from the mouth of a cave to pool at the bottom of the chasm. At the other end, it flowed out again, rushing over rocks in a frothy white torrent until it met the waterfall that plunged over the cliffside. Droplets of water misted over the falls and caught the sunlight to create a colorful rainbow. A few rope ladders dropped from the edge of the chasm to the large pool below. A group of people had waded into the water, bending to draw water into earthen jugs.

A loud whoop suddenly echoed from the chasm, and Kesari shifted her gaze just in time to see a Sularan child jump from one of the rocks jutting over the water. She gasped. He was going to hurt himself. Her body tensed in anticipation of the pained scream that was sure to come.

But it didn't. Instead, the child plunged into the water. After a few seconds, he resurfaced with a bubbling laugh. Another child dove in after him, screaming delightedly all the way down. Kesari spun around. A whole line of children stood at the top of the chasm, waiting for their turn. The youngest couldn't have been more than four or five, and the other kids all cheered for him when he stepped up to the edge and went leaping over the side. Even Saya let out a whoop.

Two of the boys standing in line perked up at the sound of her voice and turned to look at her. They grabbed the arm of the older boy in front of them and pointed. He shielded his eyes and followed the line of their fingers.

Saya raised a hand to wave at him and called out a greeting in Sularan.

The older boy shouted as he broke into a run. "Saya! Saya!" After a brief hesitation, the other two followed, pumping their shorter legs as fast as they could to keep up. All three of them were calling to Saya now, and soon there were three more figures running toward them from all directions, laughing and hollering. They came closer and closer but didn't seem to have any intention of slowing. Kesari took a few steps away from the edge of the chasm. The pool below might break her fall, but that didn't mean she wanted to be knocked in.

A boy of about ten rushed past Kesari from behind and slammed into Saya, wrapping his arms tight around her waist. The three boys who had spotted her first came next, the younger ones attaching themselves to both of her legs while the older one grabbed her by the hand and chattered away excitedly. Two more boys appeared seemingly out of nowhere and latched onto what was now a mass of arms, legs, and smiling faces. Saya's laugh cut through the commotion of their voices as she ruffled their hair, shoved them playfully, and raised one of the smallest ones up onto her shoulders.

"Who are they?" Amar whispered to Mitul, but he only shrugged and shook his head in response.

Saya turned to her friends as the boys continued to chatter. "These are my brothers," she said proudly, still grinning.

She spoke a few words to the boys in Sularan. They disentangled themselves from her and turned to stare at Kesari, Lucian, Amar, and Mitul. Now that they weren't all clustered together, Kesari could make out individual faces. The oldest was a hair shorter than Saya, all lanky teenage limbs and a face somewhere between boy and man. The youngest two were twins, identical in every way except for their clothing. There was a little bit of Saya in all of them. One had her same full lips and piercing eyes. A few had her strong, straight nose. Another held exactly the same posture, shoulders straight and body completely still, but with muscles tensed like he could spring into action at any moment.

"They're *all* your brothers?" Mitul asked.

Saya nodded and pointed to the oldest boy. "This is Halos, he's fourteen. Hidaver is thirteen and Hursit is ten. This rascal is Hadar, he's eight. And then the twins are six—Hilmi and Hirza."

The twins shook their heads exuberantly and started to protest. One of them jumped up and down while the other held up seven fingers.

Saya laughed and turned back to her friends. "It's very important to them that you all know it's their birthday in a few days. They'll be seven."

The two boys smiled proudly, a matching gap showing where their front teeth had yet to grow back in.

"We have another brother," Saya said. "Hazim. He's sixteen, so he's away on haseph now, too."

Kesari had to count the boys again. Six brothers here and one on haseph, and all of them younger than Saya. She'd never seen or even heard of a family so large. In Atrea, her sibling group of three had been considered average, and two or three children were common in Kavoran families as well. Tarja healers could easily prevent pregnancy, and even in Atrea, most cities had at least a few of those. There were Tarja among the Sularans as well, but perhaps they had different ideas about family planning.

"You have *seven* little brothers?" Kesari asked. She tried to keep the incredulity from her voice, but it slipped out anyway.

"And you're the only girl?" Amar said, as if he couldn't quite believe what he was seeing either.

Saya nodded. "That's right. Seven younger brothers, and I'm the only daughter. And before anyone asks, yes, all of us have the same mother and father." She recited each statement in a flat tone, like she was used to answering such questions.

"It's nice to meet you all," Mitul said, smiling at each of the boys.

"Nice to meet you," a few of them repeated back in accented Kavoran.

A sudden hush seemed to fall over the entire settlement. The oldest of Saya's brothers present—Halos, if Kesari was remembering correctly—turned around. Saya turned with him, facing a large tent that sat above the rest on a rise of flat ledge. There, a woman had emerged, standing straight and tall in front of the tent's opening. Her hawkish gaze immediately fell on the group.

Saya's smile fell. She inhaled a deep breath and began walking toward the tent, her brothers fanning out around her.

Kesari wasn't sure whether to follow or stay put, but Amar and Mitul both started forward, so she fell in beside them. The woman watched, saying nothing, her expression unreadable. She held herself with a rigid dignity that radiated authority. As they drew closer, Kesari could make out the subtle age lines creased into her weathered face. Her attire was more colorful and decorative than that of the other Sularans in the settlement, and her ash brown hair had been woven into a pair of long, elaborate braids that fell over her shoulders.

"Who is that?" Kesari whispered to Mitul, not really expecting him to have an answer.

"I have no idea," he replied, then glanced at the still silent Sularans around them. "Someone they all respect."

"Or fear," Amar said.

Saya's brothers stopped walking when they were still several paces away from the tent. Kesari, Amar, and Mitul took the cue and stopped as well. Only Saya continued on, opening her palm out to one side in greeting. She said something in Sularan. A few long moments passed before the older woman responded, her voice low and as coarse as the desert sand.

They spoke for a few minutes. Kesari had no idea what either of them were saying, but she didn't dare ask anyone to translate. A frown pulled at the woman's face, and Saya's words took on an increasingly agitated tone. At one point, she gestured to Amar, and the woman fixed her golden-eyed stare on him. He stared back, unblinking, until her gaze returned to Saya. The older woman spoke a few more short, clipped words before retreating into her tent.

Saya's shoulders sagged as she turned to face Kesari and the others. The hubbub of Hayathu rose back up around them as people resumed their work and play. Halos stepped forward and said something to her, which brought some small semblance of a smile to her face.

"Well?" Amar said. "What was that all about?"

Saya straightened. "The Masahi welcomes us all as guests. She'll make arrangements for a meal in honor of our visit tonight."

"That's all?" Mitul asked.

Saya nodded curtly.

"That was a long conversation just to find out about dinner," Amar said.

Saya pursed her lips and pushed between her brothers. She started to walk off, alone.

"Where are you going?" Amar called, annoyance cutting into his tone. When he received no answer, he started after her. "You can't just—"

Halos stepped into his path. "Let her go."

"What's her problem?" Amar asked. He nodded to the tent on the ledge "Who is that woman?"

"The Masahi," Halos replied. "She is our leader."

"Like a queen?" Kesari asked.

The boy raised an eyebrow. "Not quite. Each Sularan tribe chooses one person to represent them on a council. 'Masahi' is the title given to the highest-ranking council member." He raised one shoulder in a half shrug. "In this case, that person also happens to be our mother."

Kesari wouldn't have guessed that, given the complete lack of warmth or even familiarity in the reunion between Saya and the older woman. Amar and Mitul looked equally surprised. Apparently, Saya hadn't mentioned that part of her personal history to either of them.

"The Masahi is disappointed in Saya," Halos went on. "She's been away on haseph for two years now, and we've all been awaiting her return. For her to come back now without having completed her journey is upsetting, especially to our mother."

Mitul cocked his head to one side. "It was my understanding that there's no time limit on when a person has to complete their haseph."

Halos nodded. "Yes, but there are…expectations. Especially for someone like Saya."

"What expectations?"

"She's the eldest child of the Masahi. She may take our mother's place on the council one day, and our people are watching to see what she does with her haseph. Will she prove herself worthy of that position, or should they start looking elsewhere for a leader?"

The grandiosity of Saya's planned haseph made a lot more sense now. She wasn't simply looking for a worthy offering to bring back to her tribe. She was looking for a way to prove herself, and what better way to do that than by providing a means by which the Sularans could protect and preserve their entire way of life?

"Some believe she's chasing a mirage," Halos went on. "They think whatever she's doing out there won't amount to anything, that she's wasting her time. Our mother is beginning to fear this, too."

Kesari watched Saya's retreating figure grow smaller against the bright blue sky. What must it be like, to live under the weight of such heavy expectations? And yet, she was still trying to do what she thought was best for her people. She was still pushing forward. Did that not make her a leader already?

Kesari couldn't say she would have been able to do the same if she'd been in Saya's position. She would have frozen, or run away, or broken down. She hated that those was her default responses to hardship. Not strength, but weakness. Not persistence, but a desire to give up. Because some things were just too difficult, too terrifying, too painful.

But wasn't all of this difficult and terrifying and painful for Saya, too? On some level, it had to be. And if she could find the strength to keep trying in spite of that, maybe Kesari could learn to do the same.

AMAR

AMAR SAT ALONE AT THE EDGE OF THE CHASM, PEERING DOWN AT the reflections of stars in the pool below. Behind him, the notes of a song drifted through the settlement as Mitul and some of the Sularans played their music, sometimes taking turns and sometimes weaving their melodies together. Mitul had pleaded with Amar to play with them, and he had, for a little while. But his heart hadn't been in it, and he'd snuck away at the first opportunity. Now, the kanjira lay silent in his lap beneath still fingers.

On the other side of the chasm, Kesari, Saya's brothers, and several other Sularan children had started up a game that involved chasing Lucian around the tents. Their squeals of laughter echoed across the sand as the Spirit Tarja darted away, always just out of reach. One of Saya's youngest brothers perched on Kesari's shoulders, and a wide grin stretched across the girl's face. It was the first time Amar had seen her look so much like the child she still was, her bright eyes devoid of the world-weary sorrow that usually lingered there.

They were all so young, so full of life and energy. Watching them made him feel old in a way he couldn't remember ever feeling before, as if the full weight of all his years had finally caught up with him. How many years, he didn't know, but the sensation pressed against his skin and sank deep into his bones. He didn't belong here, and it wasn't because he was a foreigner. Maybe he didn't belong anywhere.

Soft footsteps approached from behind, and Saya sat down next to him. It was the first time he'd seen her since the day's earlier conversation with her mother. "You're a terrible host," he said, casting her a sidelong glance. "You drag us halfway across the desert to meet your family, then leave us here alone with them all day."

"Sorry." She picked up a few pebbles and tossed them over the edge of the chasm one at a time. "I didn't think coming back here was going to be so…"

"Uncomfortable?" Amar suggested.

"Humiliating."

She looked so morose about it, a vulnerable young woman exposed beneath the warrior's hardened exterior. He bumped his shoulder against hers and tried a joke. "You never told us you were a princess."

Her frown deepened. "Who said that?"

"The Masahi is your mother, isn't she? Halos said you'd likely be the one to take her place someday, which makes you…well, maybe not royalty, exactly, but something like it."

She raised an eyebrow. "You do realize we don't have the same concepts of royalty that Kavorans do?"

"Yes, but I'm not entirely wrong, am I? Otherwise, you would have finished your haseph with something simple a long time ago."

"That's true," she admitted.

"Why didn't you tell us? Or did you, and I'm not remembering that part?"

"It wasn't important. And I liked being just Saya, for once." She let out a sigh. "I was never just Saya here. There were always expectations of who I should be and what I should do. There still are."

"Ah, yes. Expectations," Amar replied sagely, tossing a rock and watching it fall until it hit the water. "That must be exhausting. Of course, I have no idea what that's like, people expecting you to be somebody you're not or do things you don't remember ever agreeing to."

She shoved him hard enough to nearly tip him over, but when he looked at her, she was smiling. "Point taken," she said, "but I don't think it's quite the same thing."

"Semantics," he replied with a shrug, allowing a grin to break across his own face. He'd spent so much energy on keeping his companions at a distance, but now he found himself wondering if it would be so bad for them to be friends again. Maybe they were already starting to get there.

Saya opened her mouth to say something else, but a sudden lull in the music and conversation behind them made her stop. They both turned to see where everyone's attention had shifted. The Masahi stood outside her tent once more, waiting a few seconds for the remaining noise to die down.

"Today has been a happy day," she said in Kavoran, her voice laced with the barest hint of an accent. Her eyes found Saya. "My eldest child has returned after two long years away from home, and although she cannot stay, we welcome her and her companions to Hayathu. Tonight, we invite them to share our meal, celebrate a reunion of friends and family, and rest their weary bodies before we say farewell tomorrow." She extended her arms. "Amar, Mitul, Kesari, Lucian, and Saya, we open our arms and our hearts to you in friendship and hospitality. I believe the food is ready. Please come and take the first portion as our honored guests."

Her hawkish eyes narrowed ever so slightly. Beside Amar, Saya stiffened and raised her chin a little higher as if to brace herself. Perhaps this was some of the humiliation she'd spoken of, the discomfort of being treated as a guest in her own home and by her own mother.

She started toward a large slab of rock where food had been laid out in woven serving baskets and earthenware dishes. Amar followed, and Mitul, Kesari, and Lucian soon joined them. Saya showed them how to use one of the large pieces of flatbread to hold their food. There were several different kinds of vegetables, all seasoned with colorful spices whose aromas melded together pleasantly. Little cakes topped with a pale pink fruit had been arranged in a basket, and steam wafted up from a bowl of rice prepared in traditional Kavoran fashion, a gracious gesture from their hosts.

A ghayat had been cooking on a spit nearby for most of the day, and Amar's stomach rumbled as he drew closer to the savory smell of its meat. A Sularan man sliced a few pieces from the animal's haunches and laid it on top of his flatbread, which was now so full he had to carry it with both hands. Only after they had all walked away from the rock slab did the rest of the Sularans approach to get their own meal.

Saya led them to a spot near one of the many campfires that had been set up throughout the settlement. They sat on the cooling sand with their food in their laps and dug in. Amar hadn't eaten since breakfast that morning, and his appetite was voracious. He ate like he hadn't had a decent meal in weeks, and to be fair, he hadn't—not compared to this. It was some of the best food he'd ever tasted, at least as far as he could remember.

Mitul watched him for a few seconds, then shook his head. "How can you be older than I am and still have the appetite of a teenage boy? It doesn't seem fair."

"He still has the body of a teenage boy," Lucian said. "Is it so surprising that he eats like one, too?"

"But where does all that food go?" Saya asked. "It's not like he's using it to get any taller or put some more hair on his chest."

"I'm perfectly happy with my height," Amar mumbled through a mouthful of rice. "And my chest hair is none of your concern."

Kesari stifled a giggle behind her hand.

"Where did you wander off to earlier today?" Mitul asked Saya. "You missed out on some terrific musical performances, if I do say so myself."

"I was visiting someone," she replied, glancing up. Her face brightened, and she pointed to something out past the rocks and the campfires. "Him, actually."

It took Amar a moment to spot the dark figure silhouetted against the night. He stood apart from the settlement in the empty desert beyond, alone except for the horse beside him. His body was swathed in loose-flowing fabrics that fluttered around him in the breeze.

"Who is he?" Amar asked.

"Zefar," Saya replied. "He's an outcast."

"Someone who didn't finish his haseph?" Kesari asked.

Saya nodded. "He worked as a mercenary in Kavora for a time. Now he lives alone, close by but not fully a part of the tribe. He taught me to fight when I was younger. I used to love listening to his stories."

The man had left his horse with some of the other animals and was now skirting around the edge of the settlement, disappearing behind rocks only to reappear somewhere else a few moments later. It was a little unnerving, how quietly and quickly he moved, like he was made of nothing more than smoke and shadow. The hilt of a dagger protruded from the top of the sash around his waist.

"Wait," Mitul said with a frown. "You've told us about this man before."

That must have happened before Amar's last death because he couldn't remember ever hearing about Saya's mercenary mentor. Then again, he hadn't made an effort to pay attention to much of anything his companions had told him until recently.

Saya nodded and stared down at her food, suddenly bashful. "Yes, well, he's actually the one who told me about Amar."

Mitul gaped. "You mean he's…"

Saya nodded, but Kesari and Lucian looked as confused as Amar was.

Before he could ask for clarification, the man himself stepped out of the shadows mere paces from where they were sitting. Several of the nearby Sularans cast dark glances in the newcomer's direction and began to mutter amongst themselves. A few even picked up their food and walked away.

The man didn't seem to notice, or perhaps he simply didn't care. His eyes were the same gold as Saya's, and he fixed his stare on Amar, a smirk curling the corners of his mouth beneath a stubbly mustache. The thick scars that marked his face gave him a grisly, ferocious appearance. One hand rested on the hilt of his dagger, and Amar's fingers itched to grab his own blade. If only he hadn't left it in a tent with his other things, but he hadn't expected to need it here, and it had seemed rude to carry it around when their hosts had been so welcoming.

"Well," the man said in a voice as smooth as polished steel. "You're still alive and well, I see. And not a day older than the last time we met, you lucky bastard."

"Be nice, Zefar," Saya said coolly.

"I'm always *nice*," he replied cheerfully. He was still staring, a cold recognition in his eyes.

Amar bristled. Something about the man felt wrong, though he couldn't pinpoint what it was. "Do I know you?" he growled.

Zefar's smile widened, and he rubbed the top of his thumb over the hilt of his dagger. "You mean you don't remember?"

"I don't remember much these days. Tell me who you are." He said it as much to Saya and Mitul as he did the stranger. They both seemed to know something of his history with the man, and as usual, annoyance at this critical gap in memory flared within him.

"Who am I?" Zefar tossed back his head and laughed. "I'm the man who killed you."

Amar scowled and mentally ran through what he'd been told of his previous lives. Mitul claimed to have seen Amar die three times. The first was at the hands of thieves in Jakhat who'd come to rob them. The most recent time had been that incident with the Visan woman. But his second death—Saya had only said it was a run-in with a mercenary, one of her people. Amar had never heard the full story, but this man had to be the one responsible.

He stood up and squared his shoulders to Zefar. The Sularan was a good head taller than him, and his teeth gleamed wolfishly in the firelight. Amar crossed his arms. "Explain."

"You truly don't remember, do you?" Zefar said, a hint of mocking in his tone. He glanced at Saya. "It's just like you said."

The last of Amar's patience fizzled out. "Skies above, will someone tell me what you're all talking about? Or do I need to beat it out of you?"

Zefar's grin widened. "Is that a challenge?"

Mitul stood and put a hand on Amar's arm. "Please, let's all sit down and have a civilized conversation."

Amar took a step back, still eyeing the dagger at Zefar's hip. The man let go of the hilt and raised his hands in a gesture of peace. Amar waited until he'd lowered himself cross-legged onto the ground before returning to his own seat.

"Well?" he said, glancing between Mitul and Zefar. He didn't care who did the talking as long as somebody did it soon.

"It happened five years ago," Mitul began. "By then we were already travelling throughout Kavora, searching for a Tarja who could tell us about your immortality. We stayed out late one night, and you joined in on a game of dice with a few other travelers."

"Where were you?" Amar asked.

"I was…occupied elsewhere."

"You told me you'd wandered off to flirt with a handsome man," Saya interjected.

"Well, yes," Mitul replied sheepishly. "If I'd known what was going to happen, I never would have left your side, though that may have been what saved my life. You left the tavern with a friend you'd met there, and you were both killed. Brutally." He cast a dark glare at Zefar.

"Killing's always brutal," the mercenary replied with a nonchalant shrug. "It wasn't anything personal, you understand. I was simply doing a job."

Amar's jaw tightened. "You murdered me."

Zefar let out a longsuffering sigh. "Yes, that's what I said earlier, isn't it? Have you not been paying attention, or are you just dense?"

Amar lunged at him, and they both went toppling into the sand. He pinned Zefar's neck against the ground, but the mercenary only let out a choking laugh, amusement dancing in his eyes. Fiery heat surged through Amar. He let out a wild roar and punched his killer in the face.

Someone grabbed his shoulder from behind. Zefar seized the opportunity to throw him off and stood. In the blink of an eye, his dagger was in his hand, but Saya put herself in front of him before he could use it.

"I should kill you!" Amar yelled, straining half-heartedly against Mitul's strong grip. Kesari had taken hold of his other arm, her eyes wide. She was terrified, but not of the mercenary—of *him*.

Amar swallowed and tried to slow his racing pulse. His anger may have been justified, but he'd crossed a line attacking Zefar like that. What was he going to do? Kill the man in the middle of a meal prepared by people who'd shown him only kindness and hospitality? His cheeks burned as he looked around at the staring faces of dozens of Sularans, their expressions troubled by the scene he'd created.

He wrenched his arms free and glowered at Zefar. The man wasn't even in a fighting stance anymore. He'd returned the dagger to its sheath and stood calmly with crossed arms and a smug smile on his face. It was only Amar who looked like the troublesome instigator now, outraged and disheveled while the outcast mercenary appeared the picture of composed dignity.

He sat down with a huff. The last bites of his food had scattered onto the ground, and a dog had wandered over to pick up the pieces. Zefar returned to his own seat, and after a few wary glances between themselves, so did the others.

"I understand you're upset," Zefar said as the usual chatter around them resumed. "But you didn't actually die, so I don't see what the real harm is."

"You have no idea what I lost!" Amar snapped. He was half-tempted to finish his fight with the man but managed to stay seated.

Zefar raised his eyebrows and waited a few seconds. "Would you like to hear my side of the story? You might find it interesting."

"Go on, then," Amar muttered.

"Oh, that wasn't very polite. I think I'd like to hear a *please*, if you don't mind."

"Zefar," Saya warned in a low voice.

"Fine," the mercenary said with a sigh. "As your friend here was saying, five years ago, you were brutally murdered by a devilishly handsome mercenary. Of course, this man had no other motive than to make a decent living for himself, and thus cannot be faulted for his actions."

Amar rolled his eyes. "Just get on with it."

"All right, straight to the point then. You should know that I was especially well compensated for this particular job, but that wasn't the only reason why it was so strange." He paused here, and Amar waited a few seconds for him to continue, but he didn't.

"Why was it so strange?" he asked grudgingly.

Zefar's eyes gleamed in the firelight. "I'm so glad you asked. You see, my employer wanted me to wait a while after the killing was done so I could watch the bodies. She wouldn't tell me what I was supposed to be watching for, only that I would know it when it happened. I was to report straight back to her about whatever I saw."

He paused to uncork a flask strapped across his shoulder and took a long drink. Amar waited silently, clinging to the last remnants of his patience, until Zefar finished drinking with a satisfied smack of his lips.

"There you were," he continued at last. "Lifeless, bloody, your body growing colder with each passing hour. You were absolutely dead—I'd made sure of it. And then suddenly, you weren't. Come sunrise, you started to breathe again, and then you simply sat up, looked around like you were confused, and wandered off. It was the most unbelievable thing I'd ever seen." His lips twitched up in another grin. "And can you guess what my employer's reaction was when I returned to her with this absolutely unbelievable piece of information?"

Amar shrugged.

Zefar leaned forward conspiratorially. "Nothing," he breathed. "She had no reaction at all. It was as if that was exactly what she'd expected would happen. She didn't even care that you weren't dead, which was what she'd hired me for in the first place. She paid me a little extra for my trouble, and that was the end of it."

A strange response indeed. Amar's curiosity about the death itself shifted to something else—something far more important about Zefar's story. "Who was she?"

"I don't know. I never found out, and it's not uncommon for my employers to want some measure of secrecy."

"You must know something," Amar said.

"Information like that usually comes at a price."

Amar was really starting to regret not strangling the man, but before he could speak any of the dozens of threats running through his mind, Saya stepped in. "You killed him, Zefar. You at least owe him some answers."

"I don't think it actually counts as killing someone if they don't stay dead, so I'm not sure—"

"Please," Saya said, exasperation heavy in her voice. "For me. Tell him what you know about the woman."

For a moment, Zefar's carefree expression faltered, and he shrugged. "She was a Kavoran Tarja, from Jakhat. She used magic to hide her face, but she was always dressed in very fine clothing. The way she spoke made me think she was used to ordering other people around. I always assumed she must have been a noble or some member of the imperial court."

"We've never been able to figure out who she might have been,"

Mitul said. "To be honest, we haven't put much thought into it. We only heard that part of the story when we met Saya."

"When Zefar told me about you," Saya said, "I knew I wanted to find you for my haseph. But learning the cause of your immortality always seemed to be more important than learning who this woman might be. Whoever she was, she seems to have lost whatever interest she had in you."

"It happened so long ago," Mitul added. "And we haven't had any more run-ins with mercenaries or hired assassins since."

"What about the girl who killed me last time?" Amar asked.

Saya shook her head. "She's a skilled Tarja, but she's no mercenary. I doubt they're connected. A wealthy Kavoran noble wouldn't hire some young, untrained refugee to hunt you down."

Mitul nodded in agreement. "If that noblewoman knew of your immortality, she may have shared that knowledge with others. It's more likely our Visan huntress heard some rumor and decided to come after you."

"Which means there could be others," Amar said. He scowled at Zefar. "Especially if the rumor spreads."

"Oh, don't look at me like *I'm* responsible," Zefar said. "It's not a story I tell often. Saya's the only one I thought would be crazy enough to believe it."

"I'll take that as a compliment," she replied.

"As it was intended." He gave her a wink. "I would certainly never want to disrespect our future most esteemed Masahi."

She shoved her shoulder against his with a grin, and Amar tried not to let himself be unsettled by the fact that she was so friendly with a man who'd once murdered him.

He stared into the dying embers of the fire, trying to fit these new pieces of information into what he already knew. Who was this woman who'd hired Zefar to kill him, and why would she do that? Had she really lost interest in him, or had she simply lost track of him over time? Perhaps she was someone from his past, or perhaps—

He sighed and kicked a little sand onto the coals. He might have been able to come up with clearer answers to those questions had he known more about his past, but there was no point dwelling on it now.

He would only frustrate himself following those thoughts in endless circles. He needed more information. He needed his memories back, but that wasn't going to happen until they reached Atrea, found Jameson, and figured out what to do about this curse. And there was no guarantee Jameson would actually be able to help him.

But he couldn't let himself dwell on that, either. He couldn't afford to lose hope when it was the only thing keeping him going.

ALEIDA

ALEIDA AND VALKYRA KEPT UP A STEADY PACE, FOLLOWING THE Adrati River southwest toward Chatanda and making far better progress on horseback than they had on foot. The closer they got to the town, the more apprehension Aleida felt about seeing her brother. How would he react to her unannounced visit? How would *she* react upon seeing his condition? Would his body's deterioration be worse than she expected after more than a year apart, and if so, would she be able to conceal her emotions? *Should* she? Would Tyrus be truthful with her about the state of his health, and if he was, what was she supposed to do with that information?

On sleepless nights when these questions and others kept her awake, she busied herself with refining the drawings she'd made of Amar and his companions. She would close her eyes and try to recall every feature from their confrontations, sometimes retracing the lines on a new sheet of paper to add more detail or alter the parts her fingers hadn't gotten quite right the first time. She'd have to ask around about them again once she and Valkyra reached Atrea, and she wanted to make her representations of them were easily recognizable.

Two weeks after leaving Valmandi, they finally arrived in Chatanda. Located near Kavora's southwest border, the town itself was surrounded by the fields and farms that were a common sight in this province. Dozens of Visan refugees had migrated here after the invasion, and the settlement seemed to have grown even more since Aleida had last visited. Many of the older buildings had been repaired or renovated, and carefully cultivated gardens grew where there had once been only weeds and rocks.

She found her brother in Hasan's apple orchard, just where she'd known he would be. He sat on a bench under the shade of a large tree, and he was so busy murmuring something to Feros that he didn't see her at first. Aleida smiled as she watched him ruffle the strix's neck feathers with his knuckles. He looked happy. Pale and thin and sunken-eyed—not as healthy as she'd hoped—but happy.

Feros stiffened and turned his head toward Aleida. Tyrus lowered his hand and followed the strix's gaze, shielding his eyes against the sun with his free hand. A hand which trembled, the fingers contorting in an odd sort of way, like he had to fight to keep them under his control. A wide grin broke across his freckled face when he saw her, and he waved.

Once, he would have sprung up and run to her. The last time she'd seen him, he'd still been able to walk with a cane. Now, he didn't even try to stand, and the cane was nowhere in sight. His bony legs didn't look strong enough to support him, most of the muscle having been eaten away by Storm Withering Syndrome—the same disease that would eventually lay waste to the rest of him.

A piece of Aleida's heart shattered, but she tried not to show it as she kicked the horse into a trot and rode to him. Feros gave a disgruntled shriek, flying into the branches above as she approached. She dismounted and threw her arms around her brother's frail shoulders. His bones jutted sharply against her skin, and she gulped back the knot forming in her throat.

Still seated, Tyrus put his own arms around her shoulders and laughed. "Aleida! I can't believe it's really you. I didn't think I'd be seeing you anytime soon." His voice was losing its boyish pitch, instead taking on a deep timbre that reminded Aleida of their father.

She blinked against the sudden burning in her eyes. He'd changed so much in the year she'd been gone. "I've been away too long," she said. "It's good to be home."

"How long are you staying?"

She let him go and stood back with her arms crossed. "Oh, you're that eager to get rid of me, are you?"

"Can you blame me?" Tyrus replied. "You're a giant pain in the ass whenever you're here."

She shoved him in the shoulder, but not half as hard as she would have before he got sick. "I can't stay too long, lucky for you. I'll have to leave tomorrow."

"Ah. Still chasing after that cure, then." He winked, but the quick smile he flashed didn't light up his eyes the way it should have.

"I'm close, Tyrus. I'm so close. And as soon as I get my hands on that cure, I'll come straight back here. I'll make you well, and we'll never have to be apart again."

Tyrus grimaced and shook his head. "Oh, don't say that. I miss you, but not that much."

His jokes eased some of the sting of her guilt, the way they always did. Aleida resisted the urge to ruffle his hair. He'd been too old for that for years now.

"Valkyra," Tyrus said, nodding to the Spirit Tarja perched on the horse's saddle. "It's good to see you again. I hope you're keeping this one out of trouble."

"I do my best," Valkyra replied. "She's quite stubborn, as you know, and not very good at taking directions."

Tyrus laughed. "Oh, I know. She always did like to be in charge."

"Where's Hasan?" Aleida asked, glancing around the orchard. There was no sign of anyone else through the trees.

"Don't be rushing off to bother him already. He's busy, but I'm sure he'll show up for lunch before too long." A teasing grin brought a dimple to Tyrus' cheek. "The two of you will have plenty of time to whisper about me behind my back."

"We wouldn't have to whisper if you'd just be honest about how you're really doing," Aleida retorted.

Tyrus shrugged. "Oh, I can do honesty. My legs don't really work anymore, I'm losing strength and control in my arms and hands, and most days I'm exhausted." He spoke matter-of-factly, his face dispassionate. "That's what Storm Withering Syndrome does to you.

Nothing surprising about it. I'd much rather hear about your adventures. I'm sure they're far more exciting than anything that happens here."

Aleida sighed. She wasn't likely to get any additional specifics out of Tyrus, so she'd have to put her questions and worries aside until Hasan returned. She unbridled the horse and let him wander into the orchard to graze, then sat down on the bench next to her brother. Valkyra flew over to join them, curling herself into a ball in the sun.

Tyrus prompted her with a raised eyebrow, and she recounted the more exciting parts of her journey from the past year. She pulled out her drawings to show him some of the sights she'd seen and the people she'd met, including Amar and his friends, though she didn't tell him the extent to which she had pursued them, or why. Tyrus had a gentle soul, and he wouldn't have approved of her using violence to find a cure for his illness, no matter how dire his situation. Once, Aleida might have agreed with him. But she had grown hard and fierce and cold these last several years. She hoped that in doing so, she'd been able to preserve some part of Tyrus' gentle spirit. A different kind of strength, but no less important.

They talked for hours, until Aleida's stomach started to growl and she looked up to realize that the sun had long since passed its noonday height. "Where is Hasan?" she asked again with a frown. "He doesn't leave you out here all day, I hope."

"He does because I ask him to." Tyrus nodded to a pile of books and papers on the ground beneath the bench. "I'm supposed to be studying and practicing my letters, but most of the time, I just read stories and daydream. It's a lot more interesting than the history and mathematical assignments he gives me."

Aleida chuckled. "He's only trying to put that big brain of yours to good use. Papa always said you could be an academic at one of those fancy Kavoran schools if you wanted to."

Tyrus grimaced at the idea. "That sounds incredibly boring."

"What is it I hear you two laughing about over here?" called a deep, kind voice from behind them.

Aleida turned to see Hasan walking toward them, his barrel chest filling out a long, saffron tunic that fell past his knees. His head was wrapped in a deep blue turban, and a droll mouth smiled from beneath a graying moustache over a bushy beard. He raised a hand to greet them. His numerous rings glinted in the sun and sent specks of light dancing over the dark skin of his cheeks.

Aleida stood and bowed to him in the traditional Kavoran way, but he extended his arm to her instead. They clasped each other by the wrists, the way Aleida might have greeted another Visan. "It's good to see you," he said. "You should have written to let us know you'd be returning. I would have prepared a feast to welcome you."

"That's not necessary," she replied. "I'm only passing through."

Hasan clicked his tongue. "Do you really need to go gallivanting off so soon? Surely you can stay a while. We've missed you."

The implication in his tone was clear, something Hasan had tried to persuade Aleida of many times before. *Your brother needs you. Stay here where you belong.* But Aleida couldn't do that in good conscience. Not when there might still be a way to save Tyrus. She was of far more use to him looking for a cure than she would be sitting by and watching helplessly as his body deteriorated.

"I wish I could," she said. "But I really do need to leave in the morning. Today is all the time I can spare."

Hasan frowned at her for a moment, then glanced down at Tyrus. "We can discuss it later. You two must be hungry. Come up to the house and we'll eat."

Aleida went to retrieve her horse. She slipped the bridle over his head and led him back to the bench. Hasan had bent over Tyrus, who wrapped his arms around the big man's shoulders and allowed himself to be hoisted onto his feet. His knees bent inward at a stiff angle, and his legs began to shake as he shifted his weight onto them.

"Slow down," Hasan said. "Let me hold onto you for a second."

"I'm fine," Tyrus insisted. His voice came out in a shallow huff, like he was trying to catch his breath.

Aleida brought the horse up beside him. "Here, get on."

"You'll have to help me up," he said.

Hasan positioned Tyrus in front of a stirrup. Aleida bent and fit his heel into her cupped palms. She raised him up while Hasan steadied him and helped him swing his other leg over the saddle. Valkyra jumped from the bench onto Aleida's shoulder, and she led the horse to the elegant little house at the edge of the orchard.

A spicy aroma wafted through the open door, already seeming to warm Aleida as she breathed it in. She'd always enjoyed Hasan's cooking. They tied the horse to a fencepost and helped Tyrus dismount. He nearly collapsed when he hit the ground, but he only laughed as Aleida caught him. "Sorry. I'm so clumsy these days."

She forced herself to smile back and positioned herself under his shoulder. He was taller than her now. He had been even the last time she'd seen him, but it still caught her off guard. A part of her still looked at him and expected to see the towheaded, dirty-faced little boy who had tagged along on all her adventures, whether she wanted him there or not.

Hasan came around to Tyrus' other side, and they helped him into the house together. He did his best to match his steps to theirs but stumbled a few times along the way. He was sucking in ragged breaths by the time they sat him down on a chair inside.

"Is there anything I can do for you?" she asked.

He shook his head. "I'll be fine."

Hasan lifted the lid from the pot cooking on a low earthen stove. The smell made Aleida's stomach growl.

"It's almost finished," he said, setting the lid back down. He headed for the door and gestured for Aleida to follow him. "Would you be so kind as to help me gather some herbs from the garden?"

"Of course," she replied.

Tyrus shook his head. "There you go, off to whisper all your secrets about me somewhere I can't follow. That's fine. I'll have you know I'm a very good eavesdropper."

Aleida rolled her eyes dramatically at him before following Hasan to the door. Valkyra stayed behind, perched on the windowsill. "Don't worry, dear," she said to Tyrus. "We can share our own secrets here, once they're gone."

The sound of his laughter followed them outside. They walked around to the back of the house and down a short path to a large garden full of vegetables, herbs, and flowers. The plants were all green and healthy, so vibrant they looked more like a painting than real life. Hasan could make anything grow and would coax even the most lifeless plants back to vitality.

Of course, it helped that he was a Tarja. He'd spent years training in the skills needed to help living things heal. It was part of what made him such a good caretaker for Tyrus. Aleida watched the man fondly as he knelt to examine some flowers. The day Hasan had taken a pair of Visan orphans under his wing had been the best thing that had happened to them since the invasion.

She knelt in the dirt beside him and began to select the herbs that were ready for picking, the same way he'd taught her years ago. "How is he really?" she asked while they worked.

"You saw for yourself. He's not doing as well as he tells you in his letters."

She'd guessed as much. "How bad?"

"His toes and feet have already darkened. It won't be long before the same thing happens to his hands."

Aleida frowned. Poor circulation was one of the hallmarks of Storm Withering Syndrome. The *storm* part of the name came from the grayish-purple tint a person's extremities took on in the later stages of the disease, like storm clouds. It meant Tyrus' heart was already starting to fail.

"He was doing so well," she said. "I thought he'd have more time."

Hasan gave her a grim look. "Honestly, I'm surprised he's survived this long."

"I'm sure that's only because of your care and attention. I can't even begin to express how much it means to me."

He shook his head. "There's no need for that. Tyrus is like a son to me. There's nothing I wouldn't do for him."

"I know, but still, thank you."

Hasan nodded and placed gentle fingers at the base of a plant that was starting to droop. It perked up a little as he channeled altma into its roots, and the leaves brightened to a more vibrant shade of green.

"Aleida," he said quietly, "I'm sorry. I've done all I can, but I don't think he's going to live much longer."

She bit down on her bottom lip to stop the tears welling in her eyes. She didn't want Hasan to see her cry or know how terrified she was.

"This illness is devastating," he went on. "There is no cure. I don't know what you think you're looking for out there, but your brother is only getting weaker."

"I know."

"Do you? His pain worsens every day. Today has been a good day for him. Most days are not so good. His time in this world is coming to an end, and you should be here to see him through that."

"No." Aleida dug her fingers into the soil. "I'm so close, Hasan. You have to trust me. I know of a way to cure him. It's his only chance."

He sighed. "I understand why you want to keep chasing after this. He and I have waited every day, hoping you'd come back with some miracle for him. But we're past that now. You did your best, and he needs you here."

"I can't just sit here and wait for him to die."

"Don't think of it that way. He puts on a brave face, but he's scared. You can help him find courage. You'd be giving him some comfort and helping him pass on to the afterlife with dignity."

"No!" Aleida choked out the word through the knot in her throat. "Don't say that. He's strong. Don't you dare give up on him."

Hasan put a gentle hand on her shoulder. "You know I would never do that."

She pulled away from him, clenching her jaw and rapidly blinking back tears. "How much time does he have?"

"It's impossible to say exactly."

"You must have some idea. A few days, a few months, a year?"

"I don't know."

"I just need a little more time," Aleida said quietly. "He can hold on a little longer. I know he can."

"Maybe. But is it really fair for you to ask that of him?" He fixed her with a sad, piercing stare. "Who are you really doing this for, Aleida? You, or him?"

She wanted to slap him. How dare he ask her that? Of course, she wanted to keep Tyrus alive. She couldn't bear the idea of losing the last of her family. But he wanted to live, too. He was only fourteen years old. He still had so much life ahead of him.

"For him," she hissed. "*Everything* I do is for him."

"Then please, I beg you to reconsider. Stay with him. Do this one last thing for him. It's the best you can give him now."

Aleida returned his gaze with a glare, picked up the herbs she'd gathered, and walked back to the house with all the heat of an erupting volcano burning inside her chest.

That night, after eating a delicious supper and hearing Tyrus recount some of the local gossip, Aleida lay awake on the bed Hasan had made for her on the floor. She stared up at the ceiling, listening to her brother's snores. They'd talked late into the night, until Hasan finally insisted that they settle down and get some sleep. Tyrus had protested the suggestion at first, but when Aleida admitted she was feeling rather tired, he'd fallen asleep in minutes.

She hadn't found sleep so easily. Her mind was a torrent of worries—things she had no control over but still couldn't seem to let go of. She kept hearing Hasan's voice in her head, reminding her of how little time Tyrus had left. A cold sense of dread had been weighing her down all day, and no matter how many times she told herself she wouldn't let her brother die, that fear would not release her.

Giving up on sleep, she pushed herself up to sit with her back against the wall. Valkyra fluttered down from her perch on the windowsill and settled onto her knee. The dragon's white fur gleamed a bright silver in the moonlight. "What's troubling you, child?" she asked in a voice barely louder than a whisper.

"Tyrus," Aleida said. "He's not doing as well as he seems. Hasan thinks the end is near." She almost managed to get the words out smoothly, but her voice cracked a little at the end.

"And what do you think?"

"I don't know. Hasan said I should stay here so I can be with him when—" Her eyes started to burn again, and she took a few breaths before continuing. "I don't know what to do. I don't want to give up on saving him, but I can't stand the idea of him being alone if it really is too late."

"He's still alive, Aleida. There's still hope."

"You don't know that."

Valkyra brushed her silky tail against Aleida's hand. "What I know is that you won't be able to find peace if you give up on him. You vowed to do everything in your power to save him."

"But what if I can't? What if this is all for nothing, and he…dies alone?"

"That would be truly awful," Valkyra said. "But how much worse do you think you would feel living with the knowledge that there might have been a way to save his life, and you didn't pursue it to the end?"

Tears slid from Aleida's eyes and landed on her shirt in little dark spots. She wiped them from her cheeks quickly, but they kept coming. "I don't want this to be the last time I see him."

"It won't be." Valkyra's voice was as sure and as solid as stone. "We'll find the immortal man and his friends, and we'll use his secret to save Tyrus before it's too late. You have to believe that."

She nodded and rubbed a few more tears away with the palm of her hand. She did believe it. The only alternative was accepting that her brother was going to die, and that was something she simply couldn't do. Not yet. Not ever.

If there was even a sliver of a chance to save Tyrus, she had to go after it. Even if that meant leaving him alone in some of the darkest moments of his life.

Valkyra woke Aleida early the next morning, and they made preparations to leave. Now that she'd decided her best course of action, Aleida was anxious to get moving again. They still had a long way to go around the desert, and she didn't want Amar getting too far ahead of them once he and his friends reached the other side.

She was saddling the horse when Hasan came outside. He crossed his arms and watched her with a disapproving scowl but didn't say anything. Like Aleida, he was stubborn, and he must have known it would be pointless to try to talk her into staying now that her mind was made up.

"Did you at least take some food from my larder?" he asked.

She shook her head. "You don't need to worry about that. I'll be fine."

He clicked his tongue. "I refuse to let you leave my house with an empty stomach or an empty pack. Come. We can fill your bags while breakfast is cooking, and then you'll sit and have a proper meal with us before you go."

She followed him back inside the house without protest. Tyrus was up and sitting in a chair by the window, his blond hair still sticking out in wild tufts like he'd just climbed out of bed. "You weren't going to ditch me without saying goodbye, were you?" he asked.

"Of course not. I'm only getting ready." She smiled and ruffled his hair the same way she used to when he was younger. He swatted her hand away.

Hasan set about making breakfast and began to pull food from his larder. There were round juicy apples and dried apple slices, hard cheeses and breads he'd baked himself, salted pork and fish caught fresh from the river. It was enough food to last Aleida several weeks. He divided them into piles for her and wrapped them up in paper and cloth, giving her instructions about what needed to be eaten soonest before it went bad and what could wait a while. By the time they had packed everything away, her pack and the horse's saddlebags were full to bursting.

They ate a hearty breakfast of buckwheat pancakes and honey-sweetened apples. Aleida tried not to focus her attention too much on the way Tyrus' hands trembled as he raised bites of food to his mouth. He ate everything he was given and even took seconds, so at least his appetite hadn't failed him yet.

She eyed his bony legs and the collarbones jutting above the neck of his shirt. How could he be so thin if he was really eating enough? Was he only trying to keep up appearances now for her sake, or was the disease simply stripping his body of all useful nutrients?

They sat around the table and talked for a while after breakfast, until the itch to continue her journey became overwhelming and Aleida stood up to leave. "I should get going."

"Already?" Tyrus slid himself forward in his chair and motioned for Hasan to help him up.

"You don't need to get up." She took a step toward him but stopped as Hasan came around to his side.

The Tarja put one of his own burly shoulders beneath Tyrus' and raised him to his feet. "It's time for him to begin his studies for the day anyway. And fresh air is almost as good as any healing magic."

"I sincerely doubt that," Tyrus said, "but I enjoy it anyway."

They all walked out into the sun together, and Aleida turned to her brother. "Take care of yourself, all right?"

"Isn't that what Hasan's here for?"

"Well then don't give him a hard time," she said, nudging Tyrus in the ribs. "Do what he says, and try to keep up your strength until I get back."

"I'll take good care of him," Hasan said.

"I know you will." She ignored the tightness in her chest and put her arms around Tyrus' shoulders. "I'm sorry. I wish I could stay longer."

He raised his free arm to wrap around her back. "I know."

"I'll return as soon as I can, I promise. I'll make you well again, and everything will go back to normal. You just have to be strong a little longer, all right? You have to keep fighting. You can do that for me, can't you?"

"I promise," he said.

She held him tighter, unwilling to let go. What if this was the last time she got to hug him like this? "I'm so proud of you."

"I'm proud of you, too," he mumbled. "But you're squeezing me to death."

She forced herself to pull away and turned to Hasan. "Thank you for everything." There weren't enough words to express the depth of her gratitude, but someday, she hoped she'd find a way to show him how much she appreciated all he'd done for her and Tyrus. "May Artex bless your life with his most wondrous creations."

"Go in harmony, Aleida," he responded, dipping his head to her. "I hope you find what you're looking for."

With an old, familiar weight on her shoulders, Aleida turned, mounted her horse, and steered him toward the road that would lead her south to Atrea. She didn't permit herself to look back.

KESARI

SAYA ROUSED KESARI AND THE OTHERS EARLY THE NEXT MORNING. She had already refilled their water stores and went to load everything onto Berna's back while the others readied themselves to leave Hayathu. When they exited their tent, she was saying goodbye to each of her brothers. Some of the younger ones clung to her, whining what Kesari could only assume were pleas for her to stay. Two of the older ones managed to pry the twins away long enough for Saya to walk to where her mother stood, watching the lively, noisy interactions between her children with serene repose.

Saya looked tense as she approached the Masahi, but she'd barely gotten a few words out when her mother threw her arms around her shoulders and pulled her close. Saya's eyes widened in surprise for a moment, then she put her own arms around the woman. When they parted, the Masahi brushed a few strands of Saya's hair behind her ear, her eyes shining with tears. They exchanged some final words before Saya turned and nodded resolutely to Kesari and the others. It was time to leave.

The boys lined up to give her a final embrace, and Kesari's heart thrummed with a melancholy pang as she watched them. There was so much love evident between them, an entire lifetime of memories and laughter, fights and reconciliations, shared experiences and shared blood.

A family that was whole—something Kesari had once had.

They walked away, leaving Hayathu behind to finish their long trek south across the desert. Saya never turned back, but Kesari did, and even when they had gone a fair distance, she could still see six figures standing in the sand, watching their sister grow smaller and smaller against the horizon.

"Is everything all right?" Lucian asked as she turned back to face the landscape ahead.

Kesari nodded and attempted to force a smile onto her face.

"Then why do you look so sad?"

"It's nothing."

Lucian drifted a little closer to her ear and spoke softly. "Your family is waiting for you, too, you know."

"My family is better off without me."

She had repeated the words to herself so many times they barely sounded real anymore. The conviction behind them, however, was still very real. She had broken her family. They would never be whole again, and no matter how much she missed them or how many times Lucian reminded her they must be waiting for her, she could not allow herself to go back.

It took them another three weeks to reach Atrea, by which time Kesari had developed a painful sunburn despite her best efforts to prevent it. The landscape had slowly begun to change during their last two days of travel, until they found themselves in the grassy plains and milder weather that characterized much of western Atrea.

Saya found the road again, and they changed out of their desert clothing into more comfortable attire. Kesari took to wearing Rajiv's worn blue coat again, reveling in its comforting weight against her shoulders. A few short days later, they reached the town of Malfram, where Jameson Weatherford reportedly lived.

At the first signs that they were nearing civilization, Lucian retreated back into his lantern. Tarja were uncommon enough in Atrea, let alone Bonded Tarja and Spirit Tarja pairs. Before leaving home, Kesari wouldn't have minded the extra attention their uniqueness drew, but now, she was grateful for Lucian's discretion.

The town had been built at the edge of a lake fed by Atrea's largest river. Most of the buildings were made of wood and brick, and the roads were hardpacked earth. The people here had pale complexions and dressed in typical Atrean fashion, with women in long, flowing dresses and bonnet hats while the men donned high-collared shirts, tailcoats, and trousers. Several of them stared at the foreign newcomers with quizzical looks as they passed. Other parts of Atrea were more diverse, including Kesari's hometown of Deveaural, but Malfram generally didn't see too many travelers or foreigners.

They found a small inn at the edge of town, and the innkeeper was willing to trade them a hot meal, two rooms, and some coin for Berna, who would no longer be needed now that their travels through the desert had ended. Saya kissed the donkey on the nose and patted her cheek before handing the reins over to the innkeeper.

"Ask him about Jameson," Mitul said to Kesari. She was the only one of them who spoke Atrean and had now become a translator for the others.

She turned to the innkeeper. "We're looking for a Tarja, Jameson Weatherford. We were told he lives here in Malfram somewhere. Have you heard of him?"

The man's eyes immediately brightened. "Oh, yes! The Great and Honorable Wizard Jameson. He's very famous around here. Or rather, he's our town's claim to fame. He was born and raised right next door to my grandmother, you know. She used to take care of him sometimes when he was a boy. The stories she could tell you about all the mischief he got up to." He chuckled a little and shook his head.

"What's he saying?" Amar asked impatiently.

Kesari ignored him and continued her conversation with the innkeeper. "Do you know where he lives now?"

"Sure. The king sent for him himself, asked him to come to Deveaural and serve the crown. He's been there for over a year now."

"Oh." Kesari's last hopes shattered like glass. They'd come all this way, through the forests of Kavora and the scorching Sularan desert, only to learn that the man they were seeking lived in the one place in Atrea she couldn't go.

"What did he say?" Amar asked, more insistently this time.

"He's not here," she answered numbly. "He moved to Deveaural."

Amar's expression shifted to match her own disappointment. Kesari turned back to the innkeeper, thanked him again for the room and the hot meal, and followed the others out of the stables.

"I'm sorry," Mitul said, putting a hand on Amar's shoulder. "It's frustrating, but Deveaural's not much farther. Right, Kesari?"

"No. Probably a week's journey, and the road is easy."

"See?" Mitul said brightly. "We're almost there, and we've got a good guide. We'll have our answers soon enough."

Kesari dug her toe into the dirt. "Actually, I don't think I'll be going the rest of the way with you."

"What?" Amar snapped. "Why not?"

"I can't." She wished Lucian would back her up, but he remained silent in his lantern, black eyes peering up at her through the glass.

"I thought you were from Deveaural. Don't you know the way?"

"Yes, but…I don't want to go back there."

"Kes," Mitul said gently, "I don't know why you left home, but whatever the reason, we can help you face it. You've done so much for us already, and we'll do whatever we can for you. We need you. Won't you take us the rest of the way?"

Kesari's heart began to gallop as a wave of dizziness spread from inside her skull and through the rest of her body. Her mouth felt thick, her breaths constricted by a sudden tightness in her throat. She could smell smoke. It filled up her lungs, the heat from a fire pressing against her skin.

"I'm not—" She backed away from the others. "You'll be fine without me. I'm sorry." She turned, headed for the inn, and was inside and up the stairs before she even fully registered what she was doing. Once inside her and Saya's room, she slammed the door behind her.

Still fighting off waves of breathless panic, she sank to the floor. Lucian floated out of his lantern as a tiny spark and hovered in front of her face. He expanded to his usual size, constricted back down, and expanded again. "Breathe, Kesari," he said softly. "Just breathe."

She did, timing her inhales with his expansions and her exhales with his constrictions. Safe. She was safe. There was nothing here that could hurt her. The fire, the smoke, the screams—it was only a memory.

Something that had happened a long time ago. Her fault, but there was nothing to be done about that now.

Breathe in. Breathe out.

It took several repetitions of this before she felt like she'd regained some control, the panic ebbing away until it was a whisper in her mind rather than a deafening scream.

"Do you want to talk about it?" Lucian asked.

She did, and she didn't. She knew talking about it would help, but she could already guess what Lucian would tell her. Maybe she needed to hear it, but she didn't want to.

She gave a resigned sigh. "Being this close to home already felt wrong. But going to Deveaural—how am I supposed to do that?"

"How are you supposed to keep running from it for the rest of your life?" Lucian countered gently.

"I'm not running. I'm just not ready yet."

He drifted a little closer to her. "I think you *are* ready, and I think you know that. You're scared, but it's normal to be scared, Kes. Fear doesn't mean you *can't* do something, it only makes it a little harder."

He didn't understand. She shook her head and pulled Rajiv's coat tighter around herself. "I know what you want me to do. You think if I go back there and face what I did, then maybe I won't want to break our Bond anymore, and everything will go back to the way it was supposed to be." Her words came out in a heated, hateful rush, scalding her throat. But she didn't care. "That's what you want, isn't it? That's all you care about."

Lucian was silent for a few seconds, his dark eyes solemn as he stared at her. Kesari stared back, warring internally with herself. She shouldn't have been so harsh with him, but she was so angry. At him, but mostly at herself.

"Even I'm not foolish enough to believe it could ever be so simple," Lucian said at last. "All I want is for you to be happy."

"I am happy," she snarled.

"Are you?"

She didn't answer him. Of course she wasn't happy, not truly. She hadn't been for a long time. How was anyone supposed to be happy after what she'd done, what she'd lost?

"What was it you told Tamaya you wanted from breaking our Bond?"

It took her a few moments to remember. "Peace," she murmured.

"Peace," he echoed. "Maybe that will come from breaking our Bond, and maybe it will come from facing your fears and your family. But either way, you'll have to go to Deveaural to find that peace."

"I don't *have* to do anything."

"You don't, but what's the alternative?"

She sighed. He was probably right, as usual. Avoiding her past these last two years had brought her only superficial comfort. She needed more than that, which meant she needed to put the past to rest for good. The only way to do that was to break her Bond with Lucian.

Her heart wrenched sharply. Breaking the Bond could mean that Lucian would die—for good this time—and she still wasn't sure she could handle being responsible for that, even if he was technically dead already. But she at least wanted to know what her options were, and for that, she needed Jameson.

Maybe going to Deveaural wouldn't be so bad. She didn't *have* to visit her family, after all. She could avoid her old neighborhood and the places her parents and sister frequented. Deveaural was a big city, with plenty of room for her to blend in and avoid being seen if she wished. It would be fine.

"All right," she said resolutely. "We'll go with them."

The others were pleased when Kesari told them over dinner that she'd decided to accompany them after all. Amar asked what had made her change her mind, but he left the issue alone when Lucian shot him a look through his lantern. Neither Saya nor Mitul questioned her about it further, much to Kesari's relief.

They left Malfram the next morning. The east-west road that led to Deveaural was wide and well-kept, and they encountered a few other travelers along the way. Lucian spent most of his time in the lantern, though Kesari still spoke to him when there was no one else around. She was more talkative with the others as well, trying to distract herself from the growing disquiet building up within her the closer they got to home. If she thought about it too much, her pulse raced and her breaths became shallow, but Lucian was always there to calm her. A few times, she was half tempted to turn around, but she forced her feet to keep moving, one step at a time.

The journey passed without incident, and after a week, Deveaural came into view over the rise of a hill. A wide expanse of buildings stretched across the horizon with the blue sea gleaming behind them. Many had been built of white stone from a nearby quarry, giving the city a shining glow in the high noon sun. Other structures were made of wood, cut from the forest that pressed against Deveaural's edges right up to the beach. A patchwork of fields extended around the outskirts of the city, melding into the fringes of the forest.

A slow smile stretched across Kesari's lips as she took in the view. Some of her dread about returning melted away as a newfound sense of warmth wrapped her like an embrace. Despite everything, this was still her home, and the familiar sights were a comfort she hadn't expected.

They followed the sloping road down into the trees below, eventually emerging into the farmland they'd seen from the hilltop. The others let Kesari take the lead, and it didn't take her long to find the familiar trails she'd walked with Mum, Dad, Rajiv, and Navya as a child. She took a meandering path, steering them far away from her own childhood home and other familiar places—the Hempstock's farm where Mum traded vegetables for milk, old man Barker's where Dad often had his tools repaired, the onion fields Rajiv had tended to the summer before he joined the Atrean Navy.

A group of girls who looked to be about Navya's age headed their way, and her heart started to pound. She made a quick turn onto a different path. The last thing she needed now was to run into her family, or anyone else she knew, for that matter. What would she say to them? Just imagining it made her hands feel clammy.

"Where are we going?" Amar grumbled behind her. "I swear you're leading us in circles."

"It's a shortcut," she replied.

He snorted. "That's a lie if I ever heard one."

"Shh," Lucian hissed from the lantern.

After a few more quick detours, they left the farmlands and reached the city itself. Buildings packed tightly together rose up before them in neat rows. Little square houses with steeply pitched roofs and tall chimneystacks lined the busy cobblestone streets, and shops displayed a variety of colorful products in polished glass windows. Carriages rolled by in droves as pedestrians hurried about their business. Some were dressed in modest attire similar to what they'd seen in Malfram, but many wore elaborate suits and gowns, accented with decorative hats, jewelry, spectacles, purses, and even a few colorful pet dragons.

There were several Kavorans among them, along with a few Visans, Sularans, and other foreigners, distinguishable only by their unfamiliar clothing and speech that was as varied as their appearances. Many travelled here to trade from across the sea, and Kesari couldn't even name all the places they were from.

She smiled again. Skies above, she'd missed this—the rush, the noise, the organized chaos of it all. Everyone was always going somewhere important, and the very air was alive with more sounds and smells than a person could ever hope to remember in a single moment. Her family lived on a quiet plot of farmland, and she'd always begged Rajiv to take her into town on the days they finished their chores early. Many of her best memories had been made right here.

Her worst memories, too.

A bitter pang twisted in her gut, but she forced the smile to stay in place as she turned back to look at her companions. "Welcome to Deveaural."

Mitul's eyes were wide and bright as he turned his head this way and that, seemingly trying to take in everything at once. Amar looked around more casually, an air of indifference in his loose posture. Saya, however, seemed agitated. She held her body as tense as ever, but her eyes darted at every new sound, making her look something like a wild, wary animal.

"Is it always this noisy?" she asked Kesari.

"It quiets down a bit in the evening," she replied. "You'll get used to it."

"Somehow, I doubt that."

Unsure of where to go now that they were in the city, Kesari caught the eye of an approaching girl and stepped toward her. "Excuse me, but we're looking for a Tarja named Jameson Weatherford. Have you heard of him?"

"Sure," said the girl. "Who hasn't?"

"Do you happen to know where he lives?"

"He's in the tower." She turned back and pointed west, toward the coast and the royal palace. For a moment, Kesari feared the girl was talking about one of the towers in the palace itself, but then she noticed a darker, conical spire rising over the roofs of the surrounding buildings.

"Thanks," she said, gesturing for the others to follow her.

"Be careful," the girl called after them. "The Wizard Jameson doesn't take too kindly to strangers turning up at random. He threatened to turn my friend Sarah into a toad once."

It wasn't possible to use magic to turn one thing into another, but Kesari didn't bother telling her that. Instead, she simply ignored the girl's warning and set off down the street.

Mitul fell into stride beside her. "What did she say?"

"Just that this Jameson might not be the friendly type." She hadn't let such a minor inconvenience stop her from pestering Tamaya or any other Tarja she'd gone to for information, and she wasn't about to let it stop her now.

"I don't care how unfriendly he is," Amar said, "as long as he can give me some answers."

The wet, salty smell of the ocean grew stronger as they continued into the city and got closer to the coast. Passing under the shade of a particularly large building, Saya stopped and craned her neck to look up.

"Is this the tower we're looking for?"

Kesari hadn't taken her eyes off the dark spire the girl had pointed out, and it still lay at least a few blocks ahead. She stopped to examine what had caught Saya's attention.

It took her a few seconds to recognize what it was—*where* it was. The city square. She'd meant to avoid it, but she'd been so focused on trying to reach the tower that she hadn't been paying attention to their surroundings. Her stomach leaped into her throat.

In the very center of Deveaural, a magnificent bell tower rose a few stories higher than the surrounding shops and houses. Three enormous bronze bells hung inside the open belfry, gleaming so brightly that Kesari had to shield her eyes against their glare.

"They rebuilt it," she said quietly, half to herself and half to Lucian inside the lantern at her waist.

"Rebuilt what?" Mitul asked. "The bell tower?"

"Why did it need to be rebuilt?" Saya asked.

Kesari's mouth went dry, and the skin on her arms prickled. She glanced nervously down at Lucian, and he floated up out of the lantern to hover in front of the others. A few people around them stared at his sudden appearance, but Kesari didn't care anymore. Her feet were rooted to the ground, the weight of Rajiv's coat pressing down on her as a dozen explanations rose to her mouth and stuck in her throat.

Lucian floated to an alley a few paces away. "Here," he called to the others. "We can get to Jameson's tower this way."

Mitul and Amar trailed after him without hesitation. Kesari forced herself to move, her lungs still tight and breathless. Saya continued to stare up at the bell tower.

"Are you coming?" Kesari called. Her voice came out with a shaking, reedy pitch.

"Coming," the older girl replied.

A few minutes later, they found themselves in front of what could only be Jameson Weatherford's residence. The tower stood alone in an empty courtyard, away from any other shops or houses at the farthest edge of a dead-end road. Thick rosebushes with blooms the color of dawn grew all around its base except for a gap where the door was. Flowering vines crept up the curving stone walls to the dark, steeply slanted roof, where puffs of pale gray smoke billowed from a narrow chimney.

Lucian and Kesari were the first to approach the door, where they found a handwritten message pinned to the wood. Kesari hadn't ever learned to read very well and could only understand a few of the shorter words, but Lucian read and translated it aloud for everyone.

"'Estate of the Great and Honorable Wizard Jameson Weatherford. No admittance after noon except by prior appointment. All violators subject to expulsion by magical force.'" He turned to them with a sly grin. "Well, that's not very friendly, is it?"

"What's a *wizard*, anyway?" Mitul asked, speaking the foreign word slowly and deliberately.

"Atreans have all sorts of strange names for Tarja," Lucian replied. "Sorcerer, wizard, witch, enchanter. Some will say each of those means a different thing, but that's rubbish. Most people here don't actually know what they're talking about when it comes to magic."

"Fancy title," Saya said with a snort.

Amar strode forward. "He can call himself whatever he likes, as long as he lives up to his reputation." He raised a fist and rapped his knuckles against the door.

The ink scrawled across the paper began to glow, and a disembodied voice read the last two lines aloud in Atrean. "No admittance after noon except by prior appointment. All violators subject to expulsion by magical force."

"What was that?" Saya asked.

"A warning," Lucian replied.

Kesari shifted back and forth on her heels. "Maybe we should come back tomorrow."

Amar shook his head, brows drawn together in a look of grim resolution. "We came all this way. I'm not waiting any longer."

He rapped on the door again but hadn't even finished when some invisible force knocked him off his feet and sent him flying backwards through the air with his arms and legs splayed out in front of him. He landed with a groan on the cobblestones, eyes wide and jaw slack.

Lucian let out a low, cackling laugh as he floated over to Amar. "That was incredible. You should see your face!"

Amar glowered at Lucian, stood up, and brushed the dirt off his backside. He walked to the edge of the road and picked up a rock half the size of his palm. Kesari backed away from the tower as he took aim.

The rock hit dead-center, then went ricocheting straight back at Amar. He barely had time to duck to avoid being struck in the chest.

Lucian laughed again. Amar scowled, the anger in his eyes burning more fiercely than ever.

Kesari looked up. There was a face poking out of a window overhead, peering down at them from several stories above. "Look!"

she called to the others, but by the time they did, the face was gone. "He was up there. I saw him."

Lucian floated up the side of the tower to the window. "Hello?" he called out. "Hello, your Great and Honorable Wizard-ness? Do you mind coming out for a chat?" He tried to float forward through the window, but some invisible barrier seemed to be blocking him. "I don't see anyone," he called down to the others.

"This is ridiculous," Amar said. He picked up another rock and sent it sailing into the air. It missed the window and clattered harmlessly off the stone walls of the tower.

He picked up another and was about to try again when a man's voice called out from behind the door. "Stop that at once!"

Amar lowered his arm and approached the door again. "We need to talk to you. Let us in." After a moment's hesitation, he added, "Please."

"Didn't you hear the message?" the man snapped back. He spoke Kavoran with perfect fluency, though his Atrean accent was thick. "It's well after noon. Come back tomorrow, or preferably not at all if you're going to keep acting like a bunch of barbarians."

Amar's face contorted with intensified frustration, and Kesari hurried to chime in before he could say something that would aggravate the wizard further. "We're sorry. We didn't mean to disturb you, but it's very important that we speak to you. Please, we won't take much of your time."

For a few moments, their only answer was silence. Then the door opened with a creak to reveal a tall, thin man in disheveled blue robes. His skin was pale even for an Atrean, as if he didn't see the sun as frequently as he should have. Thick, black hair framed a handsome face that was younger than Kesari had expected it to be. His green eyes were piercing beneath dark brows as he surveyed the strangers before him.

"Well, you're persistent, I'll give you that," he said at last. His gaze settled on Kesari and Lucian. "And you have a Spirit Tarja in the form of fire. I can't say I've ever seen that before. Curious. But I really am very busy today. You'll have to come back another time."

"We have something else, too," Mitul said quickly.

Jameson shook his head. "Whatever it is, I'm sure it's of no interest to me. Not right now. Good day."

He turned to leave. Desperate to stop him, Kesari called out, "Tamaya Takhar sent us."

Jameson stopped and glanced back over his shoulder at them.

"It's about him," Kesari went on, pointing to Amar. She could bring up her own concerns later. Right now, they needed to get the wizard's attention.

"What about him?" Jameson asked, raising a single eyebrow.

Amar stepped forward, facing the man with his shoulders squared. "Apparently," he said, "I've been cursed."

AMAR

AMAR WATCHED JAMESON'S FACE SHIFT FROM ANNOYANCE TO DOUBT to curiosity until finally, he pushed the door open and stepped out into the sunlight. His emerald-green eyes bored into Amar, searching for answers, or maybe searching for a lie. Amar stared back, unwavering.

"I suppose you'd all better come inside," Jameson said at last. He pushed the door open and held it for them as they filed in one by one.

The tower was much larger than it had appeared from the outside, but it seemed Jameson wasn't much of a housekeeper. A large, square table stood in the center of the room, almost entirely hidden beneath scattered rolls of parchment and haphazardly stacked books. Wooden crates of bottles and pouches too numerous to count sat underneath the table. A battered suit of ancient armor stood lopsided against the wall, its arms and shoulders draped with discarded robes and scarves.

Wooden stairs ran along the curved walls of the tower in a spiral, circling up to the levels above. Cobwebs clung to the corners, and particles of dust shimmered in the light. The entire place had a wet, earthy smell, like rain falling on dry ground. Mismatched chairs were scattered around the hearth without any kind of order or arrangement, and it was toward these that Jameson directed them after locking the front door.

He gestured for them to sit. He took the largest chair for himself, a plush, velvety thing that was starting to wear at the corners. Amar chose a simple wooden stool and pulled it a little closer to the fire as the others circled around in their own chosen seats. Lucian hovered faithfully over Kesari's shoulder, adding his orange glow to the flickering light of the flames in Jameson's hearth.

"Now then," the Tarja said, nodding to Amar as he settled back into his chair. "You mentioned a curse? Please explain."

Amar exchanged a glance with Mitul, who launched into the story of their first meeting. Jameson listened intently, his fingers steepled in front of his mouth as he leaned forward. Only once in a while did he interrupt to ask a question. Amar and Mitul answered each one as best as they could, and occasionally Saya, Lucian, or Kesari would chime in with their own thoughts and observations. It was all a little overwhelming, and Amar began to feel like a specimen being poked and prodded for some kind of scientific experiment.

"And Tamaya suggested that I could help you, did she?" Jameson asked when they'd reached that part of the story. "Do you know why?"

"She seemed to think you might know about curses," Mitul said. "More specifically, how they work, and how to break one."

A smirk curled Jameson's lips. "So she's finally realized all my studying is useful after all."

Amar frowned. What was it Tamaya had said about her former pupil? That he was always more concerned with magical theory than its practical applications. It now occurred to him that, even if Jameson could provide them some answers, he might not actually be able to *do* anything about the curse.

He shook away the first seedlings of frustration before they could take root. He could deal with that problem if and when it arose.

"Do you think you can help?" Mitul asked.

"That depends," Jameson replied, fixing his intense gaze on Amar once more. "What exactly is it you want help with?"

"I want to know what's going on," Amar said. "I don't even know who I am, or what caused this. I want my memories back. I want answers, and if there's some way to break this curse, I want that, too."

"Well, that sounds simple enough," Jameson said. It was impossible to tell whether he was being serious or sarcastic. He turned to Kesari and Lucian. "And what about you two?"

The girl blinked, her gaze shifting away from the fire she'd been absently staring into. "What about us?"

"I didn't hear you mentioned in your friends' story until right at the end, so you haven't known them as long as they've all known each other. Judging by your accent, you're Atrean, not Kavoran, and yet somehow you ended up there and led a group of strangers back here. I'm curious as to why."

Fidgeting with the hems of her coat sleeves, Kesari glanced at Lucian. "We wanted to—that is, *I* wanted to come and see you. Tamaya said you might know of a way to…" She took a breath, as if working up the courage to speak her request. "To break our Bond."

Jameson's brows furrowed, and Mitul exchanged a surprised look with Saya. After his conversations with Lucian, Amar had suspected this was coming, but he could still hardly imagine Kesari and Lucian being separated. What would that mean for the Spirit Tarja?

"I know it sounds ridiculous," Kesari said, "and you probably think I'm a fool, but—"

Jameson held up a hand. "I'm not here to judge. I'm curious, I admit, but your reasons are your own. You should know that breaking a Bond is no simple matter. There are tremendous risks involved—*life-threatening* risks."

"I know," Kesari said.

"You gave up half your life to make this Bond. Even if you do manage to break it and survive the ordeal, you likely won't get those years back."

"I thought as much."

"Lucian could fade away. Forever."

Amar looked at Lucian, but his expression was unreadable. The stakes were so high for him, and yet, he'd been entirely supportive of Kesari all the way here. Amar didn't understand it. What was it about their Bond that was so awful Kesari couldn't bear it any longer?

The girl simply stared down at her hands in her lap, saying nothing.

Jameson shifted his gaze to Lucian. "And you're all right with this?"

"It's her life," he replied evenly. "The decision is hers to make."

Jameson nodded. "Well, I suppose it's not impossible. In theory, I understand how it *might* work, though I fear it could leave both of you permanently damaged. Or worse."

"But you can do it?" Kesari asked, her voice high and shaky.

"I think I *can*, but I'm not sure I *should*." He ran a hand over his face. "I need to do some research. In a few days, I'll have more information. For all of you."

"Does that mean you know how to break this curse?" Amar asked hopefully.

"Not yet," Jameson said. "But I might be able to figure it out. It will be difficult, of course. No one really knows anymore how curses were created, let alone how to break one. But if we can get your memories back, we might be able to figure out when you were cursed, and why. That would be a start."

His gaze grew distant, and his words became mumbled as if he were talking more to himself than to the rest of them. "There are some old books on lost forms of magic I'll need to look through in the palace library, and then there's the memory retrieval. Of course, going so far back could get tricky." His eyes flitted to Kesari and Lucian. "Might be helpful to have some assistance, but if the Bond is broken…no, that won't work. Maybe we could do that after."

The Tarja was completely lost in his own thoughts now, and there was no point in sticking around to listen to his musings. Amar stood up and motioned to the others. "I guess we'll be going, then."

Jameson blinked. "Going? Nonsense! You'll stay here. I have more than enough room for guests upstairs, and this way you'll be readily available for any questions I might have or any tests we need to conduct."

Amar raised his eyebrows. "Tests?"

Jameson nodded enthusiastically. "Think of it as an experiment. Breaking a Bond is complicated enough, but that's going to be child's play compared to figuring out this curse. We'll have to prepare, make sure you're physically and mentally strong enough to handle this. I'd feel a lot better if I could keep an eye on you myself, the same as I would any of my other test subjects."

"Test subjects?" Amar was starting to feel more uneasy the longer Jameson talked. Did the man even see him as a person, or just something to be examined and studied?

"It's exciting, isn't it?" Jameson said, standing up so quickly his robes swirled around him in a dramatic flourish. "It will be the cutting edge of science and magic, bringing the two together to unravel ancient mysteries that have been lost from the world for centuries." He headed for the door, grabbing a canvas bag from the table as he passed and then stuffing his stocking-clad feet into a pair of boots near the threshold.

"Where are you going?" Mitul asked.

"To the library, of course," Jameson said, as if this were completely obvious. "Feel free to settle in upstairs. You can take any room you please. Except for the one with the green door at the top—that's mine. I'll be home before supper, and I'll change the door barrier to let you back inside if you decide to go out. Make yourselves comfortable."

He was off before any of them could respond. Amar turned and saw his bewilderment reflected in his companions' faces as they stared at the door through which Jameson had disappeared.

"What an absolutely peculiar man," Saya said, shaking her head.

Amar was inclined to agree, but Lucian only grinned. "I thought he was absolutely delightful."

KESARI

WITH JAMESON GONE, THE CONVERSATION QUICKLY TURNED TO their lodging situation, and Kesari deftly danced around the others' questions about whether she was planning to stay with family or anyone else she knew in the city. Lucian shot her a pointed look, and she shifted everyone's attention back to the wizard's offer to host them. So it was that a few minutes later, she found herself leading the others upstairs to explore the rest of the tower.

The entirety of the second level was even more disorganized than the first. It had been turned into some kind of laboratory or study, but it was difficult to see how Jameson could get any work done amidst all the clutter. They quickly moved on to the third floor, where they found three empty rooms and another winding staircase that led up to the top level.

Dust and cobwebs covered every surface, but Kesari made quick work of them with a broom she found between two bookshelves. Amar and Mitul opted to share the largest room and let Saya and Kesari take the other two. There were no beds, but they found and divided up a large stack of blankets. The bed Kesari was able to make from these was far more comfortable than what she'd become used to camping on the road. She changed into a fresh set of clothes and set her pack beside her makeshift pillow.

"You know you have a real bed waiting for you at home," Lucian said.

Kesari brushed a few tangles from her hair with her fingers and shook the dust from Rajiv's coat as best as she could. It was in dire need of a wash, and there were a few new holes she wanted to mend, but she could worry about that later. For now, she slipped it back on over her clothes, covering up the scars on her arms.

"Did you hear me, Kes?" Lucian prodded.

"Yes."

He sighed. "But you're not going home, are you?"

She slipped her boots back on. "No."

"Where *are* you going, then?"

"It's awfully kind of Jameson to let us stay here, don't you think? I figured I'd get some things from the market and make supper to thank him for helping us. We could surprise him when he gets back."

"That's a very nice idea."

She told the others, and they discussed what they wanted to cook and divided up the various tasks involved. As Kesari was the only one who really knew her way around Deveaural, it was agreed that she would do the shopping.

"I'll come with you," Saya offered. "You might need an extra pair of hands."

"That's all right," Kesari said quickly. "I can manage on my own. I'll be back before you know it."

She bounded down the stairs two at a time, letting her boots clatter against the wooden boards. If the others were still trying to talk to her, she couldn't have heard them, and that was for the best. Being back in this city had set her on edge, like there was something inside her screaming and rattling the bars of a cage. She was barely keeping it in, and she didn't want anyone else around if it escaped. She needed to be alone, Lucian's company excluded, of course.

The Spirit Tarja retreated back into his lantern as they exited onto the street. Kesari set out for the dockside market, but along the way, she couldn't resist the temptation to wander by some of her old haunts around the city. She pulled the oversized lapels of her coat up in an attempt to at least partially conceal her face. Her first stop was Bedford's Bakery, where she bought a fried scone with fresh honey, just like she, Rajiv, and Navya used to do when they were younger. Mr. Bedford gave her a look of vague recognition as he handed over her scone, and Kesari ducked her head while passing him her coins. She didn't wait for him to return her change before she darted back outside.

They kept going. As she walked, Kesari bit into the warm, sweet pastry with a satisfying crunch. A dribble of honey slipped down her chin. "Mmmm, even better than I remember." She wiped the corners of her mouth with the back of her coat sleeve. "These were Rajiv's favorite."

"I remember." Lucian said from his lantern. He was always telling me they were the finest delicacy in all of Atrea, better than anything even the king might be served in his palace."

Kesari smiled. "He used to tease you about not being able to taste them for yourself."

"He did," Lucian muttered grumpily. "Scoundrel."

She polished off the rest of the scone and licked the last sticky spots of honey from her fingertips. Her path took them past the palace with its elegant masonry and tall, spired towers, and Kesari slowed. Several bards competed for listeners' attention and coin outside the gates, and for a second, she could almost see Navya's skirts twirling around her legs as she danced to their music. They didn't like when people stayed too long to listen without tossing some token of appreciation their way, but none of them had ever been able to resist little Navya's wide-eyed innocence and childish charm. Her high, girlish laugh seemed to echo in Kesari's ears even now.

She pushed the memories aside along with the ache in her chest. Being here without her siblings made it all feel wrong somehow, off-balance. Before she moved on, she made a mental note to tell Mitul about this place when she got back to the tower. He might enjoy playing here sometime during their stay in Deveaural.

The buildings began to thin out a little the closer they got to the coast, and the sounds of music, carriages, and chattering people were replaced by seagulls' cries and the gentle rush of ocean waves breaking against the shore. They reached the docks, where ships of all types were being loaded and unloaded in preparation for their next voyage. She tried to identify each one the way Rajiv had shown her. There were agile schooners built with shallow drafts so they could navigate treacherous shoals, sturdy brigs often used as merchant vessels, frigates that were as fast as they were armed and deadly, and even a few hulking galleons anchored farther out to sea. A number of small fishing boats floated between the larger vessels.

Kesari stuck her hands deep into her pockets, closed her eyes, and inhaled the salty air. Of all the places in Deveaural she loved, the docks had always been her favorite. Rajiv's too. She could almost hear his voice on the wind, as clear as it had been the day their dad brought them here to see an enormous sea dragon some Atrean naval ship had captured.

See that ship, Kes? Someday, I'm going to sail on a ship like that. You can come with me when you're old enough. We'll explore the whole world together.

Her eyes burned. She snapped them back open and kept walking. The market was already in sight.

In addition to the typical residents going about their business, this area was also populated by a few hundred seafaring individuals—captains, sailors, fishermen, deckhands, and more than a few unsavory-looking types who may or may not have been pirates. There were even a few people in long seafarer's coats very much like the one Kesari wore, and she held her head a little higher at the idea that she almost looked like she belonged here, like she was one of them.

Almost. It was Rajiv's coat, and *he* was the one who had belonged here, once upon a time. Kesari was only pretending, clinging to scraps of cloth and memory as if that would somehow bring her brother back to life.

She slipped into the bustling market crowd. An assortment of smells and sounds bombarded her senses, and she kept an eye out for the items she needed as she wove her way between stalls and passersby. Her first purchase was a large woven basket, into which she loaded all the ingredients for a flavorful clam chowder her mum used to prepare. She was pretty sure she was remembering everything, though she didn't have any expectations of the dish turning out half as good as Mum's. Still, her mouth began to water at the very thought of its rich flavor, served with freshly baked bread and sugared strawberries in cream for dessert.

The shadows had lengthened significantly by the time she finished her shopping and headed back toward Jameson's tower. She let her feet carry her on instinct, following the quickest, most familiar route from the docks. Her path took her through the city square. She kept her eyes on the ground, ignoring the looming shadow of the bell tower above her. Her grip tightened around the heavy basket.

"Kes?" Lucian whispered. "Are you all right?"

Her breaths felt short and strained. She stopped walking and let her gaze drift up to the top of the tower, now home to that fancy new belfry instead of the old clock that had once been there. That would *still* be there, if not for…

She tried to swallow, but the knot in her throat was too big. Her mind drifted back to the conversation she'd had with Lucian in Malfram.

How are you supposed to keep running from it for the rest of your life?

Maybe he was right. Maybe facing her past really was the first step toward finding peace. After all, breaking her Bond wouldn't bring Rajiv back. It wouldn't erase what had happened here. Nothing could.

She wandered over to a stone pedestal at the base of the building. Two columns of names were engraved on a metal plate there. Fifty-three names, to be exact. Kesari didn't count them, but she knew. She couldn't read very well, but she also knew exactly where to find her older brother's name among the rest. It winked up at her in the gleam of the sun, two-thirds down the first column.

Rajiv Thomas Eves. Dead, like all the rest. Because of *her.*

She stared up at the tower again and blinked back the tears burning at her eyes, but it wasn't so easy to quell the sudden thundering in her chest or the churning in her stomach.

A familiar voice drifted from the lantern. "Breathe, Kes. Just breathe."

But she couldn't. Her racing heart threatened to explode, and her lungs were so tight she was sure she would suffocate. Ash filled her nose, her mouth, her throat. It burned her from the inside out, dry and coarse. It blew around her in the breeze, lit by tiny embers that threatened to catch her clothes and hair on fire.

The street noises behind her turned into horrified cries. She clamped her hands over her ears, but it didn't help. She could still hear them, could still feel the heat radiating from the burning tower, torrid against her skin.

Something fell on her shoulder. She pushed it off and whipped around to look for an escape.

Saya's face hovered in front of her, concern creased into her brow. She reached for Kesari. Her lips moved, but Kesari couldn't hear what she was saying through those awful, frenzied screams.

She wrapped gentle fingers around one of Kesari's wrists. Kesari allowed her hand to be pulled away from her ear so she could hear what Saya was saying.

"What's wrong?" The young warrior's voice was distorted and distant.

Lucian answered, but Kesari couldn't make out his words. She looked down at him, his flames lapping against the glass of his lantern.

She tore it away. His flames couldn't hurt her, but—no, she had to get rid of them. She threw the lantern onto the ground, along with the fiery being inside. The glass shattered. Someone yelled.

The fire was everywhere now. Behind her, in front of her, lapping at her coat, creeping over Saya's skin and hair.

And then Lucian's voice again. "Breathe, Kes. You're safe."

"We're going to die."

"It was a long time ago. No one is dying now."

"The fire." She looked around again, blinked a few times. There was no fire. But her heart continued to pound like a drum, and she could still feel the smoke suffocating her.

"You're right here in Deveaural with me and Saya," Lucian said. "We're safe. Can you feel the sun on your face? Can you feel the breeze? Take a deep breath, and you can smell the ocean."

Her breath came in shallow, panicked puffs, but she tried to focus on Lucian's voice. She *could* feel the warmth on her face like he'd said, not from a fire, but the orange glow of the setting sun. A gentle breeze blew strands of hair across her brow, and when she sucked in a deep breath, there was a whiff of salt in the air. Saya was still holding onto her wrist, and she could feel the place where their skin met, too. The screams that had seemed so real moments before melted away, replaced by happy voices engaged in ordinary conversation and the clip-clop of horse hooves on the cobblestone streets.

It wasn't real. The fire, the danger, the screams—none of it was really happening. It had happened a long time ago. Right now, she was safe.

Her heart was still racing, though not as fast as before, and her breathing became a little easier. She inhaled another deep breath as Saya led her to a nearby bench. She sat down, and Saya went back for the broken lantern and the basket, which Kesari had dropped sometime during her panic. Lucian hovered beside her shoulder, silent and watchful, but she couldn't look him in the eye.

She shook her head, trying to clear away lingering traces of the memory. She hadn't even had a nightmare that bad in months, and this had felt so much more *real*. The panic and fear had hit her with the same force as the day it had happened, like she was right back there all over again.

She shuddered involuntarily as Saya sat down beside her. "How can I help?"

"I'm fine," she replied, but her voice lacked any semblance of conviction.

"I think it's pretty clear that you're not." Saya's voice was gentle, not intrusive or prodding, simply honest and concerned. They sat there in silence for a few minutes, Kesari still trying to regain control of her frantic heartbeat and her scattered thoughts. Flashes of memory kept popping into her mind, and she couldn't fully get rid of the waves of emotion that accompanied them. She kept seeing Rajiv's back as he ran into the burning building.

If only he'd come back out. If only she'd stopped him. If only she hadn't been so reckless.

"What are you doing here anyway?" she asked Saya, more as a way to distract herself than because she actually cared to know.

"We all went out to look for you," Saya replied. "We got worried when you didn't come back after a while. I remembered passing by here earlier, the look on your face." She shrugged. "I thought it might be significant to you somehow, so I came to see if you were here."

Kesari swallowed. They all went looking for her. They cared enough about her to worry when she didn't come back. Saya cared enough about her to notice the expression on her face, *knew* her well enough to realize it meant something.

Knowing all that burst something inside Kesari, and all the emotion she'd been holding in since coming to Deveaural surged out like water from a broken dam. She doubled over, buried her face in her hands, and cried. The cuffs of her coat—*Rajiv's* coat—were soon soaked through.

She'd been running from this for so long. She'd done everything she could to shut out the memories of that horrible day, even going so far as to mark her arms with the point of a knife when the emotional pain became too great. She'd fled to Kavora, as far away as she could get from this place, and spent her days wandering the country looking for new ways to distract herself, all so she didn't have to face *this*. But here it was, staring her in the face. She'd thought she was ready; it had been more than two years. But it still hurt just as much as the day it all happened.

Saya patted her gently on the back, and eventually, the tears stopped. Kesari raised her head. "I'm sorry."

"You have nothing to apologize for."

Saya's warm smile reminded Kesari so much of her mum she almost started crying all over again. Instead, she sighed and stared back up at the tower. It was so different from the building she remembered, but there was something beautiful about the way they'd rebuilt it.

"Do you want to talk about it?" Saya asked.

"I think so." She'd meant to say *no*. A part of her still wanted to say no—a lingering, naïve hope that not talking about it would make it go away. But that hadn't worked so far, and the part of her that had burst free now longed to be heard. Before she could stop herself, the words began to pour out.

"This is why I can't do magic. I was the one who—" Her voice hitched, and she paused to collect herself before trying again. "I burned down the clocktower."

It had been summer, a few weeks before her fourteenth birthday and six months after she'd made her Bond with Lucian. The naval ship Rajiv was assigned to came into port that afternoon, and Kesari, Lucian, and Navya had arranged to meet him at the docks. They ate dinner together and had a lovely evening exchanging stories and news before they found themselves strolling through Deveaural's central square. Kesari complimented Rajiv on his new coat, which had been a gift from his captain after a recent promotion.

"She said I might even make a good captain myself someday," he said. His eyes sparkled, and his chest puffed out proudly as he peeled the coat off. "Here, Kes. You try it on."

Navya giggled when Rajiv draped the coat over Kesari's shoulders. He leaned back with his fingers on his chin to examine her. "Hmm...a little big, I think. But the color suits you."

Kesari laughed and stuck her arms through the sleeves. They fell past her fingertips and flapped loose around her arms, but the coat smelled of saltwater and the mint leaves Rajiv liked to chew, and Kesari hugged it tight against herself in the cool night air. "It's a fine coat. I think I'll hold onto it a while longer."

"Only if you show me some of the new magic tricks you've been practicing," Rajiv said.

"They're not *tricks*," Lucian sniffed in his proud, crackling voice. "Magic is an art. It takes great skill and practice."

"Show him the one where you shoot fire," Navya said, skipping ahead of them with her arms outstretched. "I like that one."

Kesari nodded and pushed up the sleeves of Rajiv's coat. "Watch this."

Several overhead streetlamps lined the square where they were walking, including a few in front of the old clocktower. No harm in helping the lamplighter with his job.

Lucian hovered close to her ear. "This isn't a good idea. You need more practice, and we shouldn't be experimenting here."

"I've gotten good," Kesari argued. "I've improved a lot this week. You said so yourself." She was tired of being treated like a little kid. Her aim was impeccable, her control over her altma honed to perfection. And Rajiv was here, watching her with the same admiration in his eyes that she'd always had for him. When else would she get a chance to show off to her big brother?

Lucian continued to protest. "That doesn't mean—"

But Kesari had already reached out a hand. She took careful aim, summoned the altma within her, and released the energy exactly as Lucian had taught her, the same way they'd practiced a hundred times at home.

At the time, she hadn't understood what went wrong, or why. Now she knew it was because she hadn't really been in control as much as she'd thought she was. The intensity of her excitement had overtaken her, disrupting the connection between mind, body, and soul that was needed to channel altma. Under better circumstances, that might not have been such a catastrophic mistake. But there in the square, with the clocktower right behind the lamp she'd been aiming for, the results had been disastrous.

The fireball that left her hands was larger than any she'd managed to conjure before, and much faster, too. It shot past the streetlamp and went through one of the windows in the lower part of the clocktower, which housed a pub and lodgings for travelers. Within seconds, the magical flames spread to engulf the entire ground level. Kesari could only watch, mouth agape, as the fire grew. Time seemed to warp around her after that, but she could still remember images and sensations in brief flashes.

Rajiv's voice in her ear, telling her he would be back, that he had to help the people inside.

Navya's hand gripping hers so tight it felt like her bones were being crushed.

Lucian urging her to move, coming so close to her face that she would have been burned if their Bond hadn't prevented him from being able to hurt her.

And then there were all the other people—the ones who coughed and choked as they emerged from the smoking tower, the ones who screamed and ran as the structure began to collapse. People covered in burns dragging disfigured corpses from the wreckage, their grief-stricken wails echoing into the night and ringing endlessly in Kesari's ears.

Navya tugged on her arm and tried to tell her something, but it wasn't until a fleeing man knocked her down that she was jolted back into reality. She scooped her little sister into her arms and ran, following a group of panicked survivors until they stopped near the palace gates.

Navya began to cry, her tiny voice full of terror. "Where's Rajiv, Kes? He said to wait for him. We have to go back and find him!"

Kesari turned to go back, but Lucian darted in front of her. "No, I'll go. You stay here with Navya."

Too exhausted to argue, or perhaps too afraid and guilt-ridden to face the damage she'd done, Kesari sat next to her sister to wait. People came out of their homes in droves with food, water, and medical supplies to help the survivors. An old woman stopped to examine

Kesari and Navya for injuries. They were both covered in ash and grime but otherwise unharmed, and the old woman simply clicked her tongue, pronounced them both extremely lucky, and continued on to help the next person.

By the time Lucian returned, Navya had cried herself to sleep in Kesari's arms. The Spirit Tarja's face was expressionless as he floated forward. Kesari's heart caved in on itself. Rajiv was gone. She knew it before Lucian even said the words.

She rocked her sister's tiny body back and forth in rhythm with her own sobs. Tears streaked down her face and fell into Navya's black curls, but the girl never stirred. People were starting to stare at the pair of them, two young girls alone in the streets at night with a magical flame. They couldn't stay here long before someone started asking questions—questions Kesari wasn't even sure how to answer. She stood, hoisted Navya onto her back, and carried her home in the dark.

By the time they arrived, she'd made a decision. It was late, but light still illuminated the windows of their small cottage. No doubt Mum had stayed up waiting for them while Dad went out to look for them himself. The ache in Kesari's chest deepened as she crouched behind some trees at the edge of their property and gently set Navya down.

She reached forward to wake her sister, then stopped herself. Navya was only ten years old, but they were home, and she'd be safe for now. Besides, what could she say that wouldn't be awful and cruel and too big a burden for Navya to handle? Better to let her sleep a while longer, have a few last minutes of peace where her world wasn't shattered and she still had two older siblings who loved her. Better to leave without saying anything at all.

And so, that was exactly what she did.

Kesari told Saya everything in a rush, afraid of the judgment she might see in the older girl's eyes if she stopped. She had to pause a few times to keep her emotions under control, and even then, a few tears slipped out. "I killed all those people," she said at last, nodding to the fifty-three names on the pedestal. "I killed my own brother."

It was the first time she'd said it out loud to another person, and somehow, that made it more real. She'd always known she was responsible for what had happened, of course, but even in her darkest nightmares, she shared that blame with someone or something else. It was Lucian's fault, too, she told herself. It was just the unstable nature of the magic itself. Sometimes, in her lowest moments, she even pretended it was Rajiv's fault. He'd had no business asking her to do magic tricks for his own entertainment.

Anything to shift the blame somewhere else, to make it so it didn't feel like a knife twisting inside her heart every time she so much as thought about using magic.

"You ran away," Saya said.

Kesari looked at her, ready to come to her own defense. But there was no judgment in Saya's voice, and her eyes were neither scolding nor pitying.

"I couldn't face my family," she said. "I left and never looked back, so being here now is—" She paused, unsure how to describe the torrent of emotions within her. Part of her was happy to be home. She'd missed this city almost as much as she still missed her family. But she was also terrified. She longed for her parents' embrace while simultaneously dreading the accusatory looks they would have for the person who'd killed their only son.

She sighed. "I've been running away so long I'm not sure I know how to do anything else."

"I'm sure your family misses you," Saya said.

Kesari shook her head. "Navya would have told them what happened. They must hate me."

"Navya would have told them it was an accident," Lucian said. "Because that's what it was. It was awful and tragic, and of course your parents must have mourned Rajiv, but it was an accident. And they've been mourning you, too. They don't even know that you're safe, or alive."

They'd had this exact conversation more times than Kesari could remember, but for some reason, sitting here in front of the clocktower and her dead brother's name, the words sunk in with a deeper kind of clarity. She nodded and let out a shaky breath. "I need to go home. I know I do. But what am I supposed to say to them?"

"The right words will come when you get there," Saya replied. She put a hand on Kesari's arm. "And you don't have to go alone."

Kesari cast a glance at Lucian. "I know."

"I think she's saying she'll come with us," he said.

"Oh." She turned back to Saya and blinked. "Thank you. I admit, I'd be grateful for the company."

"It would be my honor."

Kesari stood on legs that felt suddenly shaky. "I guess we should go now, before I lose my nerve." She looked down at the basket full of food. "But Jameson's dinner! Maybe we should take these things back first."

"Nonsense," said Lucian. "You can bring it home to your family and help your mother make dinner. I'm sure they'd appreciate that."

"That's a wonderful idea," Saya said.

"But I bought this with *our* money. We all chipped in. And won't Amar and Mitul be irritated that we didn't come back?"

"Don't worry about the money," Saya replied, stooping to pick up the basket. "You've more than earned this, bringing us all the way here. And Amar and Mitul will be perfectly fine on their own for a while. Come on."

Kesari remained frozen. It was hard to believe this was actually happening after all the times she'd put it off. Was it really what she wanted? She still wasn't sure, but she knew it was what she needed. She couldn't keep running forever.

"It's going to be all right, Kes," Lucian said gently. "And even if it's not, you're not alone."

She nodded, and with a deep breath, she forced herself to take her first, hesitant step toward home.

The second step came a little easier after that.

"This is it," Kesari said when they at last came into view of her childhood home. It was a small cottage Dad had built himself, nestled in Deveaural's countryside and surrounded by wildflowers of every color. Mum could make anything grow, and her vegetable garden was already lush and green on the east side of the house. Kesari's mouth watered at the memory of fresh peas and spicy peppers, but her stomach was still lurching with the anxiety of what she was about to face.

"It's lovely," Saya said.

Kesari took a breath and forced herself to continue on through the grassy field that separated her from her family. Her legs wobbled, like all the bones within them had turned to dust, but she wouldn't turn back now.

The door of the house opened as they reached the edge of the wildflowers, and a slight Kavoran woman with a long, thick braid stepped outside. Kesari's breath caught as her mum raised a hand to shield her eyes so she could get a better look at the approaching visitors. She stared, saying nothing, and the seconds dragged on like years. Kesari's heart thrummed against her ribcage. Maybe coming here hadn't been such a good idea after all.

Then the woman called out her name, her voice as warm and familiar as the folds of Rajiv's coat against her skin. "Kesari?"

She looked at Lucian. He offered a reassuring smile, and she raised a hand in greeting.

Mum dropped the basket she'd been carrying, hitched up her skirt, and began to run through the tall grass. "Kesari! Kesari!" She was half crying, half laughing, and when she pulled her daughter into her arms, warm tears smeared across Kesari's face.

She melted into the embrace, inhaling the scent of fresh-baked bread, wet earth, and cinnamon. Her body trembled from the effort of trying to hold back her emotions, and after a few seconds, she let it all out in a tear-soaked sob.

Mum stepped back to get a good look at her, taking Kesari's face in both of her hands. "Oh, my sweet girl. Is it really you?"

"It's me, Mum," Kesari mumbled around the knot in her throat. "I'm home."

Two new figures approached from the cottage, a square-shouldered man with pale skin and a wiry teenage girl. Dad and Navya. They both seemed hesitant, their identical dazed expressions making the resemblances between them even more apparent.

Kesari's mum, still beaming with joy, looped one arm through hers and led her to the other half of their family. Everything around them seemed to fade, but they stood out in sharp focus, so familiar and yet so changed by the years that had passed since Kesari left.

Navya had grown, no longer the little girl she'd carried home on her back the night of the fire. At twelve, she was nearly as tall as Kesari now, and the childish innocence in her dark eyes had been replaced by a steely hardness. She didn't return Kesari's smile. Her arms stayed crossed, her entire body as rigid as a knife.

Dad had blinked away the daze in his eyes by the time Kesari reached him. His ruddy cheeks were more weathered than she remembered, and he cast a look at Lucian that was difficult to interpret. He'd always been superstitious about magic and hadn't ever settled with the idea that his daughter had Bonded to a Spirit Tarja. For a single, heart-stopping moment, Kesari feared he would send them both away.

But then his eyes flitted back to her face, and the corners of his mouth lifted beneath his thick, copper beard. He pulled Kesari into a tight hug, his voice rough against her hair.

"Welcome home, Kes."

ALEIDA

Nearly a month after saying goodbye to Tyrus in Chatanda, Aleida and Valkyra finally rode into Malfram and immediately began inquiring after Jameson Weatherford. It didn't take long to learn that he'd relocated to Deveaural, and no one they talked to seemed to know anything about Amar or his friends. Aleida tried not to think too much about how long ago they might have been here. She had to keep going, even if the trail had all but gone cold. What other choice did she have?

"If Jameson Weatherford is in Deveaural, then that's where Amar will have gone, too," Valkyra said as they took to the road again. "We'll find them, dear. Don't get discouraged."

"I'm *not* discouraged," Aleida shot back.

"Good. I'm glad."

She sighed. It wasn't Valkyra's fault Jameson had moved, nor was the dragon responsible for any of these delays. She'd been the only one Aleida could consistently rely on through all of this, and she didn't deserve to be the target of her wrath. "I'm sorry. I guess I'm just frustrated."

"That's understandable."

Aleida chewed her bottom lip and nudged the horse into a trot. The same repetitive questions swirled around her mind like a whirlpool.

What would all these delays cost her? What if she couldn't find Amar in time to save Tyrus? What if she *did* find him, but couldn't make it back to her brother in time?

A part of her wanted to ask Valkyra, who always seemed so wise and would probably know exactly what to say. But she was afraid. There were no good answers to questions like these, and certainly no easy ones.

Instead, she sent out a silent prayer to the Artist. *Please, Artex, help me save Tyrus. Watch over my journey and intervene on my behalf where you can. I'm doing everything I'm capable of, but it's not enough. I need your grace.*

She couldn't bring herself to add the caveat that typically went with such prayers—*if it be your will.* Surely the caring, benevolent Artex wanted her brother to live as much as she did. She had to believe that, or what was the point of having faith in a higher power at all?

She rode on, alternating her horse's pace between a gallop and a walk. Stars blinked into view overhead, and finally, at Valkyra's warning that their mount needed to rest, Aleida stopped for the night. She set about making camp while Valkyra went hunting for fresh meat, and she'd just gotten a fire going when the rustle of wings overhead caught her attention.

She stretched out her arm, and Feros landed, his sharp talons digging into her bare skin. His feathers reeked of blood and rotten flesh. She held her breath against the stench, opened the tube on his back, and drew out its contents. Feros fluttered up to perch on the branch of a nearby tree and stared down at Aleida with his haunting, ink-black eyes.

She unrolled the folded sheets of paper and smoothed them over her leg. There was no written message this time, only a few drawings. One showed Aleida and Tyrus sitting on a bench under an apple tree. Another had Aleida leaning forward on a horse that galloped across the center of the page. The last drawing was of Hasan, chasing after a rabbit through a sea of leafy plants that could only be his garden.

Aleida smiled. The lines were steadier and stronger than they had been in the last batch he'd sent. Maybe he'd had a good day, one where his hands hadn't hurt or shaken as much as usual.

She opened her pack and tucked the drawings in with the rest of Tyrus' letters, then pulled out the sketches she'd been working on over the last few weeks to send back to him. Her journey had been remarkably dull of late, and rather than documenting the miles of empty landscape around her, she'd drawn some of the familiar characters and creatures from the bedtime stories Papa used to tell them.

There were the giant sea dragons that attacked ships or guided them through storms, depending on which version one wanted to believe. There was the great artist Cassia, chosen by Artex himself to paint the lightning that drove off their enemies. There were creatures that were half human and half beast, mythical monsters defeated by the legendary heroes of old. Aleida had even thrown in a drawing of Tyrus dressed in gleaming armor fit for a hero. His voice was strong in her memories of their childhood, pleading with Papa to make up some story featuring himself as the lead character.

Carefully, she rolled up the drawings and called for Feros. It took more than a little bribery with some dried pork to get the strix to come down from his perch, but he eventually complied. Aleida slipped the drawings into his carrier and offered him a drink from the palm of her hand. His sharp beak cut though her skin in what she half believed was a purposeful attack, and he drank the bloodied water greedily. Aleida's nose wrinkled in disgust, and she was glad when he finally flew off, back toward Chatanda to deliver her message.

Valkyra returned as she was bandaging her hand. "What happened?"

"Feros," she muttered.

"Did he bring a message?"

"Yes, but he's left already."

Valkyra's gaze drifted to Aleida's pack. "Anything you need me to read?"

"No. Only drawings this time."

"I see." She shifted her wings behind her back. "Well, I'm afraid I didn't find any food, but you still have enough to last a while. And there's something else that might be useful. Come. And bring the rest of those bandages."

She bounded across the forest floor like a fox, and Aleida tried to keep up as best she could. It was hard to see much of anything in the shadows, and she used her magic to create a glowing orb of light over one hand. After a few minutes, Valkyra stopped and waited for her to catch up, then jumped up from the ground to perch on her shoulder. "You'll want to cover your face," she said.

"Why?"

"Because we're going to harvest daravak, and you don't want to accidentally inhale any of it yourself."

She raised her shirt up over her mouth and nose. Valkyra extended one clawed foreleg to indicate the direction she should walk. After a few paces, the light from Aleida's hand fell upon a gnarled tree. Shelves of fungus grew along the lower section of the trunk, soft and pale against the rough bark. In some places, it grew so thick Aleida couldn't even see the tree beneath. She stepped closer and bent to examine the fungi, which was speckled with dark spots that reminded her of a seagull's egg.

She reached out to touch the daravak but stopped before her fingers brushed its surface. "Is it safe to touch them?" she asked, her voice muffled through the fabric of her shirt.

"Yes, but you'll want to wash your hands thoroughly after. It won't affect you unless you ingest or inhale it. Wrap it up and we'll take some with us."

Aleida spread some of the bandages on the ground and pulled a section of the fungus from the bark. It separated with a gentle tug, and she laid it atop the fabric. "I assume you're thinking this could be useful against Amar's Tarja friend."

"And Jameson, should he prove to be uncooperative when we question him."

Aleida nodded. It was a good idea. Not a complete plan, maybe, but better than charging into another fight unprepared. "Do we need to do anything special for it to work?"

"No. It should keep its potency for at least a couple of months. And then of course we'll have to find some way to administer it, but we can figure that out once we have a better idea of the situation we're dealing with."

Aleida pulled several more pieces of daravak from the tree, then wrapped the bundle up tight. She wound another bandage around it as an extra precaution before pulling her face free of her shirt. "It's a good find," she said, smiling at Valkyra. "Thank you."

"Of course, dear." She draped her silky tail over Aleida's shoulder. "I know how frightening it can be to lose your magic to something like daravak, even temporarily. But the weapons people use against you can be wielded just as effectively in your own hands. Maybe even more so. Your very existence is the perfect example of that."

Aleida frowned. "How do you mean?"

"You were orphaned by Kavoran Tarja and their magic, and yet here you are, using that same magic to fight for your brother's life. Our greatest weaknesses can become our biggest strengths, under the right circumstances."

There was a certain pride in her voice, an admiration for what Aleida had become—for what *they* had become together. But Aleida's stomach twisted, and she found no encouragement in the dragon's words. Yes, her trials had changed her, made her stronger, made her hard. She'd been thrust into the fire and hammered relentlessly, only to come out on the other side as sharp as a steel blade. The right circumstances indeed, her weaknesses turned into a weapon.

But if she was sharp and hard and strong, it was only because she'd been forced to become so. She had never asked to be made steel.

KESARI

ALONE IN HER OLD ROOM, KESARI RAN HER HAND ACROSS THE
lovingly hand-stitched blankets spread over the bed she used to share
with Navya. A lamp in one corner illuminated the space with a warm
glow now that night had fallen. Saya had returned to Jameson's tower
after dinner, but Kesari had opted to stay with her family. They'd
welcomed her back so warmly; it would have been wrong to disappear
on them so soon after that reunion.

And yet, the idea of staying here permanently didn't feel quite right
either. This had been such a long time coming, but it had happened so
fast. She was still trying to sort through it all in her head. So much had
changed, and so much hadn't. Maybe in time, she would feel like she
belonged here again.

But what if she didn't?

She stooped to open a wooden chest sitting at the end of the bed.
Dad had gifted it to her and Navya right before Kesari left home. A
bitter chill cut through her when she found a bunch of Rajiv's old
things inside, as well as some of her own. She picked up a doll Mum
had made when she was six or seven years old. It smiled at her with a
chipped-paint mouth, but she couldn't bring herself to smile back.

"None of us could bear to throw out any of that useless stuff after
you left."

Kesari jumped at the unexpected voice behind her.

Navya stood in the doorway. "It all sat in that trunk, collecting dust. Shame. I really could have used the storage for my own things."

Her voice was filled with a contempt Kesari wouldn't have previously believed her capable of. She hadn't said a word during dinner, though Kesari thought she'd caught her sister glaring at her a few times.

"Sorry," she replied. The word felt so weak and minuscule in light of everything that had transpired two years ago. She put the doll back in the trunk and closed the lid. They stared at each other in silence for a few moments. "Did you...want to come in?" Kesari asked awkwardly.

Navya rolled her eyes. "It's *my* room, you know. You can't invite someone into their own room." She walked inside anyway and sat on the bed with a huff. "Dad's out there thanking Lucian for looking after you all this time"

"You mean they're actually having a civil conversation?" Kesari asked. "They used to have such terrible fights."

"He says you haven't used any magic since you left."

"I haven't." Kesari walked over to sit on the bed beside her sister. She folded her knees up against her chest. "I didn't want to hurt anyone else."

Navya let out a snort. "Oh, of course not. Heaven forbid you should hurt anyone else. Just your family."

"Navya, look—"

"No, you look." She shook her head. "Why did you even come back here anyway? Was it because you wanted to see us, or only because you wanted to help that Sularan girl and the other new friends you told us about?"

"I *did* want to see you, I just...didn't know if I should."

"You left us." Navya clenched her hands in her lap. "I wasn't sure you'd ever come back."

"I know." The pain in her sister's voice squeezed around Kesari's heart. She'd put her in a horrible position the night she left. She'd gotten Navya home safe, but after such a traumatic event, the burden of having to tell their parents what had happened couldn't have been easy.

"I was ten years old," Navya said, her voice rising. "My brother was dead and my sister disappeared, and I had *no one*. Mum and Dad could barely take care of themselves for a while, let alone pay any attention to me. We weren't even sure if you were all right out there. You could have been dead, and we never would have known."

"I'm sorry." That weak, useless word again.

"Now you're back, and it's all I've ever wished for, but I'm still so angry at you for leaving." Tears filled Navya's dark eyes. "You didn't have to, you know. You could have stayed. Maybe it would have been hard, but we would have figured it out."

Everything inside Kesari crumbled. Navya was still so young, but so much more grown up than she remembered. "I really am sorry, Navya. I couldn't bear to stay knowing that I..." She swallowed. "I killed him."

"You didn't kill Rajiv, Kes. It was an accident."

"An accident I caused."

"No." She swiped at her cheeks with the palm of her hand. "There was an investigation, after you left. Some men from the palace started questioning anyone who was seen at the clocktower the night of the fire. They came here, and I told them everything. I told them it was your fault."

A new wave of guilt surged through Kesari. "I know it was."

Navya took her hand. "But it *wasn't*, Kes. Not entirely. I heard one of them talking to Mum and Dad after. He said the building had been in poor condition for years. He said architects had been trying to convince the king to renovate it, because it was dangerous, ready to collapse. But it wasn't ever a priority, and it kept getting worse, so it was only a matter of time before something bad happened."

"I'm still the one who set it on fire," Kesari said, new tears running down her cheeks.

"But it shouldn't have burned so easily or so quickly," Navya insisted. "Think about it. It was one little fireball. It shouldn't have been capable of doing so much damage. If we're going to point fingers, the king is as much to blame as you. Maybe even more so. And he must know that, because the royal family made payments to every family who lost someone in that fire."

Kesari shook her head. She didn't know what to do with this new information. For so long, she'd carried the full burden of blame for what had happened that night. It was something she'd known she would carry for the rest of her life, and the fact that someone else might be equally responsible did nothing to ease her conscience. She was still directly connected to the deaths of all those people, and shifting part of the responsibility onto someone else didn't change that.

When she said nothing, Navya sighed and let go of her hand. "It doesn't matter anymore, anyway. You're back. And I guess I'm going to have to get used to sharing my room again."

"I guess."

"You *are* staying, aren't you?"

Kesari chewed on her lip. If only she could give Navya the straightforward answers she deserved. She'd waited so long to come home, and the reception from her family had been better than anything she could have hoped for. She owed it to them to stay.

But didn't she also owe it to herself to do whatever was best for her? She'd had some dark days, but the time she'd spent wandering all over Erythyr had been valuable. She and Rajiv had always talked about going off on grand adventures and seeing the world one day, and that was what she'd done when she left home. The idea of staying in one place now seemed restrictive. The idea of staying *here*, in *this* place, where Rajiv's memory was still so painfully close—she wasn't ready for that.

And then there was this curse of Amar's, and Saya's haseph. She wasn't sure how any of that would play out, but she'd come this far with them already, and she wanted to see it through. Whatever that meant.

"You should stay," Navya said, more quietly now. "I'm sorry if I haven't seemed as happy to have you back as Mum and Dad. I really did miss you."

"I missed you too," Kesari said. She was too tired and too emotionally drained to make any big decisions tonight. That could wait until later. For now, it was enough to just be home.

She smiled at her sister, and for the first time since she'd returned, Navya smiled back.

AMAR

AMAR, SAYA, AND MITUL MADE THEMSELVES COMFORTABLE IN Jameson's tower over the next few days as their host came and went sporadically. He would spend hours poring over stacks of books and scrolls, only to go dashing back to the library or to consult the historians at Deveaural's most prestigious academic institution. The disheveled piles on his table grew by the day, and his mutterings to himself became increasingly frenetic. He jotted notes in a green, leatherbound journal, and he often fell asleep in his armchair with a book still propped open on his lap.

Sometimes, while Jameson was out, Amar would try to peek through his notes and the stacks of books on the table. Much of it was written in Atrean, making it impossible for him to read. Even the Kavoran notes were hard to decipher, written in a laborious, academic style. The content was all related to magic and science, of which Amar didn't have enough background knowledge to fully understand. He tried to talk to Jameson about his findings a couple of times, but the Tarja only brushed him off. He seemed to have a particular talent for immersing himself completely in his work and ignoring everything else. He probably wouldn't have even remembered to eat if Saya or Mitul didn't set a plate in front of him two or three times a day, and even then, it sometimes went untouched. No wonder the man was so thin.

Kesari and Lucian were still staying with her family, but they stopped by at least once a day to see if there had been any new developments. Jameson was as good at ignoring them as he was Amar. Sometimes, he would engage in lengthy theoretical discussions with Lucian about a specific magical problem he was trying to puzzle out, but Amar couldn't keep up with these conversations and had to content himself with being patient. He'd find out what he needed to know when Jameson was ready to share it, and not a moment sooner.

He kept himself busy by writing in his own journal, documenting some of the more notable events from his travels over the last few months. Maybe it was futile, but since he couldn't hold onto his real memories, this was the next best thing.

Four days into their stay in Jameson's tower, the Tarja was finally ready to review the results of his research. Kesari and Lucian had arrived at noon with fresh vegetables from her mother's garden and a savory meat pie, which Kesari cut and divvied up amongst the others for lunch. Jameson had just roused himself for the day and yawned as he took a full plate from her. "Oh good," he said brightly. "You're all here. I think I've figured out what to do about your predicament."

Mitul exchanged a hopeful look with Amar. "You mean you can break the curse?"

"Ah—well, not exactly. Not yet, anyway. Let me explain from the beginning." He cleared his throat and set down his plate. "Most magic is short-lived. Fast-acting, powerful, and over almost as quickly as it began. Think of the way Tarja use magic to attack or defend against an enemy in battle. Each burst of altma is gone in a second." He snapped his fingers, igniting tiny green sparks that crackled over his fingers and then disappeared.

"Of course, there are some types of magic that last longer. Healing magic, for example, or illusions. Those don't fade away quite as quickly, but they do fade, usually within minutes or hours, sometimes a few days. If you want the effects to last longer, you have to renew them by channeling altma over and over again. By nature, magic is fleeting and unpredictable. Tarja can spend years honing the skills and power needed to control it." He glanced at Kesari and Lucian. "Of course, if one is Bonded to a Spirit Tarja who already developed those skills in their lifetime, that learning process is often faster and easier, but the point is, in most cases, magic doesn't last."

"What does that have to do with my curse?" Amar asked.

Jameson's eyes brightened. "Well, as I'm sure you can attest to, a curse is different. It lasts much longer."

Amar nodded. His own curse had lasted decades, at least, and as far as he knew, no Tarja had been renewing it all those years. "How?"

"It's hard to say for sure. Much of what we once knew about curses has been intentionally erased or lost through the years. But a curse is stable, powerful, and long-lasting in a way that other types of magic aren't. My research suggests that there's really only one way to manipulate magic to be all of those things at once. You have to channel altma directly from its source—from life itself. And in a much bigger amount."

"You're talking about blood magic," Lucian said. "Draining so much altma out of a living thing that you actually damage it. Maybe even kill it."

"Yes. At least, it makes the most sense that curses would have been closely tied to blood magic. The amount of altma required to sustain one would have been tremendous."

"Isn't blood magic forbidden?" Kesari asked.

Jameson nodded. "The practice was widely condemned in Kavora a few centuries ago, and any Tarja found to be practicing it were killed or imprisoned. And that was after curses were eradicated, so any knowledge of links between the two has long since been forgotten. Most of the information I managed to dig up is purely theoretical or based in myths and legends." He paused to take a quick bite of his food and leveled his gaze at Amar. "Despite that, I do believe Tamaya was right. You are cursed. It's the only explanation for how the magic keeping you alive could have lasted so long."

"But that means he had to have been cursed before that knowledge was lost," Mitul said. "How long ago exactly did you say that was?"

Jameson shrugged. "Five hundred years ago, give or take a few decades."

It lined up with everything they'd learned from Tamaya, but still, the sheer vastness of all the time Amar had lost was dizzying. Half a millennium. How many lifetimes was that? How many deaths? How many people whose faces he had forgotten?

"You mentioned something before about getting his memories back," Mitul said.

"Ah, yes! The idea is that if we can go back in Amar's memories far enough, we'll be able to discover when he was cursed, and why, and possibly even how to break it."

"And you're sure it *can* be broken?" Saya asked.

"I don't see why not," Jameson said with a shrug. "All the stories about curses mention some way of breaking them. There's usually some kind of stipulation or condition woven into the magic itself."

"That doesn't make sense," Saya said with a frown. "Why bother with something that requires so much energy if the curse can simply be broken?"

"Lucian and I came up with a theory on that." Jameson turned to the Spirit Tarja. "You should explain. It was your idea."

Lucian smiled and seemed to grow a little larger, as if he were puffing himself up. "Let's imagine that a curse is like this tower," he said. "Now, all magic has weak points—that's unavoidable. It's unstable, it doesn't last long, or it can be diffused if you go at it just right." He hovered over to float near the wall. "If this tower was missing a few stones here and there from top to bottom, those would be obvious weak points, and there would be a high risk of the entire thing crumbling as soon as it was attacked. But if you can move your weak point to a single, hard-to-reach location—maybe somewhere at the very top—suddenly the tower is more stable, more defensible."

"You can control the circumstances it will break under," Jameson said. "And as long as those conditions are never met, the curse can continue indefinitely."

He strode over to the table and pushed aside a few stacks of books until he found his green journal lying open beneath a pile of papers. After flipping through a few pages, he ran his index finger over the notes scribbled there. "In all the stories and legends, there's usually some very specific condition that has to be met before the curse can be broken. It was often part of an incantation, which makes me think a curse had to be spoken aloud to come together properly. Some stories talk about curses that were hereditary—maybe an illness passed on to all the males in a family for a specified number of generations. Sometimes they were a little more vague—a curse on a king's land that could only be broken when he made a great sacrifice to his people, for example. True love's kiss seems to have been a popular curse-breaker, at least until people realized how common true love actually is."

"So we just have to figure out what the weak point is in my curse," Amar said. "Then we can break it."

"Yes. That's why we need to explore your memories."

"And how do we do that, exactly?"

"Magic, of course. It's a healing technique. I've used it a few times on people who've injured their heads in a fall or experienced a decline in memory as they age." He tilted his head to one side and stared at Amar contemplatively. "I've never had to go back more than a few decades, but with you, we'll be going back hundreds of years. That could complicate things."

"How?" Mitul asked. He glanced at Amar, his brows furrowing in concern.

"Magic always has risks, especially when it's experimental. And the mind is a delicate thing."

"I don't care," Amar said. "Do what you need to do."

Mitul put a hand on his shoulder. "Maybe you should give this a little more thought before you agree to anything."

"I don't need to give it more thought. I want my memories back. What's the worst that could happen—I die? I'll come right back as good as new, so what does it even matter?"

"You'll forget everything again," Mitul said.

"It's not like I haven't had to deal with that before." He said it dismissively, although if he was being honest with himself, that possibility did give him some pause. All this time, he'd tried to convince himself that his companions didn't know him, that they meant nothing to him. But somewhere in their travels together, that had changed. They were all he had, and he didn't want to lose them or forget about them again.

But he also wanted to remember whatever history he, Mitul, and Saya had shared before—a desire that only had grown more intense the longer they'd traveled together. He wanted to remember everything.

"There's a risk your mind could be damaged in the process," Jameson said. "Perhaps permanently. All of this is theoretical, and some of it is pure guesswork. I can't say for sure that any of it will work, or that it will even be safe."

"I don't care," Amar said again, his mind firmly made up. "I can't keep living like this. I'm tired of not knowing who I am."

Jameson regarded him with narrowed eyes, as if searching for any sign of fear or doubt. But Amar had none, and after a few seconds, the Tarja nodded. "All right then. But I'm going to need some help."

"I'll help," Mitul volunteered. "Whatever you need, just say the word."

"Actually, I'd prefer for you and Saya to wait outside," Jameson said. "There's someone else more suited for the job."

Mitul's shoulders slumped a little, but he nodded.

"Lucian has already agreed to be present for consultation during the process," Jameson went on. "And Kesari, I think you should be here, too."

Her eyes widened, and she stuffed her hands stiffly into the pockets of her coat. "Oh, I don't actually use magic anymore."

Jameson waved a hand dismissively. "I know, but you're more familiar with it than any of your friends. At the very least, you can keep an eye on Amar during the procedure, watch for any signs that things are amiss."

Kesari started to protest further, but Amar cut her off. "I'd feel a lot better having a friend with me."

She stared at him for a few seconds, mouth agape, and he offered what he hoped was an apologetic smile. Saya had briefly told him and Mitul what she'd learned about Kesari's history. This, of course, had made Amar feel like a complete ass for having been so hard on her before. He still owed her a real apology, but for now, this would have to do. And it was true, anyway. Whatever ordeal he was about to go through, he didn't want to face it alone.

"I...of course," Kesari stammered at last. "I'm happy to help however I can."

"Wonderful," Jameson said, clapping his hands together. "Let's finish our lunch then, and we'll get started."

Kesari sucked in a breath. "Already?"

"No time like the present," the Tarja replied.

Amar immediately began to wolf down the rest of his food. He couldn't agree more.

KESARI

"I DON'T KNOW IF I CAN DO THIS," KESARI WHISPERED TO LUCIAN.
They stood alone near the fireplace while Amar ushered Saya and Mitul
outside, his low voice reassuring them that everything would be all
right. Jameson had set about clearing the entire room, humming to
himself as he pushed the table and all its mess under the stairs and
arranged the chairs neatly around the curved wall of the circular room.
The hollow pulsing behind Kesari's ribcage had grown deeper and
stronger over the last few minutes, reverberating off every nerve in her
body. Maybe she shouldn't have agreed to this.

"You'll be fine," Lucian replied. "All you have to do is watch."

Kesari twisted the cuffs of her coat between her fingers. "Can't Saya
or Mitul do that?"

"They don't know magic the way you do. They wouldn't know what
to watch for."

"I barely know magic at all anymore."

"You do," Lucian said. "How much time did you spend learning as
much as you could about magic before we even met?"

"A lot," Kesari admitted with a rueful smile. She'd sought out every
book and story about magic she could find as a child and had pestered
any Tarja she met to answer her questions. For years, her heart's only
desire had been to wield that same power herself. Rajiv had called it an

obsession. It was why he'd brought Lucian's spirit to her in the first place, and why she had been so eager to form that Bond with him.

"You still have all that knowledge," Lucian said. "And Amar wants you here. He's going to need the moral support. The way Jameson describes it, pulling memories from a person takes a toll on their body. The fact that we have to go back centuries complicates things. He shouldn't go through that without a friend by his side."

If that were the case, then Mitul would have been the better choice, but he and Saya were already outside. The door was shut, and Jameson was guiding Amar to the center of the room, and it was too late for Kesari to change her mind. Instead, she took a deep breath, shook out her arms, and approached the two men with Lucian trailing along behind her. She could do this.

Jameson rubbed his hands together as his gaze slid over each of them. "Let's go over how this is going to work," he said. "First, I'll put Amar to sleep. He'll lie on the floor in the center of the room here, and I'll start delving into his memories." He turned to Amar. "It's safer and easier for both of us if you're unconscious during the procedure, but you should still be able to remember everything once we're finished. Typically, this works better if I go backwards incrementally, though the mind does have a tendency to snag on the important bits."

"What do you mean?" Kesari asked.

"Significant moments, traumatic events—maybe the birth of a child, a wedding, a death, or any other experience that had a major impact on the person. Our memories of those things are more powerful, and when the magic catches on an event like that, the mind wants to go through it in its entirety. It takes a few minutes for me to correct things and get back on course, and it's usually easier to let it play out."

"But that will be better for us anyway," Lucian said. "We're specifically looking for whatever event led to Amar's curse, which will undoubtedly be one of those important memories. The mind will naturally be drawn there, once we go back far enough, and we'll be able to see exactly what happened."

"Wait." Amar held up a hand. "You'll be able to *see* my memories?"

"Not just see them," Jameson said. "We'll hear them and smell them and feel them, too. As I extract them, they'll fill this whole room. There will be gaps, of course. No memory is perfect. But yes—we'll be able to see your whole life. Almost like a stage play, but far more immersive."

Amar frowned. "I didn't realize it was going to be so…public."

"Afraid we might find something embarrassing in there?" Lucian asked with a sharp grin.

"As if you've never done anything humiliating," Amar shot back. "I have hundreds of years' worth of memories, and I'm sure some of them include things I'd rather keep secret. If that's not possible, so be it, but don't go telling stories at my expense when this is over."

"Touchy."

Kesari shot the Spirit Tarja a look. "We won't say anything," she promised.

"Of course not," Lucian agreed. "I wouldn't dream of causing you any embarrassment."

Amar raised an eyebrow, clearly unconvinced.

Lucian let out a sigh, making his flames flutter. "I'd put my hand over my heart and swear on my own life, but since I don't have any of those things anymore, you'll have to take me at my word."

Amar rolled his eyes.

"What do you want me to do?" Kesari asked Jameson.

"Look after him. Sometimes people vomit, so you'll want to make sure he doesn't choke. If he starts thrashing about, he's having a seizure. We can't stop that, but you will want to make sure he doesn't hit his head. Sometimes there's bleeding from the nose or the mouth. A little blood isn't anything to worry about, but a lot is cause for concern."

"This is sounding more and more fun by the second," Amar muttered.

Jameson went on as if he hadn't heard him. "I'll also need you and Lucian to pay attention to the magic—the way it feels, the way it looks, anything out of the ordinary. I'll have to focus all my attention on Amar and his memories, so I'll be counting on you two to let me know if something seems off."

"In other words," Amar said, "don't let him blow us all up or anything like that."

His tone was sarcastic, but Kesari's stomach was twisting itself in knots. This was far out of her depth—much more so than she'd originally believed.

"Well then," Jameson said with a smile, "let's begin. Amar, please lie down on the floor and try to relax."

Amar lowered himself onto the blanket the wizard had spread out, muttering to himself. "Relax, he says. Like it's so easy after he's just listed all the ways this could all go wrong."

Kesari sat on the floor next to him, and Lucian took up a position facing her, hovering over Amar's body. Amar's jaw was set as his dark eyes darted between them, then back to Jameson, and Kesari thought she could see a hint of fear behind his determined gaze. She reached out and placed one hand over his. He flinched a little, eyes widening ever so slightly as they flitted back to her face. Then he relaxed and wrapped his fingers around hers. "I'm ready," he said.

Jameson stood at his feet and waved a hand over him a few times. A glowing dust-like substance drifted down from his palms and melted into Amar's clothes and skin. Within seconds, his eyes had fluttered shut, and he was breathing deep, heavy breaths.

"He's asleep," Jameson said. "I'll open a bridge to his mind now."

A stream of golden light snaked its way from the wizard's fingertips and into Amar's forehead. Jameson held it there for a few seconds, then the light began to fade. Kesari continued to watch Amar's face and the rise and fall of his breaths, but nothing changed. It seemed like nothing was happening at all, and she was about to voice this concern when the room suddenly filled with vivid, three-dimensional images that shifted and flickered back out again as quickly as they had appeared.

The images were accompanied by a plethora of smells and sounds, but they came and went so quickly that she could never get a firm hold on any one thing. Most of it seemed to meld together into an indistinguishable cacophony of sensations, but her eyes did manage to pick out certain familiar elements. She caught glimpses of Deveaural, the red sands of the Sular Desert, their fireside meal among the Sularans in Hayathu. For a moment, Mitul's voice floated above all other sounds as he sang to a crowd on the streets of Sharmok, and then he was gone, replaced by Lucian's smirk, Saya's strong hand clutched around her bow, Kesari pulling at the sleeves of her coat, Tamaya's wrinkled face, and dozens of other images.

Then, all at once, everything stopped.

Kesari blinked, head spinning as she tried to regain her bearings after the chaos that had come before. She looked down at Amar. He was still breathing deeply, but his eyes moved rapidly behind closed lids. Was he seeing all this in his mind as he slept? Did he think he was dreaming, or was he aware that these were all memories he'd actually lived?

The darkness of night had fallen over them, though Kesari was sure they hadn't been working that long. She looked up and could no longer see Jameson's tower room. Instead, they were on a path surrounded by trees, with the fresh, green smell of the forest blowing on a gentle breeze. The ceiling above had been replaced by a night sky full of stars, and Kesari's mouth dropped open. She'd seen plenty of clever illusions woven by magic before, but this was better than any of them. It seemed so real.

Figures came into view nearby, and their voices rang out clear and familiar. Saya and Amar shouted to each other as they fought off the young Visan woman and dodged her magical attacks. Lucian and the other Spirit Tarja chased each other through the air in a wild dance. They were all so close and so realistic that Kesari jerked back when the fight drew closer and their attacker's lightning shot out in a jagged blue line. She flinched as it passed through her shoulder but felt nothing.

Then, Amar's sword was in the young woman's hand, and the point slashed across his body with a sickening squelch. It happened impossibly fast, just as it had on the night these events had actually occurred. Kesari knew it was only a memory, but somehow it was worse, seeing it all again from this angle, this close, now that she knew Amar and thought of him as a friend. She stifled a scream as he fell. Then she saw herself and Mitul burst out of some trees, and all the awful turmoil she'd felt that night as he begged her to save Amar came rushing back like a wildfire across a dry field.

She squeezed the real Amar's warm hand and looked down at his sleeping face, at the steady rise and fall of his chest. He was still breathing, still alive, but he shouldn't have died that night. He might not have, were it not for her own selfish fears.

"I'm sorry," she whispered.

His fingers curled around hers a little tighter. Maybe it was an involuntary reflex, or her imagination, but she smiled anyway. She hadn't been able to save him then, but she could help him now.

"Well, that was...gruesome," Jameson said. His hands still hovered over Amar, fingers moving in subtle shifts as if he were playing an instrument no one else could see. No one except for perhaps Lucian, who watched the wizard with dark, flinty eyes and a distinct lack of his usual smirk.

"Is everything all right?" Kesari asked.

"Yes," Jameson replied, "but this is turning out to be a bit more difficult than expected. It's like all his memories are locked up in a cell behind a dozen stone walls. I'll get through them, though. Let's keep going, shall we?"

The torrent of memories began to fly by once again. Glimpses of Amar, Mitul, and Saya traveling together filled the room. Moving farther back, Saya disappeared, leaving only Mitul and Amar. Mitul's face lost some of its wrinkles as the memories went by, but Amar's maintained its same, unchanging youthfulness.

They stopped on another memory, at night again, but now in a city street. "Hang on a minute," Jameson said. "I'll get us moving again."

"How far back are we?" Lucian asked as a pair of figures appeared. One was Amar, but Kesari didn't recognize the other man. They staggered up the street side-by-side, and their raucous singing bolstered her suspicions that they were drunk.

"Not nearly far enough," Jameson grunted. A thin sheen of sweat had broken out on his brow, but below his outstretched hands, Amar dozed on peacefully.

A third man stepped out of the shadows and plunged a knife into Amar's chest. Before his companion could react, the assassin pulled out a second blade and slashed his throat. The killer's face caught the moonlight as he turned, and the haseph-mark scars there were unmistakable.

"Zefar," Kesari murmured, recalling the tale the Sularan mercenary had told them in Hayathu.

"It's a good thing Mitul wasn't with him," Lucian remarked. "Though I do feel sorry for that other poor soul."

Jameson's face looked a little green. "How much violence has this man endured?"

"Only way to find out is to keep going," Lucian said.

"I'm not so sure I want to."

The blur of memories started back up, moving faster this time. Mitul appeared in some of them, the gray streaks in his dark hair and beard fading away the farther back they went, until he was a man of about thirty. He and Amar now sat at a low table in what looked like a tavern, eating a meal of curried chickpeas and flatbread. The rich aroma made Kesari's mouth water, even though she still had a full belly from lunch.

"You don't have to come," the Amar in the memory said to Mitul.

"Nonsense," Mitul replied. "Of course I'm coming. Someone needs to look out for you."

"I'm perfectly capable of looking out for myself."

Mitul raised an eyebrow. "And what happens if you die out there on your own? Someone should be there to remind you who you really are."

Amar shook his head. "You should stay. You have a whole life here. What about Kamaal?"

Mitul lowered his gaze and went silent for a few moments. "He'll understand." He raised his eyes to meet Amar's. "You're my brother. I can't let you do this on your own."

They faded away, and new images spun all around Kesari. Mitul appeared in several of them, soon becoming a teenager and then disappearing altogether. There were no more familiar faces in the rapidly shifting memories after that. Amar's eyes darted behind his eyelids at a matching rate of speed, and his brown skin began to glisten with sweat, though the temperature in the room was still quite cool.

"What happens if we go too fast?" Kesari asked.

Jameson didn't answer. His eyes were fixed on Amar, the muscles in his face tensed in concentration as his fingers continued to tap out their silent rhythm.

"He has to find a balance," Lucian explained. "We have to go back a long way, and maintaining a bridge like this for too long can be dangerous. So he can't go too slow, but he can't go too fast, either."

Kesari pointed to Amar's face. "Should we be worried?"

"He's all right for now," Lucian replied. "I think."

This was hardly comforting, but she didn't know what else to do except watch Amar for any further signs of distress.

The memories hit another snag, and a battlefield filled the room. Along with it came a hundred different horrifying sounds and smells. Armored men and women screamed and ran in all directions, and Kesari's nose burned with the stench of smoke and blood. It reminded her too much of the fire at the clocktower, and she wanted to close her eyes, but that wasn't going to help. She squeezed Amar's hand and focused on the feeling of his skin against hers to keep herself from slipping into her own memories.

At Jameson's feet, another Amar was sprawled out with three arrows sticking out of his chest. His breaths were wet and ragged, and blood dribbled from one corner of his mouth. His shaking hand twitched toward a sword on the ground—the very same sword he still carried.

Jameson hurried the memories along. There were more battlefields, several of which Amar died on. Kesari stopped watching, instead focusing on the real Amar in front of her, but she couldn't completely ignore the sounds and smells of war and death all around her. At one point, she made the mistake of looking up to see him leading about a dozen other soldiers over mountainous terrain. A group of enemy Tarja came upon them. There was a flash of light, and then Amar and every single one of his companions began to bleed from deep gashes made by invisible weapons. The horror on his face as he watched his friends die seared itself into Kesari's mind.

Sweat beaded on the real Amar's face, which was now contorted in a grimace of pain. His hand grasped hers so tightly she had to pry his fingers loose. She reached a hand to his forehead. The heat hit her palm before she even touched his skin. "I think he has a fever," she said to Jameson.

"That's normal," the wizard answered. His voice was strained now, and a few strands of black hair clung to his damp forehead.

Amar's entire body suddenly went rigid, then began to convulse. Jameson had warned that a seizure could happen, but seeing it sent Kesari's heart racing. She put her free hand on Amar's shoulder. "It's all right. You're all right."

He kept shaking, and she looked up at Lucian helplessly. What was she supposed to do to help him through this?

"Watch his head," Lucian reminded her.

Kesari stripped off her coat and placed it under Amar's head.

"Hold on," Jameson said. "Let me find something happier."

The battlefield faded away, and now they sat in front of a blazing campfire. A thin layer of snow covered the ground, and the smell of roasting meat and burning wood filled the air. The people seated around the fire were the same soldiers Kesari had seen slaughtered by Tarja minutes before. Two of them, a man and a woman, stood in the center of the circle holding hands. Amar stood in front of them, smiling as he spoke the words of a Kavoran marriage vow. The couple kissed, and there were cheers and whistles from the other soldiers, who soon closed in around them to offer congratulations.

The groom pushed through the crowd to find Amar, who embraced him with a firm pat on the back. "Thank you," he said.

"It was my honor," Amar replied. "May you both have a long and happy life together."

The man stared at his bride with a look that couldn't possibly have been any happier. "I'm sure we will," he said, "if we can get through the rest of this war."

Jameson's voice cut through the memory. "How's he doing now?"

Kesari looked down at Amar. The seizure had stopped, and the muscles in his face had relaxed a little. "Better."

The wizard nodded. "Good. Now let's try to get to the beginning before anything else goes wrong."

The tower became little more than a swirling mass of colors as Jameson pulled them through Amar's memories at a breakneck speed. Occasionally, the images stopped for a split second, caught on Jameson's magic like cloth on a protruding nail. War seemed to be the common theme. Whatever decade it was, wherever in Erythyr Amar's memories took them, he was always a soldier. Jameson managed to pull free and keep moving before these memories could play out for very long, but Kesari still saw more blood and violence than she thought she'd ever witness in her entire life. She shut her eyes against the visuals and tried not to vomit from the stench and the noise and the dizzying speed at which they flew through it all.

"Don't look up," Lucian said, picking up on her distress. "Stay focused on Amar."

She followed his advice and put her hand to the man's damp forehead again. His fever was getting worse, and a few times, his muscles began to spasm. Jameson kept moving, never allowing one memory to take over long enough to cause a reaction as severe as that first seizure. At least, not until they came to a particularly stubborn event that seemed insistent on not being overlooked. It settled into every crevice of the tower with all the weight and density of a boulder.

They now appeared to be in a tiny, one-room house with packed-earth floors. Amar knelt over a bed in the corner, head bowed and shoulders slumped with his hands clasped in front of him. Three long, lumpy objects wrapped in blankets lay on the bed. They almost looked like...

Bodies. They were bodies. One was long and slender, but the other two were so tiny it made Kesari's heart ache to look at them. Hot, heavy air permeated the house with the rancid stench of sickness and human refuse.

The Amar who knelt over the bed let out a whimper, then broke down in quiet sobs as he buried his face in the blankets. "Why?" he asked pleadingly. "Why did they have to die?"

The real Amar began to convulse again. His body writhed and twisted more violently than ever, and it was all Kesari could do to keep him from slamming his skull against the hard floor. His eyes flew open, rolling back in his head so far that only the bottom edges of his irises were visible. He began to gasp for air in rapid, strangled breaths.

"Jameson!" Kesari called out.

"I know," he hissed. "I'm trying to get us out of here, but his mind is stuck on this."

"Try easing back on the connection a little bit," Lucian advised.

"If I do that, it could sever completely, and we may not be able to reestablish it."

"You're forcing it too much," Lucian said. "Let him take the lead."

Jameson's face twisted in concentration, and after a few seconds, the house with the dead bodies faded away. A field of tall grass and wildflowers at sunset replaced it. Amar now stood in the doorway of a small house and watched a boy of about five run through the grass. A tiny girl toddled after him. They both had the same eyes—Amar's eyes, dark and hooded, with long black lashes. They were exactly the sizes of the smallest bodies he had cried over in the previous memory.

A woman in her late twenties came up behind him in the doorway and wrapped her arms around his waist. He turned around and kissed her deeply. They put their foreheads together, and the woman laughed softly.

On the floor in front of Kesari, Amar's seizure continued. A thin trickle of blood began to flow from his nose.

They moved to a new memory. The same woman from before, now a few years younger, cradled a small bundle as Amar wrapped his arms around both of them. He kissed the top of the woman's head and stroked the baby's tiny cheek with a finger.

Another memory. This time, Amar brought flowers to the woman, who only looked a few years older than Kesari. A giggling group of friends surrounded her, and they teased the girl as she accepted Amar's flowers. He puffed out his chest and held his head high, but his gaze slid shyly down to the ground when she smiled at him.

Amar's convulsions became even more thrashing and violent. "Why isn't it stopping?" Kesari cried out. "These are all happy memories. Shouldn't it be getting better?"

"I don't know," Jameson said. Beads of sweat stuck in the creases of his brow and ran down the sides of his face. "I can't get him to let go of this one."

Kesari gave Lucian a pleading look as blood continued to flow from Amar's nose. The Spirit Tarja looked from Jameson to Amar, then back at Jameson. "Maybe we should stop."

Before the wizard could respond, the tower went spinning in a chaotic tornado of color again. Jameson grunted, his hands suddenly stiffening over Amar's body.

"What are you doing?" Lucian asked, a spark of anger in his voice. "You're going too fast! He's getting worse."

"I'm not doing this," he hissed between gritted teeth. "*He* is."

Kesari glanced up at the memories that flickered into clear view every now and again. More battlefields. Amar talking with some friends. Amar riding a horse through the forest. Amar as a child brandishing a wooden sword against an older boy.

"There!" she called out.

"He's so young," Lucian said. "That has to be from before the curse."

"We need to go forward," Jameson said as his fingers resumed their frantic tapping pattern. The memories began to shift more slowly, but still wouldn't settle on any one thing. "How is he doing?"

"A little better," Kesari replied. Amar's breathing had returned to normal, and though his body still gave an occasional twitch, his movements weren't nearly as fitful as they'd been before.

A forest sprang up all around them, then transformed into some sort of great hall hung with red and white banners. A blooming lotus flower adored every one. The hall became a richly-decorated private room—the kind of room Kesari imagined Empress Dashiva herself might live in. The lotus motif appeared again—on the pillows, carved into a tall armoire, laid out in white tile on the floor beneath an ornate washbasin. She barely had time to take it in before they were back in the forest.

"When is this?" Lucian asked.

"If I've been keeping track correctly," Jameson replied, "I'm guessing this is about six hundred years ago."

Amar rode through the forest as a young teen, a red banner hanging over him and his black steed. It caught the wind to reveal the white lotus symbol again.

"What do you think that is?" Kesari asked.

"I don't know," Lucian said. "Some clue about where he is, perhaps, but I don't recognize it."

Jameson merely shrugged.

The memory shifted again, but this time, it finally seemed to settle on something. They were in the same room as before, but now it was only dimly lit by a few candles. Amar sat upright in the bed with an open book perched on his lap. He appeared to be the same age Kesari knew him as now—the same age he'd been for centuries. He was clad only in a pair of loose pants made of silk, and his bare chest rose in slow, even breaths as he concentrated on the book he was reading.

A series of muffled noises filtered into the memory—crashes and clangs and shouting voices. Amar stiffened, his eyes darting to the door. It flew open and slammed against the wall with a bang. A young woman burst through it, breathing heavily.

Her eyes found Amar, and an expression of pure hatred contorted her face. He gave her a quizzical look and opened his mouth to speak, but whatever he'd meant to say to her was drowned out by the distressed moans of the real Amar.

His body started to writhe once more. Whatever this memory was, it wasn't a happy one. Kesari adjusted the coat under his head to provide a better cushion, but there was little else she could do for him. Blood trickled from his nose again, and a new stream started at one of his ears.

There was a flash of light, and Kesari looked up in time to see the young woman in the memory stretch her hands out. Her mouth moved, but her words were inaudible. Twin tendrils of crimson light shot out of her palms to wrap themselves around the Amar in the memory.

The memory itself seemed to be slipping out of Jameson's control again. The sounds were almost completely muted now, and the images became abstract, rippling and shifting like smoke. A violent wind tore through the tower. It swirled around them and pulled at Kesari's clothes and hair. Amar went rigid and let out a long, pained cry that seemed to carve out everything inside her, leaving her hollow.

Mitul and Saya burst into the tower, the worry on their faces morphing into sheer horror when they caught sight of Amar. "What are you doing to him?" Mitul demanded, rushing to his side and dropping to the floor. He grabbed his friend by the shoulders as the convulsions started again.

"I'm trying to stabilize him," Jameson snapped.

Saya flung herself down next to Mitul and Amar. "You have to stop!"

Jameson remained where he was, hands stiffly outstretched and every muscle taut as he tried to bring the altma swirling around the room back under his control. Kesari didn't know if the others could sense it the way she did—the prickling energy in the air, the uneasy sense of imbalance—but something had gone very wrong here.

"He can't stop," Lucian explained over another pained cry from Amar. "If the connection is severed too quickly, the damage could be permanent."

For a moment, Kesari saw Amar lying on the ground exactly as he had the night they met, bleeding from a fatal wound while she stood by, helpless and frozen. That same sense of powerlessness started to creep over her, and she recalled his words to her in Sharmok.

Are you going to help, or are you just going to sit there and watch that person suffer?

She wasn't powerless anymore. She never had been. She had magic, too, and she could use it to support Jameson and help Amar.

A shiver tingled up her spine and ran into her fingertips, the altma within her begging to be used. A voice in the back of her mind whispered that this was folly, that she didn't know what she was doing, that she would only make things worse.

She chose to ignore it, instead focusing on the unseen connection between her mind, body, and spirit the way Lucian had once taught her. It was like stretching a long unused muscle, difficult and painful, yet somehow exhilarating. She consciously acknowledged the emotions without trying to snuff them out, placed her hands on either side of Amar's head, and channeled her altma.

At first, nothing happened. Then, there was a faint prickling in her core that rippled through the rest of her body. She honed that energy to a point and sent it down her arms, through her fingertips, and into Amar's body.

His convulsions subsided. Not entirely, not all at once, but little by little, he stilled. Lucian hovered next to her, saying nothing, but his silent support gave her a little extra courage in the face of the sheer terror threatening to swallow her up. There were so many ways this could go wrong, so many ways she could hurt Amar more than she was helping him. But that hadn't happened yet. The healing magic she'd channeled seemed to be working, and Lucian would tell her if she started to do something wrong. This time, she would listen to him. This time, she wouldn't let Amar die.

After a couple of minutes, he lay completely still, his chest rising and falling in deep, even breaths. The magical energy in the room had died down. Kesari could still feel it, more strongly now that she was reconnected to her own altma, but it wasn't out of control. When she looked up, all signs of Amar's memories had vanished from the room. Jameson slumped into one of the chairs against the wall, looking exhausted and more disheveled than usual.

"He's going to be all right," Lucian said, drifting down to hover in front of Kesari's face. "He needs rest now. You can stop."

She nodded shakily and pulled her fingertips away from Amar's head. Her hands trembled, and as the connection to her altma receded back into dormancy, terror engulfed her.

What had she done? What could she possibly have been thinking, using her magic like that?

She gently pulled the coat out from beneath Amar's head and wrapped it tight around herself, but the sensation wasn't as comforting as she'd hoped it would be.

A gentle hand fell on her shoulder, and she turned to see Mitul smiling at her. His eyes were soft and wet with tears that hadn't yet fallen. "I don't know what you did or how you did it, but thank you."

"You saved him," Saya said.

"No, I didn't. I just——"

"You did," Jameson murmured from his armchair. "You helped him relax enough to let me ease him out of the memories and back to the present. If you hadn't intervened, I'm not sure I would have been able to bring him back alive and unharmed."

"Is he?" Mitul asked, gazing back down at Amar. "Unharmed?"

"As far as I can tell," Jameson said. "He'll need a good, long rest, I expect, but there shouldn't be any lasting damage. He'll wake up as good as new. Better, in fact, because he'll remember who he was before all this." The wizard stood up and swept a few stray strands of hair out of his face. "I think I'll go and take a bit of a rest myself, if you all don't mind. I haven't had that much excitement in a long time, and I don't think I'm particularly well-suited for it."

He gave a curt nod to all of them, but his piercing green eyes lingered on Kesari. "You really ought to reconsider severing your Bond. You have the potential to become a talented healer with some practice."

Kesari's cheeks warmed. Her, a Tarja healer? That was the last thing she wanted.

Wasn't it?

Something stirred within her that had been silent for a long time—a whisper of the dreams she'd had as a child. Magic was a gift, a tool, something that could be used to make the world better. Once, that was all she'd wanted. Maybe that dream was still within her reach, but...

But she had ruined everything. She had been reckless, and because of her and the power she wielded, people were dead. She didn't deserve to be a Tarja.

"Give it some thought," Jameson said as he headed for the stairs. "Nothing has to be decided right away."

AMAR

AMAR REGAINED AWARENESS SLOWLY AND LABORIOUSLY, ONE HALF of his mind still stuck in a dream while the other clawed its way back to the waking world. Lifting his eyelids was a chore that required immense strength, and when he succeeded, he immediately regretted it. Sunlight from an open window pierced straight through his skull and intensified the pounding in his head. The ache of his muscles came into sudden, sharp focus as the rest of his mind caught up with him in full consciousness. A groan passed through his clenched teeth. It felt like he'd been run over by a passing carriage and then thrown down a few flights of stairs.

But the physical pain was nothing compared to the sudden agony that tore through his heart as hundreds of newly recalled memories swirled through his mind. He tucked his arms around himself and rolled onto his side, unable to stop the tears that filled his eyes and ran down his face to wet his pillow.

There were so many faces, each with their own story now erased by time. Friends he'd come to know and love over centuries only to watch them die. Soldiers he'd fought alongside and soldiers he had killed. People he had learned from and people he had taught. He buried his mouth against his pillow to stifle his own sobs, but there was nothing he could do to stifle the pain.

He wept for the friends who'd already left him. He wept for Mitul, Saya, Kesari, and Lucian, who would eventually leave him, too. He wept for Padma and Tarik and Asha, the wife and children he'd loved more than anyone else in the world. And in the depths of his self-pity, he wept for himself—for the man who had suffered loss again and again, who had died and forgotten and started life anew more than fifty times, who now remembered everything in such excruciating detail that it threatened to consume him.

Some might have said his immortality was a gift, and there had been times when Amar wondered if they were right. Now, he saw it fully for the curse it was. The urgent desire to rid himself of it made him want to crawl out of his own skin.

Someone knocked on his door and quietly pushed it open. "Amar? Are you awake?"

Kesari. Sweet, gentle Kesari, who feared her own magic but had selflessly used it to help him at the end. He'd been so lost, overcome by anguish and terror. The soft touch of her hands and the steadying influence of her magic had given him something real to cling to in the overwhelming tumult of all those memories. He wiped a hand across his face as he sat up and turned to face her. Lucian floated in his usual spot over her shoulder.

"How are you feeling?" she asked.

"Terrible," Amar replied. "Everything hurts."

Kesari frowned. "Jameson pushed you too hard at the end. I don't think he meant to, but the magic was so out of control by then."

"You brought me back," Amar said. "That was very brave of you."

"It was," Lucian agreed.

Her eyes went to the floor. "I didn't think you'd remember."

"I remember. I owe you my gratitude, and I think I owe you an apology, too."

"Oh, you don't have to—"

He held up a hand. "I've been unkind. I resented you for not using your magic to save me before, and that wasn't fair."

"It's all right," Kesari murmured.

"Saya told me about your brother."

She stiffened and wrapped her arms around her stomach, clutching the fabric of her coat in her fists.

"It's not exactly the same," Amar went on, "but I do know what it's like to lose people and to feel like it's your fault they're gone." The heartache deepened as dozens of remembered faces floated through his mind. "I hope you can find healing. I hope we both can."

She gave him a thin smile and nodded. "Me too."

"Mitul will want to know you're awake," Lucian said. "He sat up with you all night until Saya made him go to bed, but he'll be furious if he finds out you woke up and no one told him."

Amar started to rise, but Kesari shook her head. "I'll go get him. Wait here."

She left the room with Lucian trailing along behind her.

A few minutes later, there was another knock at the door, and Mitul stepped inside without waiting for an invitation. He grinned when he saw Amar sitting on the edge of the bed and strode over with his arms outstretched.

For a second, he hesitated, then seemed to disregard whatever uncertainty remained and threw his arms around Amar. The gesture felt like a welcome home after a long time away, and Amar's eyes pricked with new tears, as joyful as they were sorrowful. He blinked them away as he returned his old friend's embrace.

Mitul let him go, looking him up and down, then sat next to him. "How are you?"

"I'm not sure," Amar answered.

"You look better. But of course, having a seizure on the floor and bleeding from your nostrils is a pretty low standard of comparison." He said it jokingly, but there was a lingering darkness in his eyes. After a few seconds, he asked, "Do you remember everything now?"

"Not everything, I don't think, but a lot more than I used to. I remember you most of all." Maybe it was because those memories were more recent, or maybe it was because Mitul had been by his side for so long and had seen him through multiple deaths. The man was nothing if not loyal. It was more than Amar deserved, and his response to that loyalty had been resentment and mistrust.

He looked his friend in the eye. "I'm sorry."

"There's nothing to apologize for," Mitul said, clapping a hand on his shoulder.

He shook his head. "You've sacrificed so much to see this through with me, and I haven't fully appreciated it."

"I've sacrificed nothing that wasn't worth giving up to help my brother."

"What about Kamaal?" Amar asked, repeating the question he'd asked so many years before, when they first started this journey together.

A wistful look passed over Mitul's face, and he twisted the silver and turquoise cuff around his wrist—a gift from Kamaal, Amar now remembered. "That was a long time ago."

"You were so happy with him." A fresh wave of guilt rippled through him. It was a familiar feeling, one he'd carried before, but he'd never brought the subject up with Mitul so directly. He'd always told himself he was trying to avoid making the other man uncomfortable, but the truth was, he'd been avoiding his own discomfort. Not talking about it made it easier to ignore some of the guilt. "You only left to help me. You could have stayed in Valmandi and built an entire life with him."

"And I would have tortured myself wondering whether you were safe out here on your own." Mitul lifted his gaze to meet Amar's. "I couldn't make Kamaal come with me, and I couldn't bear to stay and speculate on what might happen to you. Leaving was *my* choice. I regret nothing."

Despite his words, Amar still felt the need to apologize again. "I'm sorry."

Don't be. Tell me what else you remember."

"People, mostly," he said with a sigh. "And they're all dead."

"I suppose that's the curse part of immortality, isn't it? You get to live forever, but no one else does."

Amar nodded and looked past Mitul to stare out the window, knowing that if he saw his friend's expression when he told him the next part, his emotions would overcome him again. "I had a wife once, you know. I had two children—Tarik and Asha. The plague took them all, and I didn't get so much as a fever. I've lived dozens of lifetimes, and my children never had a chance to grow up. How is that fair?"

"It's not," Mitul said. "But few things in life are. I'm sure you've learned that again and again in six hundred years."

"I have to find a way to break this curse. I'm not saying I want to die today, or tomorrow, or anytime soon. But I want to grow old and know that someday, I'll die like everyone else. I've lived too long already."

"Do you remember anything about how you were cursed?"

"Not much. Pieces." He remembered the girl who had cursed him, her eyes brimming with hatred. He remembered the tendrils of red light that had closed around him when she'd used her magic, and he remembered snatches of his childhood before that. He'd lived in a palace somewhere, surrounded by trees and decorated with the symbol of a lotus flower. But there was nothing more solid than that.

"Do you know why it happened or how to get rid of it?" Mitul asked.

He shook his head. "Maybe Jameson can try again." He knew even as he said it that it was a bad idea.

"I don't think that's safe," Mitul replied. "Things got so out of control the last time. Who knows what could happen to you if you try again?"

Amar sighed and pinched the bridge of his nose. They'd come all this way, and he still didn't have all the answers he needed. How long would he have to chase them?

"There might be another way," Mitul said. "Jameson still has a few ideas. He's downstairs poring over his books again and writing notes. We can talk to him whenever you're ready."

"I'm ready," Amar said.

They headed downstairs, where the Tarja stood at his table in the center of the room, dark hair shrouding his face as he leaned over a thick tome. Muttering to himself, he flipped through the pages and didn't seem to notice Amar and Mitul entering the room. Saya and Kesari stood on either side of him, watching him work, and Lucian hovered over one of the open books on the table. They all looked up as Amar approached.

"It's good to see you up and about," Saya said with a grin. "Are you feeling all right?"

"Better," Amar replied, then nodded to Jameson. "What are you looking for?"

The man beckoned him closer with a sweep of his hand. "Let me tell you what we've learned while you were asleep."

Amar approached the table, and when Mitul pulled up a chair for him to sit in, he accepted it gratefully. His body didn't ache quite as much as when he'd first awakened, but he still felt weak and drained. Just coming down the steps had made him lightheaded.

"Do you recall the lotus symbol that kept appearing in your earliest memories?" Jameson asked.

Amar nodded. "It was in a palace, maybe the emblem of some noble house. It seemed important, but I don't remember much more than that."

Jameson flipped through the book in front of him until he came to a page that had the same symbol on it. "I've come across that symbol before, in my studies of Erythyr's ancient history," he explained. "It seems it was the royal emblem of the kingdom of Shavhalla."

Shavhalla—the name sounded familiar. It had been his home, he was certain, but he couldn't remember anything about it. Nothing except what he'd seen with Jameson's help—riding through a forest, a well-furnished room in the palace, the angry face of the girl who'd cursed him.

"My mother used to tell me stories about Shavhalla," Kesari said. "I thought it was a legend."

"So did I," Mitul agreed.

Saya shook her head. "I'm not familiar with it."

"Shavhalla was said to be one of the richest and most powerful kingdoms in ancient times," Mitul explained, "until a great tragedy occurred and it fell into ruin. Some stories say it was destroyed in an earthquake. Others claim the spirits of the forest became angry with the people of Shavhalla, so the trees swallowed it up and hid it away forever with magic."

"I'm not so sure about any forest spirits," Jameson said, "but like most legends, there is a grain of truth to these tales. Shavhalla was real, as far as I can tell. There are several reliable ancient sources that mention it, but we don't know for certain what happened to it. It seems to have disappeared, perhaps because it was destroyed, or perhaps hidden by some enchantment, as the legends claim." He flipped to a new page in his book, the margins filled with hand-written notes. "In the centuries that have passed, the forest has grown denser all around it, and those who've dared to search for it are seldom heard from again. The few who have returned claim the area is heavily guarded by demons and worse. The very land itself seems to be haunted, maybe even cursed."

Something cold prickled against the back of Amar's neck. "Cursed. Do you think that has anything to do with *my* curse?"

"I wouldn't be surprised," Jameson replied. "In your memories, we saw you well-dressed, living in luxury and comfort inside the palace. You must have been someone important, maybe even the king of Shavhalla himself. Whatever happened to you would have been important, too. It would have been recorded somewhere, and those records could very well still be inside whatever's left of that palace."

"You're saying we should go there," Saya replied. "And where *is* Shavhalla, exactly?"

Jameson pushed a pile of books aside with a wide sweep of his arm and unrolled a map of Erythyr, which he spread out on the table in front of him. "It should be right about here," he said, pointing. "Deep within the Vihaara Forest at the foothills of the mountains."

"That's all the way in northern Kavora," Saya said, disappointment heavy in her voice. Amar could understand her frustration. She'd come so far trying to find a way to save her people, and for every question that had been answered, two more seemed to spring up. Both of them had yet to find what they were searching for.

"Wouldn't it be easier to just go back into my memories?" Amar asked.

Jameson shook his head. "I wouldn't attempt it, even if I thought it would help. The procedure ended up being a little more intense than I could have predicted. It was nearly as dangerous for me as it was for you, and I value my own safety too much to try it again."

Saya crossed her arms and stared down at the map. "All right. I guess we're headed to Shavhalla, then."

"I guess we are," Mitul agreed.

Lucian turned to Jameson and chuckled humorlessly. "So, to make sure I'm not missing anything here, you want them to go to a haunted city in the wildest forest in all of Erythyr, survive whatever enchantments are guarding the place, steal a bunch of old records that may not even exist anymore, and just hope that if they *do* exist, they'll tell them how to break this curse?"

Jameson shot him a look. "Well, when you say it like that, you make it sound utterly hopeless."

Kesari, who had been silent during the entire conversation, glanced up at Lucian. "Them?" she said softly.

"What?"

"You said *them*. Not *us*."

The grin faded from Lucian's flickering flames. "I assumed we weren't going. You still have a Bond to break and years' worth of time to catch up on with your family."

"I think I may need to reconsider breaking our Bond," she said quietly. Despite the softness of her voice, a new spark flickered in her eyes, the hint of something bold that made her look almost like a different person altogether. "And as for my family..." She looked around the room between all of them. "I have one right here, too. And if you're all headed into an ancient, enchanted palace in a cursed forest, it seems to me you might need a Tarja."

Amar smiled at her, genuinely happy that she'd decided to come with them. "We'd be lucky to have you."

Lucian made a pointed, crackling noise that sounded a bit like someone clearing their throat.

"And you, Lucian, of course."

The Spirit Tarja let out a laugh that was, for once, not the least bit sarcastic. "Well then," he said, "it looks like you all get to enjoy my delightful company a while longer. I can't think of any greater privilege. You're all very lucky."

Kesari rolled her eyes and swiped at him with her hand. He darted away and flipped in a circle up to the ceiling, cackling to himself all the way.

KESARI

Kesari held her pack open while her mum inserted several brown paper parcels tied with string. Her dad watched from the doorway, jaw working as he chewed on his bottom lip.

"I hope it's enough," Mum said, clicking her tongue as she stowed away the last parcel of food. "I don't want you going hungry out there."

"It's plenty. Thanks."

"Do you have enough money?" Dad asked in a low, gruff voice. "We could spare a little more coin if you think you'll need it."

"No, I'm fine, really."

It made her feel like a very small child again, the way they fretted over her. When she'd told them her plans to accompany the others to Shavhalla, they'd tried to talk her out of it. Mum had cried, and Dad had raised his voice the way he used to during his worst arguments with Lucian. The knot of guilt over leaving them still twisted inside her gut, but as she'd explained to them last night, this was something she had to do. She'd come so far with Amar and the others, and being with them had helped her feel more like herself—like the person she'd lost to the fire two years ago. But that feeling was new. She was still trying to figure out who she was and who she wanted to be, and she couldn't do that if she stayed here, where her past was so near, dragging her down with cruel, sharp claws.

She had to go. Knowing she had a family and a home to return to made leaving both easier and more difficult.

Her parents had come around by morning, or at least they'd pretended to. They still didn't fully understand or approve, she knew, and their unspoken misgivings hung in the air like an invisible wall. But they were trying to be supportive in their own way, Mum with her home-cooked food parcels and Dad with his offer of coin they both knew full well he couldn't spare. She gave them both a hug before slinging her pack over her shoulder and heading out the door.

Navya waited outside with Lucian, and their hushed conversation trailed off when they saw Kesari. "I thought you were going to stay," Navya said, her shoulders squared as she turned to her sister with crossed arms.

Kesari winced at the accusatory note in her voice. "I know. But I won't be gone so long this time, and I swear I'll come home as soon as it's over."

Navya's brows drew together, and she blinked rapidly, like she was trying to hold back tears. "Why does everyone else get to be more important to you?" she choked out.

A shuddering crack ran through Kesari's heart. She glanced at Lucian, but he had no words of advice to offer, and the dark voids of his eyes were completely expressionless.

"It's not that they're more important," she said, taking a step toward Navya. She wanted to offer a better explanation, but the younger girl leaned away, donning a mask of cold indifference. Even if she *could* explain herself, Navya wouldn't hear it. The best she could hope for was that her sister would come to forgive her in time.

"I'm sorry," she said, knowing the words were useless but having nothing better to replace them. "Take care of yourself. I'll see you soon."

She gave her mum and dad one last embrace and walked away from her childhood home, feeling Navya's glare on her back all the way to the road.

"Are you sure you want to do this?" Lucian asked. He hovered beside her, and a few people stared curiously as they went by. Kesari was still trying to get used to the attention, but in light of her efforts to

overcome her fear of her magic—not to mention the broken lantern—
it was better that Lucian stayed out in the open. She was a Tarja, and
hiding her Bond with him wasn't going to change that.

"I think so," she answered. "More sure than I am of anything else,
anyway."

"If it's what you want, I'll support you, of course. But if you change
your mind…" He hesitated a moment. "I think you should know
Jameson and I did find a way to break Spirit Tarja Bonds. That's still
an option, if you want it."

She didn't—at least, not right now. But curiosity prickled at her.
"How?"

"The process itself is less complicated than we imagined," Lucian
replied. "The link between us comes from our sharing the same life—
your life—which is what allows altma to flow from me to you. But it's
still my altma creating the Bond, which means I could take control of
it, with enough focus and effort. I'd be taking control of you in the
process, but then I could sever our Bond, and we'd no longer be
connected. It would be difficult, and the cost to either of us would still
be great. But it's possible."

"What would happen to you?"

"I'd probably linger for a while, until my altma faded away and
allowed my spirit to move on."

Kesari frowned. "So you'd be gone. Forever."

"Yes, but don't let that be the determining factor in your decision.
As I've said before, I already lived my life. This life is yours, and it
should be your choice." He darted ahead of her to hover in front of
her face. "Whatever you feel is best, I'm with you."

Kesari nodded. After all the time she'd spent searching, to finally
have what she'd been seeking came as a relief. She *could* break her Bond
with Lucian, but she no longer wanted to. Doing so would only mean
running from her problems again, and she wasn't so certain anymore
that escape would bring the inner peace she wanted.

"Thank you for letting me know," she said. "But for now, I'm afraid
you're stuck with me."

"And it's my honor," Lucian said, grinning at her with his jagged
smile.

When they arrived back at Jameson's tower, the others were already waiting. They'd finished packing everything they would need for their journey and were now going over a few last details with Jameson regarding Shavhalla. The wizard folded up a map marking the presumed location of the ancient city and handed it to Amar, who stuck it into his journal.

"You'd better get going," Jameson said. "Your ship leaves right at noon—the captain was very adamant about that. She won't wait."

He'd been gracious enough to book them passage on the ship himself, asking only that they return with whatever incredible discoveries and knowledge they found in Shavhalla. He was so excited by the prospect of exploring the lost city that Lucian had tried to convince him to come along, but ultimately, the wizard had decided he wasn't particularly well-suited to life on the road and insisted on staying in the safety of his tower.

"Where can we find this ship?" Mitul asked, slinging his satchel over his shoulder.

"It's at the far south end of the docks, near the castle," Jameson replied. "An Atrean naval frigate. The *Vindicator*, captained by a woman named Olivia Rutledge."

Kesari exchanged a glance with Lucian. "That's Rajiv's ship!"

"Your brother?" Saya asked.

She nodded. "He joined the navy as soon as he was old enough. He only served for a couple of years, but that was the ship he was assigned to. He used to say Captain Rutledge was the best in the entire Atrean Navy, even if she did used to be a pirate."

"Used to be a *pirate*?" Jameson said. "I had no idea. Though that does perhaps explain why she was willing to break protocol and ferry a few travelers all the way to Pahari."

Mitul, Amar, and Saya exchanged worried looks, and Mitul tentatively asked, "How does a pirate end up serving in the Atrean Navy?"

"She helped them with something years back," Kesari said. "Worked with them to capture another group of pirates who'd crossed her, if I'm recalling Rajiv's stories correctly. But she did such a clever job that the navy decided they'd rather have her as an ally than an enemy. They turned on her, and once they'd captured her, they offered her a choice: execution or enlistment."

"Not much of a choice," Amar said.

"Exactly. They gave her the worst ship in the whole fleet at first, just to make sure they could catch her if she decided to cut and run, and they assigned all the sailors no one else wanted to her crew. But she earned their respect and loyalty, and she eventually convinced the navy to give back the ship they'd stolen from her. She renamed it the *Vindicator*. Rajiv used to say she'd never have a respectable name among the powers that be, but they know they're lucky to have her on their side."

"I think I'm starting to like the sound of this captain," Saya said. "Let's go meet her."

They bid farewell to Jameson and headed for the docks. Kesari spotted the *Vindicator* almost immediately, easily remembering its pouncing lion figurehead from all the times she'd spent waiting for Rajiv to come into port. She'd met Captain Rutledge a few times, but she wasn't sure the woman would remember as their encounters had always been brief. As they approached the ship, she straightened the collar of her freshly-washed coat in an effort to make herself look more presentable.

They found the wide dock where the ship was stationed engulfed in a flurry of activity. A tall, red-haired woman barked orders to various crewmen, who scurried to obey. "Check those guns, Hensley. Lieutenant Kain, I expect our stores to be filled by the time I return. Master Gambol, chart our course and have the crew make ready to set sail."

"Aye, captain," came a chorus of replies.

Captain Rutledge spun around on her heel. Her long coat billowed out behind her in the wind, the same color and style as the one Kesari now wore but adorned with various insignias befitting her officer status. Her sharp, gray eyes fell on the newcomers, and a cutlass swung from her hip as she marched toward them. A thick scar cut across her face from beneath her left eye to her jawbone, making her smile appear more than a little roguish. "Do my eyes deceive me, or is that one of Rajiv Eves' rascally little sisters?"

Kesari grinned back at her. She *did* remember, or at least she remembered her association with Rajiv. "Kesari," she said, in case the woman had forgotten her name or which of Rajiv's sisters she was. "It's good to see you again, Captain."

The woman looked her over appraisingly. "You've grown up a fair bit since the last time we met. And you look more like him, too." She gave Kesari another smile, this one sad and almost apologetic. "He was a good man, your brother. Might have made a fine officer one day. We were all sad to lose him."

"That's very kind of you to say," Kesari replied, staring at the dock beneath her. She doubted Captain Rutledge knew it was her fault Rajiv was dead, or she wouldn't be acting so nice right now.

"What brings you here?" the captain asked, her eyes flitting to the others.

"We're coming with you," Kesari said. "To Pahari, I mean. We're the ones the Wizard Jameson asked you take."

"What a delightful coincidence!" Captain Rutledge replied. "Almost makes me regret charging the man double for your passage, but I expect he can afford it, great important wizard like that. Come aboard then, and I'll have Nate show you where to stow your things." She led them to the gangplank, calling out in a clear, ringing voice as they walked. "Nate! Come here, please."

A freckle-faced boy of about twelve scampered across the ship's deck and down the gangplank to stand in front of Captain Rutledge, waiting for instruction.

"These are the guests I mentioned. I trust you made space for them below deck. Why don't you show them to their quarters?" She turned back to Kesari and raised her hand to the brim of her hat. "Welcome aboard the *Vindicator*." Then she was up the gangplank and marching the deck, shouting orders to the crew as she oversaw their last preparations to set sail.

The space Nate had found for them ended up being four bunks at the far end of the crew's quarters below deck. It was small and cramped, and there was barely enough room for them to stow their belongings, but Kesari didn't mind. She didn't plan on spending much time there anyway.

After shoving her pack under her bunk, she turned and surveyed the rest of the crew's quarters for a few seconds. There were so many beds, and one of them had been her brother's. She'd have to ask which one later. Surely some of the crew would still remember him.

She followed the others back upstairs to the top deck, where Captain Rutledge began shouting orders to set sail. She stood at the helm, head high and proud with her long, auburn hair streaming in the wind behind her. "Hoist anchor! Unfurl those sails and put her to sea."

White sails flapped open above them, and the ship pitched forward a little as wind filled the canvas. Saya's eyes widened, and she gave Kesari a look that suggested she was going to spend the next few days feeling very ill. Amar and Mitul flashed each other a grin as the ship left the dock for the open ocean. Kesari gave Deveaural one last glance, then turned around and set her gaze on the endless blue expanse before her.

ALEIDA

THE LATE EVENING SKY WAS DARK AND CLOUDED WHEN ALEIDA AND Valkyra arrived in Deveaural, the only light shining from a few gas streetlamps and the windows of buildings that lined the cobblestone roads. Despite neither of them having been to the city before, finding Jameson Weatherford's tower was a simple matter with the assistance of a friendly passerby.

Now, Aleida stood in the shadows of a darkened shop down the street, studying the tall, circular building nestled in its own little garden. Smoke rose from a narrow chimney on the roof, and a faint yellow glow emanated from a window at the top of the structure, but there had been no other signs of activity in the time she'd been watching. It seemed Jameson was alone, but Valkyra flew closer to peer inside. She returned after a few minutes.

"He's in bed reading a book," she said. Her tiny claws pricked Aleida's shoulder as she landed. "As far as I can tell, it's only him, though there is a sign on the door threatening violence should he be disturbed outside of normal business hours."

Aleida nodded and turned to the horse behind her. He gave a soft nicker as she reached into one of the saddlebags. She pulled out a scarf and some gloves, which she used to cover her nose, mouth, and hands, then reached into the opposite bag and withdrew the carefully wrapped daravak she'd collected near Malfram. If Jameson cooperated, there wouldn't be any need for it, but it didn't hurt to have options, especially when dealing with a Tarja as powerful as his reputation suggested.

They approached the tower. A paper sign printed with clear Atrean letters was posted on the door—the warning Valkyra had mentioned, no doubt—but Aleida ignored it. She raised her gloved fist and knocked.

A voice spoke seemingly out of nowhere, but the Atrean words were incomprehensible to her. "What was that?" she whispered to Valkyra.

"The same warning written on the page. You might want to brace yourself before you try again."

"What do you mean?"

Valkyra nodded to the door. "It might hit back."

Aleida channeled altma and sent it flowing into her muscles. She shifted into a wider stance, knocked again, and immediately felt the thrust of energy that exploded from the door and slammed into her. Even with her own magic strengthening her body, she barely managed to stay on her feet.

There was still no response from the Tarja within, and after a few seconds, Aleida recovered her breath, channeled her altma again, and knocked a third time.

The blast that followed was much stronger, and she staggered back a few steps. Her ribs and sternum ached from the force of the blow, and she could barely take a breath. Curse this Tarja and his abominable tower!

She glared up at the window. A head appeared, black hair shrouding a pale face, and a man's voice called down to them in Atrean.

"He's telling you to leave," Valkyra translated.

"I figured that," Aleida muttered. She called back to Jameson in Kavoran, hoping he would know the language. "I need to talk to you. I'll break your door down if I have to, but it would be a lot easier for both of us if you'd come here."

Jameson angrily muttered something she couldn't make out.

"It will only take a few minutes," she said. "I promise. I just have some questions."

He sighed. "Fine, then. Wait there."

They waited. And waited some more. Aleida paced back and forth in front of the flowering shrubs. Surely it didn't take that long to descend a few flights of stairs. Maybe she should break the door down after all.

Finally, it flung open. Jameson's mouth was turned down in a sour frown as he held up a glowing orb of light and regarded her through narrowed eyes. "What do you want?"

"I'm looking for some people who passed through here. They were coming to see you."

"I see lots of people," the man replied. "And I don't make a habit of sharing their business. It wouldn't be professional."

He started to shut the door, but Aleida took a step forward and put a hand out to stop him. "Please. It's important that I find them. My little brother's life depends on it." She reached into her pocket and pulled out a crumpled drawing of Amar—one of several she'd done on the road on the way here. "This is him. He would have come here asking you about a curse. He's immortal."

Jameson's green eyes widened, and he looked her over again. Aleida could see the cogs in his mind turning as he pieced together what little he knew of her—foreign clothing, Visan accent, the white dragon perched on her shoulder. She summoned as much altma as she could hold, allowing the energy to wind itself tight within her. This was going to be a fight.

"You're *her*," Jameson said.

She tensed. "Tell me—"

A blast of magic to the chest cut off her words and flung her back onto the cobblestones. She pushed herself upright as a flurry of books came hurtling toward her. She managed to dodge or deflect most of them with her own magic, but one caught her in the side, and a thick volume struck her in the nose. Blood seeped out, soaking through the scarf she still wore around her face. The door slammed shut.

Cursing, Aleida barreled straight into it, using all the strength she could channel into her body to knock it down. Jameson gave a yelp and headed up the stairs, his oversized robes swirling around him. Aleida shot a bolt of white-hot lightning after him, but he put up a glowing barrier that absorbed the attack. At the same time, a disembodied suit of armor charged at Aleida with its sword raised. She ducked just in time to avoid decapitation.

"He's getting away!" Valkyra called out. She flew up the stairs after the Tarja, and Aleida continued to fend off the attacking suit of armor. She ducked under its arm and got close enough to touch its metal body. With her own magic, she sought out the altma that had been used to animate it and absorbed every last bit into herself. The armor froze in place with its sword poised directly above her, unable to deliver its fatal blow. Aleida sucked in a breath but didn't stop to enjoy her relief. She darted for the stairs, taking them two at a time in her pursuit.

Valkyra reappeared in front of her. "Watch out!"

One of the stairs dropped out below Aleida's foot. She jumped over the gap only to hit her knee against another step which had sprung up higher than the rest. The entire staircase was roiling and buckling and in some places vanishing altogether, but years of climbing seaside cliffs in Libera had made he nimble and quick. She caught a glimpse of Jameson's robes fluttering around the next bend and redirected all of her altma into her feet, giving herself an extra burst of speed.

She rounded a corner and ran right into Jameson before she saw him, but quickly recovered her bearings and tackled him to the ground. They tumbled down several steps until they reached the landing below, and she finally managed to pin his arms to the floor.

A burst of light shot from his fingers to a tapestry on the wall. The fabric wrapped itself around her ankles and dragged her back. She maintained a firm grip on the man's arms as Valkyra dug into her pocket and pulled out the bundle of daravak. Pieces of the mushroom scattered across the floor, but the dragon seized one in her claws and shoved it up against his nose even as the tapestry started to win its fight with Aleida. After a few more seconds of struggle, it released her, and Jameson's limbs went limp.

"Daravak," he spat. "How dare you use such dishonorable tactics on another Tarja?"

"I tried to ask you nicely." She kept him pinned to the floor with her own body and brought her face closer to his. "Tell me where he is."

"Gone," he replied with a smile that was much too smug for a Tarja with no magic.

"But he *was* here," she replied. "How long ago? Where did he go?"

"I'm not helping you."

Aleida's blood burned through her veins. If Amar was gone, she had no time to beg for answers. She needed results. *Now.*

She sent a shock of altma through the man's body. He cried out, and she looked away from the pained grimace on his face.

"Where did he go?" she asked again.

"I don't know," he choked out.

"You're lying."

Valkyra scurried up Aleida's back to whisper in her ear. "He won't talk unless you really hurt him."

She swallowed. She'd never enjoyed this particular method of forcing information out of people, but Valkyra was right. If this was what she had to do to save Tyrus, what did it matter whether she liked it or not?

She put her palm against Jameson's forehead and released another current of lightning. He screamed and thrashed. Her hands started to shake, but she kept the current flowing a few moments longer.

When she stopped, the Tarja trembled and let out a weak groan. Aleida swallowed the bile in her throat and tried to shut out Mama's voice in the back of her mind, reminding her about Artex's teachings of kindness and compassion. It had been a long time since she'd forsaken such virtues in favor of doing what was necessary.

"Where is Amar?" she asked.

Jameson only whimpered in response.

Aleida extended her hand, nauseated before she even touched his skin. This time, she didn't draw out the magic as long as before. Maybe the man would finally come to his senses and answer. "Where did he go?"

His breaths came out in quick, shallow pants. Had she gone too far? Would he even be able to speak to them now?

Valkyra turned to Aleida, her expression as serene and composed as ever. "Again."

"No," Jameson croaked out. "No more, please. I'll talk."

She stood up and hoisted him to a sitting position against the wall. He whimpered and leaned against it, as limp as a sack of potatoes. He didn't speak for a few seconds, and Aleida stepped closer, trying to ignore the way he winced in her shadow. "Where did Amar go?"

"Shavhalla," he responded. "I sent him to Shavhalla. There are records there that might tell him how to break the curse."

A familiar panic chilled her blood. If Amar broke his curse before they could reach him, they wouldn't be able to transfer it to Tyrus, and even Valkyra didn't know how to recreate a curse of immortality. They had to catch up to him before that could happen.

"How long ago did he leave?"

"Yesterday," the man said, straightening a little. "Before noon. I bought them passage on a navy frigate escorting a merchant vessel to Pahari."

"What ship?"

"The *Vindicator*, captained by a woman named Olivia Rutledge."

"And the merchant ship?"

"I don't remember." Jameson's words tumbled out in a frantic rush. "But it was bigger, probably slower."

Aleida pursed her lips. They were closer than she'd thought, less than a day behind their quarry. If they could find a fast ship willing to take them up the coast, they still had a chance of catching up. "Any idea where we can hire a ship?" she asked Valkyra.

"Maybe. But one of us should stay here to guard him."

She frowned. "Why not leave him and be on our way?"

"I think it's better if he comes with us," the dragon replied. "We may need his help to find Shavhalla, or we may need to interrogate him again if we find out he's lying. He might even be a useful hostage when we next meet Amar and his friends."

Aleida gnawed at her bottom lip. Bringing Jameson along could slow them down, but Valkyra made a compelling argument. And if the man dared do anything to hinder their progress, they had ways of encouraging cooperation. "Fine," she said. "But how are we going to pay for passage?" They had long since run out of what little money they'd had to begin with.

"Oh, we won't be paying for our own passage, dear." Valkyra's silver eyes drifted back to Jameson, the corners of her mouth curving in a demure smile. "A famous Tarja like you, employed by the king himself—I'm sure you have plenty of coin to spare, don't you?"

The Tarja's face seemed to pale even further. "I—that's not—you can't just—"

"Stop sputtering," Aleida snarled.

He flinched. "Fine, all right. Money. I have money. Just please don't hurt me anymore."

Aleida bit back the apology hovering behind her lips. She grabbed Jameson around the arm and pulled him unceremoniously to his feet. "Good. Let's go get it."

He led her upstairs to the top floor and through a green door. The room behind it was as cluttered as the rest of the tower, but in a way that felt almost cozy. She watched his every movement like a predator, ready to strike should he try to escape or fight her off again. But for now, at least, the man seemed fully subdued.

He walked to a small chest in one corner of the room and dug around inside. After a few seconds, he withdrew a bulging pouch that was the size of both of his fists clasped together. It weighed heavy in Aleida's grasp when he handed it over to her, the coins inside making soft, metallic sounds as they rubbed together. She knew without even opening it that it was more money than her family had ever had at any one time in her whole life.

She tied the pouch to her belt and nodded back to the door. Keeping Jameson in front of her where she could see him, they made their way back downstairs.

Valkyra was waiting for them on the ground level, riffling through the books and notes spread across a large table. She turned to them as they approached, her eyes locking with Jameson's. "What are all these notes about Spirit Tarja Bonds?"

He rubbed at the back of his head. "Oh, that was for the other two. Kesari and Lucian."

"The Tarja who was with Amar?" Aleida asked.

"Yes. They wanted to break their Bond. I was trying to figure out how to make the process safer."

"But it's impossible to break a Bond."

Jameson shook his head. "It's certainly not recommended, but it is possible. Although to do so would come at a great cost to the parties involved."

"Did you break it for them, then?" she asked. If he had, that would be to her advantage. She doubted the girl would be much of a fighter without her magic. One less foe for her to face, should it come to that again.

"No. They decided they didn't want that after all. Almost a shame, after all that research. I was very curious to see what might happen."

Aleida rolled her eyes. That was just her luck. Any glimmer of something good happening for once, and it was snuffed out like a flame in the wind. She sighed.

"I see our generous host has decided to part with some of his wealth," Valkyra said, eyeing the pouch at Aleida's waist. "I'll go to the docks and see if I can find us a ship. You'll keep an eye on him?"

Aleida nodded and followed the dragon to the door. She started to open in, but Valkyra fluttered up to her shoulder, furry muzzle brushing against her ear. "Be careful with him," she whispered in Visan. "He might look harmless now, but he didn't earn his reputation without being both clever and talented. We don't know what tricks he's plotting."

"I know," she replied. "Hurry back."

The dragon flew out the door with an elegant swish of her long, silky tail, and Aleida closed it tight behind her. When she turned, Jameson was watching her with a curious expression. "What's her name?" he asked. "And yours."

She narrowed her eyes. "Why?"

"Seems we ought to properly introduce ourselves, don't you think?"

Aleida considered Valkyra's warning, but surely there wasn't any harm in telling the Tarja her name. If they were going to be dragging him along with them, they'd all become well acquainted soon enough. "I'm Aleida. Her name is Valkyra."

"Valkyra," he mused. "Hmm. She must have been a very powerful Tarja to have taken on that form, but I can't say I've ever heard of her."

"Not every powerful Tarja feels the need to live in a great big tower and take on lofty titles," Aleida retorted.

"Fair enough." He out an enormous yawn and slumped into an armchair near the fireplace. "I must say, I'm rather exhausted from all that fighting and torture and thievery. If you don't mind, I think I'll take a nap."

He said it in such a carefree way, but Aleida cringed anyway. What would Mama and Papa say if they could see her now? What would

Tyrus say? Would they still be proud of her and the lengths she was willing to go to for her family, or would they be disappointed?

She was still mulling this over as Jameson tipped his head back and promptly began to snore.

The night dragged on, and Valkyra didn't return. Aleida retrieved her belongings from the horse still waiting outside, packed a bag with some clothes for Jameson, and helped herself to his food stores. Afterward, there was nothing to do but wait. She grew more impatient with each passing hour. All she could think about was how fast an Atrean naval ship was, how far ahead Amar must be by now, and how much farther he was getting as the seconds passed by. Jameson remained in a deep slumber, which only irritated her further as her own exhaustion sank in. She didn't dare close her eyes and take her attention off the man for any prolonged period of time.

At last, there was a scratching at the door, and she opened it to let Valkyra in. "What took so long?"

The dragon held her nose in the air. "It's not easy finding a fast ship with a crew willing to chase down a navy frigate. I think I did magnificently, given the circumstances."

Aleida sighed. She needed to sleep. Once she had a few hours rest, she wouldn't be so agitated. "Sorry."

Valkyra fluffed her wings out behind her back. "We can set sail as soon as we get to the docks, so if you're done complaining…"

Needing no further prompting, she shook Jameson awake. "Time to go."

"You're leaving?" He sat up and pushed his shaggy black hair out of his face.

"*We're* leaving," she reminded him, then tossed him the bag she'd set next to her own. "I packed you some things for the trip while you were sleeping."

"Are you certain you want me to come?" he asked pleasantly. "I'm not much of an adventurer. I'm afraid I'd only slow you down and get in your way."

Valkyra hopped from the table onto Aleida's shoulder and leveled her keen gaze at the man. "If you do either of those things or cause us any other sort of trouble, I can promise you'll regret it."

Aleida adopted her own cold expression to back the Spirit Tarja's threat. Jameson looked between them, sighed, and said, "All right, no trouble. I understand."

Aleida motioned to the door. "Lead the way."

"Wait," Valkyra said. "Put an illusion over him. He's bound to attract attention out there."

Jameson visibly deflated. Perhaps it had been his plan all along for someone on the streets to recognize him and save him from his captors.

Aleida had never been particularly skilled with illusions. It took a few attempts to create something passable, but by the time she was done, the scrawny man was disguised as a burly sailor with an unremarkable face. As long as no one looked too carefully, the illusion would hold up long enough to get them to the docks. For good measure, she channeled altma to put a barrier over his mouth, which would prevent anyone from hearing him should he try to cry out for help.

They made their way to the docks without incident. Aleida had never seen so many ships in one place since Libera fell to ruin, and even then, there hadn't been *this* many. Valkyra directed them to a well-maintained vessel at the farthest end of the port—a brig, if she was correctly remembering Papa's lessons on the different types of Atrean ships they'd watched from the shore near home.

She had never seen the crew of these ships before, but she was fairly certain that the unsavory group of people standing before her now were pirates. One wore a great brimmed hat with ragged feathers and frayed edges. Another had so many piercings that she could hardly distinguish the flesh of his ears from the metal. On the deck of the ship, she spotted a one-armed woman with a wooden peg for a leg. Another man leered at her with a grin full of holes where there should have been teeth.

This was the crew Valkyra had found to help them hunt down Amar?

The man with the ragged hat stepped forward and bowed low to all three of them. "Greetings, Mistress Aleida." He spoke Kavoran with a heavy accent she couldn't place. "Me name's Cutter, and I'll be yer captain on this voyage. I trust yer Spirit Tarja has informed you of the details of our arrangement?"

Valkyra chimed in before Aleida could respond. "You take us to the *Vindicator* and help us board her. You can have whatever you see fit to take, except the man we're hunting."

Aleida nodded to show she understood.

"Excellent," the captain said. "And our payment?"

She dug through her pack for the pouch Jameson had given her, the contents of which she'd divided up and stowed away in various other places on her person and amongst her belongings. The pouch itself was still fairly heavy, and Cutter's eyes gleamed greedily as she passed it over to them. He shook it a little and smiled when the coins jangled, then waved them forward. "Come aboard, then. I've got a lovely bunk set up for you in the officer's quarters."

"And him?" Aleida took hold of Jameson's elbow. "Any chance you could lock him up somewhere safe for me?"

Cutter smirked. "Of course, miss. It would be our pleasure." He whistled, and the man with the earrings seized Jameson by the arms and dragged him up the gangplank. The Tarja's eyes were wild with fear, but no sound escaped his lips through the barrier Aleida had placed there.

"We'll set sail as soon as yer settled," Cutter said, turning to walk up the gangplank with his coat billowing out behind him.

Aleida hesitated for only a moment, then followed. Her eyes drifted to the bow of the ship, where the name *Hound's Hatred* had been crudely scratched into the wood. A chill breeze blew through the salty air, and a spray of seawater misted over her skin. She shuddered, and not only from the cold water. Everything inside her screamed that getting aboard a ship with a bunch of pirates was a terrible idea. But she could take care of herself.

Besides, if this was what she had to do to save Tyrus, what did it matter whether she liked it or not?

KESARI

KESARI LOVED EVERYTHING ABOUT LIFE ON THE *VINDICATOR*. SHE
loved the pitch and roll of the deck beneath her feet, and she loved
clinging to the sail lines and leaning out over the sea to stare at the froth
made by the ship's passing. She loved the clean, salty smell of the air
and the dolphins that sometimes leaped and frolicked around the
vessel. At night, she loved looking out as far as she could see, where
the sky seemed to melt into the water with no horizon to separate them.
She loved watching the lamps come on like stars in the merchant ship
they were escorting, setting it aglow as it trailed behind them.

Maybe it was a new sense of freedom or just knowing that Rajiv had
once walked this same deck, but being on the *Vindicator* made Kesari
feel brave. After their first night at sea, she asked Lucian to start
training her to use her magic again, and he was more than happy to
oblige. She spent most of her mornings meditating under his direction,
working to align the energy of her mind, body, and spirit so she could
better channel altma and then keep it in her control. To test her
abilities, she stuck with simple, safe exercises that were easily contained.
Still, the practice proved to be far more difficult than she remembered
it ever being before.

"Don't fight your emotions," Lucian reminded her after one
particularly frustrating morning. She'd been trying to mend a small tear

in the fabric of her coat, but it wasn't working "If you're fighting them or trying to shut them out, your mind can't be fully in harmony with the rest of your being."

"If I don't fight them, they get out of control," she retorted. "That's what happened before." When she'd burned down the clocktower, it was because she hadn't kept her excitement in check, and she couldn't allow something like that to happen again.

"Shutting out your feelings only puts you at war with yourself," Lucian replied. "You can't channel altma like that—not in a way that's safe or effective. Try again."

She did, again and again, day after day, spending hours upon hours reflecting on her feelings and the turmoil that had been writhing inside her since Rajiv died. Most days, she cried, but Lucian was always there to talk her through it. And little by little, as she acknowledged the conflict within herself instead of trying to ignore it the way she'd always done before, it began to subside. Not completely—she suspected she'd hold some piece of it forever—but at least enough that she could feel its power over her starting to weaken. Enough that she could, sometimes, leave her past in the past.

When she needed a break, Kesari spent her time wandering the ship and pestering the crew about her brother. She'd quickly figured out which ones had served on the *Vindicator* at the same time he had. They told her stories that made her laugh and stories that made her cry, and every memory they shared gave her a little more strength to carry her grief. It wasn't the tight, constricting thing it had once been, pressing on every part of her so that she suffocated under its weight. The loss was still heavy, something she'd carry the rest of her life, but she was strong enough to bear it.

"I forget, sometimes," she confided in Lucian one night as they stared up at the stars. "Just for an instant, I forget that I burned down that clocktower. How terrible is that? I shouldn't *ever* forget—not after what I did."

"You can't spend the rest of your life agonizing over your mistakes," he replied. "Rajiv wouldn't have wanted you holding onto them forever."

He was probably right, as usual, though it was still difficult not to feel guilty on the nights she went to bed and realized she hadn't thought much about those mistakes all day. But she was happy. For the first time in years, she was truly and unconditionally happy.

Amar and Mitul seemed equally happy, having rekindled their old friendship now that Amar had regained his memories. They frequently played music together for the sailors at night, much to everyone's delight. Saya, however, was utterly miserable. She spent their first three days on the ship vomiting over the bulwark. Even after the seasickness passed, she constantly walked about with a strained expression that was very unlike her usual calm confidence.

Late one night, after Amar, Mitul, and most of the sailors had gone to bed, Kesari and Lucian wandered up from the crew's quarters to find Saya standing at the starboard side of the ship, staring out across the ocean beyond. The merchant vessel, the *Golden Raven*, drifted silently behind the *Vindicator*, close enough that Kesari could see its sailors' shadows in the lantern light. Farther in the distance, another ship was silhouetted against the moonlit sky. Another brig maybe, like the *Raven*, but it was hard to tell from this distance.

She leaned against the bulwark next to Saya. "It's good to see you out here looking so healthy."

The older girl gave a wry smile. "If I stand still like this and look out there in the dark, I can almost pretend I'm staring at the desert and forget I'm on this cursed ship."

"Not much of a sailor, then."

"Not like you. But I shouldn't complain. It's this ship that's bringing me closer to finishing my haseph. A little seasickness is a small price to pay."

Kesari had been so wrapped up in her own concerns lately that she hadn't spared much thought for Saya or her haseph. They'd learned so much from Jameson, and the implications were bound to have an effect on the young warrior's own goals. Even if they found Shavhalla and the answers Amar was seeking, would they discover what Saya needed? Would they learn how to replicate his curse to give immortality to the Sularans?

"Do you still think you'll find what you're looking for in Shavhalla?" she asked.

Saya shrugged. "I like to believe I will, but maybe I'm just too stubborn to admit I've wasted all this time on something that won't work. And that's if it's even the right thing to do in the first place. Immortality is…" She trailed off and shook her head. "You saw. All of Amar's deaths, all the people he lost."

"He told you?"

"He told Mitul. Mitul told me enough. I think I finally understand why Amar doesn't want his immortality. And why it might be a bad idea for me to offer my own people that option, assuming we *do* find a way to recreate the curse."

Kesari wasn't sure how to respond. Her own feelings about life, death, and immortality were complicated, to say the least. Because of their Bond, she and Lucian shared a life, which meant she had essentially given up half of her remaining lifespan from the day their Bond was formed. If she reached the age of fifty, she'd be lucky. She knew how precious life was, how valuable every year could be, and there was still so much she wanted to do with whatever time she had left. The prospect of living forever was undeniably enticing. And yet, she'd seen the pain in Amar's memories. He'd lost so many people, and she knew the pain of loss, too. To experience that pain a hundred times or more would be unbearable.

"Immortality could save your people," Lucian said, using the same argument Saya had made a hundred times before. "If war does break out between them and Kavora, it could be the *only* way to save them."

"But is it worth the cost?"

"If it prevents them from being wiped out?" Lucian said. "Yes. Of course it's worth it."

"The same conclusion I came to," Saya said. "But it's more complicated than that, isn't it? This is a curse we're talking about. If we find a way to recreate it, there's no guarantee we can contain it. The Masahi and our leaders would make every effort to do so, but in time, it could get out. Others could use it or build on the framework to create their own curses. Things are bound to go wrong, tampering with such powerful magic."

"So what are you going to do?" Kesari asked.

"I've been asking myself that for days, but I still have no idea. I suppose all I can do is hope we'll find more answers in Shavhalla. At the very least, there should be something there that would be a worthy offering for my haseph, even if it's not what I originally set out to retrieve."

She made no effort to hide the disappointment in her tone. She'd poured so much time and energy into her haseph, and facing the possibility that it had all been for nothing couldn't have been easy for her. Kesari laid a hand on her arm. "You'll figure something out."

Saya turned her eyes back to the sea, but murmured voices behind them drew Kesari's attention. One sailor hurried toward the door that led to Captain Rutledge's cabin. He'd come from the helm, where Master Gambol and another sailor stood passing a long spyglass between them, their voices rapid and hushed. She followed their gazes back to the brig she'd spotted in the distance earlier. It was closer now, and still closing in rapidly.

"That was fast," she said, nodding to the ship.

The dark spots that formed Lucian's eyes seemed to narrow as he studied the approaching vessel. "Too fast. There must be magic propelling it."

She started to ask how that might work, but a noise like a sudden thunderclap drowned out her voice. Behind the *Vindicator*, the *Golden Raven* shuddered as a cannonball struck her stern.

Kesari's heart gave a sudden lurch, and she turned to Lucian in a panic. Captain Rutledge burst through the door of her quarters, fully awake and alert despite having undoubtedly just jumped out of bed. "What the devil is going on?" she shouted up to her helmsman.

"The *Raven's* under attack!"

"Yes, I *know* that. By whom? Why did no one sound the alarm?"

"Apologies, Captain. They were trailing so far behind, and then—" He shook his head. "I've only seen a ship move that fast with a Tarja's help."

Captain Rutledge took the spyglass offered by her yawning cabin boy and peered out at the attacking ship. "Pirates," she said in the same calm tone one might use when announcing that dinner was ready. "Well, don't stand there gawking, Nate. Get the crew up here. All hands on deck!"

The boy took off, crying out the captain's orders at the top of his lungs, and a second cannon shot rang out as the *Vindicator's* crew poured onto the deck. Kesari and Saya hugged the bulwark to avoid being run over in the commotion. Amar and Mitul soon joined them.

"What do we do?" Mitul shouted over the roar of angry sailors and the boom of another cannon blast.

"Stay out of the way," Amar replied. "And don't get killed."

Captain Rutledge stormed past them then, pausing when she caught sight of them all standing at the bulwark. "What are you all doing? Go down and help load the cannons. That shouldn't be too hard, even for a bunch of land lubbers. And you, fire creature!"

"Me?" Lucian asked, hovering forward a few paces.

"Do you see any other fire creatures on my ship? I want you to fly overhead and report back to me with what you see. If you can manage to set their sails ablaze, so much the better."

She turned on her heel and resumed shouting orders to the rest of her crew. Lucian shot off into the sky without so much as a word to Kesari, and she suddenly felt absolutely and terrifyingly alone.

"Come on," Amar said. "Let's see if we can help with the cannons." He headed for the stairs that led to the deck below, and Kesari followed behind the others.

It was even louder below deck than it had been above as shouts echoed around the crowed space and the crew hurried about, loading the cannons and firing them off as fast as they could manage. She lost count of how many blasts went off. They all seemed to ring together in her ears and echo inside her skull, punctuated by the crack of splintering wood and the screams of injured sailors. The *Vindicator* shook with the recoil of her cannons and the hits she took from enemy fire.

Someone shook Kesari by the shoulders. She blinked, realizing she'd been standing frozen against the wall. A man's face swam into view—the ship's surgeon. She didn't remember his name.

"You're the Tarja girl, aren't you?" he said, and she nodded. He gripped her by the arm and dragged her toward the front of the ship. "I could use your help. Come on."

He led her into the sick bay, a part of the ship she'd only ventured to once before. It was a small space and already filling with the wounded. Their pained expressions looked even more grotesque in the flickering lantern light.

"Help me tend to them," he said, releasing her arm. "Use your magic to heal them if you can."

Flashes of memory began to flicker at the edges of her mind. Smoke and fire, people screaming, a crush of bodies as they swept past her trying to get away from the burning clocktower.

She clenched her fists, felt the sharp press of her fingernails digging into her palm. It wasn't real. It was in the past, not happening *now*. She was here, on a ship—Rajiv's ship—and there were people who needed help. She had to do something.

Trying to brush away the last of her memories, she headed for the first person she laid eyes on—a young woman bleeding from a nasty head wound. "Let me take a look at that," she said, and was proud of herself when her voice only shook a little.

The woman took her hands from her scalp, and Kesari pulled away strands of her hair to reveal a long, deep gash underneath. She could see the skull through the torn, red flesh and had to fight a sudden wave of nausea that roiled through her stomach.

"What's your name?" she asked, both to distract herself and the woman.

"Evie."

"It's nice to meet you, Evie."

"You too, miss." She offered a tremulous smile. "How bad is it?"

"Not too bad. Nothing a bit of magic can't fix."

She instantly wished she could take the words back. She was hardly ready for this, and Lucian wasn't even here to guide her through it. What if she made a mistake? What if she hurt this poor woman more than she was already hurt?

The ship gave a sudden violent shudder, and a few of the lanterns flickered out. Evie grabbed hold of her hand, then dropped it with a shy, embarrassed look. "Sorry. Just a bit scared, I guess."

"It's all right," Kesari said. She grabbed a clean rag from a nearby table and pressed it against the wound.

"This is my first time out at sea," Evie said.

"Mine too."

"This part's worse than I imagined. I thought fighting pirates would be exciting, but it's rather terrifying, isn't it."

Kesari nodded. "That it is."

A pair of sailors came in carrying one of their comrades, who was so bloody she would have thought he was dead had he not been screaming. Evie watched them go by with wide eyes. "There's others needing help more than me, miss. You should go to them first."

Kesari's heart pounded. The woman was right, but if she couldn't even handle a little cut, what good could she do for those with more severe injuries? She shook her head and pulled the cloth away from the wound. "This will only take a minute."

Taking a deep breath, she closed her eyes and listened to the turmoil of emotions inside her. "I'm afraid," she whispered.

She said it more as an acknowledgement to herself, but Evie responded anyway. "I think we all are."

Somehow, that made Kesari feel a bit better. She channeled altma into her fingers and pressed them against Evie's scalp. Working slowly and carefully, she began to send her magic into the woman's skin, using it to feel for any deeper damage and close up the wound. Fear lingered in the back of her mind through the entire process, but she didn't fight it or try to suppress it. She didn't need to. It was there, but she didn't have to let it control her.

"That feels a lot better," Evie said when she had finished. She gingerly touched the skin around the wound, which was now little more than a raised scar, and smiled. "Thank you."

"You're welcome."

"Go on and see to the others, then. I'll be all right now."

Kesari took a deep breath and turned around to face the wounded men and women crowded into the room. There was so much pain and suffering here, just like there had been the night the clocktower burned, but she was no longer helpless. She was terrified, yes, but she could also be brave and competent.

With that, she immersed herself in the work of cleaning and bandaging wounds, setting broken limbs, and using her magic to help the injured however she could. Before too long, her fear subsided to little more than a gentle undercurrent beneath her concentration.

AMAR

A MAR'S LEGS STRAINED TO KEEP HIM UPRIGHT AS ANOTHER CANNON
blast rocked the ship. He put a hand against the wall to brace himself,
his pulse pounding in his ears loud enough to compete with the
shouting voices all around him. He hadn't been in a fight like this for
years, and never one aboard a ship. It was different, in some ways—
the cramped space, the inability to see his foe on the enemy ship, the
scent of gunpowder so heavy it burned his nostrils. But in all the ways
that mattered, it was the same. Mingled cries of pain and fear, the rapid
rhythm of his heartbeat, the familiar desperation to do whatever it took
to save his own life—and his friends'.

He whipped his head around to find Mitul and Saya. Both were still
standing, though Mitul appeared to be in a state of shock with wide
eyes and a gaping mouth. Amar grabbed him by the shoulder and shook
him until the man's eyes focused on his own. "Stay by me, all right?"
he shouted above the din.

Mitul nodded.

"Oi! You three!" A broad-shouldered woman in an officer's coat
jabbed a finger at a nearby cannon. "Man that cannon. Come on, make
yourselves useful."

Amar swallowed. He didn't have the first inkling of what manning
the cannon might entail, but he shuffled forward anyway. Better to

fight back than stand here waiting to be killed or maimed. The ship gave another lurch. Mitul stumbled into him from behind and they both went sprawling into the side of the cannon.

"Get up, man!" a sailor said, grabbing Amar by the scruff of his shirt and hauling him to his feet.

"What do you need us to do?"

"Grab these lines, quick now."

Amar took up a position behind the sailor while Mitul and Saya went to the other side of the cannon and grabbed the rope there. A burly man was already loading the shot into the barrel. As soon as he was done, another man shoved in a rammer on a long wooden stick.

"Get ready, lads," the first sailor said, tightening his grip on his own line.

Amar followed suit. Mitul and Saya did the same. Both of them looked like they were about to throw up.

As soon as the rammer was out, the first sailor put all his weight into pulling his line. "Heave!"

They did. Amar's muscles strained from the effort. The rope slipped through his palms a little when another lurch shifted the cannon's weight. He was going to have some painful blisters in the morning, assuming they lived through this.

He set his jaw. They *would* survive to see the morning. They had to.

With a few more shouts from the more experienced sailor in their group, they righted the cannon's path and heaved again. It rolled forward to press against the wall, barrel protruding out the open gun port.

"Hold her steady, lads," the sailor called.

At the rear end of the cannon, the officer who'd initially given their assignment stood by. She crouched to sight down the barrel, her hand wrapped around the cord of the gunlock. For the space of a single breath, nothing happened.

"Fire!" She yanked the cord. There was a massive blast, and the cannon shot backward with the recoil. At least a few of the other cannons had gone off at nearly the same time, and Amar's very bones seemed to shake inside his body from the force of the volley.

A thunderous rumble came from outside as the enemy ship fired back. Wood cracked and splintered somewhere to his right, and he ducked as cries rang out. Suddenly, he was back on the battlefields of Kavora, ambushed by a group of enemy Tarja. His comrades fell around him one by one, their dying screams echoing in his ears until he fell, too.

He shook his head and blinked away the old memories. Another shot was already being loaded into the cannon. He glanced over at Mitul and Saya, both still alive and unharmed. Mitul's lips curled up in a forced smile that looked more like a grimace, and Amar's heart lurched. The man was an artist, not a warrior. He shouldn't even be here. Were it not for Amar, he wouldn't be.

"We're going to be all right," he called out to Mitul over the cannon. So help him, if they got out of this, he'd do everything in his power to make sure his friend never had to risk his life like this again.

The sailor called over his shoulder to them. "Ready, lads! Heave!"

Amar was more prepared for the deafening sound and the recoil that came with this blast. Over and over again, they repeated the process, their own attacks periodically interrupted by enemy fire. The air became hot and thick with the stench of sweat and gunpowder. Several of the men had already stripped off their shirts, and Amar did the same, but even that made little difference. His hair stuck to his forehead in damp clumps, and he wiped away the moisture that dripped down his face with the back of his hand.

A sudden cheer rose up from somewhere down the line of cannons. "What's happening?" he asked the officer beside him. Sighting down the length of the cannon, she had the clearest view of the battle through the gun port.

She repositioned herself and let out a victorious cry of her own. "Their ship has caught fire! They can't outmaneuver us with their sails all burned up like that."

Lucian. It had to have been him who set the enemy's sails ablaze. Amar grinned and joined in on the celebrations with a whoop. One of the officers called for a cease fire, and Mitul and Saya threw their arms around each other in a joyful embrace. Amar stepped around a sailor to get closer to the gun port and peered through the opening. The flaming pirate ship glowed like a giant torch against the darkness.

A flash of light came from one of the open gun ports, and a low rumble echoed through the night. One last parting shot from the enemy they'd already defeated. Amar jerked back, but the cannonball struck the *Vindicator* a few paces away from where he was standing.

Wood splintered all around him. He flew backwards with his limbs splayed out in front of him, until something hard broke his momentum and knocked all the air from his lungs. Black splotches crept over his vision, and all sound seemed to have been sucked from his surroundings. He tried to take a breath, but his lungs were on fire, useless.

He sat perfectly still where he'd landed. A sharp pain pulsed at the back of his head, but nothing else seemed to be injured. He'd been hurt a lot worse than this before. If he gave his body a little time to recover, he'd be all right.

Someone grabbed his shoulder, and Mitul's face swam into full view as the dark splotches in his vision began to dissipate. "Amar?" The man's voice cracked. "Please, say something!"

He took a slow, painful breath and croaked out a single word. "Hurts."

Saya stooped over him. "What hurts? Do you need to see a healer?"

He groaned and shook his head. "I think I'll be all right."

"We're taking you anyway," Mitul said. "Can you stand?"

"I said I'm all right. Just give me a minute."

Mitul nodded and inhaled a shaky breath. His eyes looked wet, but it was hard to tell for certain in the dim light.

"Are you crying?" Amar growled. "Please don't tell me you're crying over me."

"You could have died," he replied.

"I *can't* die, remember?"

"You know what I mean." He shoved Amar in the shoulder, but only with a fraction of the force he might have used in normal circumstances. "I just got you back. I don't want you forgetting me all over again. I'd say that warrants a few tears, wouldn't you?"

"I guess," Amar said, forcing a little extra gruffness into his voice. Between the intensity of the skirmish and the reminders it brought of people he'd lost in battles past, he was starting to feel more than a little emotional himself. But now was not the time or place to let those feelings out.

He slowly raised himself to his feet. Mitul offered him an arm, and he took it gratefully. "Come on," he said once he'd steadied himself. "We should check on Kesari."

KESARI

AT SOME POINT, THE *VINDICATOR'S* INTERMITTENT SHUDDERS AND jarring lurches stopped, but the sick bay remained in a state of tumultuous chaos as the wounded continued to be brought in for treatment. Kesari had sunk into a rhythm while she worked and was so absorbed in what she was doing that she didn't even notice Lucian had come in until his voice startled her from behind.

"You're doing well here."

"I'm trying," she replied, heading for a nearby washbasin to rinse her hands. They turned the already-pink water a deeper shade of red. "Is the fighting really over?"

"Yes. We won."

She let out a grunt. It was hard to see anything that involved this much pain and suffering as a victory. "I suppose you helped with that?"

"I set the ship on fire, but it took longer than I wanted it to. I ran into a bit of trouble with that Visan woman and her Spirit Tarja."

Kesari raised her eyebrows. "They're here?"

"On the pirate ship. We can assume they were the ones to organize the attack."

"They're still coming after Amar," she said, drying her hands on a nearby rag that looked relatively clean. "Did you tell the others?"

"No. I wanted to check on you first, make sure you were all right."

He grinned. "And look at you! I can feel the magic all around this room. You've done a lot of good here tonight."

Kesari gazed around at all the bandaged sailors, the bloodied rags, the red-stained floor. The pained cries of earlier had subsided to a few, quiet moans, and aside from that, the room felt almost peaceful. Lucian was right—magic practically thrummed in the air around her, pulsing against her own altma. She'd channeled more of it tonight than she'd even allowed herself to feel in the last two years combined.

What had she been thinking?

The rhythmic trance she'd fallen into snapped, and whatever had kept her going until now suddenly drained out of her. Her bottom lip trembled, and her legs started to shake. She backed up against the wall and slid to the floor before her body collapsed. Her heart started to race as familiar waves of panic washed over her.

"I was so afraid," she said, tears forming in her eyes. "I didn't know what I was doing. I needed you here."

"I'm sorry. I would have stayed with you if I'd known, but I thought I'd be more useful out there." He hovered a little lower until his gaze met hers. "But Kes, you *didn't* need me. You did all this on your own."

"What if I'd messed up? I could have hurt someone."

"You didn't, though."

"But I could have."

"Look at me, Kes." She did, and he smiled at her. "You didn't hurt anyone. You helped them. I'm sure you saved some of their lives. Your magic did that."

She wasn't sure why those words made her cry even harder, but they did. Her magic had helped this time, and that was exactly what she'd wanted so desperately ever since she was a child. But what about next time? What if she lost control again?

For a while, she sat there on the floor with her arms wrapped around her legs and her entire body shaking. Amar, Mitul, and Saya found her like that. They gathered around her, raised her up with gentle touches and soothing words, but she barely heard them. In a daze, she followed them back to her bunk, where she lay with her knees curled up beneath her chin as tears continued to roll down her cheeks.

Lucian hovered above, whispering to her that she was safe, that she had done well. The others whispered too, and she caught her own name in worried tones among their words. They probably thought she was pathetic. They probably thought she was losing her mind. They were probably right, on some level, but she was too exhausted to care.

She closed her eyes and forced herself to take slow, deep breaths until the tears stopped, and she finally succumbed to a mercifully dreamless sleep.

PART III

THE WOMAN WHO LOST HER HEART

ALEIDA

THE MUSCLES IN ALEIDA'S ARMS BURNED AS SHE ROWED A DERELICT little dinghy away from the *Hound's Hatred*, but the sensation was nothing compared to the vehement rage and disbelief that burned within her. She'd come so close only to have Amar slip away once again. Those idiot pirates! If they'd just listened to her and taken the *Vindicator* before focusing their attention on the *Golden Raven*, she might have captured Amar, and they'd all have what they wanted.

Captain Cutter had gotten himself killed mere minutes into the fight, and the crew spent the rest of the battle in disarray trying to prevent the *Hound's Hatred* from being pummeled by the *Vindicator's* cannons. Aleida had hoped to help them get the upper hand using magic, but even that had failed. She and Valkyra had instead been forced to focus their attention on the firey Spirit Tarja, who had eventually succeeded in setting the entire ship aflame.

Before long, relentless cannon fire left the *Hound's Hatred* crippled and taking on water at an alarming rate. Aleida had been reluctant to give up, but at Valkyra's urging and seeing no other option, she decided to abandon ship. They'd hurried down to the brig to retrieve Jameson, already up to his waist in seawater. While the pirates were still fighting, the three of them managed to lower a dinghy into the ocean and escaped before the entire ship went down. Now, Aleida could barely make out the dark silhouettes of the *Vindicator* and the *Golden Raven* in the moonlight. There was nothing left to be seen of the pirate vessel.

Valkyra lay coiled in Aleida's lap. Her cold gray eyes watched the Wizard Jameson for any sign of mutiny. He sat across from them, hunched and shivering in soaked robes. "How far until we reach land?" he asked between chattering teeth.

"Not far," Aleida replied. The *Vindicator* had traveled a northeast route right up the coastline, so they weren't too far out to sea. But her arms were already shaking with exhaustion, and she didn't trust her own emotions enough right now to ease the rowing by channeling altma. Instead, she thrust the oars at her prisoner with a harsh growl. "Your turn."

"Oh, I'm not really cut out for this sort of work," he replied nonchalantly. "If only you hadn't taken away my magic. I know a few tricks that could make this a lot easier."

"And I know a few tricks that could make your life miserable if you don't cooperate," she snapped back. "Now row."

With a sigh, Jameson wrapped his hands around the oars and began to row. Aleida continued to glare at him with barely contained rage as the true object of her fury sailed farther and farther away aboard another ship.

It was nearly dawn by the time they reached land. They rode the breaking waves right up to the shore and stumbled out of the dinghy unceremoniously. Jameson tripped and collapsed onto the sand, where he lay motionless without even the slightest attempt to get back up. Every muscle in Aleida's arms and back screamed at her to lie down and rest, but she refused to listen.

She nudged the man's feet with her toe. "Get up. We need to keep moving."

"Agreed," Valkyra said. "If any of those pirates managed to get off the ship, they'll be coming ashore soon, too. They won't appreciate us stealing one of their boats and abandoning them in the middle of the ocean."

Jameson groaned in protest but pushed himself up anyway. When Aleida pulled out the soaked bundle of daravak to dose him again, he barely put up a fight. All she had to do was let a few crackles of lightning jump between her fingertips, and he inhaled the stuff on his own.

They walked inland, heading northwest away from the beach. Valkyra guessed they were somewhere north of Libera, a suspicion that was confirmed when they came to the edge of a river delta shortly after noon. Only then did they stop to rest. Jameson flopped onto the ground beneath the shade of a large tree and fell asleep within seconds.

Aleida took a few minutes to spread out the contents of her pack in the sun. Most of them were starting to dry already, but the papers and art supplies in her leather case had been soaked through. She clenched her jaw in frustration as she carefully pulled apart Tyrus' letters and her own drawings of Amar and his companions. Her charcoal sketches were smeared into shapes that were beyond recognition in most places, and the ink from Tyrus' letters bled across the paper in such a way that both the words and his drawings were indecipherable. She put her fingers to the pages and used magic to pull as much moisture out of them as she could, though that did little to improve their appearance. Defeated and drained, she propped herself up against the trunk of a tree, crossed her arms, and went to sleep.

It was dark when she awoke. Her eyes immediately went to the spot where she'd last seen Jameson. He was still there, snoring heavily. It took her a few seconds longer to spot Valkyra. She perched on a boulder near the river, moonlight reflecting off her white feathers and the silver scales of two large fish at her side.

The dragon stared into the water, completely motionless. She might have been carved from marble were it not for the soft fluttering of her fur in the breeze. Then, in a sudden graceful maneuver, she dove, her wings pressed flat against her lithe body. She made no sound and barely more than a ripple when she broke the water's surface. When she reemerged, she carried another writhing fish in her claws. It was bigger than she was, and her wings strained with effort as she lifted it onto the boulder. She pinned it there until its movements ceased.

Aleida stood and walked down to her. Valkyra shook the water from her fur, the movement starting at her head and rippling down to the end of her tail. "I thought you might be hungry," she said, nodding to the fish.

"Starving," Aleida replied. Now that she'd rested, hunger was her most immediate concern. "I'll make a fire."

She carried the fish back up the riverbank and set about collecting fallen twigs and branches. It didn't take long to get a good blaze going, and when Valkyra came to join her in front of the fire, she carried some freshly harvested daravak to replenish Aleida's stores. Aleida dosed Jameson with it again while he was still sleeping.

He began to stir and woke soon after, sniffing the air as he stretched his lanky arms over his head. "Mmm, that smells good. I'm so hungry I could eat a whole ocean full of fish."

Aleida said nothing. The meal would take a while longer to cook, so she began to gather up her papers still spread over the ground. They were dry now, the pages crisp and warped. She studied one of the drawings Tyrus had sent and frowned. She could barely tell what it was anymore. He must have spent so much time trying to get it right. It would have taken him a great deal of effort, given the state his hands were in. He probably shouldn't have bothered, but he had, for her. Their drawings were all they had of each other when they couldn't be together.

And now, they were ruined.

Her eyes burned as tears threatened to form, but she blinked them away. She shoved the pages back into her leather case and bent to collect the rest. There was no saving these drawings, but Tyrus would have no trouble making more once she'd saved him.

"What are those?" Jameson asked, walking over to stand above her. "Oh dear, they're all ruined. What a shame."

"It doesn't matter," Aleida snapped. She wasn't sure if she was trying to convince him or herself. "They're just letters. I've already read them."

"And drawings, too." He plucked one of the papers from the ground. "These are quite good...or at least, this one is. Did you make this?"

Aleida yanked it away from him and glanced at it before stuffing it into her case. It was a portrait of Amar and remained in decent condition, thanks to the magical durability she'd channeled into the paper and ink while drawing it. It was one she'd carried around in her pocket to show people while asking about him. But even magic couldn't completely thwart the effects of a good soak in the ocean.

"Where exactly is Shavhalla, anyway?" she asked, anxious to change the subject.

"Oh, about three weeks' journey from here, maybe a little less. It lies deep within the Vihaara Forest." He picked up another paper, studying it for a few seconds before handing it to her. It was one of Tyrus' letters.

"Stop that," she muttered, yanking it away from him.

"Stop what?"

"Don't touch my things."

He hung his head, looking supremely offended. "I was only trying to help."

"Only trying to snoop, you mean."

Valkyra fluttered up to Aleida's shoulder. "Looking for information to help you escape, perhaps?"

"Can you blame me?" the man asked. "I didn't ask to be dragged along on this little adventure of yours, and neither of you have been very nice to me. If you'd only tell me what you want, I'd be happy to oblige, and we can go our separate ways in peace."

"So willing to sell out your friends, are you?" Valkyra said.

"They're not friends," Jameson retorted. "They were pleasant enough, but I'm not a hero and I never claimed to be selfless or brave. All I want is to get out of this alive and unharmed, and you've made it perfectly clear that won't happen if I cross you. But perhaps we can make a deal. I'll tell you how to get to Shavhalla, and then you can leave me here and be on your merry way."

Valkyra's mouth curved up in a reticent smile, but Aleida could sense the hostility beneath it. She didn't trust him, which meant Aleida wasn't about to, either.

"It's better if you take us yourself," she said.

"I beg to differ," he muttered sullenly.

She said nothing to counter his protest but raised her hand and sent tendrils of lightning dancing through her fingertips. Jameson flinched at the implied threat. She kept channeling her altma a few seconds longer, just for good measure. "How long before Amar reaches Shavhalla?"

He cocked his head to one side, considering the question. "They'll arrive in Pahari in the next day or two. From there, it should only take them a couple of weeks."

That wasn't so bad. They'd lost less time than Aleida had feared. "We could still catch up to him," she said to Valkyra.

The Spirit Tarja only nodded. Aleida stuck her leather case back inside her pack and sat down near the fire. The food looked ready. She grabbed one of the sticks speared through roasted fish and onion, handed it to Jameson, and took another for herself.

"Why exactly have you two been chasing Amar all this time?" the man asked as they ate. "What do you want with him?"

"That's none of your concern," Valkyra replied.

"They thought it might be something to do with his immortality."

Aleida exchanged a quick look with Valkyra but said nothing.

"I can't see what use that would be to you," Jameson went on. "It's *his* curse. It's not like you can magically use it to make yourselves immortal."

Aleida frowned. She still had her own doubts about Amar's curse, and hearing the Tarja voice them aloud stung. Was he right? Could Amar's immortality be useless to Tyrus?

No. That was fear talking. Valkyra had always been so certain, and she was a skilled and powerful Tarja in her own right. Even now, her expression was kind and reassuring, and she rolled her eyes at Jameson as if to say what a fool he was.

That made Aleida feel better. What did he know, after all? In life, Valkyra must have been far more powerful than he was. She probably knew all kinds of things he didn't, and if she said there was a way to use Amar's curse to save Tyrus, Aleida believed her.

She had to. The only other choice was giving up, and she would never be willing to do that.

AMAR

THE DAY AFTER THE BATTLE, AMAR, MITUL, AND SAYA WORKED alongside the crew of the *Vindicator* to repair whatever damage they could as the ship continued its course to Pahari. The *Golden Raven* had taken far more damage than the *Vindicator*, and some of the sailors and the surgeon from the navy ship went over to assist the crew of the *Raven*. Kesari and Lucian went with them, and they didn't get back until late that night.

Unable to sleep, Amar found himself on the upper deck of the ship when they returned. Most of the sailors trailed down to their quarters on the lower decks while others took up their assigned night duties. Kesari stayed behind, leaning against the portside bulwark of the ship and staring out across the water. The coastline beyond was barely more than a darker strip of shadow in the night.

Lucian found his way over to Amar. "No sleep for you either?"

"I tried," he said. "I can't stop thinking about that Visan woman and her Spirit Tarja."

"That is a disturbing thought, I admit."

"How do they keep finding me? And why?"

"This may surprise you," Lucian said ruefully, "but some of us would love the opportunity to live longer than the time we were given."

"Trust me, the novelty wears off after a few centuries."

"I can only imagine. They do seem rather obsessive about tracking you down, though. I assumed we'd lost them a long time ago, but it seems we should have been more appreciative of their tenacity."

Amar crossed his arms as a chill breeze blew across the deck. "Do you think there's any chance we've lost them for good now?"

"After all the efforts they made to find you again?" Lucian said. "I wouldn't count on it. We should probably watch our backs a little closer from now on. Things could have ended much differently if we weren't aboard a well-armed ship with such a competent captain."

"That's what worries me." Not so much for himself, but he didn't like to think of Mitul or the others getting caught in the crossfire of his next fight with the woman. He nodded to Kesari. "How is she?"

"Still a bit shaken, I think. But she did well today. She helped a lot of people."

"That's good."

"I hope so." Lucian sighed. "I think she felt like she *had* to use her magic last night, like she didn't have a choice, and I wish that hadn't been forced on her. I'm not sure she was really ready for it. But she has a good heart, and she wants to help. I tried to talk her out of going to the *Raven*, but she wouldn't hear it."

Amar chuckled and shook his head. "Used to be no one could talk her into using her magic at all."

"She's come a long way." There was a note of pride in the Spirit Tarja's voice, and he grew a little bigger. "You should go talk to her."

"Me? What would *I* say?"

"Anything. I think she could use a friend right now, and I'm more of a...well, not a parent, but something like it. She's had enough of my advice for one day."

Amar shrugged. He wasn't sure what good it would do, but it seemed to be important to Lucian, so he walked over to the bulwark to stand beside Kesari.

"Oh, hello," she said, making a poor attempt at a smile.

"Nice night," he said, looking up at the stars. "Peaceful."

"I guess," she replied.

The conversation lapsed into silence while Amar struggled to think of something to say. He hadn't spent much time with Kesari since they'd left Deveaural, but there were subtle changes in her demeanor that made him understand why Lucian might be worried about her. On the surface, she seemed more confident, and Amar had assumed her willingness to use her magic was a reflection of that. But there were cracks in her armor, a subdued sense of sadness that seemed to weigh her down and diminish some of the vibrance in her eyes.

"Some of the sailors were talking about you today," he said at last. "The Tarja girl who healed them and their friends. You made a good impression."

"I'm glad," she said with that same, forced half-smile.

He pursed his lips. This was stupid. He didn't know how to help her feel better. In six centuries, he hadn't figured out the many nuances of human relationships. He hadn't wanted to, and he still didn't. Because even now that he had his memories back, what was the point? He'd outlive every single one of them if he didn't die again and forget them first. The threat of losing it all still loomed over him like a shadow.

But Kesari had been there for him when he needed her most. He had to at least try.

"What about you?" he asked. "You helped everyone else, but how are *you* doing?"

She shrugged and shook her head but said nothing.

"Well, it was very brave of you to step in like that. It couldn't have been easy."

She didn't respond for so long that Amar almost gave up and walked away. At last, she said, "I was terrified the whole time. I thought I was going to mess up and hurt those poor people even more."

"But you didn't."

"No, but I could have."

"I was scared, too," Amar admitted.

She sighed. "Of course you were. It was a battle. We could have died. But you didn't have to be afraid of yourself, did you?"

She sounded almost angry, desperate for someone to understand her and yet furious that he didn't. He'd said the wrong thing, as usual.

"You're right. I wasn't afraid of myself—not this time. But I'll tell you a secret." He drummed his fingers against the edge of the bulwark. "I've spent most of my life being scared."

She looked at him, brows furrowed and eyes searching. "Scared of what?"

"Losing the people I care about. Losing everyone."

"You've lost a lot of people already," Kesari said gently. "It's understandable."

"Maybe, but I've let that fear hold me back in a lot of ways. I think you know a little about what that's like?"

She looked down into the dark water below. "I just don't want to hurt anyone else."

"And I don't want to lose anyone else. But think of all the good things we're both missing out on if we let that fear stop us."

He leaned forward on his elbows and nudged his shoulder against hers. "I'm an old man, Kes. I know I don't look like it, but I am. And if I could give one piece of advice to an impressive young lady like yourself, it would be this. Don't be like me. Don't let fear hold you back from living. There's so much good you could do with that gift— so much good you've done already. And if that's what you still want to do, then do it."

Her only response was a slow nod, and they stood there staring out into the night in silence, watching the sea slip by beneath them.

After two more days of sailing, the *Vindicator* docked at Pahari alongside the *Golden Raven*. Captain Rutledge came to see Amar and his friends off when they disembarked.

"I hope you find what you're looking for out there," she said, giving them all a salute. "Kesari, it was an honor to serve with a member of the Eves family once more. Rajiv would have been proud of who you've become."

She smiled. "Thank you, Captain."

"If any of you ever need to take to the seas again, my crew and I would be happy to have you aboard." She turned to Amar with a wink and a crooked smirk. "Though perhaps you might warn us the next time you've got such determined enemies on your trail."

He bowed his head to hide a sheepish grin.

"Thank you for all of your help," Kesari said.

"Aye, it was no trouble. Good luck and safe travels to the lot of you."

They bid her farewell and waved goodbye to the crew. It took them the rest of the afternoon to get out of Pahari. First, they had to stop for supplies, a task which proved difficult once vendors pegged them for tourists and then competed with each other for their business. Solicitations from the most determined didn't stop even once they'd bought everything they needed, and they struggled to extricate themselves as quickly and politely as possible. When they finally left the city, Amar found himself looking forward to the comparative solitude and silence of the forest.

They didn't have to walk far to reach its borders. A well-trodden road ran along the riverbank into the trees, but by the time they stopped to make camp for the night, the road had turned to little more than a game trail, and the trees and underbrush had grown so thick they couldn't see very far ahead. The entire forest seemed to have an immense, overpowering weight to it. Some of the trees within its depths might have been the oldest in all of Erythyr.

While the others prepared a meal, Amar took out the map Jameson had given him, which was simply a page traced from an old book about one explorer's travels to Shavhalla. The records indicated she hadn't actually entered the lost city, but she claimed to have made it close enough to see some of the ruins from a distance. She was one of only a handful of explorers to have made it back from the venture alive and of sound mind, which made her maps and firsthand reports the safest ones to rely on. Still, there would likely be plenty of guesswork involved in their own navigation once they got closer.

Hovering overhead, Lucian illuminated the map, and Amar pointed to a space in the middle that had been left empty. "Shavhalla should be around here. Jameson said if we follow the river, we'll eventually come to a series of bridges and stairs that will take us there."

"We should head down to the riverbank tomorrow," Saya suggested. "I'd feel better if we stayed near the water. It wouldn't take much to get lost in here, and at least that way, we'll be able to find our way back out if we need to."

The others nodded in agreement, and Amar returned the map to his pack. "Let's eat and get some rest, then. We have some long days ahead of us."

For the next several days, they followed the river's path through the dense green forest. The terrain was rocky and uneven near the riverbank, and beyond that, the trees and underbrush grew so thick as to be almost impossible to navigate. The canopy overhead cast every step in heavy shadow, and their progress was slow, even with Lucian taking the lead to alert them of any obstacles ahead. In the darkest sections of their path, Kesari helped to light the way with an orb of magical light encasing her palm.

They made camp each night wherever they could find a clear space, pushing aside some of the ground cover as needed so they could all lie down. The night brought eerie sounds and a darkness so thick that not even the light from Kesari's magic could penetrate it far. Lucian kept watch while the others slept. Some nights, he would wake them when the sounds of wolves and other predators drew a little too close for comfort. Only once did the wolves come near enough to see, and they retreated when Lucian's flames grew larger, but Amar kept his sword and his pistol close by when he slept. Whatever dangers lurked in the darkness, he was ready to defend himself and his friends.

His anticipation grew with each step, and he began to look for signs in their repetitive surroundings. Signs that they were nearing Shavhalla, but also signs of the familiar. Something from his childhood, maybe, some memory that would come back to him with the right cue. But the trees all looked the same, and there was nothing telling in the sounds, smells, or textures all around him.

At the end of the second week, the ground began to slope up in front of them. They were nearing the foothills of the mountains deep within the forest. Shavhalla couldn't be too far now, and Amar began to worry that they'd missed the bridges and stairs Jameson's explorer had written about. In the eighty years since she'd traveled here, it was entirely possible that the structures she claimed to have seen were no longer standing. Surely if they were on the right track, they would have come across some sign by now.

Despite Amar's concerns, they pressed on. Late into the afternoon,

Lucian stopped abruptly, then floated a short distance ahead as if to get a closer look at something.

"What is it?" Amar called to him, already quickening his own pace to follow.

"I think I've found our bridge."

The others' footsteps crunched through the foliage behind him. In Lucian's dim orange glow, Amar could see what appeared to be a series of tree roots and branches woven together and extending out over the bank of the river. Kesari held out her hand, and her orb of light sprung from her palm. As it floated toward the river, Amar stared in amazement at what he saw.

The woven tree roots crossed the entire width of the river to the opposite bank, forming a natural bridge. It was only wide enough for two people to cross side by side, but it still looked sturdy and safe even after untold years of disuse. Sidewalls made of more roots and branches extended up to about waist-height, with moss and flowering vines laced between their intricate crisscrossing.

The beauty and simple ingenuity of the structure tugged at something in Amar's chest, and the barest hints of a memory floated across his mind. A man's laughter, the jostle of riding horseback, the taut pull of a bowstring in his hands.

Had he been here before? He must have been, so many lifetimes ago. But the memory was gone as quickly as it had come, nothing more than a passing shadow.

Mitul put a hand on his shoulder. "Is everything all right?"

He blinked and nodded. "It's getting late. We should make camp here."

They did, and after they'd eaten, Mitul took out his saraj and played for them. Amar left his kanjira in his pack, unable to focus his attention on anything but that sliver of memory which had come and gone so quickly. He stared through the flickering campfire to where the edge of the bridge was visible in the dim light, replaying the man's laughter over and over again in his head. Who was he, and why did the sound fill his heart with both pain and joy at the same time?

He ran a hand through his hair and tried to recall it again, but if there were any more pieces of the memory scattered through his mind, he couldn't find them.

Mitul was playing a slow, sad tune now, the same one he'd played at the request of the audience back in Sharmok. It took on a more haunting quality here in the shadows of the Vihaara Forest, and Mitul's low rendition of the chorus sent a shiver up Amar's spine.

Where he has gone, none may follow.
When he will come home, none can say.
Sleep now little prince, no darkness to haunt you.
We await your noble return one day.

A noble return. It was a nice idea, something fit for songs and stories, but Amar didn't expect anyone to be waiting for him in Shavhalla. He'd be lucky to find anything there at all.

Mitul continued to play even as the last embers of their campfire died away and the others all lay down to sleep. The song and the vague memory of the man's laughter followed Amar into his dreams.

AMAR

BY THE TIME THEY AWOKE THE NEXT MORNING, LUCIAN HAD SCOUTED ahead to find a path that would take them north to the first ruins of Shavhalla. He led them up uneven stairs cut into rocky hillsides and over more woven bridges like the one at the river. They passed beneath similarly woven arches blooming with multicolored flowers, and the birdsong from the canopy above grew clearer and more melodious as they left the river's rushing water. Brightly colored insects and other tiny creatures fluttered, crawled, and hopped across their path. They even saw a pair of small blue and gold dragons, who watched their passing from the branches of a tree with dark, curious eyes.

By late afternoon, Lucian was hurrying them on, eager to show them something he'd found while scouting their path in the night. "Come on. It's not much farther now."

"What is it?" Amar asked.

"You'll see." He darted through a gap and around a bend in the trees ahead. Amar had to twist his body sideways to squeeze through, but once he had, he saw it.

A twin set of statues were positioned on either side of a stone bridge. No water flowed beneath it, but there was a shallow depression in the ground where the river might have once been. The bridge was much wider than the others they'd seen, and the statues appeared to be identical. One had toppled onto its side and was now overgrown with moss and creeping vines. The other stood a few heads taller than Amar, depicting a being with the body of a woman and the head of a tiger. She cradled a blooming lotus flower in her hands, which had been delicately carved from a different kind of stone—some kind of pale crystal. Illuminated by Lucian's flames, it gleamed against the gray and mossy green of the statue's hands.

"The white lotus," Lucian said proudly. "Like we saw in your memories."

Mitul ran his fingers along one of the flower's smooth petals. "We must be getting close."

Amar stared up at the tiger's face, again searching for something familiar. His thoughts were a spinning haze, unfocused and without direction. He felt like he was caught between the past and the present, like nothing around him was quite real, or maybe *he* wasn't quite real. He shook his head to try and clear the fog, then followed Lucian and the others across the bridge.

When they reached the other side, the haze in his mind thickened, and more fragmented memories crept into his awareness. Voices. Smells. Colors and shapes. All of them too vague to grasp onto and sort out.

An eerie heaviness pressed against him, and he slowed, peering through the trees. All the warnings from Jameson's research crowded his thoughts. Shavhalla was haunted and cursed. There were malevolent spirits here who would harm unwitting travelers. People who set out to explore the ancient city disappeared and were never heard from again.

His hand found his sword hilt before he was consciously aware of what he was doing.

"Something's not right," Saya hissed, stringing her bow and pulling an arrow from her quiver. She too searched their surroundings with wary, narrowed eyes.

"It's quiet," Mitul said softly. "Listen. The birds have stopped singing."

Only then did Amar notice the uncanny silence around them. There was almost no sound at all, aside from their own voices. Even the rustle of leaves in the wind seemed to have quieted. A cool, misty fog hugged the ground and clung to the trees around them.

They could still turn back. Whatever awaited them in Shavhalla, maybe it wasn't worth the risk.

But he didn't really believe that. He'd been searching for so long, and now he was so close to finding real answers. Of course it was worth the risk.

"This way," he said, and he led them on. The others followed without question.

A few paces ahead, the path leading from the bridge turned into a road, paved with stones meticulously cut and lain together, not unlike the cobblestone streets of Deveaural. How the road had remained clear of the forest's overgrowth was a mystery, but it led on straight and true.

As they walked, silhouettes began to emerge from the gray green fog in front of them. Their vague shapes and shadows sharpened in the mist as they drew nearer, becoming the stone edges of what had once been proud buildings and beautiful sculptures. Now, blocks of stone and rotting wood lay in piles near half-collapsed homes and temples. Missing limbs and heads left the statues grotesquely disfigured, but some of their defects were masked by the vines snaking over their surface.

Far more chilling were the skeletons that lay scattered about the ruins, some still completely intact while others, like the statues, were missing important pieces. Pale skulls stared at them with fleshless grins and empty eye-sockets as they passed.

"What a dreary place," Lucian said. His voice was grating in the silence. Amar couldn't have agreed more, but he didn't say it. All he could do was force himself to put one foot in front of the other, ignoring the growing unease that prickled against every nerve in his body. There was something unmistakably *wrong* about this place, even if he couldn't figure out exactly what it was. Something to do with Shavhalla's curse, no doubt, and maybe even his own.

They passed under an archway carved with intricate designs and came to a long disused fountain covered with flowering vines. The buildings were denser in this part of the ancient city, and less broken. There were more skeletons, too, most of them whole and clad in ragged but vibrant clothes and jewelry. A glimpse of what the place might have once been like flitted through Amar's mind, and he could almost see the scene play out in front of him, full of life and color and sound. He wasn't sure whether the image was part of a memory or merely something he'd imagined, but it was beautiful.

Twilight began to creep over their surroundings. The deepening shadows felt somehow thicker here than they had in other parts of the forest, as if the night were a suffocating blanket being pressed over them. Neither Kesari's magical light nor Lucian's glow seemed as bright as before, and they all clustered a little closer together as they continued on.

Amar stumbled over something in the road. He caught himself on his hands as he fell and looked down. His fingertips brushed the curves of a bony ribcage belonging to a skeleton lying on the ground. He yelped and jumped up, wiping his hands on his pants as he backed away from the human remains. Under other circumstances, Lucian or Mitul might have teased him about his panicked response, but no one was laughing at the situation now.

"There's no use trying to go on like this," Saya said. "We'll have to wait until morning."

Mitul was already setting down his bag near the base of a tall statue that stood at the side of the road. "This is as good a place to rest as any."

"Or as bad," Lucian muttered.

"Shhh!" Saya hissed, pointing to something behind them. "Look."

Amar followed her gesture, peering into the darkness down the road. Pale blue lights could be seen in the distance, with more appearing even as he stared.

"Where are they coming from?" Mitul asked.

"More importantly, what are they?" Amar said.

None of them had any answers for these questions, so they set about making camp and tried to pretend there was nothing strange about the mysterious lights. That became harder to do as new ones flickered to life every minute or so, each appearing a little closer than the last. Everyone shifted their belongings so they were sheltered behind the towering statue and watched the darkness carefully while they ate. The lights came closer, hovering in the air and bathing everything in an eerie blue glow, but there was still no way to tell what they might be or where they'd come from.

A sudden gust of wind tore at Amar's clothes, followed by a longer, steady breeze that sounded like a sigh. Movement in the corner of his eye caught his attention, and he turned to see the legs of the nearby skeleton shifting on the other side of the statue. Some kind of animal disturbing the bones, probably.

Except they hadn't seen or heard any animals since crossing the stone bridge.

He gripped his sword as he stood to investigate. Saya and Lucian went with him.

"What are you doing?" Mitul hissed.

Before he could answer, the skeleton rose up. He took a step back and raised his sword defensively in front of him. How was it moving? It should have been impossible. There was nothing to even hold the individual bones together, but there it stood, as tall and straight as a flesh-and-blood man. Blanched fingers straightened the ragged fabric of its tunic into place over bony shoulders. It didn't so much as look at Amar and the others before sauntering off down the road with long, confident strides. Another skeletal figure joined it after a few paces, emerging into the blue light from some shadowed place in the trees.

Amar shivered, and Saya hissed a few words in Sularan under her breath. Lucian floated ahead, as if he were thinking of following the animated skeletons, but stopped. "They must have been here for centuries," he mused. "That's what all the legends say."

"What about it?" Saya asked.

"How long do you think it takes a human skeleton to fully decompose?"

Amar didn't know the answer, but he could tell what Lucian was getting at. The skeletons, their clothes and jewelry, even the ruins themselves—it was all remarkably well preserved for having been abandoned for centuries. Maybe that was part of whatever curse had befallen Shavhalla.

Kesari and Mitul crept forward to stand beside them, and more skeletons passed by as they all stood there watching the road. A pair of children wearing dried flower crowns and necklaces chased each other with mouths open in silent laughter, followed by a person pulling a rickety wood cart with rotted sides. A headless skeleton in a flowing dress stirred a vague sense of recognition in Amar's mind, and he got the impression that it wasn't because he'd already seen the lifeless bones and their gown on the journey here.

Sometimes the blue lights trailed after the skeletons or danced around them, causing their shadows to morph in bizarre shapes. Before long, even stranger companions joined the parade. The statues scattered throughout so much of Shavhalla came to life, walking amongst the trees with surprising grace and quiet steps. Even the great statue near their camp eventually stirred and followed the procession. The blue lights hovering near its head revealed a dog-faced man with four muscular human arms, each wielding a stone dagger. He paid them no mind as he passed, but Saya had to make a quick sidestep to avoid being crushed beneath his foot.

They watched the strange scene for what felt like hours. Some of the skeletons and statues lingered in their general vicinity, gathering in pairs and small groups with gestures that suggested speech, though they were voiceless aside from the faint whispers of the wind through their teeth. Others walked in and out of the ruins of buildings, as if they were ordinary people going about their ordinary business. They congregated within the last vestiges of what might have once been a temple and knelt as if to pray. They stood in the remains of market stalls and bartered for goods that only they could see. Two of them patrolled the streets with swords at their sides and metal armor glinting in the cold blue light. A statue of a winged tiger prowled after them. They passed within a few paces of where Amar and the others stood, but like the rest, paid them no mind.

"Should we stay here?" Kesari asked hesitantly. "Do you think it's safe?"

"If they were going to hurt us, they could have done it already," Saya replied. "I don't think they even know we're here."

Lucian's eyes narrowed as he watched the passing guards. "Who's to say that can't change at any moment?"

"I'm not going back," Amar said resolutely. He didn't know if they were entirely safe in what was turning out to be a city more haunted and cursed than any legend could have prepared them for. If the others wanted to leave, that was their choice. But he couldn't bring himself to turn back now, no matter what the danger might be. The magic of this place called his name as loud and clear as any audible voice. He could feel it, all the way down to his very bones. It was a call he had to heed.

Mitul placed a hand on his shoulder. "If you're staying, so am I."

Saya gave him a nod, her eyes hard and fearless.

"We all are," Kesari agreed.

"I'll keep watch," Lucian said. "Make sure our enchanted friends stay friendly. I'll let you know if they become a threat."

They returned to their camp, and despite the uneasy tension that had settled over him, Amar couldn't help smiling to himself as he lay down beside his friends to sleep. As strange and unnerving as Shavhalla had been so far, it was exactly where he needed to be. They'd come to the right place. Finally, after all these years, the answers he'd been seeking were within his reach.

ALEIDA

ALEIDA WAS BEGINNING TO HATE THE VIHAARA FOREST.

Farther inland, in the western part of Kavora where she'd begun this chase, it hadn't been so bad, but here the trees seemed to close in around her like an impenetrable green prison. Her clothing hung heavy against her skin with sweat and the air's humidity. Unknown creatures wriggled and scurried in the shadows, and every few minutes, she swore she could feel something crawling over her skin. Once there really was something there— a great ugly spider with long, furry legs. She yelped and swatted it away, much to Jameson's amusement, but he reacted with even less decorum when a snake slithered out from under his pack the next morning.

If anything, he was even more miserable in the forest than Aleida was, and he didn't hesitate to let her know it. It was more tiresome to tell him to shut up than it was to ignore him, which was her newest tactic, but even that wasn't working as well as she'd hoped it would. Jameson's whining voice grated on her nerves with every step. She had half a mind to leave him here to find his way back to Deveaural on his own, but Valkyra insisted they keep him close. Who knew what he might decide to do to them once he got his magic back? And besides, he'd proven useful already. Without him, they would have been wandering aimlessly. He was the only one among them who knew how and where to find Shavhalla.

Of course, that also meant he could be lying to them, leading them around in circles wherever he pleased. But Aleida had made clear to him the terrible fate that might befall him should he misguide her, and he seemed genuinely fearful of her threats.

They were fifteen days into their journey upriver when Jameson stopped and pointed triumphantly to something through the trees. "See! That's it. There's one of the bridges I was telling you about. We're close now."

Night had already settled over the forest, and it was difficult to see what he was pointing to. Aleida expanded the glowing orb of light in her hand and sent it floating ahead several paces.

"There!" he grabbed her arm. "Do you see it?"

She shot him a glare but halted the light's movement and tried to see what he was so excited about. There wasn't any bridge, just a cluster of roots and branches tangled together at the edge of the river. She took a few more paces forward and squinted.

The roots and branches *were* the bridge. They'd been woven together in intricate knots, extending from this side of the riverbank all the way to the other. It was barely wide enough for two people to cross alongside each other.

She walked up to its edge. "It doesn't look very sturdy." She took a tentative step onto it and hopped a little to test its weight. It didn't so much as bend beneath her feet. Even when Jameson stood beside her, it held firm.

"It must have been made with magic," he said, kneeling down to study the bridge's weaving. "At least partially. A little altma would have helped with the growth of these plants, too."

"I don't care how it was made, so long as it leads us to Amar." She grabbed the back of his robes and tugged until he stood up. "Let's go. We can make camp on the other side."

"I'll go catch us some dinner," Valkyra said. She leapt from Aleida's shoulder and flew out over the river, where she was quickly swallowed up in the shadows.

Aleida and Jameson crossed the bridge to the opposite bank. Once there, the Tarja inspected the ground before sitting down. Aleida started looking for firewood, but she hadn't gone far when she spotted a circle of rocks near the beginnings of an overgrown path. The center of the circle was charred and black, covered with only a few of the fallen leaves that were strewn across the entire forest floor.

She grinned. A campfire, and a fairly new one at that. Amar and his friends couldn't be too far off. She'd believed they were going the right way all along, but to have a real sign of it now was encouraging. She called Jameson to her position and made her own fire amongst what was left of Amar's.

"We have a visitor," he said as she got a nice blaze going.

Aleida looked up, tensed to confront whoever or whatever had come to disturb them. Leaning casually against a tree trunk, Jameson nodded to the branches over her head. She craned her neck, and there sat Feros, orange firelight reflected in his large black eyes.

"Get down here," she said to him, holding out her arm.

He blinked at her and let out a low, angry screech, but didn't move.

She sighed and dug around in her pack for the last of the fish she'd saved from a previous meal. Only when she held it out to Feros did he deign to flutter down and perch on her arm. She opened the container on his back and withdrew Tyrus' latest letter.

"You have a strix," Jameson said, curiosity and wonder in his voice. "I always thought it might be useful to get one for myself. Of course, the tamed ones are so rare these days the price must be outrageous."

"You can thank Empress Dashiva and Nandini Kumar for that," Aleida growled. Breeding and training strixes was a Visan tradition stretching back centuries, but like the rest of her people, all the masters in that field had been killed or displaced during the invasion.

"A shame," Jameson said, and there seemed to be a genuine hint of sympathy in his voice. Not only for the loss of trained strixes, but for the Visan people. Maybe even for Aleida herself.

Or maybe she was imagining it. She shook Feros from her arm, tossed him the rest of the fish, and unfolded the paper. Hasan's neat handwriting was scrawled across one side of a single page, but there was nothing else. No drawings from Tyrus, no shaky letters written in his own hand.

Aleida frowned. He must not have been feeling up to writing anything himself. Maybe he was starting to lose more control of his hands. The letter would tell her more, of course, but since she couldn't read it, she had no way of knowing what it said until Valkyra got back.

"Not the news you were hoping for?" Jameson asked.

She quickly smoothed her expression into one of indifference. "I'm not sure. I can't read it."

"Bad penmanship?" he asked. "I could take a look, if you'd like. My own handwriting is so terrible I can decipher almost anything."

"That's not—" She shook her head. "Never mind."

Understanding flickered in his eyes. "You mean you can't read. At all."

She didn't answer, but her cheeks burned, and she recoiled against the heat that rose in her stomach. She must seem so stupid to him, this great, renowned Tarja who had probably studied at one of the best academies in all of Erythyr.

But why should she care what he thought? He was her prisoner, and she didn't need his approval or respect. No shame. Not for him, not for anyone.

"Is it about your brother?" he asked.

Her eyes narrowed, and she clutched the letter a little tighter. Had he seen part of it somehow? "What makes you think that?"

"Strixes can only bond to a few people," Jameson said. "Traditionally, people who share the same blood, right? That way it's easier for them to track whoever they're bound to, wherever they might be."

"Maybe it's from my mother or father," she snapped. "You don't know me well enough to make assumptions."

"True. But you mentioned your brother's life depends on you finding Amar. That's an awfully big responsibility for someone so young, and I can't imagine your parents would send you out here alone, so…" He trailed off, shrugged, and knelt beside the fire.

Aleida sat down and stared into the flames herself. She turned the folded sheet of paper over and over in her fingertips, unanswered questions needling at her. Why hadn't Tyrus written anything himself? How much worse had his condition gotten since she left Chatanda?

The last time this had happened, it was because he'd fallen ill and couldn't get out of bed for a week. He'd pulled through in the end, but she'd been in a panic for almost a month before his next letter came. She wasn't sure she could bear to go through that again.

And what if it was worse than that? What if Hasan was the only one writing to her because Tyrus was....

She shoved the thought down before it could drown her.

There was a rustle in the bushes. She glanced over her shoulder, hoping to see Valkyra returning, but it was only Feros pouncing on something in the leaves. With an exasperated sigh, she fixed her gaze on Jameson. Before, when he'd tried to look at her letters and drawings, Valkyra suggested he might be trying to get information, something to use against them and make an escape later. But they were taking so many precautions. Surely escape was next to impossible. And what harm could one letter do, really?

She stood and strode toward him, holding out the paper. She couldn't bear to wait. "Read it to me."

He looked up at her, a question in his eyes, and she nodded. He took the letter, unfolded it carefully, and began to read. "Dear Aleida, I am very—"

"What are you doing?" Valkyra shot past her like an arrow and wrapped her claws around the paper in Jameson's hands. One of the sharp points caught on his skin, and he yelped. The dragon wrested the letter out of his grasp. Blood oozed up from a thin gash across the heel of his palm.

"I just wanted to know what it said," Aleida replied.

"And you couldn't have waited for me?" Valkyra's silver eyes flashed in the firelight. "You have no idea what he's plotting. He can't be trusted."

"It's only a letter."

"It's *information*. Information that could give him power over you. Over both of us. Information he could use to—"

"I get it!" she snapped. "I'm sorry, all right? I got impatient. Something's wrong with Tyrus, and I—"

"Shh," Valkyra hissed, casting a dark look at Jameson, who had wrapped his injured hand in one of the sleeves of his robe. She gave Aleida a pointed look, her mouth pressed together in a thin, annoyed line.

"I'm sorry," Aleida said tersely, impatience threatening to boil over inside her. "Please read it to me."

Valkyra let out an exasperated sigh, but smoothed the letter out on the ground. She switched to Visan so Jameson couldn't understand what she was saying. Her Visan wasn't perfect, and it always took her a little extra time to make the translation, but at least she was reading now instead of lecturing.

"Dear Aleida, I hope this letter finds you well. Tyrus wanted to write you himself, but he's had some bad days this last week and doesn't have much energy. There has been a sickness going around the village, and I'm afraid we weren't able to prevent him from being exposed to it. It's not anything serious, only a fever and some nausea, but of course with his condition, any illness is cause for concern. I'm taking good care of him, don't worry. I make sure he gets enough to eat and drink, and I've used what healing magic I can to ease his discomfort and speed his recovery. He looks at your drawings every day, and I know that helps him, too. Sometimes friends come to check on him or bring him gifts. So many people here care for him. The boy could befriend a tiger if he tried."

Aleida laughed a little at this. It was true. Tyrus had always had a much easier time making friends than she had, though she'd never begrudged him for it.

"He's been in good spirits," Valkyra continued. "Sick, but coping with it better than I expected, all things considered. He should make a full recovery, and I'm sure he'll have more to tell you in his next letter. Please be careful out there, and hurry back as soon as you can. He misses you. We both do. Your friend, Hasan."

Relief washed over Aleida as she took the letter back from Valkyra. "Thank you," she said. It wasn't the best news, but it was certainly better than all the worst-case scenarios that had been running rampant through her mind. "And I really am sorry. I should have been more careful."

"We can't trust him, dear. Not even for a second."

"I know." Aleida studied their prisoner with a new level of caution. His brows were furrowed in concentration as he examined his injured hand, and he looked completely harmless with his disheveled robes and dirt-smeared face. Without his magic, he couldn't harm her, and he'd done little more than bemoan his fate during their travels together. He seemed more like a bumbling fool than a respectable Tarja, but that didn't mean he wasn't still one of the most powerful men in Atrea. She sometimes forgot that. An easy error, but one she couldn't afford.

Whatever he was plotting, she couldn't let herself be fooled or distracted. Not when she was so close to reaching her goal. She watched him warily as she threw more wood onto the fire. The next time he tried to strike up a conversation, she wouldn't mistake his questions for idle curiosity.

KESARI

KESARI WOKE BEFORE DAWN AND FOUND AMAR ALREADY UP, standing with Lucian near the edge of the road. She went to them, and together they watched the few remaining blue lights that lingered in the gray morning. Both the statue and the nearest skeletons had returned to their original fixed positions from the previous night.

"You're up early," Amar said as she approached.

"I could say the same to you."

He only grunted in response.

"He didn't get much sleep," Lucian said. "Nervous about returning to his childhood home and all that."

Amar scuffed the toe of his boot against the ground but didn't disagree. "Do you think it's too early to wake the others?"

Kesari shrugged. "I'm sure they won't mind. We're all willing to do to whatever you think is best."

He nodded and headed for their camp. She stayed with Lucian, watching the blue lights wink out of sight as the morning sun began to brighten the forest. "Did anything interesting happen last night?"

"Aside from walking skeletons and statues coming to life, you mean?" Lucian replied. "No, that about sums it all up."

"You don't think they could hurt us, do you?"

"I'm not sure. Last night they only seemed interested in going about their own business, but that doesn't mean they won't harm us if we get in their way. We should be ready to fight if we need to."

"With magic, you mean." Her stomach knotted at the thought.

"Well, you don't exactly have any other weapons to speak of. Besides, the best way to fight or defend against something magical is usually with more magic."

Kesari frowned. Hopefully it wouldn't come to that. She was barely starting to get comfortable with using her magic for healing. Using it to fight was something entirely different. If she was her friends' best protection against whatever magical foes they might come across, they could be in real trouble.

She returned to the remains of the campfire to retrieve her pack. Saya divvied out some dried fruit for their breakfast, which they ate as they started down the road. They passed more and more skeletons the farther they walked, along with more statues and the ruined remains of various buildings. All were lifeless in the morning sunlight, but perhaps they would reanimate again once darkness fell. Or, maybe, last night's activity had been some sort of special occasion.

The buildings seemed to be more well-preserved the farther they went. Some were almost entirely intact. Amar stopped at one, and they all ventured inside. Even the furnishings remained untouched by time. A family of skeletons sat on the floor around a low table, ceramic plates arranged in front of them, cups clasped in bony fingers. Amar picked up one of the plates and traced his finger over the flowering swirls painted along the rim.

"Do you remember any of this?" Mitul asked.

"I don't know. Some of it seems so familiar, but I can't quite place it." He stared down at the skeleton seated below him, its colorful robes decorated with intricate patterns and beadwork. "These people were wealthy, I think. A noble family, maybe…" He trailed off as he set the plate back down, then turned and let his eyes wander around the rest of the room. His next words were barely audible. "Friends of my family."

"Amar?" Saya asked after several long moments of silence.

He blinked a few times, as if coming out of a daze. "Let's keep going. The palace isn't far."

Kesari exchanged a look with Saya, who only shook her head in confusion. None of them had seen a palace. Perhaps Amar was starting to remember more than he was letting on or even fully aware of.

He led them on, through winding streets that were starting to feel more and more like a maze. A few minutes later, they ducked through a partially collapsed archway and emerged into an open city square lined with more statues. At its center stood an empty fountain covered in moss and vines, and beyond that, the ornate towers and domed roofs of a palace rose into the air.

Where the rest of Shavhalla had been crumbling and half-hidden beneath the forest's overgrowth, the palace remained almost entirely untouched. The surrounding trees likely would have been cleared away when the city was still thriving, but the forest hadn't encroached onto the palace grounds in the centuries that had since passed. There were none of the skeletons they'd seen scattered throughout the rest of the city, and as they approached the wide stone steps leading to a set of heavy doors, the silence around them seemed to deepen.

The architecture was similar to that of the imperial palace in Jakhat, and though it wasn't quite as large, it was still an impressive structure. White marble towers reached toward the sky, their surfaces glistening like diamonds in the light of a sun that shone far brighter in this open space than anywhere else in the forest. Bell-shaped roofs gilded with gold topped each tower, including the largest one in the center. A myriad of designs and figures had been carved into the exterior walls of the entire structure, depicting what Kesari assumed were stories of the glory, majesty, and mythology of the people who had once lived there. Polished columns surrounded the perimeter, held up at their bases by stone tigers, horses, birds, and dogs. Some were inlaid with gleaming jewels on their chests and foreheads.

An arching set of double doors formed the entrance, each side engraved with one half of a lotus flower that was at least as tall as Kesari. Amar stopped when they reached it, staring up at the doors with his eyes narrowed and his lips pressed tight. His thumb ran over the pommel of his sword, but otherwise, he didn't move. The others stood behind him, waiting, but whatever thoughts were running through his mind, he didn't share them.

"Shall we go in?" Mitul asked gently.

Amar gave that same, dazed blink again and nodded. He put both palms flat against one of the doors and pushed. It glided open with ease, and the palace's shadows fell over them as they stepped over the threshold.

The inside was as neat and clean as the exterior had been, without so much as a speck of dust or a misplaced bauble to be seen. Strong angles and elegant arches made from stone suggested the prowess and grandeur of the nobility who had lived within these walls. More animal statues and vibrant tapestries lined the halls, and everywhere Kesari turned, the repeating symbol of the white lotus immediately drew her eye. It was carved into the walls, woven in tapestries, and laid out in a tiled pattern on the floor. It even adorned the chest plates of the stone guards standing erect and watchful at either side of the hall opposite the entrance.

Amar approached one of the armored figures, his footsteps echoing in the empty room. Lucian darted ahead to inspect it himself. "Impressive craftsmanship," he said. "It looks almost—"

The statue whipped a scimitar from the sheath at its hip and sliced through the Spirit Tarja's flames. In the split second it took his shape to reform, Amar had his own blade drawn, and Saya had leapt in front of Kesari and Mitul with her bow at the ready. Sparks flew as the metal of Amar's blade collided with the statue's stone weapon. On the other side of the hallway, the second guard drew its sword and crouched low in a fighter's stance.

Saya fired a shot to stop its attack on Amar's unguarded back. The arrow glanced harmlessly off its surface. She strode forward a few steps and took another shot, but that only succeeded in drawing the guard's attention to her. It started to charge, but Amar was there in a split second, forcing it to fight him instead of Saya.

Mitul grabbed Kesari by the arm. "Can't you and Lucian do something?"

She didn't know if she could, but she had to try. She took stock of her mental and emotional state—the fear clamoring inside her head, the panic that rose as one guard swung its blade at Amar's neck, the almost hysterical relief that came when he managed to dodge the blow.

She couldn't make any of those feelings go away, but they didn't get to control what she did next.

Sucking in a deep breath, she stretched out her hands and channeled her altma.

All she managed to produce was a mere flutter of the great wind she'd tried to summon.

Lucian flew to her side, hovering near her ear where she could hear him above the clangs and clashes of the battle in front of her. "You're all right. You can do this."

"I'm trying," she said through gritted teeth, reaching for her altma again. The faintest stirrings of her old nightmares were beginning to creep into her mind, but she shoved them back down.

"You're holding back," Lucian said. "You're afraid."

"Of course I'm afraid! What if I lose control again?" Rajiv's face, the clocktower, the fire, the wails of the injured and mournful—they all spun in a whirlwind through her mind.

Amar feinted, and Saya ducked under a heavy swing from an enemy blade. The stone guards were slow, but they could easily wear an opponent down with sheer strength and endurance. Both Amar and Saya were already breathing heavily, and if their weapons couldn't harm the statues, they were fighting a losing battle.

Kesari had to do something, and fast.

"*You're* the one in control," Lucian said, his voice soothing amidst the tumult. "Not the fear."

Kesari channeled her altma again. This time, she knelt and put both hands on the tiles beneath her. There was only a moment of hesitation, and then a rumbling echoed up from the floor. She directed all her altma down into her fingertips, through the tiles, across the foundation beneath it, and back up into the room.

Stone burst up through the tiles, scattering chunks of rock and ceramic everywhere. The very earth itself wrapped around the legs of both stone guards. With another twist of Kesari's palms, they were dragged to the ground, where more stone morphed to lock their hands and weapons against the floor.

Saya, Amar, and Mitul all froze in place, but Kesari didn't look at their faces. She couldn't—not yet. Instead, she stood on trembling limbs and strode to where the two guards were already attempting to pull free. In a few more seconds, they'd succeed, but she wasn't going to give them the chance.

She took another deep breath, closed her eyes, and thought of destruction—fire burning, wood crackling, an entire building collapsing in ash and smoke. She placed a hand against each of the guard's helmeted heads and channeled her altma again. Cracks began to spread across the stone, emitting an orange glow that seemed to emanate from within. After a few seconds, the fissures split open wide, and the guards crumbled to the floor in pieces.

She let out a breath and slowly turned around to face her friends. They stared at her with wide eyes. Something squirmed in her gut, but then a wide grin broke across Saya's face, and Kesari's fears dissipated.

"That was incredible!" Mitul said, stepping closer to examine the pile of rubble at her feet. "You were amazing. How did you do that?"

She blushed. "Magic?"

Lucian laughed. "That it was. You were exceptional."

"I'm glad you stepped in," Saya said. "We couldn't have won that fight without your help."

She started to smile, but it turned into a frown when she saw the blood running down Saya's leg. A long gash cut across her thigh under the torn fabric of her pants.

"You're hurt!" she said, rushing to her friend's side. She knelt to examine the jagged wound. A dizzying cold washed over her as she remembered the tiles and rock that had shot through the air when she used her magic. "Was that me?"

"You didn't mean to."

Her heart caved in on itself. "You all could have been hurt because of me. You could have died."

Saya put a hand against Kesari's jaw. "No. We all *lived* because of you. You saved us, Kes. And now you're going to use your magic to fix my leg. Right?"

Kesari squared her shoulders and nodded. "Yes, of course." She looked around and spotted a set of stairs down the hall. "Come on. Let's go sit down."

The way Saya limped suggested the injury was worse than she had let on, and when Amar and Mitul placed themselves on either side of her for support, she didn't protest. They made it to the stairs, and she gingerly lowered herself onto them with Kesari sitting beside her and Lucian hovering above to illuminate the injury.

Kesari poured water over the wound to wash away some of the blood, but more kept pouring from it in a steady flow. She tried to offer reassurance in what she hoped was a steady tone. "You're going to be all right."

"I know," Saya replied calmly.

She sounded so sure, like there was no doubt in her mind that Kesari was capable of healing her. Somehow, that gave her all the confidence she needed. She gently placed her fingers beside the jagged edges of the wound and channeled her altma with careful, determined focus. Little by little, she sent the energy to all the places where there was damage, repairing it from the inside out, just as she'd done with the injured sailors on the *Vindicator*. When she was finished, there was only a thin red line of raised red scar tissue that would hopefully fade with time.

"How does that feel?" she asked.

"Much better." Saya pushed herself up and tested her weight on the injured leg.

"Shall we keep going?" Mitul asked. He glanced at Amar, who was already pacing the hall anxiously, looking at each tapestry with a concentrated frown before moving onto the next.

Saya eyed the remaining stone chunks that had once been their attackers. "Yes, but let's try to avoid running into any more of those things."

"I can fly around first," Lucian suggested. "Take a look and make sure there aren't any more surprises lurking in the corners."

"That's a good idea," Mitul replied. "Amar, what do you think?"

He didn't answer. He didn't seem to have heard them. He'd stopped pacing now and was staring up at a painting on the opposite wall, which depicted an armored man sitting on a horse. He had a regal look about him, sharp features composed in a proud and dignified expression. Red banners bearing the white lotus symbol streamed behind him.

From where Kesari and the others sat, they couldn't see Amar's face, but his entire body had gone rigid. His hands were clasped tight behind his back.

Mitul took a few steps toward him. "Amar?"

He turned around, but his eyes slid past them, up the stairs that led to the next level of the palace. Without saying anything, he made his way to them and began to ascend.

"Amar, wait!" Mitul called out, already following him. "You don't know what's up there."

If Amar heard him at all, he gave no indication. Instead, he broke into a sprint, taking the steps two and three at a time while the others scrambled to catch up.

AMAR

AMAR RAN.

He ran even as his friends continued to call his name, pleading with him to stop. He ran up the steps so fast his foot missed one, and he slipped and cracked his elbow against a sharp edge. He picked himself up and kept running, around the balustrade and down the hall. He ran past five more pairs of stone guards identical to the ones below and didn't stop to see if these came to life as well. He ran past familiar doors and the memories that flitted across his mind with each one, until at last he came to the most familiar door of all—the one his feet had known their way to even as his consciousness was still trying to puzzle out new pieces of information.

The tapestries, the sound of his feet against the tiled floor, the painting of the man on the horse, the texture of the worn handle against his palm—it was all starting to fit together. So many of the answers he'd been seeking lay behind this door.

He turned the handle, pushed the door open, and stepped into his old bedroom.

It looked the same as when Jameson had gone through his memories—a wide bed covered in luxurious pillows and blankets, crimson curtains hung over a window that would offer a perfect view of the sunset, an ornately carved chest beside a painted armoire.

He approached the chest. The tumultuous sounds of a new skirmish breaking out echoed from the hall behind him. He should go back to help his friends, but he didn't. They had Kes, and he couldn't bring himself to turn around now. His feet carried him closer and closer to the chest until he was kneeling beside it. He opened the clasp and reached inside.

His fingers closed around something thick and rectangular. He pulled the object out—a book—and began to flip through its pages.

The memory he'd been grasping for came back to him in a rush.

Darshak stood atop the tallest tower of the palace and watched his father's silhouette disappear into the trees. An army of three thousand men trailed behind him in an impressively disciplined block. The red banners streaming above them seemed to glow in the fiery light of sunset. They looked glorious and noble and already victorious, and there was no doubt in Darshak's mind that they would return triumphant.

An ache filled his heart as he watched them, and he couldn't stop the sigh that escaped with his next breath. His mother reached out and ruffled his shaggy black hair, like he was still a little boy and not a nearly grown man. It was embarrassing, but since there was no one else around to see, he resisted the urge to pull away from her.

"You'll be riding off in your own battles soon enough," she said. "For now, I'm happy to keep you here where I can look after you."

Rather than pointing out that he was far past needing to be looked after, he forced a smile. She worried too much, but it would have been useless to tell her she shouldn't. She'd already lost one son in her husband's wars, leaving Darshak the sole remaining heir to the Shavhallan throne. At seventeen, he was old enough to ride into battle at King Kairav's side, but his mother wouldn't hear of it.

He watched the soldiers until the last one had disappeared from view, then turned and put a hand on his mother's arm. "I'm going to bed."

"Goodnight, little tiger," she said, patting his hand before he went inside.

He headed down two flights of stairs to the second floor of the palace. A guard opened the door to his bedchamber, and a servant came in a few minutes later with a basin of hot water and a clean towel for washing. Darshak shed his heavy royal robes and the tunic underneath, washed his face and hands, and lit a few of the lamps and candles around the room. He selected a book from one of his shelves and climbed into bed.

It was a dull read containing a history of some of Shavhalla's greatest battles and conquests over the last two centuries. His father had given it to him months ago and expected him to be finished with it by the time he returned from battle. He wanted a report on what he'd learned—some kind of test, no doubt, and one Darshak was already failing. The book was thick, and he wasn't even halfway through it yet. He was going to have to read much faster if he wanted to finish by the time the king returned.

He started to skim through a chapter about one of his great-grandfather's conquests, in which he'd raided a wealthy city in the mountains. According to the record, he'd fought valiantly against the defending army, laying waste to their entire city and defeating even their most powerful warriors. Those who surrendered were sold to northern slavers, as was Shavhalla's customary practice. Those who refused were simply cut down.

From there the text went on to dissect in detail the various tactics which had led to such a victory, and Darshak's eyes started to glaze over. This was probably one of the more important parts of the book and something his father would ask him about later, but he couldn't seem to focus. The words all started to blend and jumble together in his head, and after a few minutes, he drifted off to sleep with the book still open in his lap.

He woke with a start some time later and looked around the room with bleary eyes. The candles had burned low, and there were heavy footsteps outside his door. "She went this way," said a muffled voice. The footsteps quickened their pace.

Whoever had spoken seemed troubled, almost frantic, and only the palace guards had any reason to be up at this hour. Darshak started to get up to see what was going on, but there was thump on the other side of his door, and he froze.

He glanced at the opposite corner, where his sword leaned against the armoire. It was too far away to reach, but if he needed to, he could make a run for it.

His door opened, and a shadow cloaked in black glided inside. The figure shut the door quickly and whirled to face him. A pair of striking brown eyes under thick lashes met his gaze. The rest of the girl's face was gaunt and dirty, but her eyes were so captivating that it took Darshak a moment to notice the tension in the rest of her body.

"Who are you?" he asked.

She only glowered back at him, hatred exuding from her entire being. Though she stood between him and his sword, she didn't look dangerous. She was much smaller than him and at least a couple of years younger. He kept a close eye on her, but if she meant him any harm, he'd have no trouble taking her down.

He tried a different question. "What are you doing here?"

She raised her hands and pulled back the hood of her cloak. Her hair was cropped short, all jagged edges, as if it had recently been hacked away with a knife. A heavy metal collar encircled her neck—a slave's collar.

What was a slave doing in the palace? What was a slave doing in Shavhalla at all? Shavhallans didn't keep slaves themselves, and it was only north of the mountains that the practice was common. Had this girl come all the way here on her own?

"My name is Mahati," she said. Her voice was strong in a way Darshak hadn't expected and carried an accent he didn't recognize. "You don't know me, and I didn't come here looking for you, but since King Kairav isn't here, you'll have to do."

He frowned. "I don't understand."

"You will." She stretched out her hands, and her palms began to glow with crimson light.

Magic. Darshak's heartbeat quickened, and he made a dash for his sword. Mahati shot a hand toward him, and he flew back, knocked down by an invisible force. The light in the girl's hands grew, and the very air around her seemed alive. It swirled through her hair and tugged at the fabric of her cloak. Beneath it, her thin frame was clad in clothing even the poorest of peasants would have considered rags.

Voices came from the hall—the guards, looking for this girl, no doubt. Darshak called to them. "Here! She's in here!"

Bodies pounded against the other side of the door, but no one came in, and Mahati made no move to escape. She'd likely sealed it shut with magic, and the guards would need a few minutes to break through.

The girl's lips twitched as she drew a knife from the makeshift belt around her waist. Darshak scrambled backward on the floor, but she didn't turn the blade on him. Instead, she sliced into one of her own palms. Her blood spilled out, dark against the bright red glow still emanating from her hands.

She took a few steps closer to him. Darshak tried to go for his sword again, but he couldn't make his body obey him. He sat there on the floor, frozen, staring up in horror at this waif of a girl and the ferocious hatred burning in her eyes.

"Your father took *everything* from me," she said in a low growl. "I wanted him to suffer like I have, to live in endless loneliness after everything he cares about is gone. I wanted him to experience my pain, not just for one lifetime, but for eternity. That is what I would have cursed your father with, but since he's not here..."

She raised her hands. The red glow grew tendrils that wrapped around Darshak until it engulfed him. Warmth seeped into his skin, intensifying to a searing heat. He held back a cry as Mahati began to speak.

"Prince Darshak Kaur, son of King Kairav Kaur, with the blood of my own body and the life within me, I curse you with immortality. You will watch all you hold dear wither and die while you linger on, unbroken by time, illness, or death itself. Your soul shall be bound to the physical world for as many lifetimes as it takes you to atone for the atrocities of war. Only then will you find peace."

Everything inside Darshak burned. His body was nothing but fire and pain. A scream burst from his lips, but the sensation ceased abruptly, and the red glow of Mahati's magic disappeared.

She fell onto her hands and knees, shoulders trembling as she pulled in weak, rasping breaths. There was more blood under her palm than there should have been from the small cut she'd made there.

Before Darshak could say anything, seven guards burst into the room, and together they pinned the girl's bedraggled form to the floor with a violence that was undeniably excessive. Through the mass of armored bodies, he caught a glimpse of her face. She looked pale and drawn, but her eyes were wild, and she gave him a smirk as the guards hauled her to her feet and dragged her away.

"Amar? Where are you?"

He shut the book, blinking back the moisture that had sprung to his eyes with the sudden rush of understanding. Outside the door, his friends called him again.

Amar. That was his name now. The boy Darshak had been erased by centuries of lost time, and the name no longer fit. He was Amar to his friends now, and that was the name he would keep.

"Amar!"

"I'm in here," he responded, and a few seconds later, they entered the room, breathless and disheveled. They must have had to fight their way through several guards. "Sorry. I shouldn't have run off like that. Is everyone all right?"

"We're fine," Mitul said. "What about you?"

He nodded and stood up, still clutching the book in his hand—the same one he'd been reading the night he'd been cursed.

"This is the room we saw in your memories," Kesari said. "You were cursed right here."

He nodded. "I remember now. Not everything, but I remember the curse." He told them about his father, a king of conquests and brutality, and about Mahati and the night she'd made her way to his room. He could see her so clearly in his mind now that he wasn't sure how he'd ever managed to forget the proud defiance in her stance, the hatred in her eyes, or the sheer force of her power as she'd spoken the curse.

"It wasn't even about you, then," Mitul said when he had finished. "Your father should have been the one cursed, not you. That doesn't seem fair."

"It's not," Amar said. "But what happened to *her* wasn't fair, either." He surprised even himself with the defensiveness in his voice. A part of him was angry at the girl for condemning him to this fate, but he couldn't bring himself to hate her. He'd seen enough wars in his many lifetimes to know the pain and suffering they brought. "She wanted revenge, and if she couldn't inflict it on my father directly, I was the next best option."

"But the curse is still about your father, right?" Mitul said. "Atoning for whatever atrocities his wars caused. How?"

How indeed? The misery wrought by King Kairav's wars was surely endless. Did atonement include every act of violence that had caused suffering, or was it limited to the specific acts that had impacted Mahati? How was Amar supposed to know? How was he supposed to atone for any of it when so much time had passed and when he wasn't even the person directly responsible for those atrocities?

He shook his head. "I have no idea."

"Well, what do you think Mahati was referring to?" Saya asked. "What sorts of awful things did your father do?"

The easier question might have been what sorts of awful things his father *hadn't* done. Amar—Darshak—had been aware of this on some level, even as a boy, but it was only looking back now with centuries of experience filtering his view that he could see the full extent of those horrors.

Images of his childhood flashed through his mind—strong hands lifting him high into the air, his father teaching him the sword, his booming laugh at supper. Hard, dark eyes, but always warm and kind when he looked at Amar.

Then, other memories. The painting of a warrior king in the palace's entry hall. A funeral for the older brother he'd lost in one of his father's battles. Gifts given to him every time the king returned home, stolen from the cities he'd conquered and the people he'd enslaved.

His stomach roiled.

"My father was a self-serving monster," he said at last, looking down at the book in his hands. "Like his father and grandfather before him. Shavhalla prospered only because of the wealth we stole from others. I can't even begin to number the atrocities my father must have committed."

A shiver ran across his skin. If he hadn't been cursed, would he have ended up following in King Kairav's footsteps? He liked to believe he was better than that, but he wasn't sure if he'd always been, or if that had only come after several lifetimes.

Saya turned from where she'd been examining a tapestry on the wall. "Do you happen to know how Mahati performed the curse?"

"Some kind of blood magic," he replied tersely. He'd mentioned that detail already when recounting the memory to them, but he knew what she was getting at. She wanted to know for her haseph.

"Yes," she said. "But *how?*"

"Does it matter?" As far as he was concerned, forbidden magical practices like that should stay forbidden.

Before she could respond, Lucian posed another question. "What happened afterward? Any connection to your curse and whatever befell the rest of Shavhalla?"

"I don't know. That part's still blurry." He looked down at the book in his hands, and an idea occurred to him. He headed for the door, gesturing for his friends to follow. "But I think I know where we can find out more. Come on."

The others followed dutifully. If the records room was as well preserved as the rest of the palace, they were sure to learn something worthwhile there. They might even find the answers Saya was looking for, and that might finally convince her that this pursuit of hers was a terrible idea.

Amar could only hope.

KESARI

AFTER THEIR MOST RECENT HOSTILE ENCOUNTERS WITH GUARDS, Kesari and the others were much more cautious about navigating the palace's hallways. Amar gave Lucian some quick directions, and the Spirit Tarja flew ahead to scout out a safe route to the lowest level of the palace. Once there, Amar led them to a pair of tall wooden doors, which he flung open to reveal an enormous library.

The exterior walls were lined from floor to ceiling with shelves upon shelves of books and scrolls. More shelves were arranged in rows throughout the room, along with several tables bearing additional books and various scientific instruments. A few motionless skeletons sat at the tables, as if they'd been there studying when they'd died. Others lay in crumpled heaps on the floor, clothes bundled around their bones.

Kesari's jaw dropped as she took it all in. She'd never seen so many books in one place. Before now, she hadn't imagined there even could be so many books in one place.

"Welcome to the records room," Amar said, striding through the doors with his arms outstretched.

Lucian's voice was full of awe as he hovered to the nearest shelf. "This is even bigger than the library at my old Tarja academy."

"It's incredible," Mitul said.

"Incredibly useless," Saya muttered. She flung an arm out and swept it across the room. "How are we supposed to find what we need in all this?"

"Not by complaining about it," Amar said. He went to the nearest shelf and began scanning the spines of some of the books it held.

The young warrior's shoulders slumped. "It's going to take ages. Some of us don't know how to read at all, and we certainly can't read the ancient language of some cursed city that's been lost for hundreds of years. You'll have to go through every single book and piece of parchment in this entire room."

"If that's what it takes," Amar replied, seemingly unbothered by this.

"Do you even know what you're looking for?"

"History. Some written account of when I was cursed and what happened after."

Saya waited a few seconds, as if expecting more. When nothing came, she crossed her arms. "Anything else?"

"What else is there?" He didn't turn around, but his voice was tense.

"What about my haseph? I need to know how to replicate your curse, and frankly, I'm not sure you'll tell me if you come across something useful. You've made your feelings on the matter perfectly clear."

Amar closed the book he was holding with a snap and raised his gaze to meet hers. The muscles in Saya's jaw tightened, and Kesari exchanged a nervous glance with Lucian and Mitul. The beginnings of an argument hung in the air like storm clouds.

"You're right," Amar said. "I'm not sure I *should* help you with this. It's a terrible idea to bring this curse to your own people, and if you haven't figured that out after all our time together, that's further proof of why you shouldn't do it."

"I know the risks," Saya shot back. "I've seen what this curse has done to you. But that's better than us being destroyed, which is exactly what will happen if the Kavorans continue to come into our homeland and steal our resources. Just because war hasn't broken out already doesn't mean it won't soon, and I'd like us to be ready when that happens."

Kesari stuck her hands in her pockets and backed away, slipping between two nearby shelves. Lucian followed, and they began perusing the books as their friends' argument continued.

"You don't even understand what you're talking about," Amar said.

"Neither do you. And what gives you the right to decide what's best for my people?"

"Forgive me, I didn't realize you spoke for all of them."

"I don't, but they should have the right to decide for themselves what's best. How can they choose if they aren't even given the option?"

"Why should they have the option?" The pitch of Amar's voice rose sharply. "Curses, blood magic—it's forbidden for a reason. It's too dangerous, and I won't be responsible for putting that evil back into the world now that it's gone."

"Look," Mitul jumped in. "I think we're all a little—"

Saya cut him off. "I didn't come all this way with you so you could refuse to help me in the end."

"I never agreed to—"

"How many times have we fought side by side? How many times have I protected you and helped you? Now I'm asking for *your* help, and you refuse?"

Their bickering continued, occasionally interrupted by Mitul's attempts to placate them. Kesari did her best to tune them out as she continued her exploration of the library.

"Can you make sense of any of this?" she asked Lucian, running her fingers over the strange characters stamped into the spine of a book.

"There are a few books with Kavoran titles, but so far, none of them look very useful."

"So we really could spend days in here trying to find what we need."

She stepped over the legs of a skeleton leaning against a bookshelf and worked her way to the back of the room. There stood a section of larger cabinets housing a variety of artifacts and artworks. Kesari opened one of the cupboards to find more than a dozen crowns neatly arranged inside, all different shapes and sizes and crafted from various materials. Some were made to encapsulate the top of the head while others were left open. Intricate metal-wrought designs and gleaming jewels adorned most, but others were smooth and simple, carved from stone or wood.

She picked up a circlet of polished crystal and set it on her head.

"How do I look?" she asked, turning to Lucian.

He grinned. "Fantastic. Although I'm not sure it matches the coat.'"

Kesari laughed and turned her attention to a stack of paintings leaning against the wall. She began to flip through them. Most reminded her of the figures they'd seen sculpted into the exterior of the palace and throughout the rest of Shavhalla. The colors were vivid, and there wasn't a single place on the canvas not taken up by some elaborate pattern. A few of the paintings were more realistic— sprawling landscapes of the city and the forest, portraits of nobles, and an unfinished piece depicting...was that Amar's family?

She dragged the painting out from behind the rest and rotated it to the proper orientation. Four figures stood around what she could only assume was the Shavhallan throne. The background and the subjects' faces had all been completed, but their bodies and clothing were unfinished, as if the painter had been interrupted.

The man seated on the throne looked a lot like the one in the painting upstairs—the one that had sent Amar sprinting to his old room. He seemed a bit younger here, jet black hair devoid of the gray streaks in the other painting. On his head sat a crown of gold with a plume of red and white feathers at its center. A tall woman with long black hair stood beside him, and to either side of them were two young men—their sons. The youngest was still just a boy.

"Is that Amar?" Lucian said, hovering in front of the older son.

Kesari examined the painting closer. He did look a lot like Amar, but there was something sharp and more like his father in his facial structure. "I think it's the older brother."

"Ah, right. So that means..." Lucian drifted to the younger boy's face. "Skies above, it is him."

All four of the figures wore crowns, though none of the others' were quite as extravagant as the king's. Kesari turned back to the crowns in the cabinet behind her. She picked up one that was almost identical to the one Amar wore in the painting. Looking at it gave her an idea, and she hurried back to the library's entrance to tell the others.

Amar and Saya's argument had devolved into a heavy silence, and

Kesari cleared her throat a little to try to get their attention before speaking. "I found something interesting."

They turned to look at her, their eyes immediately drifting to the crystal crown still sitting atop her head. Mitul arched one eyebrow and gave her a smile, but Saya and Amar did not look amused.

"What is it?" Saya asked.

She led them back to the painting. Amar inhaled a sharp breath when he saw it, and he crouched down to get a better look in Lucian's firelight.

"I remember this," he said. "That's my mother and father, King Kairav and Queen Anaya." His fingers traced their faces, then moved to the young men beside them. "My oldest brother, Devran, and then me. I think I was twelve or thirteen when this was painted."

"It's not finished," Mitul observed.

"No." Amar stood up. "After Devran died, my father paid the artist and sent him away. I never saw this again, but I remember my mother asking about it a few times. I think she wanted it for the memories, but for my father, it was too painful. He wouldn't let her have it." He stared at the painting for a few more seconds before turning to Kesari. "Thank you for showing me this, but we should get back to searching the rest of the books."

"Wait," she said. "I have an idea about that, actually. A way to make it faster."

Saya's eyes brightened. "How?"

"You remember the skeletons from last night?"

"Of course."

"They were all just going about their business," Kesari went on. "Working and shopping and talking to each other, like they were still alive. Some of the ones here in the library might have worked here. They could help us find what we're looking for."

The idea sounded a lot more ridiculous out loud than it had in her head, but to her great relief, no one laughed.

Mitul tilted his head to one side. "You want us to ask a bunch of reanimated corpses for help?"

"Yes?" She blushed and stared down at her feet. "Only if you think it's worth trying."

"That's assuming they come to life again tonight," Saya said. "And I'm not sure that's something we should hope for, after the fight we had with those guards earlier."

"It's a good idea," Lucian said to Kesari. "We should at least try. Otherwise, we could be here for a very long time."

Amar tilted his head. "We could use the help, but they didn't seem to know we were there last night. How are we supposed to get them to listen to us, if they can hear or see us at all?"

"The guards we fought certainly knew we were here," Lucian said, "and maybe some of the skeletons will, too. At least here in the palace."

Kesari nodded and held out the same crown Amar was wearing in the painting. He hesitated, then took it gently, like he was afraid it might break in his hands.

"If they can hear any of us," she said, "maybe they'll listen to you. You were their prince, once. We just have to help them remember that."

AMAR

AMAR STOOD IN HIS OLD ROOM, HOLDING UP THE SMALL MIRROR HE'D found inside the armoire. He'd traded his worn travel attire for a set of red and gold silk robes, also from the armoire, and a pair of finely crafted shoes with toes sweeping up to a delicate point. An embroidered sash draped from his left shoulder and hung over his arm. His hair had been rinsed in the washbasin and brushed back so the thick waves no longer obscured his face.

"And now, the final piece," Mitul said, raising the golden crown and setting it carefully atop Amar's head. It was only the two of them inside the room. Saya, Kesari, and Lucian waited outside and watched for any more guards who might attack, but Mitul had insisted on helping Amar make himself presentable. He'd taken to the task with great enthusiasm, and Amar appreciated the assistance. His head still felt foggy as old memories seeped into his mind, and he wasn't sure he would have been much use trying to get himself ready on his own.

"There you are." Mitul smiled at him in the mirror. "Prince Darshak Kaur of Shavhalla, finally returned home after centuries."

Amar tried to smile back, but it felt forced. Mitul saw a prince, but Amar just saw a boy. A boy he hadn't been for centuries, with eyes too hard and weary for such a young face. He was so much older now than he had been the last time he'd stood here. Seeing himself in a crown and the rich attire of a Shavhallan prince only reminded him more acutely of what he'd lost since then, of all the years he'd spent wandering this world and losing the people he cared about.

People like Mitul.

Outside, the sun was already setting, casting golden light and long shadows into the room. If the dead were going to rise again, it wouldn't be long now, and they would soon put Kesari's theory to the test.

"Well, your majesty, what do you think?"

Amar cringed. "Please don't call me that. I never wanted…" He stopped himself and let out a sigh. Once, he *had* wanted to be a prince, a king. But that was a long time ago. "This is all so unexpected."

"I can't even imagine. You're handling it remarkably well."

He grunted. "Am I? Because I feel like I'm on the verge of going mad." He walked to the window and stared out at the roofs of the buildings surrounding the palace.

"Talk to me," Mitul said, coming to stand beside him. "What's troubling you?"

Amar took a few moments to sift through the thoughts swirling around his mind. "Ever since I found out I was cursed, I assumed it must have been for something *I* did. But it wasn't. I know my father was a terrible man who did terrible things, and if anyone deserved vengeance, that girl did. But…" He wasn't sure how to finish the sentence without sounding like he was discounting Mahati's suffering.

"It doesn't seem fair," Mitul concluded.

He shook his head. "Why am I the one who has to atone for something I wasn't even responsible for?" His voice came out harsher than he'd intended, but didn't he have some right to be angry? His curse had been intended for his father, and he'd only been swept up in it because Mahati had been out of options. "It's frustrating, knowing all the pain and misery I've endured since then was because of someone else's choices."

"Was it all pain and misery?" Mitul said, and a lopsided smile tugged at one corner of his mouth. "We've had some good times together, haven't we?"

"Of course. But the good parts only make the inevitable losses more bitter."

"Or do the losses make the good parts sweeter?"

Amar groaned. "Are you trying to turn this into some kind of philosophical debate?"

Mitul laughed. "I wouldn't dare debate philosophy with a man who's lived as long as you. But could I get you to consider framing things another way, oh wise and ancient one?"

He rolled his eyes but couldn't suppress a grin of his own. "Fine. Let's hear it."

"Well, the way I see it, life is full of pain, isn't it? You know that better than most. And I can see how that would make a man want to keep to himself and push away anyone who tries to get close. After all, loss can't hurt you if you don't care about losing anything."

"Exactly," Amar said.

"But that must be a terribly empty way to live."

He didn't have a response for that. For so long, he'd thought of himself as an outsider. He'd kept himself at a distance from others because, even when he couldn't remember his previous lifetimes, something inside him knew staying distant was best. Mitul was one of the only people he'd truly grown close to in decades, and that wasn't so much because of his own choosing as it was because of Mitul's loyalty. Even so, there had been times when Amar had intentionally pushed his friend away.

Despite that, Mitul had followed him all over Erythyr looking for answers. He'd watched over him and given him whatever information he could when Amar didn't even know which questions to ask. Amar wouldn't have made it here without him—without any of them. Mitul, Saya, Kesari, Lucian—each had played a part in getting him this far, and though they all had their own motivations for seeing this through, they'd also done it for *him*. Because they considered him a friend. All this time, they'd been reaching out to him, offering help and concern and companionship even as he hid behind his walls.

Maybe Mitul was right. Despite all his best efforts, trying to distance himself from others hadn't exactly made his life any easier. There had still been devastating losses and more grief than any person should have to bear, but there had also been joy, colorful spots of good amongst all the bad. And maybe those things were worth pursuing, even if it meant making himself more vulnerable.

A few blue lights flickered to life in the fading gray of dusk. Amar raised the mirror to his face and frowned as he took in his prince's attire once more. "Do you really think this will work?"

Mitul shrugged. "Lucian seems to believe it will, and he's usually right about these sorts of magical things."

Amar raised an eyebrow. "Fair point, but I'm not sure even Lucian was prepared for all we've found here."

There was a sharp knock on the door, and it opened before either of them could answer. Kesari stuck her head inside, her brows drawn together. "Oh good, you're finished. Come on. Lucian spotted a couple of guards coming our way. Maybe you can try to talk to them before they attack."

Amar picked up his sword from where it leaned against the wall and exited the room. Hopefully he wouldn't need the weapon, but he wasn't about to confront the intimidating statues without it.

Four of them were already coming up the hall, their stiff, heavy footfalls echoing through the empty palace. A few of the blue lights floated in the air behind them. Saya stood with her bow at the ready, jaw set. Amar stepped past her, placing himself between his friends and the guards.

When they had drawn a little closer, he put one palm out in front of him and gave a command in a language he hadn't spoken for centuries. "Halt."

The guards drew their swords and kept coming.

"Amar…" Saya said, an anxious edge to her voice. Her feet shuffled into a new position behind him.

He tried again, drawing himself up a little taller and leveling his gaze at the guards. "I am Prince Darshak Kaur, son of King Kairav Kaur, and I command you to halt."

The guards took one more step, then shifted into a rigid at-attention position, swords lowered at their sides and helmeted heads turned toward Amar. They seemed to be awaiting further instruction.

He took a few steps toward them. "I've been gone a long time," he said, still speaking in Shavhallan. "I'm still not sure exactly what happened here, but I'm trying to find out. I'd like to break whatever curse has come over this place…over all of you."

He approached the closest guard and stared up at its stone features. Its armor was exactly the same as what the palace guards had worn when he was a boy, and now that he was closer, he could see subtle differences between each statue. One was a little shorter than the rest while another was a bit wider around the chest. Another had a chiseled braid extending from beneath its helmet to drape over one shoulder. The fourth was missing a finger.

"You were all alive once, weren't you?" he said quietly. "The curse must have turned you to stone."

The guard he was looking at gave a subtle nod.

Amar backed away from them and gestured to the others behind him. "My friends and I mean no harm. You've done well protecting the palace all these years, but I need you to let us come and go in peace."

The guard nodded again.

"What are you saying?" Saya asked.

He glanced back at her and held up a finger. "Thank you," he said to the guard. "I'm afraid I have little memory of what happened here after I was cursed. Is there any way you could tell me?"

The guard pointed to where his mouth would have been beneath his helmet and shook his head.

"That's all right. I was hoping to find a record of those events in the library, but it's enormous and I don't really know what I'm looking for. Is there still a scholar or a record-keeper around here who could help us?"

The guard stood motionless for so long that Amar almost repeated the question. Finally, it gave a nod, turned, and motioned for him to follow. He did, and the other three guards fell into stride on either side of him like a protective shield. Behind them, the others shuffled forward as well.

"Where are they taking us?" Mitul asked.

"To someone who can help, I think," Amar replied.

"Who?"

No sooner had he spoken than a door opened up ahead of them, and a skeletal figure in a flowing green dress stepped out into the hallway. Saya drew in a sharp gasp and muttered something under her breath.

The skeleton turned toward Amar and gave a deep curtsy. He found himself responding with an automatic bow, and the woman turned and went on her way, accompanied by a few glowing blue lights that danced around her waist and in the empty spaces of her eye sockets.

"It's like they can see us now," Lucian said. "Or at least, they can see Amar. I was a little skeptical before, but this was good thinking, Kes."

"It was only a hunch," she replied.

They continued though the hall, back down the stone steps to the entryway and then to the underground level that housed the library and several other rooms Amar hadn't bothered to check. They passed a few more skeletons on the way, some already going about their business while others were just rising from their daytime slumber. Most gave Amar some sort of acknowledgement, whether it was a bow or a curtsy or simply a respectful nod in his direction. He responded in kind but hurried his group along as quickly as he could.

The guard leading the procession stopped in front of a narrow door at the foot of the stairs. Amar wasn't sure whether to knock or simply go in, but before he could decide, the door opened. A stooped skeleton with a missing jawbone stood in the doorway, the top of his head wrapped in a crimson turban ornamented with a silver pin in the shape of a lotus. His attire was white, a loose tunic and pants suitable for everyday wear by Shavhallan men. He did not bow. Empty eye sockets gaped at Amar, and after a few seconds, he tilted his head to one side as if posing a question.

"Um…hello," Amar began in Kavoran, then remembered who he was speaking to and started over in Shavhallan. "Hello. I'm sorry to disturb you. I'm Prince Darshak Kaur…as you probably know already since everyone else here seems to." He grimaced at the clumsiness of his speech. Who was this man? And why did he suddenly feel like a child again standing in front of him? He cleared his throat. "We're looking for information. I was hoping you could help."

The skeleton gave no sign of acknowledgement, but after a few seconds, he made a circular gesture with his hand as if prompting Amar to continue.

He glanced back at his friends, who waited expectantly, then continued. This was sheer foolishness, talking to a skeleton, but he had no better options. "I don't remember much of my life here. I don't know how Shavhalla was cursed, and I'd like to find out so I can set things right, if there's a way to do that. Do you know of any records that might have been written about those events? We started searching but weren't sure where to look."

The skeleton regarded him in silence for a few more seconds, then stepped out into the hall. He headed for the library, waving a hand over his shoulder for the group to follow. They did, but before they reached the library doors, Amar stopped and spoke to the stone guards flanking him.

"You can wait here or return to your normal duties, if you'd like. I don't think we'll need any more protection." He wasn't entirely sure that last part was true, but he was feeling more than a little self-conscious with the guards following him like…well, like a prince in need of protecting.

The shoulders of one of the guards slumped a little, but they all turned away and marched back up the stairs single file. Amar and the others quickened their pace to catch up with the jawless skeleton waiting patiently inside the library, and once they were all across the threshold, he closed the doors behind them.

He led them through the maze of bookshelves. They passed a few other skeletons on the way, all clad in simple white clothing. Eventually, they stopped in front of a set of shelves at the back of the room, near where Kesari had found the paintings and crowns earlier. Their guide reached for a pile of scrolls on the highest shelf, unrolled a few, and tossed them aside before looking through some others.

"How do you think he's seeing what's on those?" Kesari whispered behind Amar. "He has no eyes."

"No idea," Lucian answered.

The man tucked one of the scrolls under his arm and continued to rifle through others. When he'd collected a second scroll and a sheaf of loosely bound papers, he gestured to a set of chairs at a nearby table. Amar followed him, and as they sat down across from each other, a bony hand pushed one of the scrolls toward him.

He started to unroll it as his friends gathered around and had it halfway open when he paused and looked up them. His eyes found Saya's. These scrolls could contain information that would fill the most critical gaps in his memory, and that knowledge gave him more hope than he'd had in a very long time. But he wouldn't have made it here without the others, and regardless of what he thought of Saya's haseph, he owed her something. She deserved answers, too. What she did with them afterward was not his choice to make.

"There's one more thing," he said to the skeletal man. "We need information about how exactly I was cursed with immortality. I've never heard of anyone else like me, so I take it the practice wasn't common even when it happened to me?"

The skeleton shook his head.

"I'm not sure if you know this, but curses don't exist anymore. The knowledge of how to create them has been lost for centuries. We need to know how it was done. Specifically, how to make someone immortal." He cringed a little as he said the words, and his insides squirmed when the skeleton only stared back at him, head tilted questioningly. "It's important," he added. "It could save a lot of people. My friend—" he gestured to Saya. "She needs this."

The skeleton turned his empty gaze to Saya as if seeing her for the first time. Then he raised two fingers to his teeth, as if he were trying to whistle, and lowered them again.

"What was that about?" Saya asked.

"Your haseph," he replied. "I asked if he could show us anything about how to curse someone with immortality."

Her eyes widened. "But you said—"

"I still don't think it's right. But that doesn't mean you're wrong. And it's not my decision."

The young woman's eyes glistened, but she raised her chin and blinked rapidly before tears could form. "Thank you."

A second skeleton approached, clad in a feminine white dress that reached to the floor. She and the other skeleton conversed for a few seconds, or at least, that was what they appeared to be doing. She gestured for Saya to follow her, and the two of them set off through the bookshelves together.

"Wait!" Kesari called. "I'll come with you."

She and Lucian hurried off to join them, leaving only Amar, Mitul, and the skeletal scholar at the table.

Amar returned his attention to the scroll in his hands. He opened it up. It wasn't very long, and the words were written in a hasty, summarized format rather than complete sentences. He could read the Shavhallan letters easily enough, but it still took him a few seconds to realize what he was looking at.

"It's a military report," he said to Mitul, skimming over a list of troop positions and attack formations, the final tally of dead and wounded, and an inventory of the spoils the army had taken.

"What does it say?" Mitul asked, leaning in closer though he couldn't read the words himself.

"Not much." He raised his eyes to the skull across the table. "Why are you showing me this?"

The skeleton reached forward, and Amar lowered the scroll for him to look at—or feel, or sense, or whatever he was doing. A pale finger ran down the edge of the scroll, then stopped and tapped an area near the bottom. Amar took a closer look.

Estimated enemy casualties: 1,200

Enemy combatants taken prisoner: 0

Enemies captured for sale: 216

Amar's eyes fixated on that single, horrific word at the end. *Sale.* Two hundred and sixteen human beings stripped of their freedom and dignity and sold like animals. And this was only from one attack, a single raid out of dozens or possibly hundreds his father had undertaken. His stomach churned, and he put a hand to his own neck as he remembered the metal collar locked around Mahati's.

"She was one of these, wasn't she?" he asked, tapping the number on the scroll.

The skeleton gave a slow, heavy nod.

Mitul looked between them. "What is it?"

"The girl who cursed me—this is a report of my father's attack on her town. She and two hundred and fifteen others were captured and sold to slavers."

"Skies above." He shook his head. "How awful."

"It's no wonder she came back for vengeance." Amar selected the next scroll from the pile. This one was an account of the night Mahati had sneaked into the palace, found her way to his room, and inflicted the curse on him. It had been written by someone named Ranjan, as indicated by his name next to the title *royal scribe* at the top of the paper. It read like a report taken from Amar himself, or rather, from Prince Darshak. Most lines started with phrases like, *Darshak reports*, and *Darshak stated that*, but it didn't contain much in the way of new information. Mahati had been arrested following their encounter, as he'd already guessed, but rather than being executed, she was imprisoned in Shavhalla's dungeons.

As he recounted this information to Mitul, the skeleton reached forward again. This time, he tapped the name at the top of the scroll, then pointed to himself.

"You're Ranjan?" Amar asked.

The skeleton nodded, and Amar studied him again, trying to conjure up a face from his past that belonged with that name. The white clothes, the red turban, the slightly stooped posture—recognition flickered in his mind at last. He could almost see the wrinkled, whiskered face of his old teacher settling over the skull in front of him.

A smile pulled at his lips, but he quickly schooled his expression into something more somber. The Ranjan he remembered had been a strict instructor who demanded respect and discipline from everyone, even the prince himself. "It's very good to see you again, teacher."

Ranjan gave a slight nod.

Amar rolled up the scroll and shifted his attention to the sheaf of papers. There were a lot of them, so he skimmed to pick out the most relevant parts and summarized them for Mitul as he went.

"These are from after Mahati was arrested. They locked her in a cell and interrogated her. She was forced to eat daravak every day to suppress her magic, and..." he paused, a sick feeling settling in his gut as he read over the bottom of one page again. "They tortured her. My father tortured her himself, trying to get her to break the curse." His heart shuddered at the callous but detailed descriptions of violence the king had inflicted on the poor girl.

"Could she even have broken it if she wanted to?" Mitul asked quietly.

"I'm not sure. She claimed she couldn't." He flipped the page and read on. There were more descriptions of Mahati's interrogation and torture, along with reports of similar fates shared by other prisoners. Were these all part of the wartime atrocities he was supposed to atone for?

He shook his head. His father had been a monster. So much time had passed since he'd seen the man, and he barely felt any connection to him now, but he couldn't shake off the truth of his heritage. The king had committed such terrible crimes that the stain of his actions had followed his son through centuries, leading right back here to the ruins of a city that had been cursed because of his continued cruelty.

Wait...how did he know *that* was the reason for Shavhalla's curse? He sat back in the chair, rubbing at his temples as his brain struggled to dredge up another old memory.

"What is it?" Mitul asked.

"I think my father was responsible for what happened here," he said. "To Shavhalla, I mean. He's the reason the whole city was cursed."

"What do you mean?"

"I'm not sure yet." He picked up the next sheet of paper, hoping to find a clue that would give him more answers. After skimming through a few more pages, he found what he was looking for. "Yes—this is it! Here, it says Mahati threatened to destroy Shavhalla if the king didn't release her and the other prisoners. No one took her seriously because they were giving her daravak. She shouldn't have been able to use magic at all, but I think she found a way. I remember."

Not everything. He could only remember that part of his history in fragments, and the pieces didn't all quite fit together, but he remembered *something*. It had happened several years after his own curse. Five years, maybe, or ten—he wasn't sure. He'd been away hunting with some friends when it happened.

"*What* do you remember?" Mitul prompted when Amar's silence stretched on.

"I wasn't here," he said, still trying to sort through the pieces in his mind. "I was in the forest, near the river. There was a burst of light— the same red light from when I was cursed. It shot up into the sky, and I raced home as fast as I could, but I didn't make it. The light spread through the forest, over me and my friends, and then everything darkened." He shook his head. "I think that must have been the first time I died."

Mitul's head tilted to the side. "What happened when you came back to life?"

"I didn't know where I was or what I was doing alone in the forest. I found two bodies nearby—the friends who had gone hunting with me, but I didn't remember them. And then I left, started wandering around until I found my way to a village near the river."

He looked across the table at Ranjan, who sat with his hands clasped together in front of his jawless skull. "She must have killed everyone in the city," he said. "But I still don't understand how. Even a curse shouldn't be that powerful, should it?"

Mitul only shrugged, and what did either of them really know about the capabilities of magic? Especially when it came to curses. He stood up from the table and began speaking to Ranjan in Shavhallan once more. "What happened to her, in the end? Mahati. Did she leave once she'd cursed this place? Did she help the other prisoners escape?"

Ranjan stood and motioned for Amar to follow him. He did so without a moment's hesitation.

"Where are we going?" Mitul asked, scrambling to catch up.

Before Amar could answer, Ranjan turned and pressed his palm against the man's chest. He recoiled, and a look of disgust slipped across his face as he stared down at the bony appendage. He recovered quickly, replacing his aversion with a sheepish smile. "Sorry. I know it's not your fault you're in this state."

If Ranjan understood him, he gave no sign, but Amar could picture the disdainful scowl on his old teacher's face. He kept his palm on Mitul's chest and, with his other hand, motioned again for Amar to follow him.

"Stay here with the others," Amar said.

Mitul's eyebrows shot up. "And let you go wandering off with the mysterious skeleton man by yourself?" He gave Ranjan a sidelong glance. "No offense."

"It's fine. I'll be right back."

"Do you even know where you're going?"

He shrugged. "No, but this is something I need to do. Alone, it seems."

"You know what happens to people whenever they say that, right? Bad things. Very bad things." Worry etched deep creases between Mitul's brows. "You've *died* when I've left you alone before, and I didn't follow you all the way here so you could put yourself in danger again. Tell him. You're the prince. He'll listen if you tell him I have to come along."

Amar nearly snorted at the idea of Ranjan taking orders from him. "I'm sorry. I can't."

The musician's voice became a plea. "Amar."

"Mitul," he replied evenly. "I'll be right back. I promise. He's not going to hurt me."

"But—"

"Go find Saya and the others. Get some sleep if you can. You can all wait for me here until I return."

"And what if you don't?"

"Then you'll come find me, like you always have."

Ranjan put his hands behind his back, his posture stiff and impatient.

"I have to go," Amar said. "I'll be fine."

Mitul sighed, but none of the worry faded from his eyes. "All right, then. But please be careful."

He smirked. "Oh, let's not be ridiculous. When have I ever been careful?"

ALEIDA

AFTER AN EARLY MORNING START AND A LONG DAY SPENT LISTENING to Jameson's constant complaints, Aleida was exhausted and irritated by the time they stopped to make camp. They'd found themselves wandering in circles for most of the afternoon, which Jameson unhelpfully insisted must be part of "the curse of Shavhalla." It was only when Valkyra had flown up into the forest canopy and scouted ahead that they were able to get back on track.

By this point, the night had grown late, the darkness heavy and oppressive. Valkyra led them to the nearest landmark—a stone bridge flanked by two statues, one fallen while the other remained upright.

"This is it," Jameson said through labored breaths, shrugging off his pack. "The entrance to Shavhalla. See the lotus flower in her hands?"

"I don't care what it's got in its hands," Aleida muttered, "so long as we're going the right way."

"I can keep scouting ahead while you eat and rest," Valkyra suggested. "We don't want to get lost again tomorrow, and we should be getting close enough to the others that I could find them now."

Aleida hoped that was true. She didn't want to guess how much time they'd lost wandering around today, but if they were entering Shavhalla, they must be near Amar and his friends as well. Presumably, they'd be staying in the ancient city for a while trying to solve whatever mystery lay behind Amar's curse. Hopefully, they wouldn't succeed before she found them.

She nodded to Valkyra. "That's a good plan."

The Spirit Tarja opened her wings and leapt into the night sky. Aleida built a fire and divided up what was left of their fish between herself and Jameson. She also gave him his nightly dose of daravak, taking care to cover up her own face to avoid inhaling any of its fumes. He had long since resigned himself to this suppression of his magic and breathed the stuff in with barely a grumble. Aleida hovered an orb of light in front of him to watch as he sucked in several deep breaths.

Satisfied, she sat cross-legged on the ground to eat. A glimmer on the other side of the bridge caught her eye, and she stood back up, peering past Jameson into the darkness.

"What is it?" he asked, turning around.

"Those blue lights. What are they?"

There were three of them, but two more lit up farther back even as she watched. They bobbed between the trees like tiny lanterns, but she couldn't see anyone or anything that might have created them.

"I read about this," Jameson said, his voice animated with curiosity and wonder. "Some people say they're spirits, doomed to linger in the physical realm for eternity. It's part of the curse of Shavhalla."

She rolled her eyes. "The curse of Shavhalla. You keep going on about that, like this place is haunted or something. You don't actually believe the stories, do you? They're just nonsense."

"Are they?" he asked, raising an eyebrow.

She sat back down with a glower. "Never mind."

He ate his fish in silence, but his gaze remained fixed on her, green eyes bright in the firelight. She pretended not to notice.

"I have a story for you," he said at last. "A ghost story. Fitting, given where we are, don't you think?"

"I'm not interested," she growled.

"Oh, I think you should be," he replied. "How else are we going to pass the time until Valkyra comes back?"

"Why do we have to talk at all?"

"You're a very unpleasant travelling companion, do you know that?"

That was laughable, coming from him, but she didn't say so.

Jameson tilted his head to one side. "If you'd rather, we could talk about your brother. I was so invested after you agreed to let me read his letter last night. You must have been very worried about him. And honestly, after that opening line, I was getting worried, too."

She bristled. "You didn't even get a chance to finish reading it."

"I didn't get a chance to finish *saying* what I read."

"And what is it exactly that you think you read?"

"'Dear Aleida,'" he recited. "'I am very sorry to tell you that your brother...'"

"My brother what?" she hissed, eyes narrowing. His words didn't match the ones Valkyra had read last night, and the dragon's warning about his schemes hadn't left her mind. If Jameson thought he could manipulate her into believing whatever he told her, he was going to be disappointed.

But that didn't quell her curiosity.

"My brother *what*?" she demanded again.

He shrugged. "I don't know. I didn't see the rest. Valkyra made sure of that."

"It wasn't any of your business, anyway. I shouldn't have asked you to read it."

"Well, it turned out all right in the end, didn't it? You seemed relieved after she told you what it said." The statement came out more like a question, and his head tilted ever so slightly.

"What about it?"

"I find it interesting, that's all. The way the letter started, it sounded like bad news. 'I'm very sorry to tell you...' What was it they were so sorry to tell you, I wonder?"

"Nothing," Aleida replied. "That's not even what it said. You must have translated it wrong."

He blinked. "Because I'm Atrean? I lived and studied magic at one of the best academies in Kavora for almost a decade. I read, write, and speak it fluently. Do you really think I can't translate a simple letter?"

"Then you lied."

"Why would I—" He stopped himself, and the confusion on his face gave way to a wry smile. "Ah, I see. That's what *she* told you, isn't it?"

Aleida clamped her mouth shut. They shouldn't even be having this conversation. Better they not speak at all so she didn't have to entertain whatever game he was playing.

"You know, there's something I've wondered ever since Amar first told me about you two," Jameson said. "Are you aware that the complexity of a Spirit Tarja's form is almost always related to the power and abilities they possessed in life?"

She did know this, but she said nothing, chewing the last bites of her meal and resolutely ignoring her captive.

"It's rare for a Spirit Tarja to even be capable of taking a form that can speak and move. You've seen Amar's friend Lucian, haven't you? The fire Spirit Tarja. Even his form is remarkably complex compared to what most Tarja are capable of when they die prematurely. The fact that Valkyra was able to take the form of an actual living creature means she would have been a very powerful Tarja indeed when she was alive."

Aleida knew this already, too. She wasn't an ignorant child, and she didn't appreciate Jameson talking to her as if she was. "What's your point?"

"Don't take offense, but why would one of the most powerful Spirit Tarja in existence choose to form a Bond with an underage, orphaned Visan refugee?"

She opened her mouth, wanting to throw out all the reasons Valkyra had given her when she'd asked that exact question herself. It was because Valkyra had taken pity on her and Tyrus and wanted to help them. It was because she'd had limited options and trouble finding anyone willing to make that Bond. It was because, being so young, Aleida had a longer natural lifespan remaining to share with Valkyra, which made her an advantageous choice over older partners she might have Bonded to.

But Jameson wouldn't believe any of that, and even if he did, he would twist those reasons and use them as a wedge to drive Aleida and Valkyra apart. It was all part of whatever scheme he was concocting to escape. It had to be.

Still, the seed of doubt that had lain dormant in the back of her mind since her earliest days with Valkyra seemed to sprout anew.

"I think it's time for that little ghost story I had in mind," Jameson said, tossing a few fallen branches into the fire.

"I think it's time for bed."

"One story, then bed. Otherwise, I'll make a lot of noise and keep you awake all night."

"I can *make* you shut up," Aleida replied in the most threatening voice she could muster.

"Yes, but you don't really want to do that, do you? You don't enjoy the torture and the violence you think you have to inflict on people to make them do what you want. Besides, doesn't that go against the compassionate teachings of your Visan god?"

She scowled. "Fine. Tell your story."

Jameson flashed a satisfied grin. "All right then. Once, some years ago, there lived an emperor who ruled over a powerful and wealthy nation. Many of the citizens were gifted with magic, and the nation had the most powerful army of Tarja in all the land."

"Does this nation happen to be Kavora?" Aleida muttered.

"Shh. Listen. For most of his reign, the emperor had no heir, and it was his sister who was in line to ascend to the throne. That all changed when the emperor remarried, and his new wife finally gave birth to a son. The emperor himself died shortly after, and as the boy was still only a baby, the emperor's sister began to rule as regent. Her dearest friend, a powerful Tarja, became her closest advisor."

This was all sounding awfully familiar. Aleida glared at Jameson in annoyance but allowed him to continue without interruption.

"Two short years later, the boy heir and his mother were tragically killed by assassins. This left the empress regent as the sole remaining heir to the nation's throne, and thus, many began to suspect that perhaps it was she who'd ordered the boy's assassination. Others speculated the boy might still be alive, having miraculously escaped the attempt on his life. The new empress denied these claims, of course, but people continued to whisper about the lost prince and their empress' convenient ascent to his throne."

"This is just the story of Prince Savir," Aleida said in exasperation. "Why would I care about any of this? Is *he* your ghost?"

"The story isn't finished," he replied calmly. "And no, he isn't. May I continue?"

"Get it over with, then," she said, half out of genuine curiosity and half out of frustration that she'd suddenly become so intrigued. What more to the story was there? If the lost Prince Savir wasn't the ghost in his ghost story, then who was?

Jameson cleared his throat and went on. "As the years passed, the empress and her Tarja advisor worked together to expand the power and influence of their nation. They absorbed various provinces into their country and even went so far as to invade a small, peaceful nation at the edge of their borders. It was the advisor who pushed for this invasion, believing the smaller nation could offer a wealth of resources and a strategic defensive position to hold off potential invaders."

Aleida clenched her jaw. He was talking about Vis now and the invasion that had killed thousands and made refugees of many thousands more. So this *was* a story of Kavora's history. With Savir out of the picture, the key players were Empress Dashiva along with her long-time friend and most trusted advisor, Nandini Kumar. Just thinking of the woman made her seethe. Nandini was the mastermind behind the invasion of Vis, and if anyone was to blame for everything Aleida had lost, it was her.

"The advisor continued to push for greater power and bigger conquests," Jameson went on, "but the empress grew tired of war. She wanted her country to enjoy peace and prosperity under her reign, and so, despite all its great military strength, the nation stopped expanding its borders." He picked up another stick and prodded at the fire, creating a flurry of smoke and crackling sparks. "Peace was tenuous at first. Neighboring countries didn't know yet whether to trust this change of course, so when the advisor took actions that put a further strain on those relationships, the empress lost patience. She stripped the advisor of her title and her power and ordered her to be arrested for treason."

"Are we getting any closer to the point of this little history lesson?" Aleida asked.

He ignored her question. "Unwilling to spend the rest of her days in a Tarja prison, the advisor fled. The empress' best warriors pursued her and eventually tracked her down. Their orders were to take her alive, or if that wasn't possible, to drain her of all her altma before they executed her. Given how dangerous and powerful she was, the empress didn't want her dying prematurely and becoming a Spirit Tarja."

Aleida knew the rest of the story. There had been a time when she'd taken pleasure in imagining Nandini's end again and again. Sometimes she even embellished the details, making them more gruesome, more punitive toward the woman who had taken so much from her. It had been a darkly comforting ritual.

"The warriors fought her," Jameson said. "She killed some of them, but they finally overpowered her, and she attempted to end her own life with her magic. But her powers were weakened from the fight, so she didn't die right away."

"But one of the Tarja warriors drained away the last of her altma before killing her," Aleida said quickly. "Because of that, she didn't become a Spirit Tarja. She got what she deserved for her cruelty, and she died in disgrace. The end."

Jameson nodded. "That *is* how the story's usually told. Though I heard a slightly different version of the ending once, from a teacher—a man who was one of the Tarja warriors sent after the traitorous advisor."

"What do you mean?"

"Well, he had some doubts about whether they'd really managed to drain away all her altma before she took her last breath. He thought there was a slight possibility that she became a Spirit Tarja after all. Her ghost may still be tethered to the physical world by whatever remaining magic she possessed when she died."

Aleida waited for him to continue, but he said nothing more. "That's it?" she asked. "That's your ghost story?"

He shrugged. "I didn't think much of it either, until I spent some time with the two of you."

"If Nandini was still alive, someone would know about it by now. Besides, what does that have to do with me and Valkyra?"

Jameson stared at her without saying anything. He simply raised an eyebrow, the same look he'd given her when he'd asked a question of his own.

Why would one of the most powerful Spirit Tarja in existence choose to form a Bond with an underage, orphaned Visan refugee?

"You think Valkyra is Nandini Kumar?" She wanted to laugh at the idea, but a prickling feeling at the base of her skull gave her pause. Her mind began to fill in gaps she'd been too preoccupied to notice until now.

The battle between Nandini and Empress Dashiva's warriors had happened almost three years ago along the banks of the Adrati River, less than a day's journey east of Chatanda. Aleida and Tyrus were both living there by then. Hasan had recently diagnosed Tyrus with Storm Withering Syndrome, so she'd had more pressing concerns when news of Nandini's fate reached them. Valkyra had found her a day or two later, a shimmering spirit in human form, offering her hope and power and a chance to save her brother's life. A chance she'd taken without hesitation.

She shook her head, remembering all the ways Valkyra had helped her, all the times she'd patiently taught her how to use her magic, the nights she'd sung her to sleep and chased away her nightmares, the gentle reassurances she'd offered that kept her going when her doubts were strongest. Valkyra cared about her, and Tyrus. She always had. In many ways, she'd been like a mother to them.

"You're lying," she growled, glaring at Jameson across the fire. "You're trying to turn us against each other, like she said you would. You don't know anything about her. She's done nothing but help me."

"Have you ever asked yourself why? What does *she* get out of trying to save your brother?"

"Nothing," Aleida shot back. "But she's not doing it for herself. She wants to help us."

"Forgive me," the man said, and there was something genuinely kind in his voice. "But from an outsider's perspective, that doesn't make sense. She's a powerful Spirit Tarja. She could have formed a Bond with anyone, and she chose you. You're telling me she did that merely out of the goodness of her heart? Do you honestly believe that?"

"She's *not* Nandini. It doesn't make sense."

The more she thought about it, though, the more it *did* make sense.

If Nandini had become a Spirit Tarja after her death at the river, she wouldn't have had more than a few days to form a Bond with a living partner. Chatanda would have been the closest settlement, but much of its population consisted of displaced Visan refugees who wouldn't have welcomed a Bond with anyone responsible for invading their home. Of course she'd have had to lie about her name, and it would have been smart for her to find someone who wouldn't ask too many questions. Someone desperate enough to take the opportunity she was offering without thinking too much about it.

Someone as desperate as Aleida had been.

More pieces shifted into place. In Valmandi, Valkyra said she'd broken Aleida out of prison with the help of Magistrate Ashaya, a man known to have been a friend of Nandini Kumar. Aleida had even asked her if she'd known Nandini.

I knew her. But we weren't friends.

Technically true, if Valkyra *was* Nandini. But it had bothered Aleida that Valkyra hadn't mentioned this piece of information to her before.

And then, of course, there was the fact that Nandini was said to have been one of the most powerful Tarja to ever live. In death, she would have been exactly the kind of Spirit Tarja capable of taking on a more complex form. A talking dragon, for instance.

Aleida clenched her fists and tried to slow her racing thoughts. Even her breaths had become shaky and shallow. This couldn't be happening. It *wasn't* true.

But...what if it was?

She grabbed her pack and riffled through it until she found the letter Feros had delivered last night. Clutching it in stiff fingers, she stood and marched to Jameson, where she thrust the paper into his face. "Read it," she said through clenched teeth.

He took the letter calmly and smoothed out the wrinkles where she had crushed the paper. In a low, steady voice, he began to read.

"Dear Aleida, I am very sorry to tell you that your brother passed away last night."

The ground gave way beneath her feet. She sank down, chest heaving, a single word reverberating in her mind again and again.

No.

"His condition has declined rapidly ever since you left," Jameson continued, "and there has been a sickness going around the village this past week. I took every precaution to prevent him from being exposed, but he became ill, and there was little I could do but ease his suffering.

He spent his last hours looking through your drawings. I know they brought him comfort in the end."

Tears welled up in Aleida's eyes, burning trails into her skin as they ran down her cheeks. "You're lying," she said hoarsely. "You're making things up. It's not true."

"I'm sorry," Jameson said softly.

"No!" She lurched for him, grabbed him by the front of his robes, and yanked him forward so his face was mere centimeters away from hers. "He's not dead!" she screamed. "Say it—tell me you're lying!"

"I didn't know. I was only reading—"

She cut him off with a cry, wild and animalistic, and channeled her altma. Jameson cringed, and she barely stopped herself from unleashing it against him. Instead, she shoved him away and bent over. Her palms pressed against the dirt, and she redirected her magic downward until the ground rumbled beneath her. The stone statue at the end of the bridge wobbled and fell, narrowly missing Jameson. Aleida pressed her hands against her head, her entire body shaking with sobs.

Somewhere deep inside, buried beneath layers and layers of obstinate hope, she knew it was true. Hasan had warned her this would happen. He'd wanted her to stay so she could be with Tyrus at the end. She'd refused, foolishly believing she could still save him, asking him to hold on for just a little while longer. An unfair, selfish request made by a weak little girl who couldn't bear the thought of being alone in the world.

All her efforts, all her stubborn hope and steadfast determination— it had all been for nothing. Tyrus was gone, and she hadn't been there to comfort him when his spirit left this world for the afterlife. Instead, all he'd had were her stupid drawings.

She had failed him, in every sense of the word.

"Aleida!" Valkyra's voice cut through her thoughts like a blade, sharp and cold. "Are you all right, dear? I heard a scream and came as fast as I could."

Feathers brushed against her knees as Valkyra alighted on the ground in front of her. A sudden surge of hatred filled Aleida's veins, throbbing painfully against the back of her eyes as she stared at the Spirit Tarja through tears.

"Oh, sweet child, what's wrong?" Gentle worry laced the dragon's soft voice, and she cast a backward glance at Jameson. "Did he do something?"

"You lied to me," Aleida said in a barely controlled whisper. "You told me Tyrus was sick, but he...he's dead, isn't he?"

Her eyes narrowed. "You let him read the letter?"

"You've been lying to me all this time."

"It's *him* that's lying. You're really going to trust him over me? I told you he would try to manipulate us if we weren't careful."

"*Stop!*" Aleida screamed. She swiped at Valkyra with her hand, but the Spirit Tarja jumped back at the last moment, and her fingers raked through empty air. "You're the one who's been manipulating me."

She stood, and Valkyra rose with her, her wings fluttering in the air to keep herself aloft. "What's gotten into you?" she asked. "What lies did he tell you?"

"I know who you really are."

Her stern expression faltered, and Aleida waited for the denial that would surely follow. She *wanted* her to deny it. If she denied it, if she could offer up a reasonable explanation for everything, Aleida might be able to believe her. Maybe Valkyra wasn't really Nandini Kumar. Maybe she hadn't been manipulating her all this time.

Maybe Tyrus was still alive.

Seconds passed, no longer than the space of a few heartbeats. Then Valkyra looked back at Jameson. "You are far too clever for your own good, aren't you?" Her voice was no longer soft and silk. Instead, it carried something hard and threatening. This wasn't the denial Aleida had been hoping for.

"Nandini Kumar," the Tarja said. "You've fallen a long way since your days at the empress' side."

"A temporary setback, I assure you," Valkyra replied. She shifted her attention back to Aleida. "Now then, what to do about you?"

"It's true then. But Tyrus—you said we could save him." A new rage filled her, and she struggled to keep her emotions in check as she reached for her altma. "You swore to me!"

"I have sworn a great many things to a great many people, dear. Only the naïve are foolish enough to believe everything they're promised."

With a sweep of her arm, Aleida hurled a crackling bolt of lightning at the Spirit Tarja. It struck her directly in the face and flashed around her for an instant, but she remained unharmed. She attacked again, but Valkyra didn't even flinch. Instead she laughed, the sound loud and harsh in the night's stillness.

A sudden burning surged from the center of Aleida's chest and through the rest of her body to her extremities. There was a sharp yank on her altma, something she wasn't doing herself and couldn't control. She couldn't move. She could barely breathe. Her insides felt as if they were being ripped from her body. The agony was worse than anything she'd ever felt, a burning, tearing sensation that made her wish to die just so the pain would end. She screamed.

And then, as quickly as it had begun, the sensation ended. Aleida collapsed onto the ground, her body weak, drained, and trembling. She lay on her side, hugging her knees. Through blurred vision, she watched as a glowing blue light took shape—a woman's shape.

She recognized it as the Spirit Tarja who had come to her three years ago in Chatanda, offering power in exchange for half of what was left of her natural lifespan. She was less vibrant than Aleida remembered her being before, a little more translucent and ghostly. Her physical dragon form was gone. Now, she was only a spirit

Horror filled Aleida at the realization of what that meant. Valkyra had severed their Bond.

That explained her sudden weakness. She had shared her life with Valkyra. Separated like this, did half of her life force stay with the Spirit Tarja? Or perhaps even more? Maybe she was going to die, right here, right now.

Her eyelids fluttered closed, but a new cry prompted her to force them back open. Valkyra floated toward Jameson, who had backed himself up against the fallen stone statue. "Madness!" he shrieked. "You can't do this! We're both Tarja. If you force a Bond, you could kill us."

"My magic is stronger than yours," Valkyra said evenly. "Do not tell me what I cannot do."

She wrapped her ghostly arms around his body, which stiffened instantly. His eyes rolled back in his head, and after a few seconds, his spine arched farther than it should have been capable of, as if the bones within were being pulled apart. He let out a scream, which was abruptly cut off as his body snapped back into a more natural position. There he stood, arms limp, eyes blank, an empty shell of the panicked man he'd been seconds before.

Valkyra's glowing spirit form morphed into something smaller, solidifying as it lost its shine. She looked exactly as she had before, a silky white dragon with soft feathered wings and liquid silver eyes. She fluttered around Jameson like a bird, examining her handiwork from all angles with a cruel smile.

"Excellent," she mused to herself. "I wasn't entirely sure that would work. But if I can overpower a great Tarja like you, the immortal will be easy prey." She settled onto the man's shoulder and stared ahead. "Come. Let us leave this place."

Jameson began to walk with a mechanical rigidity, heading back in the direction they'd come from earlier that night. Aleida willed herself to reach for him as he passed, to grab him by the ankle and tell him to stop. But she couldn't move, couldn't speak. Valkyra didn't so much as glance down at her, and soon, they had disappeared into the dark spaces between the trees.

The last embers of the fire were dying, and darkness began to creep into the edges of Aleida's vision. The initial rush from all the action was beginning to wear off, and the searing pain in her body intensified as she struggled to move. With great effort, she clawed her way to the letter Jameson had dropped, lying on the ground a few paces away. Her muscles clenched, and her lungs burned from the effort. She felt gutted, like something vital had been ripped out of her and she was bleeding out, though there was no blood or any other visible sign of injury.

She'd been so foolish. She should have been able to see through Valkyra's lies from the start. She shouldn't have been so trusting. Now Tyrus was dead, and she hadn't even had a chance to say goodbye. With a cry of rage and self-loathing, she managed to pull herself forward the last little bit and grabbed at Hasan's letter.

Her hands shook as she clutched the paper, and she closed her eyes, one cheek pressed against the ground. Fallen leaves tickled her nose. Her throat was dry. She wanted water, but the effort it would take to retrieve her canteen from her pack was beyond her right now. Perhaps if she slept first, she'd get some of her strength back.

Or perhaps she would drift off into an eternal slumber and die. It didn't really matter either way.

Nothing mattered anymore.

AMAR

AMAR FOLLOWED RANJAN THROUGH THE HALLS OF THE PALACE, which were illuminated only by the moonlight and the ghostly blue orbs drifting through the empty air. They passed by several more animated skeletons and walking statues, who acknowledged Amar with nods and bows but remained ever silent. Ranjan took him past the painting of his father and down another long hall to a door that opened to the rear of the palace.

Outside, the night was cool and silent except for the barest whisper of the breeze through nearby trees. Amar's gaudy slippers made no sound as he and his old teacher padded down the walkway to a plain, square building behind a spiked iron gate. A pair of stone guards allowed them to pass without a word, and Amar looked up to see skeletal figures in high towers watching them as they entered the building.

There were no windows, but a few lit torches illuminated the interior, along with the same blue lights which populated all of Shavhalla. Ranjan conversed silently with the nearest skeletal soldier, who handed over a ring of keys before nodding to Amar. He nodded back and followed Ranjan to a set of narrow stairs leading underground.

He grabbed a torch off the wall before descending, but he didn't end up needing it as much as he thought he would. They reached the bottom of the steps and turned a corner into a space filled with dozens of glowing blue lights—more than he'd seen congregated together in one place thus far.

The air became heavy and thick as they passed rows upon rows of iron-barred cells, each one barely large enough for a narrow bed, a bucket for waste, and a single person. Most of them contained all three of these things, though the people had turned to walking skeletons, like everyone else in Shavhalla. They clutched the bars of their cells and stared out at Amar. A few reached for him, pale fingers grasping at his clothing. Others shrank away and huddled into a corner if he looked at them, as though they didn't want to be seen.

A memory flashed through his mind, brief, but vivid. Hopeless eyes, emaciated bodies, pained cries and gruff voices asking questions, blood spraying across the stone, the stench of human refuse and despair. He'd come here with his father once, right before he was cursed. The experience had repulsed him so much he'd never returned, even when King Kairav insisted he would have to get used to such things if he wanted to be a strong ruler one day.

Had his father truly believed that, or was it something he told himself to justify the terrible things he did?

Ranjan stopped and turned to unlock one of the cells. The door swung open, and he stepped back to give Amar room to enter.

This cell was exactly like all the others, a bucket in one corner and a thin straw mattress on the floor. But it was empty.

No, that wasn't right. There in the corner lay a small pile of…something. Amar squinted and stepped closer, holding his torch above the debris.

Bones. Human bones. Only these weren't animated like all the rest. They weren't even attached to each other anymore, instead lying strewn out along the wall. It was as if the person they belonged to had simply lain down, skin and muscle and other tissue disintegrating until only the fragmented skeleton was left. A set of metal shackles lay near several tiny bones that might have belonged to a hand or foot, and near the skull was a metal ring just big enough to fit around a person's neck.

A slave collar, like the one Mahati had worn.

He turned to Ranjan. "Is this her?"

His head bobbed up and down.

Amar knelt beside her remains and set down his torch. He picked up the metal collar, and a single vertebra fell out. He caught it before it hit the floor and laid it carefully beside the other bones, then examined the collar. There were jagged scratches and dents on the metal. He imagined someone hacking away at it with a stone or a knife or whatever tool they could get their hands on, trying but ultimately failing to break free.

A hard lump pressed against his throat. This girl had been through a lifetime of pain and suffering. It was no wonder she'd harbored so much anger, no wonder she'd turned all that rage on those connected to her suffering, whether they were personally responsible or not.

The curses Mahati had placed on him and on the people of Shavhalla may have been unfair and cruel, but life had been unfair and cruel to her, too. And it wasn't like he was completely blameless. Prince Darshak might not have ridden into battle with his father or personally sold human beings into slavery, but he hadn't spoken up against it, either. He'd had more power and privilege than most, but he'd done nothing to stop these horrors. Instead, he'd remained willfully ignorant, sometimes even choosing to turn a blind eye when the truth made him uncomfortable. And the rest of Shavhalla hadn't been much better.

Unfair or not, Amar could understand how, from Mahati's perspective, those curses were justice.

Some of the anger he still carried for her melted away. That fury would get him nowhere now. She was dead, and he was still cursed. The best he could do was move forward and try to set things right. Starting here, with her.

"I'm sorry," he whispered to the lifeless bones.

There were still so many questions he didn't have clear answers for, but he could guess what must have happened. Sometime during her imprisonment, Mahati had reclaimed her magic and used it to place a curse on all of Shavhalla. They'd all died, like Amar and his two friends in the forest that day, but their bodies and the city itself had been locked in their own prison—one where time slowed, delaying the effects of decay and deterioration. And it seemed the souls of those Shavhallans still lingered here, reanimating corpses and statues by night.

But not Mahati. While other skeletons paced in their cells, she lay still. She hadn't been able to escape her prison while she was alive, so perhaps she'd sought freedom in death. A curse strong enough to affect an entire city would have required a tremendous amount of power, and the power that fueled a curse came from blood. She may have even sacrificed her own life in its creation.

Amar shook his head. The anguish she must have felt to resort to something like that, to use her regained powers not to escape, but to hurt those who had hurt her.

She shouldn't be here. Even though she was only bones now, it wasn't right. This wasn't a peaceful resting place—not for her. Amar unfastened the embroidered sash at his shoulder and spread it on the empty mattress beside him. He reached for the nearest bones. They were dry and cracked and felt much too light to have ever belonged to a living person. He was gentle with them as he laid them on the sash and reached for more.

Ranjan joined him after a few seconds, squeezing past him to the corner of the room, where he bent and plucked more bones from the ground. He handed them to Amar one at a time, and they began to fill the empty spaces on the sash. There were so many of them, and when they'd collected all the most obvious ones, Amar stood, holding his torch aloft to make sure he hadn't missed any.

"We have to get them all," he said. He didn't want to leave any piece of the girl in this cell.

Ranjan lifted the edge of the mattress, and Amar searched underneath for bones they might have missed. He found another vertebra in the far corner of the room, and a smaller bone behind the bucket near the door. When he was absolutely certain they'd collected everything, he gently pulled the corners and edges of the sash together and tied them in a knot. Then he followed Ranjan back out of the cell, up the stairs, and into the fresh air.

When they returned to the palace, they found Mitul, Saya, Kesari, and Lucian waiting in the main hall. Kesari sat against the wall, her head tipped back and her eyes shut. Lucian hovered faithfully nearby. Mitul was hunched over his saraj, softly strumming a few chords and mouthing words under his breath.

Saya saw him first. She clutched a single book in one hand, and she smiled at him as he approached. There was a certain ease in her expression that he didn't think he'd ever seen before. "There you are," she said warmly.

Mitul's eyes immediately snapped to him, and he stood so quickly he nearly dropped his saraj.

Lucian chuckled a little as he watched the musician fumbling. "Mitul was starting to worry about you. But only a little."

"Can you blame me?" the man said. "You said you'd be right back."

"And here I am," he replied.

"You certainly didn't hurry."

Kesari yawned and looked up at him from the floor. "What's that you're carrying?"

Their gazes shifted to the bundle in his hands. He hesitated, unsure of how to tell them what he'd found. "This is Mahati," he said at last. "Or what's left of her. She deserves to be properly laid to rest."

For a few seconds, no one spoke. Mitul shifted back on one foot, away from the bundle of bones. Then Kesari shrugged. "There was that temple we passed. We could bury her there."

"It has to be somewhere else," he said. "Outside the ruins. Shavhalla wasn't a happy place for her. I know it's late and you're all probably tired, but I need to do this as soon as possible. She's been trapped here too long." He clutched the bundle a little tighter. "Are you ready to leave?"

They exchanged looks, and Amar knew what a strange request this must seem, asking them to go out of their way for a girl who'd been dead for centuries. But they all nodded, picked up their things, and headed for the stairs.

Amar turned to Ranjan. "Thank you for everything."

His old teacher nodded, then did something he had never seen him do to anyone, not even the king himself. He bowed. Only a little, but it was enough to express his respect. Amar returned the gesture.

"Goodbye," he said, then followed his friends, and together they walked out of the palace and back into the ghostly nighttime streets of the cursed city.

KESARI

KESARI'S FEET FELT HEAVY AND SLOW AS SHE FOLLOWED THE OTHERS through the streets of Shavhalla. Amar led the way at a brisk pace, his path illuminated only by the glowing blue lights hovering all around them. Occasionally, the skeletons and animated statues they passed would turn to him in acknowledgement, but they stayed where they were, watching from a respectful distance. He still wore the ornate robes and gilded crown that marked him as their former prince, and while they paid no attention to Kesari and the others, they didn't ignore Amar the way they had only the night before.

Had it really been that recent? So much had happened in the last day. She'd explored an ancient city straight out of legend, learned that one of her friends was the former prince of that city, and—perhaps most surprisingly of all—used her magic to fight against the cursed beings they found there.

She still couldn't quite believe it. Mere weeks ago, she'd yearned to get rid of her magic. She would have never thought herself capable of using it in combat, where there was so much potential for her to lose control in the chaos of heightened emotion. The experience had been stressful and terrifying and exhilarating in a way that both scared her and filled her with joy—the same joy she'd felt when she'd channeled altma for the very first time. But despite all the emotions surging through her, she'd stayed in control.

She brushed her fingers against the worn fabric of her coat and smiled. Rajiv would have been proud of her. More importantly, she was proud of herself. She was a Tarja. Acknowledging that simple fact still brought some discomfort, but not enough that she wanted to run or scream or tear the magic from her being. It was part of who she was, and even if she wasn't quite ready to embrace it, she at least wouldn't reject it, and that felt like a step in the right direction.

She quickened her pace until she drew up beside Saya, who hadn't said anything since leaving the palace. She still held onto the journal she'd taken from the library. Its pages were filled with handwritten notes and diagrams, addendums scribbled hastily in the margins every now and then. None of them had been able to decipher much, but Lucian's assessment of the diagrams suggested that the journal was, in fact, a detailed analysis of the same curse Amar had suffered.

"How much farther do you think we'll go?" Saya asked, glancing over at her.

She shrugged. "We won't be out of Shavhalla until we cross that stone bridge, I imagine. It should be getting close."

Saya's fingers tapped against the worn leather cover of the journal. "I was hoping he'd have a chance to look at this before we left, but he was in such a hurry I didn't get a chance to ask him."

"You could ask him now. Maybe he'll stop for a break."

She shook her head. "I don't want to bother him. He already doesn't approve of what I'm doing. I just hope this has what I need."

Kesari nodded. "And if it does, then what?"

"Then I'll take it back to my people and present it to our leaders. Hopefully, they'll accept my offering and my haseph will be complete. There will be a ceremony. I'll finally get to become an official member of my tribe, and the leaders will decide what to do about the curse."

Kesari gnawed at her bottom lip. She hadn't considered that their group might be splitting up when there was so much that remained unfinished. They still hadn't broken Amar's curse, and in some ways, their journey to Shavhalla had left them with more questions than answers.

"What about you?" Saya asked. "What will you do?"

It was a good question. What *would* she do? When she'd first decided to travel here with the others, she'd wanted to help Amar break his curse, but she had no idea what he was planning to do now. Should she stay with him? Would he want or expect that? Mitul would go with Amar whatever he chose, but Saya was leaving, and maybe Kesari should, too. She could go back home, like she'd promised Navya. She had a family waiting for her, after all. Was it wrong to keep them waiting even longer?

Her stomach flipped over at the idea of returning to Deveaural. She wasn't sure if that was residual panic from the years she'd spent deliberately avoiding anything to do with home, or if it meant she still wasn't ready to go back. It felt like there was more to see and do and accomplish before she returned, but she couldn't pin down anything more specific than that, and it wasn't like the others couldn't function well enough without her. They'd been doing perfectly fine long before she and Lucian came into the picture.

So why did the idea of leaving them behind make her want to cry?

"I don't know," she said in answer to Saya's question.

"I only asked because I thought, if you wanted to, you might come with me. I could use the support and knowledge of a Tarja when I bring this back to my people. We don't have many, and most of them have never ventured very far beyond the desert. Your perspective could be valuable."

"You think so?"

"Of course. You're a skilled Tarja, Kes. Surely you can see that by now. Stop undervaluing yourself."

Lucian floated a little closer to her ear. "She's right, you know."

"You don't have to make a decision right now," Saya said, tucking the journal into the bag slung over her shoulder. "And it's perfectly fine if you can't or choose not to. I just thought, if you're not doing anything else and if you wanted to, I'd be happy for the company."

"I'll go," Kesari said. She didn't need to think about it. As soon as Saya had asked, she'd wanted to go, and if she could truly be helpful, all the more reason to do it.

The older girl grinned. "Good."

They had come to the bridge now, and a few paces ahead, Mitul and Amar stopped walking, peering across to the other side. There were far fewer blue lights here, and without their glow, the shadows had grown darker. It was difficult to see much of anything.

"What is that?" Mitul asked Amar as the others came to rest beside them. It took Kesari a few seconds to spot the lump they were staring at. It lay right in the middle of the path, something that definitely hadn't been there when they'd passed through the day before.

"Maybe some kind of animal?" Saya suggested.

"I'll have a look," said Lucian, and he flew ahead, casting firelight over the bridge's stone walkway as he went. When he drew a little closer to the lump, he called back, "I think it's a person."

Kesari exchanged a look with Saya. They hadn't seen a single living person in days. What would anyone else be doing all the way out here?

Lucian's light fell over the figure, and Kesari sucked in a sharp breath. The clothes, the sharp features, the brown hair and pale skin—it was that woman, the one who'd trailed them all the way through Kavora, into Atrea, and even up the coast by sea.

Saya immediately fitted an arrow to her bowstring. Amar passed Mahati's remains over to Mitul, then drew his sword. Together, they began to approach the woman. Kesari hung back with Mitul for a few seconds, but her magic meant she could fight, too. She should probably do more than stand by. She scrambled to catch up with Amar and Saya, channeling altma in preparation for an attack.

The young Visan woman remained motionless. She might have been dead, or perhaps this was some kind of trap. One of her hands was wrapped around a crumpled piece of paper, and the smell of a campfire wafted from where a pack lay propped against one of the fallen statues.

"What's she doing here?" Saya asked, prodding the woman with her toe. She still didn't move.

"I don't know, but keep an eye out for the dragon," Amar replied.

Kesari knelt, reaching under the woman's jaw to check for a pulse.

"Careful," Saya warned, her arrow still trained on their enemy's face.

A faint vibration fluttered against Kesari's fingertips. "She's alive." She rolled the woman from her side onto her back. Her stomach rose and fell in shallow, barely noticeable breaths, and she remained unresponsive when Kesari shook her shoulders. There was no blood or any other sign of injury, but something was clearly wrong for her to be so lifeless.

"How did she find us?" Saya asked.

"No idea," Amar replied. "Probably the same way she's found us every time since we first crossed paths."

"What's that in her hand?"

Kesari pried the paper away from her fingers, handed it to the others over her shoulder, and continued to assess the woman. She reached out with her altma, trying to sense whatever internal damage had caused her to lose consciousness. There didn't seem to be anything wrong with her physically, but deep inside, she was injured. Not a bodily wound, but something else.

"It's a letter," Amar said. "Assuming it was written to her, her name's Aleida. Someone named Hasan sent it. Apparently, her brother just died."

Kesari felt a sudden twinge of sympathy for the unconscious woman. She too knew the pain of losing a brother. But that didn't explain the state Aleida was currently in. She frowned at Lucian as he came to hover in front of her. "There's something wrong, but I'm not sure what. It's not anything in her body, I don't think, but it's like there's a gap somewhere. A big, empty hole."

"What about her mind?" Lucian said. "Can you pull her back into consciousness?"

"I don't know."

"Wait a minute," Mitul said. "Why would we want to do that?"

"We should kill her," Saya said. "She's dangerous. She's attacked us three times now, and if we leave her here, she'll only come after us again."

Mitul grimaced. "That seems a bit harsh, but I see your point."

"No one's killing anyone," Amar said. "Not yet, at least. I want to know why she's been hunting us. We need to ask her how she found us and where her Spirit Tarja is now."

"That's it!" Kesari said. The hole she'd sensed in Aleida—it was in the same place she always reached for when she channeled her own altma, something that was very much a part of her, but not in a physical sense. It was the connection she shared with Lucian—the same connection Aleida would have shared with her own Spirit Tarja. Only now, it was gone. "She severed her Bond. I don't know what happened to the Spirit Tarja, but they're not connected anymore. I'm sure of it."

That also explained the state Aleida was in. Anyone Kesari had ever spoken to about breaking her Bond with Lucian had warned that the process could leave one or both of them seriously hurt, if not dead.

"Can you heal her?" Amar asked.

"I can try," she replied

Saya let out an irritated sigh and muttered something under her breath in Sularan.

"Good," Amar said. He sheathed his sword and took Mahati's bones back from Mitul. "I'm going to look for a place to lay her to rest."

"I'll help." Mitul said. "Lucian, do you mind lending us some light?"

The Spirit Tarja looked at Kesari. "Are you going to be all right here?"

She nodded.

"I'll stay with you," Saya said. "Our new friend won't be too happy to see us when she wakes up."

Amar, Mitul, and Lucian ventured off into the trees, and Kesari bent over Aleida again. She pressed her fingers against the young woman's forehead, reaching out gently with her altma to search for any damage inside her mind.

It was slow going, and she didn't dare rush the process. The mind was a delicate thing, even when it wasn't injured, and the deeper her magic went, the more damage she found. It was subtle, nothing more than a prickling sense that something was off, which made it difficult to know for certain what the lasting impacts of that damage would be. She was careful to send only the tiniest sparks of healing magic into Aleida's body to see what would happen before proceeding with anything more. Every now and then, she had to stop to calm her own fears and doubts, but they weren't as overwhelming as they'd once been, and it was easier to stay focused with Saya's calm presence beside her.

By the time she was done, Aleida was still adrift in a deep sleep, but no longer locked in unconsciousness. There was nothing more to be done about the hole Kesari had sensed in her. It would have to heal on its own but would likely stay with her for years, if not for the rest of her life.

She was suddenly very glad she'd decided not to go through with her plan to sever her own Bond.

"Will she wake up?" Saya asked.

"We'll have to wait and see. I've done everything I can for her now."

The older girl frowned. "I still think we'd be better off killing her, but I suppose that's Amar's choice."

There was a rustling noise behind them, and they both turned to see Mitul and Lucian emerging from the trees. "Where's Amar?" Saya asked.

"Waiting," Mitul answered. "If you're done here, Kes, he wants your help digging a grave. We don't exactly have any shovels lying about."

She nodded, and Saya hoisted Aleida's smaller, slender frame onto her back with a grunt. The young woman stirred a little and murmured something unintelligible but did not wake. They followed Mitul and Lucian into the trees, leaving the bridge to Shavhalla behind them.

AMAR

THE SPOT AMAR HAD CHOSEN FOR MAHATI'S FINAL RESTING PLACE wasn't far from the road, a tiny clearing nestled in the bushes and surrounded by moss-covered trees. Flowering vines snaked up their trunks and into their branches, and the ground was covered in long, soft grass.

An owl hooted from somewhere above while crickets chirped their nighttime song. It was so much louder here than it had been in Shavhalla, so full of life, yet still peaceful and beautiful. The girl would have liked it here, or at least, that was what Amar hoped.

After changing out of his princely clothing, he'd started to clear a shallow depression in the ground, but without tools, it was taking longer than he wanted. He'd sent Mitul back to see if Kesari could help with her magic. Now, he turned his attention to a different project.

Using a small hunting knife from his pack, he peeled away a patch of moss and bark on the nearest tree trunk and began to carve into the wood underneath. He scratched out Mahati's name in Kavoran letters and had just finished going back over them with deeper cuts when the others arrived. Saya was carrying Aleida, and she paused to lay her on the ground—none too gently, Amar noted. The young woman appeared to still be unconscious.

"Did you fix whatever was wrong with her?" he asked Kesari.

"Some of it," she answered. "For the rest, I'm not sure there is a fix. We'll have to see how she feels when she wakes up."

He nodded and pointed to the spot he'd started to clear away. "Do you mind making that deeper?"

"Sure." She knelt beside the makeshift grave and placed her palms against the ground. The dirt began to shift with a gentle rumble and the snap of roots forced aside. After a few seconds, there was a hole large enough for the remains Amar had carried from Shavhalla.

He returned to where he'd set them, still wrapped in his silken sash. His crown sat nearby. He'd packed away the rest of his clothes but didn't feel quite right keeping the crown. It was such an obvious symbol of the young man he used to be, and he'd grown so distant from that person in the centuries that had passed since. He picked it up along with Mahati's bones and carried them to the grave, where he crouched to lower them into the ground. Sitting atop the bundle, the crown's hard edges gleamed in the moonlight.

Mitul, Kesari, and Lucian all gathered around as Amar stood. He stared into the grave in silence for a few moments, unsure what to say. He'd wanted to give her some kind of ceremony, proper burial rights, a heartfelt tribute—something more than a mere hole in the ground in the middle of the forest. All of this seemed so trivial, a hollow gesture that would never be enough to make up for everything she'd suffered.

But it was the best he could give her, and even if it wasn't perfect, it was still something he needed to do.

"I'm sorry, Mahati," he said at last. "You lived such a short, hard life, and even though I wasn't the one who did those terrible things to you, I think I owe you an apology, on behalf of my kingdom and for my own inaction. I should have spoken up, used my power to stop what happened to you and others like you, but I didn't."

He paused a moment, scuffing the toe of his boot against the dirt. "I've seen a lot of war and loss in the years since you cursed me, but I've seen hope and love, too. I have you to thank for the lessons I've learned. I can't change the past, and I still don't know how to atone for all my father's crime, but I swear to you that I'll try. I hope this can be where it starts."

Mitul went to his satchel at the base of a tree and picked up his saraj. He began strumming a smooth, gentle melody, something beautiful and sad and serene all at once.

On Amar's other side, Saya began to speak. Her words were Sularan and mostly unintelligible to him, but the way she bowed her head and clasped her hands together in front of her made him think it must be a prayer. Across the grave, Kesari was picking flowers from some of the nearby plants. When she'd gathered more than a dozen, she reached down to place them inside the ring formed by the crown.

Something warm swelled within Amar as he looked around at all of them, standing there with him in the middle of the night. They were all exhausted and probably confused by his adamance for laying this pile of long-forgotten bones to rest. They'd followed him across all of Erythyr and into a lost city few had ever returned from, risking their own safety and facing their fears alongside him. He'd always told himself not to get too close, not to let anyone in, not to put down his walls. But standing here surrounded by friends who had done so much for him, he knew it was already too late for any of that. They were a part of him, and that was a gift, not a curse, even if it meant he'd lose them all someday.

Mitul's song ended, and he lowered the saraj as Saya spoke the last few words of her prayer. Kesari gave Amar a questioning look, and when he nodded, she knelt again and placed her hands against the ground. Dirt shifted to cover Mahati's remains, the fresh flowers, and the crown Prince Darshak Kaur had worn six centuries ago. Silence fell once more, broken only by the sounds of nocturnal forest creatures.

And then, after a few seconds, Mitul pointed above Amar's head to an open space in the canopy. "Look. The lights."

Amar followed his gaze. Hundreds of glowing blue lights filled the night sky, floating up into the air, where they disappeared among the stars one by one. A wind rushed through the trees from the north, from Shavhalla, and a sudden weightlessness came over him. His eyes burned, and he cleared his throat to stop the tears from falling.

"What is it?" Mitul asked, placing a hand on his shoulder.

Amar's eyes remained fixed on the small blue orbs, all of them souls once tethered to the world, now free to venture into whatever afterlife awaited them. His mouth lifted in a small smile. "The curse has been broken." He wasn't sure how, but he could feel it leaving, like fog dissipating in the light of the sun.

"Did you know this would happen?" Lucian asked.

He shook his head. "I only wanted to do right by her."

"And you did," Mitul said. "What about your immortality? Is that gone, too?"

The tentative hopefulness in his voice made Amar regret the answer he had to give. "No. Just the curse on Shavhalla. I think it's going to take more than a funeral to satisfy the terms of my own curse."

They watched the blue lights in silence for a few more minutes, until the last one had vanished, leaving only stars in the sky overhead. "I'm sorry," Saya said. "I know you were hoping for something better when we came here."

"It's all right," he replied.

And it was. If Shavhalla's curse could be lifted, then so could his. Someday, after he fulfilled his promise to Mahati, he would find his peace, too. For now, he had more hope than he'd felt in a long time and friends who were willing to walk by his side.

That was enough.

ALEIDA

SHE WAS DROWNING.

Her limbs flailed as she tried to reach the ocean's surface, but every time she got close, a new wave slammed her back down, the undercurrent pulling her deeper and farther away from Papa's boat. Her chest was tight from the strain of holding her breath.

She couldn't do it any longer. Water filled her mouth and nose, so salty it burned her throat and stung her sinuses. She sucked it into her lungs, unable to force it out, and her vision began to darken as she sank, sank, sank...

She woke with a start and a gasping breath. The salty burn of ocean water still lingered in her mouth. Every muscle in her body ached, and her head pounded like someone had clubbed her with the broad side of an oar.

Sunlight filtered through the trees above. She was still in the forest, alone and apparently left for dead. But since she wasn't dead, she needed to figure out what she was going to do next.

She started to sit up and groaned from the effort. Her weakness stemmed from more than the pain in her muscles. There was a feeling of emptiness in her somewhere, like someone had reached down her throat, grabbed hold of her insides, and ripped them out. When she tried to channel her altma, she felt nothing—a nothing even deeper than when she'd been under the influence of daravak.

Not only that, but her hands and feet were bound with rope. What was going on?

"Ah, you're awake," said a voice to her left.

Aleida turned, and a cluster of dancing flames came to hover in front of her. She squinted at the face that peered out from the fire. This was the same Spirit Tarja Bonded to the girl who accompanied Amar. Lucian, Jameson had called him. But that meant—

She whipped her head around to look behind her and was overcome by a sudden wave of dizziness. Her vision went blurry. She tried to blink it away, but it was like the whole world was suddenly underwater.

"Don't try to move around too quickly," Lucian said. His voice was low and rough with a jagged edge that matched the grin amongst his flickering flames. Two dark eyes watched Aleida with unblinking intensity. "You've been through quite the ordeal. I'm still not sure how exactly it's going to affect you, but you probably need a lot more rest."

She tried to turn again, slower this time. There behind her lay four prone figures around the remains of the same campfire she'd built last night. Her eyes immediately found Amar's face among them.

They'd found her, taken her prisoner. What were they going to do with her now? They hadn't killed her, so they must be planning to interrogate her. And if they weren't satisfied with the answers she gave...well, she knew what she'd do in that situation. She strained against the ropes binding her wrists and ankles. Her hands trembled so much she could barely control them.

The Spirit Tarja hovered over to his sleeping companions and began to wake them, starting with the girl he was Bonded to. She sat up blearily and rubbed sleep out of her eyes, then shrugged on the coat she'd been using as a blanket. She gave Aleida a small smile as she stood, stretched, and approached. Aleida wasn't sure whether the smile was supposed to be friendly or condescending, but either way, she wanted nothing to do with this girl and her magic.

"Stay away from me," she said, shuffling backwards as best as she could manage. Her shoulders hit the hard surface of one of the statues near the bridge, halting her progress.

The girl put her hands up and took a few slow steps forward. "It's all right, Aleida. We're not going to hurt you."

Her eyes narrowed. How did this stranger know her name already?

The letter! Where was her letter from Hasan?

"My name's Kesari," the girl said. Her friends were awake now, too, and they all crowded around Aleida like she was some kind of feral animal. Maybe she was. She must look that way to them, cornered like this, her hair bedraggled and falling into her eyes, face contorted in an angry snarl.

"Get her some water, Mitul," Amar said, and the older, bearded man behind him went to retrieve it. She recognized him as Amar's musician friend.

Kesari knelt in front of her, closer than the others, but far enough away that Aleida couldn't reach her. A smart choice. "How are you feeling?" she asked.

"Terrible. What do you want with me?"

"We just want to talk."

A plan began to take shape in Aleida's mind. They didn't know she and Valkyra had separated, and she could use that to her advantage. "My Spirit Tarja will be back for me. She's bringing help any minute now. If you don't let me go—"

Amar cut her off. "Your Spirit Tarja left you here to die. Either that, or she vanished when your Bond was severed."

Her stomach dropped. How did they know?

Mitul returned with a canteen, which he passed to Kesari. She edged a little closer and held it out. "Here, have a drink."

Her throat was dry and scratchy, but she didn't trust these people or anything they might give her. She didn't reach for the canteen.

"It's perfectly safe." Kesari uncapped the top and tilted it back to pour some water into her own mouth. "See? I'm sure you're thirsty. Take it."

Aleida scowled, but she *was* very thirsty. She grabbed the canteen and tipped it against her lips. Her hands were still shaking. Water sloshed out of the opening and splashed onto her cheeks and neck. It felt like less than half of the liquid made it into her mouth, but the cool relief soothed some of the dry ache in her throat.

Kesari smiled. "There, that's better. Hopefully the hand tremors will go away as you recover your strength. Are you hungry?"

She was, but she was still trying to decide whether she should answer the question when the Sularan woman spoke for the first time. "We should be questioning her, not feeding her. She's perfectly fine now, and I want answers. Why have you been hunting us?"

Aleida clamped her mouth shut and glared back at her.

"We saved your life," Kesari said, as if that made any kind of difference. "We're not your enemies."

"Yes, we are," the Sularan woman said. "If you don't answer our questions, we'll—"

"Saya," Amar cut in. His voice was authoritative, a warning.

She muttered something under her breath but said nothing more.

Amar crouched down to look Aleida straight in the eye. "You and your Spirit Tarja have been pursuing us for at least three months now. I'd like to know why."

"Why should I tell you anything?"

He shrugged. "Why not? You're not going to be able to hurt me or my friends in this state, and we won't harm you if you stay calm. So, let's talk."

She stared back at him defiantly, but he was right. She didn't have any real reason to withhold information from him—not anymore. Not when every reason she'd had for coming after him in the first place had been rendered meaningless.

Tyrus.

Her chin trembled, and the threat of tears pricked at her eyes. She fought to keep her composure. The last thing she wanted was to cry in front of these people.

Amar tilted his head, dark eyes searching her face. "What happened to your Spirit Tarja? Why did you break your Bond?"

Valkyra. This was all *her* fault.

The wet pinpricks in Aleida's eyes turned to tears of rage and hatred. She could no longer hold them back, and they coursed down her face in tiny drops that fell onto her trembling hands. She glanced between the faces surrounding her. Maybe Kesari was right. They weren't her enemies, but Valkyra was. And Valkyra was their enemy, too. After all, it had been her idea to go after Amar in the first place.

Maybe he and his friends could be useful. With Tyrus gone, Aleida had nothing left to live for—nothing but revenge. And with a common enemy, perhaps Amar would help her. Together, they could finally bring Nandini Kumar to justice.

Artex would not approve of this plan. The Artist taught peace and forgiveness, not destruction and vengeance. But Artex had forsaken her. Despite all her pleadings and her very best efforts, he had allowed Tyrus to die. Why should she care anymore about Artex's teachings?

"I didn't break the Bond," she said. "It was Valkyra."

"Your Spirit Tarja?" Amar asked.

"Yes." She began to explain, starting at the very beginning with Tyrus' illness and the desperate Bond she'd formed with a powerful Spirit Tarja, never questioning who the woman really was or what her true intentions were. "We hoped your immortality would be enough to save my brother."

"And what about Valkyra?" Amar asked. "What did she want with me?"

Aleida frowned. She hadn't considered that. She hadn't yet had time to think about it much. "I don't know."

"It's obvious, isn't it?" Lucian cut in. "She must have wanted immortality for herself."

"But she's already dead," said Kesari.

"Yes, but think of it. If she were to make a Bond with someone who's immortal, she could live forever."

Aleida nodded slowly. It made sense, especially considering who Valkyra really was. She'd been powerful, a high-ranking member of the Kavoran imperial court. Her life had been cut short, and to her, that must seem like an unbearable injustice. Maybe she wanted her own revenge on the people who'd thrust her from power, or maybe she wanted that power back. Someone of her station wouldn't have been content to simply fade into obscurity, and there were plenty of advantages to living forever.

"And then I suppose you started following us?" Amar prompted.

"Yes. You were hard to find at first, but Valkyra was so sure you existed, and I needed to believe her. It was the only way to save Tyrus."

"How did she find out about me?"

"I don't know." There was so much she hadn't known, hadn't questioned. Perhaps if she hadn't been so desperate, she wouldn't have been misled. She should have asked more questions. She should have been more skeptical. But that desperation was likely why Valkyra had chosen her.

"I think I know," Saya said. "Zefar."

"Your mercenary friend?" Kesari asked.

Saya nodded. "He always told me the woman who hired him to kill Amar must have been nobility or a member of the court." She turned her gaze to Aleida. "You said Valkyra was powerful, but who was she, before she died? Do you know?"

"I didn't for a long time," Aleida replied. "It was Jameson who figured it out. She's Nandini Kumar."

She watched their expressions shift as they took in this information. Even Lucian's face changed, the smirk in his flames replaced by a tiny frown.

"Wait," Kesari said. "What does Jameson have to do with any of this?"

Aleida backed up, recounting her arrival in Deveaural, taking the man prisoner, their battle at sea, and her eventual arrival here. When she spoke of the letter Hasan had sent, Amar produced it from his pocket and handed it to her. A new bout of tears threatened to spill out as she gripped the paper with shaky fingers, but she managed to hold them in. The others' faces were grim as she described her confrontation with Valkyra and the severing of their Bond.

"I think she forced a Bond with Jameson," she said at last. "I'm not sure how. It looked...*wrong*. They walked off together, and it was like he was under her control. That was last night. Or at least, I think it was. I'm not sure how long I've been out."

An eerie silence hung in the air for a few seconds. Kesari and Lucian exchanged a glance, and Mitul looked back over his shoulder anxiously, as if he expected Jameson and Valkyra to come bursting out of the trees at any moment. For all Aleida knew, that was a very real possibility.

"Where did they go?" Amar asked.

"That way, back toward the river," she said, pointing. "We'd subdued Jameson's magic with daravak. Until it wears off, there's probably not much they can do, but I know she was still planning to find you."

The scowl in Lucian's flames grew darker. "If she can sever a Bond and force a new one on someone else—even another Tarja—she has terrible power indeed."

Saya crossed her arms, casting a doubtful look at Aleida. "Is such a thing even possible?"

"I know what I saw," she snapped back.

"Jameson found a way to break our Bond," Lucian said, "and based on what he learned, Aleida's account is certainly within the realm of possibility. Especially given that Nandini Kumar was said to be the most brilliant Tarja in generations."

Amar frowned. "Well, there's a comforting thought."

"We should leave before they come back looking for you," Aleida said. It wasn't her place to tell them what to do—far from it—but she didn't want to stay here just waiting for Valkyra to find them. If the Spirit Tarja could control Jameson's magic the way she'd controlled his body, they were in for a serious fight.

"I hate to agree with her, but she's right," Saya said. "This is an easy spot for her to find us. We should go somewhere we can lie low for a while."

"Or better yet," Aleida said, "go after her and put an end to this while Jameson's still weak."

"Put an end to this?" Kesari echoed. "You mean kill him."

"It's the best way to make sure she never comes after you again." It was also the simplest way to repay her for her betrayal. Killing Jameson would mean killing Valkyra at the same time. "She's controlling him. He's not himself anymore. We'd be putting him out of his misery."

"How can you say that?" Kesari scoffed. She seemed personally offended by Aleida's callousness.

"And what do you mean by *we*?" Mitul asked.

She took a few moments to formulate a response. She needed them far more than they needed her. She was still so weak, and without her magic, she'd be useless in a fight. But that didn't change the fact that she wanted Valkyra to pay for everything she'd done.

"Let me help you," she pleaded, softening her voice. "At least let me come with you. She took *everything* from me. I need to make sure she doesn't get away with it."

Amar's eyes narrowed as he considered her proposal, and he cast a glance back at Mitul. An unspoken conversation seemed to pass between them. The musician shrugged, and Amar turned back to Aleida. "I suppose it wouldn't hurt to let you come along, as long as you don't cause any trouble."

"I promise." Tentatively, she held her bound wrists out to him. He sighed, slid his sword from its sheath, and cut through the ropes at her wrists and ankles.

"We're not killing anyone," he said firmly. "Not if we don't have to. We'll lie low and defend ourselves if it comes to that, but Jameson helped us, and I won't throw his life away so casually."

She opened her mouth to tell him how stupid that was, but he raised an eyebrow, and she stopped herself. No trouble—that had been her promise. She would keep her word.

At least, until a better opportunity presented itself.

AMAR

Before they left Shavhalla behind for good, they ate a quick meal, and Saya insisted on showing Amar the journal she'd taken from the palace. She wanted to make sure it was what she needed. Creating an immortal Sularan army was still a bad idea as far as he was concerned, but he'd promised to help her, so he skimmed over the pages anyway. He recognized Ranjan's handwriting immediately.

The contents were meager. Only a few dozen of the pages had been completely filled up, and half of them had hand-drawn diagrams which took up more space than the words. A quick scan of the text indicated that Ranjan had been studying Amar's curse, but whether that was due to a desire to break it or to replicate it, he couldn't tell. The last several pages seemed to have detailed instructions on how one might go about creating an immortality curse but, much to his disappointment, gave no further specifics on breaking his own.

"Well?" Saya asked, leaning forward when he reached the last page. She hadn't yet taken a single bite of her meal.

"It's exactly what you're looking for," he replied. "These last few pages tell how my curse might have been created. Some of it doesn't make sense to me, but with Lucian's help, I should be able to translate it for you."

She blinked in surprise. "I wasn't sure you would. You still don't approve of what I'm doing."

He shrugged. "No, but you were right. I owe you a lot, and it isn't my place to decide what's right for anyone else. I don't want to be the kind of man who stands in his friend's way."

She lunged forward to throw her arms around his shoulders, squeezing so tight she threatened to crush him. "Thank you."

"All right, all right," he grumbled breathlessly, patting her on the back. "That's enough. I said I'd translate it for you, but I still hope you don't decide to go down this road."

She let him go, still grinning, and tucked the journal into her satchel.

They left the path, hoping to reduce their chances of running into Valkyra should she happen to be skulking nearby. Lucian flew ahead of the group periodically to look for trouble and make sure they were still headed the right way, but aside from his directions, the travelers remained silent. Amar was grateful for the quiet. His thoughts were a jumbled mess after talking to Aleida, and he needed time to sort out all the new information he'd been given.

Finding a way to break his curse remained his first priority, but that could be a lot more complicated if Valkyra continued to hunt him. He hadn't spent much time or effort keeping up with Kavoran politics over the last few decades, but Nandini Kumar was infamous. And by all accounts, a force to be reckoned with. Clever. Powerful. Skilled.

Dangerous.

But what did she want with him? There had to be more to it than the desire for immortality. Someone like her wouldn't be content with simply living forever. She must have some other plan, something she wanted to *do* with her life once she Bonded to him. And it likely wasn't anything as innocent as growing the world's largest flower garden around a cozy little cottage in the woods.

He couldn't stop her from coming after him, but if he broke his curse, she wouldn't have any reason to seek him out anymore. She didn't care about him, only what he could give her. Once that was gone, she wouldn't be a threat to him.

Of course, he still wasn't sure *how* to break his curse. It could take years, and he didn't relish the idea of trying to accomplish his own goals while evading a dangerous Spirit Tarja. All of which would become doubly complicated if he died and forgot everything all over again.

On that note, he really needed to record everything that had happened over the last few days in his journal.

When they stopped for the night, however, Saya immediately put him to a different task—translating Ranjan's writings. While Mitul and Kesari prepared their supper, he sat next to her under the light of Lucian's flame, meticulously copying everything Ranjan had written onto the blank pages in the back of the journal, translating them from Shavhallan to Kavoran as he went.

Occasionally, he had to stop and ask Lucian about the correct magical term for something Ranjan had written, and Kesari helped by copying the diagrams so that he only had to label them. Aleida listened to all of it with a blank expression. Once, she wiped at her eyes with the sleeve of her tunic, but she said nothing.

It took him a few hours to translate and copy everything down. By that time, it was very late, and Mitul and Kesari had already gone to bed. He returned his quill and ink to his pack, fingers stiff and cramped from so much writing. Recording his memories of Shavhalla in his own journal would have to wait until tomorrow.

Saya took Ranjan's book from him and put it back in her satchel. "Thank you," she said. "Truly. For that and for everything else you've done to get me here."

He nodded. "I should be thanking you, too."

She fell silent, and Amar was about to go to bed himself when she spoke again. "It's not as complex as I thought it would be. Creating a curse, I mean. It doesn't seem that much different from any other kind of magic."

Lucian let out a sound that was a bit like a snort. "Except for the part where you have to channel altma directly from your own blood or someone else's. It all sounds similar in theory, but in practice, there's a lot that can go wrong. And when things go wrong with magic on this scale, they go *very* wrong. Look at Amar with his memories."

Ranjan's journal had made no mention of memory loss. He would have had no way of knowing about it, and it was difficult to say whether it was supposed to be a part of Amar's curse at all. Lucian had speculated that the recurrent amnesia may have been an unintentional side effect created by the complexities of using such powerful magic, or a mistake resulting from the pressure Mahati had been under when she'd performed the curse. After all, what was the point of condemning someone to experience an eternity of loss and suffering if they simply forgot it all each time they died?

"Only the most skilled and powerful Tarja would dare attempt a curse like that," Lucian went on. "I wouldn't, if I were still alive. Someone like Jameson might be able to pull it off, but I doubt he'd risk it either. How many Tarja like him do you have in the desert?"

"None as renowned as him, but I can think of a few who might be powerful enough. That's all we need."

Amar frowned. "That, and enough people willing to put their own lives on the line to conduct this little experiment."

"My people are not afraid of risk," Saya said resolutely. "Especially if it means giving ourselves an advantage over enemies who could destroy our entire way of life."

There was another, potentially bigger problem with her plan. Nandini. Creating an entire army of immortal Sularan warriors would give her plenty of people to form an eternal Bond with, and then it wouldn't matter if he broke his own curse. She'd have other opportunities to get whatever it was she wanted with immortality.

He didn't say this, though. It wouldn't sway Saya, and she'd likely only see it as him trying to dissuade her from her chosen course of action.

From her spot on the ground, Aleida muttered something. She'd been so quiet Amar had almost forgotten she was there.

"What was that?" he asked.

She kept her eyes downcast. "It wouldn't have worked."

"What wouldn't have worked?"

"Valkyra said if we found you, we could transfer your curse to Tyrus so he wouldn't die. But based on what was in that journal, that was never going to work, was it?"

There was a moment's pause before Lucian answered. "No, it wasn't. You might have been able to give your brother the same curse, but in the time it would have taken you to learn how to do that, his illness would have claimed his life anyway."

"I'm so stupid," she said, her voice breaking a little. "I never should have left him."

She looked so small, hunched over like that with her head drooping, eyes fixed on the ground. Barely more than a girl, and certainly not the formidable Tarja who'd fought and killed him three months ago. Pity swallowed up all the lingering animosity Amar held for her. She'd lost everything, and now even the assurance that she'd made the best choices she could for her brother had been tainted.

"You didn't know," he said.

She looked up at him, her blue eyes watery with tears. "You have to kill her."

"I don't want to hurt Jameson."

"He's already beyond saving, and you don't owe him anything. He helped us, you know. He told us everything about you, said he didn't care what we did to you as long as we spared him."

"I can't fault him for trying to save his own skin."

Hatred burned in Aleida's eyes. "If you don't kill her, she'll keep coming after you. She'll kill all your friends to get to you if she has to." Her voice was sharp, almost frenzied.

"Are you saying that because you really believe it, or only because you want her dead?"

"Both."

Amar sighed. She had a point, and the last thing he wanted was to put his friends at risk. He could try to convince them to leave, to let him do the rest of this on his own, but Mitul would never agree to that. And if his hunch about Valkyra's future plans was correct, maybe putting an end to her was the best option—not only for him, but for everyone. Before she could wreak any havoc on the world.

But that was only a hunch. He didn't know anything for certain, and he couldn't sacrifice an innocent man's life so easily.

"It's late," he said to Aleida. "Get some sleep. We can talk about it in the morning."

"But—"

He cut off her protest. "You're not wrong, but we need to have a plan. If we don't find her first, she'll find us, and either way, I want to make sure we're prepared when that happens."

KESARI

"WE *CAN'T* HURT JAMESON," KESARI SAID, SLAMMING A FIST INTO HER palm for emphasis. All morning, they'd been debating the best way to handle a fight with Valkyra and the wizard. It seemed inevitable that they would run into each other at some point, and Amar had decided killing her was the only way to make sure she didn't come after him again and threaten all their lives. It was a fair point, but Kesari had been much more comfortable with their previous plan of simply running away and lying low. Even if it was unsustainable.

"I don't *want* to hurt Jameson," Amar said. "If we can figure out a way to save him, that would—"

"Not *if*," she said. "We *have* to find a way to save him."

"There isn't much left to save," Aleida countered.

"You don't know that," Kesari snapped back. She was becoming increasingly annoyed by the young woman's presence, not so much that she regretted saving her life, but definitely enough to make her wish they'd left her there on the road afterward.

Aleida looked like she was about to say something else, but Amar cut in. "Look, if you have any ideas, I'd love to hear them. But my main priority is keeping the rest of you alive. And that should be your priority, too."

Kesari said nothing. She *didn't* know how to save Jameson, and that hurt. The only reason he was caught up in this was because of them, and she was the one who'd led the others to Deveaural to find him.

"I might know a way," Aleida said. "It's not a permanent solution, but it could buy us time to figure out something else."

Amar nodded. "Let's hear it."

"I still have some daravak. If we can capture them and use that to disable Jameson's magic, they won't be able to hurt us."

"Can't she just sever her Bond with him and force one on me?"

"I don't think so. When she Bonded to Jameson, she had to touch him to do it. If we can trap her inside a barrier, she won't be able to do that, and if Jameson's magic is suppressed, he won't be able to break free."

"A barrier," Kesari said, recalling how Aleida had trapped Amar inside one the night she killed him. "Like the one you used when you attacked us before."

"Yes. They're typically used as protection, to keep things out, but you can create one to keep something *in* instead."

Kesari looked at Lucian. "Do you know how to do that?"

"I do," Lucian said. "I was reasonably skilled in creating defensive barriers when I was alive, so you should pick it up quickly, with a little practice."

"Practice while we walk," Amar said. "We need to keep moving."

They were all anxious to find the river again and have a guide out of the forest. Lucian gave Kesari some quick instructions and observed her practice for a few minutes, then left to scout ahead. They started walking, and Kesari experimented with making barriers as they travelled. At first, they were small and weak. They fizzled out after a few seconds and were immediately burst by the pebbles Amar and the others tossed through them. She kept working at it. Aleida offered a few suggestions of her own, and by noon, her barriers were deflecting fist-sized rocks, Saya's arrows, and even the heavy blows of Amar's sword.

After that, she moved on to trapping things inside a barrier. She put them around butterflies, beetles, frogs, and birds as they crawled, hopped, and flew across her path. This made her more nervous, knowing she had the potential to hurt the creatures if she got something wrong, and her magic destabilized. Most of the animals she trapped escaped in a matter of seconds. The more she practiced, the easier it became, and by the time they stopped to rest for the night, she was creating barriers that could hold her friends and Lucian. She wasn't entirely sure she'd be ready to contain Valkyra and Jameson when the time came, but she had no other choice. It was the only way to save Jameson.

She found herself sitting beside Aleida while they ate. "Thanks for your help today," she said. "You taught me a lot."

Aleida shrugged and kept her focus on her food. Her hands shook as she raised a slice of dried apple to her mouth. It slipped out of her fingers and fell onto the ground, and she frowned at her hands as if they'd betrayed her before reaching for another piece. "They won't stop shaking," she muttered.

"I could try to see if there's anything more I can do to heal them," Kesari suggested.

Aleida gave a slight shrug. "Sure. Maybe later."

They ate in silence for a few minutes. It was a cold night, but they hadn't dared to make a fire that might draw their enemy to them. Kesari wrapped her coat a little tighter around herself and was about to try to strike up a different conversation when, to her surprise, Aleida spoke again. "I wish I could fight her myself."

"Valkyra?"

She nodded. "She ruined everything. I hate that I'm not strong enough to do more than give advice on how to capture her." The pitch of her voice rose. "Just don't mess it up, all right? You want to keep Jameson alive? Fine. But make sure *she* doesn't get away."

Kesari flinched at the fury in the young woman's eyes, but she couldn't blame her for it. She'd lost everything, and being angry was so much easier than sitting with the hurt and sorrow.

"I'm sorry about your brother," she said quietly, and when Aleida turned another furious gaze on her, she quickly added, "My brother died, too. A couple of years ago." She looked down at her boots. "It was my fault."

Aleida didn't speak for a few seconds, and when she did, her voice hitched. "How did you survive it?"

"I almost didn't," she replied, glancing at Lucian over her shoulder. "But I had a lot of help, someone who was there even when I felt alone."

The other girl snorted. "I *am* alone."

"You don't have to be." She gestured to the others on either side of them. "We're all here."

"That's not—"

"Kesari!"

One of Saya's arrows went whizzing past them at the same time Lucian shouted her name.

She stood and whipped around. A tall, shadowy figure approached through the trees. Slender fingers clutched Saya's arrow in one hand, then snapped it in half and threw the pieces to the ground. Tendrils of blue lightning began to crackle around the figure's hands and body, illuminating a familiar face.

Jameson.

He extended a hand toward them. Kesari barely had time to throw up her arms and erect a protective barrier in front of herself and her friends. Lightning struck the invisible wall and went rebounding back toward the wizard as a silky, white dragon emerged from behind his back and shot into the air.

"Get to cover!" Amar shouted, grabbing Mitul by the back of his shirt and hoisting him upright.

"You too," Saya said to Aleida. She came up beside her and Kesari with another arrow already nocked.

Jameson hurled more lightning, and Kesari put all her energy and focus into maintaining the barrier.

"Let me fight!" Aleida protested. Her eyes weren't on Jameson at all, but on Valkyra, a flash of white darting through the leafy canopy above.

"How?" Saya shot back. "You don't have magic or a weapon. You'll only get in the way."

"But I—"

"Go find Mitul!" The young warrior grabbed Aleida by the shoulder and shoved her back.

"Stay focused, Kes," Lucian said into her ear.

Kesari shifted her gaze back to her barrier, which was starting to weaken where Jameson's lightning had struck it repeatedly. Through it, she could see his face more clearly now. Streams of dried blood flowed from his nose, ears, and mouth, giving him a grotesque sort of mask that highlighted the hollow emptiness in his eyes. All the energy and inquisitive vibrance which had once been there was gone now.

Maybe Aleida was right. Maybe he was too far gone to save.

Saya loosed an arrow. It shot through Kesari's barrier and seemed to be heading straight for Jameson's chest, but he threw up a barrier of his own. The arrow fell harmlessly to the ground.

Amar fired his pistol, but even that couldn't penetrate the wizard's defenses. Saya released another arrow, then another. They weren't doing any damage, but as long as she forced Jameson to keep his barrier up, he couldn't unleash another attack on them.

At least, Kesari didn't think he could. She let down her own barrier and channeled altma to lift nearby rocks into the air, propelling them in Jameson's direction for extra distraction.

Amar ran up beside her, clutching his sword in one hand and a tiny bundle of fabric in the other. "I've got the daravak. I just need to get close enough."

"We'll cover you," Saya said, firing off another arrow.

Kesari kept up her own barrage as Amar charged at the wizard. He was closing in when Jameson's barrier exploded in a burst that sent him flying backwards. It was enough to knock Kesari and Saya back, too. Even Jameson seemed momentarily dazed.

In a blur of white, Valkyra dove from the sky and wrapped her claws around Saya's bow. The young woman held onto it, using the arrow in her free hand to try to beat the Spirit Tarja away. Valkyra didn't react, not even when Saya stabbed the arrow's point through her chest.

"The barrier!" Lucian said.

Kesari reached for her altma and channeled it around Valkyra, shaping one of the imprisoning barriers like she'd practiced all day. It only took a few seconds, but Valkyra saw what she was doing before the edges closed. She released the bow and darted into the trees, shattering the barrier in the process. Saya fired a shot after her, but she had vanished.

Amar was up and already attacking Jameson. The wizard moved with abnormal speed, always staying out of reach and dodging every attempt Amar made to close the gap.

Kesari put her hands on the ground, watching Jameson's movements as she channeled her altma. There—an opening! She sent the energy from her fingertips into the earth. A ripping sound filled the air as the ground Jameson had moved to rose up to push him off balance.

Amar lunged for the wizard's face, arm outstretched with the daravak clutched in his fist. He didn't get close enough. Lightning shot from Jameson's hand to wrap around Amar's body like long, jagged fingers, and he went down with a groan.

"Amar!" Saya screamed. She rushed forward, firing more arrows at Jameson as she went. Kesari hurled her own magic at him, too. He dodged or deflected every blow, and when Saya's last arrow was spent, he stretched out his hand.

A ball of blue fire flew from his fingertips. Kesari flattened herself against the ground. Saya tried to duck behind a tree, but she wasn't fast enough. The projectile struck both her and the thick trunk. She fell, screaming as she tried to put out the flames burning through her clothes. The bushes at her feet ignited, and the fire quickly spread over the forest floor.

Kesari ran to her. She grabbed hold of her hand and dragged her back, away from the flames. Another fireball shot over their heads. It struck a tree, which crackled and groaned as it went up in flames.

Fire. Burning. Screaming. The clocktower.

It all came back to Kesari in a rush that put her right back *there*.

Standing in the square, she clutches Navya's hand. Rajiv is inside. They're supposed to wait for him to come back. He promised he would come back.

She shook her head. Breathe. She had to breathe. She wasn't there. Rajiv was already gone. None of that was happening right now.

Right now, her friends were hurt, and they needed her. She was the only one who could subdue Jameson and Valkyra.

Beside her, Saya groaned through clenched teeth, staring at the red, charred flesh of her arm. But those injuries would have to wait. Stopping Jameson was their first priority.

Another fireball made impact close by. Kesari threw up a barrier as she turned, only to see them both right behind her—Jameson and Valkyra. The perfect opportunity.

Drawing on all her altma, she pushed out her own barrier, changing its shape and purpose as she went. From the outside, it would look like she was trying to do what Jameson had done before, using the magical force to create a devastating blast. But it was a trap, and one Kesari could only hope they wouldn't see coming.

Not until the last moment, when the barrier engulfed them both in a sphere of shimmering fog, closing, closing, closing…

ALEIDA

Kesari's barrier snapped around Jameson and Valkyra, trapping them both in an orb of magical energy. Beside Aleida, Mitul let out a victorious whoop and went dashing from cover to where Amar lay. They'd left their previous position as soon as they'd seen him fall, knowing they had to recover the daravak if their plan to save Jameson was going to work. They still needed to suppress his magic, but at least for now he was contained.

Contained. That wouldn't last long. It was only a matter of time before Valkyra found a way for Jameson to break free.

Aleida's jaw clenched. She couldn't let that happen.

Her eyes drifted to Amar's sword, which lay on the ground a few paces away. Neither man was paying any attention to it or to her. They were turned away, Mitul helping Amar to stand up, both of them checking to make sure the daravak was still in his hand. Soon, they'd be looking for the sword.

It was now or never.

She broke away from the shelter of the tree at a run, scooping up the weapon as she went. For one panicked moment, her fingers refused to close around the hilt, and she had to stop. Then the sword was in her hands, and she was charging forward again.

Valkyra was right there, getting closer with every step. Kesari's barrier prevented her and Jameson from getting out, but it couldn't stop Aleida and the sword from getting *in*. And when she plunged the blade through Jameson's heart, Valkyra would be dead.

Of course, so would he.

She pushed aside the twinge of guilt that came with that thought. Jameson wasn't even himself anymore. Surely he didn't *want* to be the puppet of a dangerous, violent Spirit Tarja. She'd be doing him a favor, killing him before he could hurt anyone else.

The tip of the blade broke through the barrier before Kesari even saw her coming.

"Aleida, no!"

It was Lucian who cried out, and in the split second that Kesari's focus shifted, the barrier rippled, weakened. Valkyra's eyes found Aleida's, and her mouth twisted into a vicious smile. Jameson grabbed the sword by the blade before it could pierce through his chest. Blood dripped from his hand as he pressed the other against the barrier. It dissolved around Aleida in a flurry of silver sparks.

The sword gave a sharp twist in her hand as Jameson wrenched it free, slicing deeper into his own palm. He cast it aside. Droplets of red arced through the air. With strength intensified by magic, he shoved her back, and she went sprawling onto the ground next to Kesari and Saya. Amar and Mitul were flung down next to her a moment later.

Before any of them could fully recover, Jameson put his hands to the ground. All around them, roots burst up in a shower of dirt and torn grass to wind around their arms and legs. Aleida thrashed against the restraints and cried out in frustration, but a new root clamped down around her neck so tight she could hardly breathe.

Beside her, Lucian was already burning through the roots that held Kesari down. She managed to sit up and shoot a single rock at Jameson's head, but the Tarja had her pinned back down in seconds. He raised a barrier around Lucian to keep him contained as well.

Kesari continued to fight against her restraints. Sparks of light shot from her fingertips, but her power wasn't enough. Tears ran down her face, and her eyes were wide and wild as she watched the man close in. She was terrified, and it was clear her magic wasn't even remotely under her control.

Aleida stretched her fingers as far as they would go, trying to reach Kesari's. They were too far. "Focus," she said, but her voice only came out as a croak. She doubted the girl even heard her.

Jameson loomed over them, his tall frame silhouetted against the fire still burning through the forest behind him. Valkyra perched on his shoulder. She held her head high and regal as she stared down at them. Her silvery gaze flitted across Aleida for only a moment, then focused on Kesari.

"You have proven to be far more trouble than I anticipated," she said in the same low, silken voice that had once brought Aleida so much comfort. "From the way Jameson described you, I thought you'd be a dainty little mouse, but there's a tiger inside you, isn't there?"

Kesari let out a whimper. More sparks shot from her fingers, but to no avail.

Valkyra let out a sigh, almost as if she was disappointed the girl couldn't put up more of a fight. "Oh, well. I suppose I ought to kill you now."

Lucian slammed himself against the inside of his spherical barrier, his flames fanning out against its contour and then reforming. When that didn't work, he made himself bigger, growing until fire filled the entire space. Still, he couldn't break free. None of them could.

All they could do was watch as Jameson knelt and placed both hands on Kesari's forehead.

AMAR

Amar pulled against his restraints with every ounce of strength in his body as the Tarja knelt over Kesari, Valkyra's threat echoing through his mind.

I suppose I ought to kill you now.

Not Kesari. Not the sweet, wide-eyed girl who'd helped him recover his memories and fought enchanted guards by his side in Shavhalla. She had a family to go back to, a bright future ahead of her. She was still only a child. *Not* Kesari.

Jameson's hands were on her head.

"Stop!" Amar yelled, but his voice was muffled beneath the others' shouts.

"She's just a girl," Mitul pleaded. "Don't hurt her."

"I'll kill you for this!" Saya cried in a voice so harsh it sounded inhuman.

"Leave her alone," said Aleida.

Lucian's voice was inaudible within the barrier, but he made his protests known with frantic movements inside his confines.

"Valkyra!" Amar roared as loudly as he could.

Her head swiveled toward him, and the others fell silent.

He closed his eyes and took a few deep breaths. It was over. There was nothing they could do to defeat her. Not now, anyway. His best option was to make sure the others all got out of this alive. Valkyra saw them as disposable, a nuisance to be eliminated. The only way to keep them safe was to make them a critical part of her victory and achieving what she wanted.

So what did she want?

"Don't hurt any of them," he said. "It's me you want, isn't it? You can have me, but not if you hurt them."

Valkyra smiled, the tiny points of her razor-sharp teeth glinting in the firelight. Then she looked back down at Kesari, who was still squirming against the roots that held her down.

A soft, glowing light emanated from Jameson's fingers and pulsed against Kesari's forehead. Her body went still.

"No!" This time, it was Saya's voice that rang out over all the others. "I'll kill you! I swear I'll kill you!"

Not if Amar killed her first.

Valkyra laughed, a clear, ringing sound that cut through Saya's screams. "Fool. Your friend isn't dead."

Saya cut herself off in the middle of another shout.

Valkyra pointed a claw down to the barrier that still held Lucian. "See? If she were dead, this one wouldn't be here anymore."

"What did you do to her?" Amar demanded through clenched teeth.

"I simply put her to sleep. I'm curious to hear more about your offer, but I couldn't have her causing any more trouble while we talk." Jameson stood, and she rode on his shoulder as he strode toward the fire still ravaging the forest. It had crept closer in the last few minutes, close enough that its heat was becoming uncomfortable against Amar's skin.

"I think that's probably enough of that," Valkyra said as she and Jameson stared into the flames. He extended his arms and pushed out his hands out. As he held that pose, the flames began to subside.

"What's your plan?" Mitul whispered while the pair was occupied.

"I have to go with her," Amar replied. "It's the only way to get the rest of you out of here alive."

The man shook his head. "No. There has to be something else. She's never going to let us just walk away."

"She will if it's the only way she can get me to cooperate."

"You can't cooperate with her. You have no idea what she'll do to you." He glanced at Jameson and Valkyra and lowered his voice a little more. "You still have the daravak, don't you?"

It remained clutched in his palm, moisture seeping through the fabric from where it had been crushed when he fell. "Yes, but without Kesari, we can't contain them."

"But if you go with her—"

"Then you'll be safe. That's all that matters. We can fight this fight another day, but tonight, we've already lost."

The last of the flames petered out, leaving behind a sudden darkness and the heavy smell of smoke. Jameson turned back around and walked straight toward Amar. He stopped when he was a few paces away, and Valkyra hopped off his shoulder to rest on Amar's chest. Her claws pushed through the fabric of his shirt and pricked against his skin.

"Now then," she said. "What was it you were saying earlier?"

"Leave them alone," he said, "and I'll go with you. I'll do what you want."

"Oh? And what's that?"

"You want to make a Bond with me so you can share my immortality. Isn't that right?

She smiled demurely. "That's right."

"Good. Then I'll Bond with you. But you have to leave everyone else alone."

Saya raised her head as far as she could to look at him. "Amar, you can't!"

"Enough," Valkyra hissed. Two new barriers began to form—one for Saya, Aleida, and Kesari, and one for Mitul on Amar's other side. For a few seconds, their shouts of protest filled his ears, then there was silence.

He met Valkyra's gaze evenly. "You can't hurt them, or I won't cooperate with you. And you need a willing partner to form a Bond."

"Not necessarily," Valkyra said, tilting her head toward Jameson. "Take this one, for example."

"Exactly. Look at him. He's practically falling apart."

The dragon ruffled her wings. "Why should that matter to me?"

"It's got to be exhausting, controlling his every movement the way you have been. Can he even think for himself at all anymore?"

Her eyes narrowed, and she said nothing for a few moments, as if she were thinking through his offer and trying to find the catch. Finally, she said, "All right, then. I think I can agree to those terms. But what guarantee do I have that your friends won't come after us?"

"You don't. Just like I have no guarantee you won't hurt them once we make our Bond."

"That is a dilemma."

"So we don't do it here," Amar suggested. "You can put the others to sleep like Kesari, and we can leave together right now."

"They could still come after us."

"Not right away."

"I could still come back to hurt them."

"We'll put enough distance between us and them to let them wake up so they can escape or fight back."

Valkyra's tail flicked back and forth across his abdomen. "There still aren't any guarantees in your little plan. For either of us."

There weren't. Once they'd left here together and formed their Bond, there would be nothing to stop Valkyra from taking control and returning to attack the others again, using his body to do the damage this time instead of Jameson's. But he still had the daravak. As soon as he got the chance, he would ingest it. That should suppress the magic that would come with their Bond so Valkyra couldn't use it against his friends.

"It's the best plan either of us are going to get," he said.

"I suppose you're right." She turned to Jameson, who walked stiffly to the barrier that held Kesari, Saya, and Aleida. He stepped through it, stooping to put Saya and Aleida to sleep with the same glowing light. The barrier vanished. Lucian remained trapped inside a smaller one of his own, watching the scene play out with coal black eyes.

Jameson stepped into Mitul's barrier and repeated the process. A chill went down Amar's spine as he looked over at his sleeping friend. He wished he'd had the chance to say goodbye—to all of them—but maybe this was for the best. This way, they couldn't try to talk him out of what he was doing.

"How long will they stay like that?" he asked.

"Until dawn. Plenty of time for us to get away from here, don't you think?"

"Let's go then." He wanted to be as far away as possible by the time the others woke up.

The roots around his wrists, ankles, and hips loosened. He sat up, shook off the dirt, and when Valkyra wasn't looking, slipped the daravak into his pocket. He'd likely only have one chance to use it, and he couldn't waste that opportunity until he was sure he needed it. No sooner had he stood upright than his limbs locked up. A new barrier had formed, clinging to every angle of his body so he couldn't move.

He tried to speak as Valkyra hopped onto Jameson's shoulder, but his mouth wouldn't move either, and the words came out jumbled.

"I'm afraid I can't hear you," the dragon said. "But I'm sure you're wondering why I've put you in there. Call it an abundance of caution. I'd be a fool to trust you completely. Now then, shall we?"

Jameson began to walk, and by no means of his own, Amar followed, hovering above the ground in his floating prison. He tried to turn, tried to get one last look at his friends, but it was no use. All he could do was stare ahead as Valkyra and Jameson took him deeper into the forest.

No more than a couple of hours could have passed when they stopped. Valkyra had Jameson withdraw the barrier trapping Amar, and he stumbled onto the ground with the sudden release. It was still night, but the trees in this part of the forest had thinned out enough that he could see a bright swath of stars through the canopy when he righted himself.

"Why are we stopping already?" he asked.

Valkyra was still perched on Jameson's shoulder, both of them safely out of arm's reach several paces away. A smile curled the soft corners of the dragon's mouth. "I think this is as good a place as any."

The icy chill in her voice sent a shiver down Amar's spine. He'd left his sword behind, and his pistol was empty, but he looked to the ground for an improvised weapon—a rock, a stick, anything he could use to defend himself. "This wasn't the plan," he said. "We agreed to get as far away as we could before we make our Bond."

"I've changed my mind. I like my plan better."

His heart raced in response to the threat in her words, but he had one card left to play. The daravak was still in his pocket.

He started to reach for it, but Jameson was faster. His hands flattened against the ground, and the area beneath Amar's feet shifted to throw him off balance. A thick tree root shot up in front of him, shedding dirt and tiny plant tendrils as it straightened. The sharp tip gleamed like it had been turned to polished stone.

He barely had time to react. The root shot forward and pierced straight through his abdomen, emerging out the back below his shoulder blades. Pain erupted through his body as it withdrew, and he slumped onto the ground. Blood pooled beneath him. His fingers scraped against his hip where they'd reached into his pocket, still clutching the bundle of daravak.

Valkyra flew from Jameson's shoulder to land on the tree root still protruding from the ground. Blood seeped into the pristine fur at the bottom of her feet, turning them red. She blurred in and out of focus as Amar's vision swam. "I'm terribly sorry about that, dear," she said, sounding not the least bit sorry at all.

"I won't—" His words came out garbled as he choked on a mouthful of blood. "I won't make a Bond with you."

"Oh, I think you'll find I can be very persuasive. You don't like me now, but we're going to be the best of friends when you come back to life. Of course, our first order of business as partners will be eliminating your companions. I can't have them interfering, you understand."

Blackness crept into Amar's vision. He was losing way too much blood, way too fast. He was going to die. And then she was going to make him kill his friends. Friends he wouldn't even remember anymore, not even after everything they had been through together.

Valkyra's silky tail brushed over the tree root, picking up more of Amar's blood. She glanced back at Jameson. "I suppose there's no point in keeping up *this* Bond anymore. As you guessed, it is rather exhausting having to control him."

She closed her eyes, her body stiffening, and Jameson let out a long wail. He clawed at his face as new streams of blood ran from the corners of his eyes like tears. His limbs twisted around his torso in a grotesque, monstrous fashion, and there was a series of sickening snaps that might have been bones breaking. With one final shudder, his wailing ceased. He collapsed onto the ground and did not move again.

Valkyra's dragon form dissipated, replaced by a shimmering light the same blue color as the glowing orbs from Shavhalla. It morphed into the shape of a woman, long hair framing a square face. She remained near the bloodied tree root, a callous smile on her lips as she down at Amar.

He clung desperately to what little remained of his own lucidity. This couldn't be the end. He couldn't let her win. Not like this.

With a cry, he pushed himself onto his back, freeing his left hand to pull out the daravak.

"Still clinging to life?" Valkyra clicked her tongue. "Let go, Amar. Everything will be so much easier after you die. I promise."

He raised his hand to his mouth, shaking with the effort.

"What are you doing? What is that in your hand?"

He released one corner of the bundled fabric, and the daravak fell into his open mouth.

"Stop that!" Valkyra screamed, her voice shrill. She bent down at his side, wrapping her ghostly hands around his wrists, but he couldn't feel them.

He chewed the bits of mushroom and forced himself to swallow. He didn't know if it would do any good, given the state he was in. But it was something, and the fact that it infuriated Valkyra had to mean there was at least a chance that it would work. Even if she did convince him to make a Bond in his next life, with the daravak in his system, he wouldn't be able to use his magic. Not for a while, at least. He could buy his friends some time, maybe enough for them to get away. Or better yet, Valkyra would realize that pursuing and confronting them wasn't worth the effort after the time it took for the daravak to run its course.

She continued to rage and scream at him as the blackness closed in. Amar shut his eyes and conjured up images of his friends' faces. Mitul. Saya. Kesari. Lucian. Faces he didn't want to forget. Memories he would cling to until his very last moments. Memories he hoped to find again someday.

Their faces were still in his mind when he let out his last breath.

KESARI

"KES?" THE VOICE THAT SPOKE HER NAME WAS SOFT AND MUFFLED. "Kes, can you hear me? Wake up."

Her eyelids were so heavy, but she finally managed to pry them open. She squinted against the brightness of Lucian's flames. "What's wrong?" It was a cold, gray morning, and he didn't usually wake her so early unless there was something wrong.

But something *was* wrong. It all crashed into her at once, making her sit up and snap her eyes wide open as she scanned her surroundings for the others. Saya put a hand on her shoulder. Mitul paced back and forth across the ground where he and Amar had been lying. Aleida was back at their camp, gathering everyone's belongings. Straight ahead were the sparse, darkened remains of the patch of forest that had burned during their fight. There was no other sign of Valkyra or Jameson, and Amar was gone, too.

You can have me, but not if you hurt them.

Amar's words—the last word's she'd heard before Jameson put her to sleep.

"Where is he?" she asked Lucian.

"Valkyra took him."

"She made Jameson put the rest of us to sleep, too" Saya explained, "and then they all left."

"We've lost hours," Lucian said. "Plenty of time for them to get far away from here. We have no idea where he is."

Mitul turned toward them, deep creases furrowed into his brow. "How are you feeling?" he asked, but there was an edge of impatience to his voice. He must be anxious to get moving and go after Amar.

"I'm all right," Kesari replied. She stood up, turning to Saya. Mitul's cloak covered her right arm and chest where the fabric had burned away, but red skin still peeked out from the edges. "Let me have a look at that," she said.

Saya carefully lifted the edge of the cloak. Her fingers shook, and her teeth began to chatter as if she were freezing. Kesari winced at the sight of the raw, blistered skin underneath. A feverish warmth radiated from it.

"That bad, is it?" Saya said with a weak smile.

"It's going to be fine."

"You'll need to use some water when you heal that," Lucian suggested.

Kesari nodded. Aleida was already approaching with their packs, and she dug through hers until she found her canteen. She channeled altma through her fingers to cool it and carefully dripped some over Saya's injury. "Sorry," she said as the young woman flinched. She didn't dare touch the skin, as painful as it looked, and instead left her hands hovering over the wound while she sought out the deeper tissue damage with her magic.

"I should be more careful," Saya said, gritting her teeth through the pain. "This is the second time you've had to patch me up in the last few days."

"I don't mind," Kesari said. "But I don't like to see you hurt."

It was a slow process, but the water seemed to help. With Mitul growing more and more restless by the second, Lucian offered to fly ahead and see if he could at least pick up Amar's trail. He returned an hour later, right as Kesari was finishing up with Saya's wounds. The skin was still a little raw and red, but Saya's face had regained its usual color and was no longer damp with sweat.

"I found something," Lucian called out as he dropped down from the sky. "Jameson's dead. I didn't see Amar or Valkyra, but there must have been some kind of fight. There's blood everywhere."

"Where?" Mitul asked.

"Come on." He flew off again with the musician right on his trail. Kesari, Saya, and Aleida followed. They practically had to run to keep up with Mitul's breakneck pace, and they were all panting when they reached the spot Lucian had found.

Jameson's body was sprawled across the ground, and even though she already knew he was dead, Kesari had to check for herself. She almost regretted it when she saw his face. The sight was even more grotesque than it had been last night. Along with the blood that had dried on his waxen skin, there was a strained twist to his muscles that suggested extreme pain. He hadn't deserved any of this, even if he had led Valkyra and Aleida right to them. Kesari put a hand to her mouth to stifle a cry and turned back to the others.

They were standing around a dark, sticky pool covering a patch of fallen leaves. A few paces away, a thick tree root protruded from the ground, its surface coated red. Flies buzzed around the whole mess, and Kesari had to cover her face with her sleeve to keep the smell from making her sick. There was so much blood.

"That's Amar's," Mitul said.

"We don't know that for sure," she replied, though the words sounded foolish as soon as they left her mouth. Who else could the blood belong to? Jameson lay several paces away, and there was no trail or sign of his body having been moved that she could see. Besides, he hadn't been bleeding nearly this much.

"She killed him," Saya said.

"Why?" Mitul's voice was strained. "He'd already given her what she wanted. If she killed him, he'd forget everything."

"That must have been why," Aleida said. "Maybe she wanted him to forget. He'll be easier to manipulate, now. She can tell him whatever she wants him to believe."

Mitul whirled on her, his eyes full of a ferocity Kesari had never seen in him before. "This is your fault," he said. It wasn't a shout, but his voice shook with the effort of a man trying to keep his rage in check. "Everything was going according to plan until you charged in with that sword. If you hadn't interfered, he'd still be here."

"I had to interfere." Aleida's jaw tightened, and she gestured to Jameson's body. "You were all tiptoeing around, trying to save a man who couldn't be saved. This all would have been so much simpler if you'd agreed to kill him from the beginning."

"Maybe we should have killed *you* from the beginning," Saya shot back. "We saved your life when you didn't give ours a second thought every time you came after Amar. Whatever it took to save your brother, right? Whatever it takes to get what *you* want, no matter who gets hurt in the process."

"What does it matter now?" Aleida hissed. "He's dead anyway. He was dead before the fight even started, so what was the point of trying to save him?" Tears brimmed in her eyes, but her scowl was all angry defiance.

"We don't kill people whenever it's convenient," Saya replied. "We're not monsters like you."

Aleida lunged, tackling her to the ground. She raised a fist to pummel Saya's face, but the taller woman had a knife to her throat before she could strike.

Before either of them could take action, Mitul grabbed Aleida by the shoulders and hauled her back. "That's enough, both of you!"

Aleida continued to glare at Saya, who stood and brushed the leaves out of her hair and clothing without looking at her.

"Amar sacrificed himself to save us," Mitul went on. "We should be making the best use we can of our second chance, not fighting with each other and wasting more time. We need to figure out what we're going to do next."

"I don't care what the rest of you do," Aleida said. "I'm going after Valkyra. She needs to answer for what she's done."

"And how exactly do you plan on making that happen?" Lucian asked. "We don't know where she's going or what she's plotting, let alone how to stop her."

"And you're not killing Amar just to kill her," Saya said.

Aleida rolled her eyes. "Of course I'm not. What would be the point if he's going to keep coming back to life?"

"Pointless or not, you seem to have a habit of coming up with reckless ideas."

Aleida opened her mouth like she was about to say something else, but Mitul cut her off. "Enough. You and I will both go after Amar and Valkyra. We need to find out more about whatever she's planning, but we can't let her know what we're doing. She already knows we're trouble, and she's going to want to get rid of us as soon as we give her a chance."

"So we go after them and...what?" Aleida asked. "Just wait?"

"Yes," Mitul said. "Because sometimes it's helpful to think about things and make a plan before you go rushing in."

"We'll need some way to get his memories back once we find him," Kesari said. "With Jameson gone, that's going to be difficult."

"You could do it," Saya said. "You were there when Jameson brought his memories back the first time. Do you remember how he did it?"

"Not exactly," Kesari replied. "I may have been there, but I didn't really participate. I mean, maybe if I had his research notes, but—"

"That's it then," Saya interrupted. "You, Lucian, and I can go back to Deveaural to get his research. We'll cut through the desert on the way, and I can finish my haseph and present my offering to my people. We'll meet up with Mitul and Aleida afterward."

"Where?" Lucian asked. "We don't know even where Valkyra's going."

Kesari's gaze flitted to Aleida. Mitul, Saya, and Lucian stared at her, too.

"What are you all looking at me for?" she asked.

"Where do *you* think she would go?" Mitul asked. "You know her better than any of us."

She shook her head. "I *don't* know her. She lied to me the entire time we were together."

"And you can't think of any clue she might have given in all that time?"

Aleida chewed on her bottom lip for a few seconds, thinking. "I don't know," she said at last. "She used to be a member of the imperial court, right? Maybe she'll go back to Jakhat, try to regain some of her old power."

Mitul nodded. "That sounds like something the old Nandini Kumar might do, if half the things I've heard about her are true."

"All right," Saya said. "So you'll go to Jakhat, and we'll go to Deveaural. If everything goes well and factoring in the detour through the desert, that should take us…" She paused a moment, thinking. "Two months, maybe a bit longer. Then we'll be headed back to Kavora."

"We can meet in Valmandi," Mitul suggested. "One month after the first day of winter, at the same inn we stayed at before."

"The Saffron Fox," Kesari said.

"Right, that's the one. We'll share whatever information we've learned about Amar and Valkyra by then, and hopefully you'll know how to restore his memories. We can make a better plan from there."

Kesari nodded her agreement. Saya and Aleida were still glaring daggers at each other, but they nodded, too.

With that decided, they made their preparations to depart. They buried Jameson right there in the forest. Kesari created another grave like the one she'd made for Mahati, and Saya and Mitul lowered his body into it. Saya offered a Sularan prayer, and Aleida produced a charcoal drawing from her pack—a portrait of Jameson himself. She hooked it onto a tree branch hanging over the grave.

Afterward, they found a sunny clearing near the banks of the river and ate one final meal together. Then it was time to say their goodbyes and head their separate ways. Kesari awkwardly held a hand out to Aleida while Mitul and Saya embraced. "I'm glad we met," she said, "and that you're on our side now."

Aleida's hand trembled in hers. "I'm on my own side."

Mitul approached Kesari, his arms outstretched. She threw hers around him and squeezed tight, breathing in his campfire scent and smiling when he gently patted the back of her head. "Take care of yourself, Kes," he said. "I can't wait to see what your magic can do the next time we meet."

Tears filled her eyes as she let go of him. She let them fall without even trying to hold them back. "I'll miss you. And your music."

He gave her head one last pat. "I'll play something special for you when we see each other again. Lucian, I trust you'll watch out for her?"

"I always do," he said.

Mitul nodded and turned to Aleida. "Are you ready?"

"Just waiting on you," she replied tersely.

He gave Saya, Kesari, and Lucian an exasperated look and shook his head, then hoisted both his own satchel and Amar's pack over his shoulder. The hilt of Amar's sword jutted up above his shoulder, reflecting a gleam of sunlight as he followed Aleida into the trees.

Kesari watched their backs for a few seconds as they walked away. For an instant, a sharp and familiar fear stabbed at her chest, and she saw a flash of a memory—Rajiv's back as he ran into the burning clocktower, never to be seen again.

But this was not the same thing. She would see them both again, and she'd see Amar, too. She had to believe that.

Saya touched her arm and motioned to the narrow path that would take them south, out of the forest and toward the desert. "Shall we go?"

Kesari wiped away the last of her tears and nodded. She hated to leave the others behind, but at least she still had Saya and Lucian. With them by her side, she could face anything.

SAVIR

IT TOOK THEM THREE DAYS OF WALKING THROUGH THE FOREST TO reach the main road, by which time Savir was growing accustomed to the gentle weight of the Spirit Tarja perched on his shoulder. Talking to her with the familiarity she claimed they shared still didn't feel quite natural, but he tried to strike up a conversation anyway.

"Valkyra?"

"Yes, Your Highness?"

"How much farther is it to Valmandi?"

"Not far," she replied. "A week, or perhaps a little more."

Apprehension curled inside him. That didn't give him very long to recover his memories, and there was so much he needed to remember. Who he was, the life he'd lived before, anything that had ever happened to him prior to waking up in the forest covered in blood with Valkyra's spirit hovering over him. She had already explained everything several times, but that wasn't the same as having the memories himself.

He went over her account again, hoping it would spark something. His name was Savir, formally known as Prince Savir Akraja Jai Sharma, son of Emperor Akraja Munar Sharma. He was the rightful heir to the Kavoran throne, secretly smuggled away to safety as a toddler when his mother learned of an assassination plot against them both. Unable to escape, she was killed, but Savir had spent the last seventeen years in hiding under the watchful care of his Tarja guardian, Valkyra.

Now that he was grown, it was time to come out of the shadows and take back his throne. He and Valkyra had set out for Valmandi to reunite him with his maternal grandparents, but they hadn't gotten far when they were attacked. Valkyra gave her life to protect him, but because she was a Tarja, her spirit lingered, tied to the physical world by the altma still within her. Savir had taken a nasty bump on the head during the fight and lost consciousness. When he came to, he found their attacker dead, blood strewn across the ground and on his shirt, which had been torn during the struggle. All that remained of Valkyra was her glowing blue spirit.

He still didn't remember anything prior to regaining consciousness, and initially, he'd been skeptical of Valkyra's account. Strangely, he knew the songs and stories about the lost Kavoran prince, but the idea that the figure in those tales could be him had been hard to accept at first. The longer she talked, though, the more it had begun to make sense. He may not have ever worn a crown or sat on his throne—not yet—but when he thought of himself as a prince, it seemed to fit. It was the *only* thing that fit, and he clung to that piece of himself hoping it would help to fill in the gaps in his memory.

Valkyra been gracious in answering all his questions and recounted the events that had led them here as many times as he'd asked, always with the same exact details. A faint gnawing feeling in his gut still gave him some doubts, but he supposed that could just as well be attributed to the uncanny discomfort of not having his memories.

And so, when she had asked him to Bond with her so she could continue guiding and watching over him, Savir had agreed. What else was he supposed to do? He didn't have anyone else, and he would have had no idea where to go or what to do next on his own. As she had pointed out, they needed each other. Besides, the power that came with the Bond was well worth the cost of the years it would take off his life.

It had taken a full day for him to start to feel or use any of his new magical abilities, but now, he was making orbs of light and twisting lightning around his fingers like he'd been doing it all his life. "Do you think my memories will come back before we get to Valmandi?" he asked as he conjured a sphere of blue lightning in his palm. It crackled there for a few seconds before fading away.

"I hope so," Valkyra replied. "It's difficult to say for certain. We'll have to wait and see what happens, but I'm sure they'll return eventually.

Savir frowned. He'd been hoping for a clearer answer.

"Don't worry, dear." She brushed her silky tail across his cheek. "I've planned for every contingency. There are such wonderful things in store for us. Just wait and see."

The story continues in
CURSE OF SHAVHALLA BOOK TWO: REVENANT PRINCE

GLOSSARY

ALTMA – an energy source present in all living things which can be used by Tarja to fuel their magical abilities

ARTEX – the Visan deity, believed to be the creator of all things; sometimes referred to as 'the Artist'

BOND – a magical connection between a Spirit Tarja and a living person which grants the living partner the ability to channel altma at the expense of sharing the remainder of their natural lifespan with the Spirit Tarja

CHANNEL (ALTMA) – the act of drawing altma from one's surroundings and using it to perform magical feats

CURSE – a specific branch of magic whose affects are longer lasting and more powerful than most types of magic; curses were outlawed in Erythyr several hundred years ago and much of the knowledge about them has been erased or forgotten

GHAYAT – a species of antelope-like creatures native to the Sular Desert that are an integral part of the ecosystem and the Sularan people's way of life

HASEPH – a rite of passage undertaken by all Sularan youth at age sixteen in which the participant is required to seek out and bring back to their tribe something of value so that they may become a full-fledged member of the tribe

KANJIRA – a small handheld drum, typically a circular wooden frame covered on one side with a drumhead made from animal skin while the other side is left open

MASAHI – the highest-ranking member on a council of tribal leaders chosen to represent the Sularan people

MESALA – a species of plant native to the Sular Desert which is the main food source of the ghayat and whose flowers can enhance a Tarja's magical abilities; sometimes referred to as 'Sularan torches'

PASHLIK – a Sularan curse word; a derogatory term for someone who is ignorant, irritating, or otherwise contemptible

SARAJ – a Kavoran stringed instrument approximately one meter in length, which is versatile for a variety of musical styles and has a rich, reverberating sound

SPIRIT TARJA – the spirit of a Tarja who died prematurely; this death causes the altma within them to tether their soul to the physical world either until the altma fades or until the Spirit Tarja forms a Bond with a living partner

STORM WITHERING SYNDROME – a fatal degenerative disease with no known cure, named for the purple and bluish skin discoloration that occurs in later stages of the disease due to poor circulation

TARJA – any person capable of channeling altma to perform magical feats; a Tarja may be born with the ability to use magic or, less commonly, may be someone who has gained those abilities by forming a Bond with a Spirit Tarja

CAST & NOTABLE FIGURES

AKRAJA MUNAR SHARMA – deceased, former Emperor of Kavora, father of Prince Savir, sister of Empress Dashiva

ALEIDA CERAN – a young Visan woman orphaned during Kavora's invasion of Vis, older sister to Tyrus, became a Tarja through her Bond with Valkyra

AMAR – a Kavoran man with a mysterious past, long-time friend of Mitul

BHAJAN VORA – king of the city of Valmandi within the Kavoran Empire, husband of Queen Indira, father of Princess Priyani, grandfather of Prince Savir

DASHIVA SHARMA – reigning Empress of Kavora, younger sister of the late Emperor Akraja

DEV ASHAYA – A magistrate of Valmandi, formerly a member of Empress Dashiva's Imperial Council

FEROS – a strix belonging to Aleida and Tyrus Ceran who often carries messages between them

HASAN KHURANA – a Tarja healer and farmer who lives in Chatanda, guardian of Tyrus and Aleida

INDIRA VORA – queen of the city of Valmandi within the Kavoran Empire, wife of King Bhajan, mother of Princess Priyani, grandmother of Prince Savir

JAMESON WEATHERFORD – an Atrean Tarja of great skill and renown, sometimes referred to by his formal title The Great and Honorable Wizard Jameson

KAMAAL RUMAN – a famous Kavoran painter

KESARI EVES – an Atrean girl with Kavoran ancestry, sister of Rajiv and Navya, became a Tarja through her Bond with Lucian

LUCIAN – Kesari's Spirit Tarja, takes the form of hovering flames and is typically about the size of an apple

MITUL RAMA – a middle-aged Kavoran musician, long-time friend of Amar

NANDINI KUMAR – deceased, former Tarja advisor to Empress Dashiva

NAVYA EVES – younger sister of Kesari and Rajiv

OLIVIA RUTLEDGE – a former pirate now enlisted in the Atrean Navy, captain of the *Vindicator*

PRIYANI VORA SHARMA – deceased, former Princess of Valmandi and Empress of Kavora (through marriage to Emperor Akraja), daughter of King Bhajan and Queen Indira of Valmandi, mother of Prince Savir

RAJIV EVES – deceased, Kesari's older brother, formerly a sailor aboard the *Vindicator*

SAVIR AKRAJA JAI SHARMA – son of Emperor Akraja and Princess Priyani, former heir to the Kavoran imperial throne, officially reported dead but believed to be alive by some

SAYA HAS SEDA – a young Sularan woman currently undergoing her haseph, companion of Amar and Mitul

TAMAYA TAKHAR – an elderly Tarja healer known for her great skill and knowledge

TYRUS CERAN – a young Visan orphan suffering from a terminal illness, younger brother of Aleida

VALKYRA – Aleida's Spirit Tarja, takes the form of a small furred and feathered white dragon

ZEFAR HAS YARATHA – a Sularan mercenary and an outcast among his tribe, Saya's former mentor

DEAR READER

Thank you so much for taking the time to read this book. I hope you enjoyed it. Now that you're finished, please consider leaving an honest review. Reviews are especially important to indie authors and can help others make informed decisions about their reading experience, which allows the book to reach its target audience.

Follow me social media to stay up to date on my writing, and please feel free to reach out. Your questions and comments about the story and characters are always welcome and appreciated.

tahernandez.com
tahernandez@tahernandez.com
Twitter: @ta_hernandez5
Instagram: @ta_hernandez5
facebook.com/tahernandez05

ACKNOWLEDGEMENTS

If there's ever been a book in me that I wanted to write more than any other, it's this one. Some of these characters have been in my head for more than a decade, and the fact that I'm finally getting their story out there is a dream come true. Of course, I wouldn't have been able to do it without the help and encouragement of the following people.

First of all, I have to thank the amazing beta readers, critique partners, and sensitivity readers who provided the valuable feedback and insights I needed to do this story justice. Jordan, Stephanie, Megan, Taylor, Michelle, Sarah, Jenn, Chris, Mandy, and Katarina—you guys made the best group of early readers I've ever had the pleasure of working with. Whatever I managed to do well in this book is only as good as it is because of you all, so thank you.

There are so many pieces of myself in this story and things I've learned from the incredible people who have shaped me over the years. To my family, my friends, my mentors and teachers—thank you for being a part of my growth. I also want to thank my husband Alex, who continues to be unyieldingly supportive of everything I pursue, as well as my daughters, who have been incredibly patient with me on the numerous Saturdays I've forgotten about lunch because I was so wrapped up in this story.

And of course, thank *you*, reader, for stepping into the world of my imagination and investing your time in this story. It means everything to me.

ABOUT THE AUTHOR

T. A. Hernandez is a science fiction and fantasy author and long-time fan of speculative fiction. She grew up with her nose habitually stuck in a book and her mind constantly wandering to make-believe worlds full of magic and adventure. She was first inspired to write after reading J. R. R. Tolkien's *The Lord of the Rings* many years ago and is now happily engaged in an exciting and lifelong quest to tell captivating stories.

She is a clinical social worker and the proud mother of two girls. She also enjoys drawing, reading, graphic design, playing video games, and making happy memories with her family and friends.

OTHER WORKS BY T. A. HERNANDEZ

THE SECRETS OF PEACE TRILOGY
Secrets of PEACE
Renegades of PEACE
Survivors of PEACE

OTHER STORIES
Whispers of Shadow and Starlight
Calico Thunder Rides Again

CPSIA information can be obtained
at www.ICGtesting.com
Printed in the USA
BVHW031416061221
623328BV00015B/737/J